THE CRITICS ARE ENCHANTED BY THE POWER OF *MERLIN'S LEGACY!*

DAUGHTER OF FIRE:
"Any collection of the Arthurian legend would be lacking without it."

—*Heartland Critiques*

DAUGHTER OF THE MIST:
"Sorcery, enchantment, mystery and romance blend together perfectly . . . Like Mary Stewart and Marion Zimmer Bradley, Quinn Taylor Evans weaves a spell that enchants, absorbs and enlightens the reader."

—Kathe Robin, *Romantic Times*

DAUGHTER OF LIGHT:
"As powerful and enthralling as the first two books. Enchantment, magic, passion and love all swirl together with evil and danger in a tale that is absolutely unforgettable!"

—Laurel Gainer, *Affaire de Coeur*

SHADOWS OF CAMELOT:
"*Shadows of Camelot* has the same romantic enchantment as the other books of Merlin's Legacy . . . This one's a heart stopper."

—*Rendezvous*

And now, the magic continues with
MERLIN'S LEGACY: DAWN OF CAMELOT

BOOK YOUR PLACE ON OUR WEBSITE AND MAKE THE READING CONNECTION!

We've created a customized website just for our very special readers, where you can get the inside scoop on everything that's going on with Zebra, Pinnacle and Kensington books.

When you come online, you'll have the exciting opportunity to:

- View covers of upcoming books
- Read sample chapters
- Learn about our future publishing schedule (listed by publication month *and author*)
- Find out when your favorite authors will be visiting a city near you
- Search for and order backlist books from our online catalog
- Check out author bios and background information
- Send e-mail to your favorite authors
- Meet the Kensington staff online
- Join us in weekly chats with authors, readers and other guests
- Get writing guidelines
- AND MUCH MORE!

**Visit our website at
http://www.zebrabooks.com**

MERLIN'S LEGACY: DAWN OF CAMELOT

Quinn Taylor Evans

Zebra Books
Kensington Publishing Corp.

http://www.zebrabooks.com

ZEBRA BOOKS are published by

Kensington Publishing Corp.
850 Third Avenue
New York, NY 10022

Zebra and the Z logo Reg. U.S. Pat. & TM Off.

First Printing: October, 1998
10 9 8 7 6 5 4 3 2 1

Printed in the United States of America

Prologue

Britain, 1068
The West Country

The door of the chamber was slowly pushed open.

Light from the oil lamp at the wall framed a slender young woman, exploding like millions of tiny flames in brilliant red hair that fell to her waist, glowing softly across pale taut features and at eyes bright with unshed tears.

Vivian's hand rested hesitantly on the latch as the light from that single oil lamp spilled past and angled across the pale sandstone floor only to be swallowed by the waiting darkness beyond.

No candles had been lit. No priest's softly murmured prayers greeted her. Only silence and the gathering darkness. If only Poladouras was here, she thought. He should be, but he was afar in the old abbey at Amesbury and would not arrive for at least a fortnight. She hesitated, her hand tightening at the latch as she hesitated.

''You are a healer,'' she silently scolded herself. ''You've seen death countless times before. 'Tis not a dreadful thing. 'Tis peaceful. She lived a long, full life, and she was deeply loved. She will long be remembered by all who knew her. Great stories will be told about her for generations to come. One can ask for no more than that.''

But in her heart other whispered words Vivian had struggled with brought fresh tears to her eyes.

You were always a part of my life, dear one. I cannot imagine that you will not be part of it now. That I will never again hear your thoughts joining with mine, giving your wise counsel; that I will never again feel your hand on my arm with gentle strength and guidance; that you will never hold the child I now carry as you held me and my sisters when we were babes.

There was no answer that whispered back from inside the chamber, or joined with her thoughts in that old way. No gently whispered words of love and encouragement in response. And Vivian cursed the mortal emotions she had once longed for, wishing she could not feel them now. Surely feeling nothing at all was better than the painful ache that tightened around her heart.

Perhaps, if she did not go inside, if she closed the door and walked away . . .

This was the hope that whispered in her mortal heart, but she knew it would change nothing. She would not find her beloved old nurse in the main hall below, easing the ache in tired old bones before the warmth of the fire. Nor would she find her in the kitchen as she had so often, instructing the cook on the preparation of the evening meal. Nor in the nursery, gently crooning ancient songs while rocking Vivian's young son to sleep.

She was not there. She was here, in this room, waiting for her.

Vivian let her other senses expand and guide her through the darkness to the pallet where the old woman lay, brought there after she was brutally struck down while trying to protect Vivian's son from the powers of Darkness.

With all her extraordinary powers—the ability to heal mortal flesh, to see the future unfolding in visions found within a blue crystal, to move as effortlessly through stone as if it were no more than air, and to summon the powers of light in a burst of brilliant flame with but a single thought—the one power she did not possess was the power to hold back death. Tears coursed down her cheeks as her thoughts reached out to the silence.

I should have sensed the danger. I should have been there to protect you as you always protected me. I am so sorry I failed you, dear one.

But she had not been there to protect Meg, and now she was gone.

Vivian slowly entered the chamber and closed the door behind her. She let her senses expand further, guiding her to the pallet where the old woman lay beneath the death shroud.

She reached out, fingers brushing the edge of the pale, sheer cloth, trying somehow to hold onto the essence of the woman who had raised her from a child. Clear and strong, as if the old woman stood beside her even now, she sensed Meg's powerful presence.

She smelled it in the lingering essence of fragrant herbs that always clung to the old woman's clothes and now drifted across her senses like eternal Spring. She felt it in the gentle warmth that had always been there to comfort her as a child and now stroked her cheek like a tender caress. She heard it in the gentle words that had always guided her and now whispered through her thoughts in the ancient way that had once joined their thoughts together.

"Do not weep for me, my child. I am at peace. I have fulfilled my destiny."

But as Vivian touched the edge of the shroud it moved as though stirred by some unseen current of air. With a gentle sigh that she felt across her senses, the shroud flattened across the pallet and Meg was gone.

Vivian gasped and jerked her hand back.

"You will not find her there."

She whirled around. Her senses expanded further, and she became aware of another presence just beyond the darkness within the chamber. It moved through her blood like liquid fire, a presence of power so strong that it was felt in every beat of her heart and it stirred within her soul. A presence that was part of her, bound to her across time and beyond the mortal world.

The words seemed to hang suspended in the cool night air that filled the chamber as a pale vaporous mist spilled through the open window.

It fell into a glowing pool that shimmered as though it caught and held the light of the stars in the heavens. Then it slowly expanded and lengthened, taking the shape and form of a man as a portal opened from one world into another.

He slowly emerged through the currents of mist, stepping from that other world as easily as stepping through a doorway from one room into another.

He was tall and lean, exuding a restless, vibrant energy beneath layers of dark blue leggings and tunic, the mist swirling around him like a glistening silver mantle that shimmered with each step he took.

He stepped through the mist, no longer an immortal creature of legend or dreams, but transformed into mortal flesh and blood. Silver hair molded his head and glistened at the close-cropped beard that framed handsome features. And his eyes were as blue as ancient crystal.

"Father?"

He opened his arms and Vivian went to him as she had countless times as a child, needing comfort, holding onto his strength and quiet understanding of things that she could not completely grasp.

He let her cry until her tears were spent, somehow understanding her need, as only fathers can, to give in to those mortal emotions that were so much a part of her.

She sighed, a soft heart-wrenching sound that pulled at his own immortal heart. No matter that she was a woman full grown with a child of her own, no matter that they were immortal creatures with powers beyond what most mortals could believe or accept. She would always be his little girl, and he would always want to take away the pain. And slay the dragons, he thought with a smile for the things that had once frightened her.

"I wanted to see her one last time . . ." Vivian whispered between jerky little sobs. "There was something . . . I wanted to tell her."

She hiccuped again, frustrated just as she had been as a child when the words got caught and wouldn't come out right.

He gently smoothed her hair. His touch was warm and comforting, easing the ache of loss. Beneath her ear, as she laid her head against his chest, the solid beat of his heart was equally comforting.

"What would you have said, daughter?" he asked as he gently stroked her hair.

"I would have told her how much I loved her, how much she meant to me." Her breath caught on a new wave of sadness. "I would have told her that I will miss her all the days of my life." She took a deep breath.

"I would have told her that I wish she might have found what I have found . . . great passion and love . . . to feel the joy of her own babe stirring in her arms . . . to see her child's first smile." Fresh tears ran down her cheeks.

"She lived her entire life giving to others." Vivian wept. "She never knew that sort of passion or joy. She never knew what it is to be loved as I have been loved."

"Is that what you truly believe, daughter? You above all should know that appearances are deceiving."

There was something in his voice that made her look up. "What else is there to believe?"

He stroked the tears from her cheek. "What she could never tell you, the truth she was sworn to keep as the price for a bargain she made."

Confusion drew her delicate brows together, his firstborn daughter so much like her mother whom he loved beyond all else in this world or the next.

Merlin smiled as he sensed her trying to probe his thoughts in the old way. He drew her with him to the window to gaze out at the stars that glittered across the universe, as he had countless times when she was a child and she sat upon his knee listening to tales of ancient kingdoms, brave warriors, magical creatures, and the powers of Darkness and Light.

"Let me tell you a story . . ." he began as he had so many times when she was a child.

Chapter One

Island in the Mist

The earthenware bowl fell and exploded on the stone floor littered with the shattered remains of previous attempts.

"You must focus your power," came the gentle admonition from the instructor.

"Focus your energy. Concentrate. With concentration you can accomplish anything. You can elevate something as simple as an earthenware bowl, or change the course of a river. Without it, your power is nothing more than chaos. Now, please try again, mistress."

The next bowl slowly lifted from the surface of the table, wobbling as the air about it quivered with an invisible stream of power. Then it began to move, precariously at first as though constantly on the verge of disaster.

Gradually it steadied and gathered momentum, circling the chamber with increasing speed. Others who had watched the morning lesson fled to the far corners of the chamber, diving for cover behind stout furnishings as the earthenware missile careened above them.

"You must visualize the bowl," the instructor reminded her pupil. "Then you must become it, guiding its flight, thinking the course it will follow. Yes! That is it! You have it. Very good, young mistress!''

The bowl gathered speed, whirling about the chamber on a dizzying, chaotic course. It streaked dangerously close to a wall, sharply banked the corner, and nicked the adjacent wall for a moment careening off course.

''You must concentrate, mistress . . . !'' the instructor warned as she sensed her young pupil on the verge of losing control once more.

There was a collective gasp of horror from those who watched as the bowl whizzed past the instructor a scant few centimeters from her head, lifting the edge of her pale blue headdress.

''Control, mistress!'' the instructor reminded again for all the good it did.

The bowl circled the room, no more than a blur. This time, it careened so close to the instructor's head she was forced to dive for cover under the table. The bowl whirled past, then circled the room once more.

''The young mistress has really done it now,'' a muffled voice was heard from the mantel at the hearth and the safety of a chink between two stones.

''You sound as if it was deliberate,'' another replied, peering tentatively around the corner of the mantel to survey the damage.

'' 'Tis a difficult thing to master, Cosmo. Some skills simply take more practice. I have faith in her. She will accomplish it in time.''

''In time we will run out of pottery, Grendel. And you and I will be sent into the mortal world to acquire more. I do not care for the mortal world. 'Tis full of mortals.''

In their most common form they were small creatures, visible to some, completely invisible to others in the mortal world where they were variously called fairies or wood sprites, associated with mystical places and thought to possess magical powers. But they could take almost any shape or form much like changelings, except they were not born of mortal blood.

Their greatest power lay in their ability to move unnoticed among mortals, by whom they were often mistakenly blamed for mishaps, mislaid items, objects that suddenly turned up where they ought not to be, and other such and stuff and nonsense.

In truth, they were companions and Guardians, sent by the Ancient Ones into the mortal world to watch over those who truly possessed great power—the children of the Light.

"Perhaps she is better suited to herb gathering," Cosmo continued. "Some simply do not have the talent or the ability."

"This one possesses both the skill and the ability," Grendel assured him. "We are not talking about a changeling. You forget who her ancestors are."

"I forget nothing, 'tis only because of what I have seen here today that I even suggest it. She is no better than the last time, when you and I both very nearly ended up transformed into mice and the next meal for Nicodemus."

Grendel shrugged. "I have been transformed into far worse. As it was, the transformation did not last long, and we managed to escape."

"Only by a hairsbreadth when we dove into that mouse hole!" Cosmo protested.

"You mean by the lengths of our tails," Grendel corrected, his eyes twinkling with mischief.

Cosmo's eyes narrowed. "It was a narrow miss and well you know it. I've not much liking for mouse holes," he continued his tirade. "The owner was not at all hospitable."

"Ah," Grendel replied with a smile at the memory, "but it was a grand adventure."

Cosmo snorted indignantly. "I prefer carefully learned lessons to bowls whizzing past my head and adventures in mouse holes. She was supposed to transform the acorns into mice. Whatever happened to good students?"

"Quit complaining. It could have been worse," Grendel, the more adventuresome one replied, his eyes again twinkling as he remembered the spell. "It could have been an owl who took after us rather than Nicodemus. And I suspect the young mistress may be a better student than she lets on."

Cosmo replied sarcastically. "Oh, yes indeed. Being carried hundreds of miles away to have our bones picked clean by an owl is most certainly preferable to swift and certain death from a cat! I do not care for flying. I do not like adventuring.

"We are simple creatures," he went on. "We are meant to have our feet firmly planted on the ground. All of this has become far too dangerous. I, for one, do not intend to be transformed into some other peckish creature or to find myself smashed by flying pottery." He moved from the safety of the mantel and straightened his shoulders.

"I intend to lodge a formal protest. I shall ask for another post. The guardians can jolly well get someone else to do this."

Grendel seized him by his tunic and clamped a hand over his mouth. With much squirming and muffled protests, Cosmo was dragged back into the safety of the shadows at the corner of the mantel. Out of harm's way.

"This is perhaps not the best time to press your complaint," Grendel whispered against his ear. "There are worse things than being transformed into Nicodemus' next meal."

Unable to protest or respond for the hand clamped firmly over his mouth, Cosmo could only reply with a muffled sound as he followed the direction of his companion's gaze. His eyes grew large and round over Grendel's hand.

Both watched as the bowl whipped past the instructor's head as she emerged from under the table, circled the room at an impossible speed then swooped back around, this time sending the instructor diving for the far corner of the room and into a pile of neatly stacked baskets. Baskets were sent flying in all directions as the bowl whizzed past, banked another corner, and then skidded to a stop above the table where it slowly and with perfect control lowered to the top of the table.

Cosmo gave in to Grendel's greater wisdom and made no further protest as the instructor slowly picked herself up off the floor, shoving aside the baskets piled on top of her.

Her feet were tangled in the hem of her mantle, and her skirt was hiked up around her knees. Her headdress was askew, and the veil had fallen forward over her eyes. She was a dreadful sight.

She finally made it to her feet, felt the air whistling around her bare, exposed knees, and hastily pushed the hem of the skirt back down into place. When she peered from under the edge of the headdress to see who had witnessed this latest indignity, Cosmo and Grendel had the presence of mind to remain hidden behind the stone at the mantel.

She silently congratulated their wisdom in not adding further to her humiliation. Scooping the veil back and straightening the headdress, she tried to restore as much dignity as possible to her appearance as befit someone of her position and importance.

"That should do for today," she announced with great understatement. "You seem to have mastered the art of levitation."

She slowly glided past, head held high beneath the skewed angle of the headdress.

"Next time," she calmly announced, "we will work on more self-control!" The door slammed behind her.

For several moments there was only silence, then a collective sigh of relief when she did not return.

Be humble and obedient at all times.

"So much for rule number one," Meg muttered, not without a twinge of regret at the deception she'd just played on her Guardian—had been playing for quite some time now.

"I know you're there," she called out to her tiny companions, still safely hidden behind the stone at the mantel. When they didn't immediately emerge from their hiding place, she reminded them, "I don't like being spied upon. If you don't come out I'll change you into mice again, and this time I will feed you to Nicodemus."

"You would not do such a thing," Cosmo declared, making no attempt to disguise his displeasure as he finally emerged from behind the stone. "Besides, so poor are you at your lessons you would never be able to remember the conjurement."

"Be careful," Grendel warned as he, too, finally emerged. "I do not think she is as poor at her lessons as she would have us all believe."

Meg laughed softly as she transformed, taking the shape and form of a large snow-white owl. Large wings unfurled and she took flight, sweeping through the chamber, gathering speed, then angling back toward the hearth. She swept low, talons outstretched.

Cosmo and Grendel fled across the mantel, scrambling over one another to escape, only to find themselves trapped where the stones at the hearth met the adjacent wall.

Rich laughter filled the chamber as the owl swept past and alighted on the ledge at the nearby window opening, transforming once more into a slender creature of sunlight and mist with the light of a million stars glittering in the folds of her gown and ancient rune crystals hanging from the belt that encircled her slender waist.

"So poor am I at my lessons that it is a wonder I can remember any of them." She concentrated her attention on a half-dozen pottery bowls on top of the table.

They rose from the surface at the same time. Then they began to spin. Some spun slowly, while others whirled about at great speed. Then they began to move in intricate, dizzying patterns, constantly on the verge of chaos yet perfectly and precisely controlled.

One by one, at breakneck speed the bowls returned to the surface of the table, stopping just short of disaster. Then, one by one, they settled with a gentle clunk into each other until they stood neatly stacked.

Cosmo stared in amazement before turning to Grendel with an expression of growing suspicion and alarm at the deception that had been played upon them and the Old One all along. Grendel did not seem quite so surprised.

"Did you see that?" Cosmo asked incredulously. "She has deceived us!"

"Better to deceive us than turn us into toads," Grendel observed philosophically. "Or *mice.*"

"Mice?" Cosmo repeated with alarm.

"Yes, you know," Grendel reminded him. "Nicodemus' favorite food? We should be going now." He pulled Cosmo along by the arm.

Cosmo's eyes grew round with understanding as he finally realized what it was that Grendel had been trying to tell him.

"Do you mean she knew how to do that all along?"

"Come along, Cosmo!" Grendel insisted as they made their way to the door.

Cosmo glanced at Meg. He laughed nervously as they both began to back out of the corner of the mantel.

"Yes, of course. We must be going now."

"I wouldn't want to keep you," Meg added as a means of sending them on their way. They were far too curious for her own good, especially considering what she had planned.

"And, of course, you'll say nothing of this to anyone," she suggested, with no need to explain the danger if they chose to mention it to anyone.

Grendel laughed. It came out as a nervous, squeaky sound that more closely resembled the nervous twittering of mice.

"Of course not, mistress," he assured her. "No doubt, you wish to tell Elora of it yourself and surprise her."

"Yes," Meg replied, thinking far ahead of the two tiny creatures. "No doubt it will be a great surprise."

"And you must practice so that everything is perfect when you tell her. She will be most pleased."

She smothered back a smile at their nervousness. Of course it served them right to have the tables turned on them, so many times had they spied on her, followed her everywhere she went, and made her every secret known to Elora. Companions they were called. More like guards in what had become like a prison that she longed to escape.

"Yes, I must practice my lessons."

"Then I suppose we should leave you alone," Grendel suggested, backing toward the door with Cosmo hovering behind him.

They had almost reached their goal. They were no more restrained by that boundary than she was, but they obviously considered it a point of safety, and escape.

"If you please," she replied sweetly, holding back laughter at their discomfort.

"By all means." Grendel bowed low before her. "Come, Cosmo," he called to his companion.

"Right behind you, Grendel." Then they both shot out the door, gone in the blink of an eye.

A student shall use her time alone to contemplate the knowl-

edge and wisdom she has gained. She shall not leave until she is given permission. Such is the humility she must learn.

So much for rule number two.

Meg waited until she was certain Grendel and Cosmo did not linger beyond the door, waiting to follow when she left. Taking no chances, she transformed, now no more than a current of air that slipped unseen out through the window.

The place she sought was in the village of the changelings just beyond the temple. No one saw her leave, nor sensed it, so adept had she become at slipping through a portal on a drift of wind or becoming one with the mist, leaving no trace behind for anyone to find.

With a single thought she was there, stepping through the mist that rose in gently purling waves across the ground as it warmed beneath the late morning sun.

Her senses immediately became attuned to everything about her, the sounds of the village—the laughter of small children at play, the singing of others, the recitations of lessons drifting out through a nearby window on the morning air.

This was the learning place, a bridge between the mortal and immortal worlds. A place which might be glimpsed in those moments between night and day when the earth hung suspended in twilight. But only by those who believed and knew where the portal opened between the worlds.

A Learned One stepped from the cottage and turned down the path in her direction. Meg quickly stepped aside. The Learned One suddenly stopped as if he sensed her presence. He slowly turned back around.

Meg drew the mantle of mist more tightly around her, becoming one with it at the same time she gathered the energy of her powers to prevent the Learned One sensing her presence.

He hesitated, like an animal that has caught an illusive scent. She felt him reaching out with his powers. But she had learned her lessons very well. He angled his head first to one side and then the other, as though trying to grasp something that escaped him. When it would not come, he eventually turned and continued down the path, frowning thoughtfully.

Rule number three: Do not be a deceiver nor use your powers against other immortals.

"At this rate, I will not have to sneak out of Avalon. I shall be cast out," she murmured as she turned and slipped across the path, a flowing, disembodied creature of sunlight and mist, impossible to see by those who did not possess the power.

She finally found the cottage she sought. As easily as the mist at dawn she slipped through the window, a silvery current pooling in the shadows near the hearth, then slowly taking shape.

The cottage belonged to the changeling, Dannelore, a half mortal who was a free-mover—those among them who moved freely between the mortal and immortal worlds.

Meg had been brought here several times by her Guardian, Elora, to learn what she must know of the mortal world that was bound to their world beyond the portal of time.

"Mortals are simple creatures," Elora had explained. "They are given to greed, warring, and barbarism. But there are some among them with minds open to knowledge. It is those we seek out, for through them there is hope for the world.

"Others, like Dannelore, live among them as enlightened ones, bringing them the knowledge of the ancient ways. But their task is not easy. There are those among the mortals who are not open to knowledge. They fear the enlightened ones. Many have been slain out of ignorance."

"But what of those whose minds are open to knowledge and enlightenment?" Meg had asked. "Are they slain as well?"

"Some are ridiculed, punished, or locked away by those less knowledgeable. Some are treated as outcasts, sought out for their knowledge of healing ways when mortals become sick or wounded. Still, a few others are held in high esteem. They are made counselors and holy men, and become leaders among their people. But even though we guide them, mortals still war among themselves. At this rate they shall destroy themselves in no time at all." She shook her wise old head.

" 'Tis a painstaking business, this evolving of mankind. 'Tis like bringing a newborn into the world, nurturing it, protecting it, and keeping it from harming itself until it is grown.''

Elora had made the comparison not long after Meg saw her first changeling babe, born in the mortal world and brought to their world after the death of the mother.

She had been fascinated by the child and filled with countless questions. She was very young at the time, and it was her first contact with a child of mortal flesh and blood. It was Dannelore who brought the child to them.

That early curiosity of things beyond her world which Dannelore was free to experience while she as an immortal was not, began a friendship that forged a deep bond.

Whenever she could, Meg sought out the changeling's cottage. There she sat for hours, listening to stories of the mortal world, tales of creatures who seemed to her too ignorant to live, the occasional wise ones who sought out Dannelore's knowledge of the ancient ways; fantastic tales of raiding and warring for which she had no logical understanding; stories of the gentle, kind mortals Dannelore encountered, including a man she spoke of often.

''For the most part mortals are very illogical, overly emotional, and smell bad,'' Dannelore had explained.

But when she spoke of the man her voice had softened and her hands stilled at the task she had been working at. She closed her eyes and described him with tender, deeply moving words. It seemed that at least one mortal was not quite so offensive.

Through Dannelore's thoughts and spoken images, Meg saw what the young changeling had seen and experienced, and far more. She experienced a depth of mortal emotion so complete and intense that it fascinated and confused her. In her innocence she had no clear understanding of what Dannelore had felt or shared with the mortal she spoke of, but she sensed that she had intruded on something that lay deep within Dannelore's soul.

Afterward, the young changeling had looked at her with eyes filled with both immeasurable joy and great sadness.

''What is it?'' Meg asked with growing alarm. ''Do you have a sickness? You look so pale and miserable.''

" 'Tis not a sickness of the flesh, but of the heart. I miss him terribly. I would gladly give up everything I have in this world to live with him in his world for whatever time we might have together.''

Meg had never heard of such a thing. The powers of a changeling were not as great as those of the Ancient Ones, but far greater than those of the mortals. Here, they lived forever. Their simple needs were taken care of. There was no hunger, disease, or war. Neither was there love or passion.

Dannelore smiled sadly through her tears. "I blame it on the mortal blood that flows through my veins. It makes me vulnerable to human emotions. But I find that I like these mortal emotions very much. Both the good and the bad.''

She attempted to explain these emotions to Meg—the simple happiness to be found on a spring morning at the sight of flowers in a meadow with the sun warming one's face after a long, cold winter; the sweetness of honey first tasted on one's tongue; the pride and sense of accomplishment when a mortal boy's broken leg healed straight and true because of her care; the simple comfort to be found before a warm fire at night when storms raged beyond four strong walls.

And then Dannelore had told her of the passion and pleasure to be found in the physical joining with a man, the inexplicable joy experienced the first time she felt new life stirring inside her.

Meg had not known that Dannelore had born a mortal child, for she had spoken of it to no one. But even as the telling of it brought her great joy, it also brought great sadness for the child had taken ill with a consumptive sickness and all Dannelore's knowledge of healing could not save her.

For the first time that long-ago day, Meg glimpsed the depth of what Dannelore had experienced in the mortal world, and felt that first longing deep within herself for things she had never known or experienced—happiness and sadness, joy and wonder, love and passion.

Afterward, she returned to the cottage many times, drawn by the deep, unquenchable longing to experience that which she had often heard of but never known. Always she was forced to sneak away, because the Guardians disapproved of her curiosity.

"You are beyond such things, child," the Old One, Elora, had once told her when Meg asked when she might venture into the mortal world.

"But Merlin is not beyond such things," she had boldly replied. "He lives among the mortals as one of them," she added with pride in the brother she had seen only briefly.

"All for a purpose," Elora had explained. "The Ancient Ones have great expectation of these mortals. There are those among them with qualities of great intelligence, compassion, and courage. It is hoped that with his guidance one among them will excel above all others and build a future for the kingdom of mankind."

"Arthur," Meg repeated the name of the mortal she had heard spoken of.

Elora had looked at her through narrowed eyes, her thoughts probing. "What know you of Arthur?"

" 'Tis said that he and his sister are not wholly mortal; that his mother the lady Ygraine lay with a changeling who had transformed himself into the form of her own husband, and the child she conceived possessed the powers of the immortals flowing through his veins."

"Bah!" Elora had replied. "Rumors and speculation. I suspect you have spent too much time in the village of the changelings and not enough time at your studies. They are given to much gossiping, something you would do well not to listen to."

" 'Twas told to me by a Learned One," Meg informed her Guardian. When Elora demanded to know the name of the Learned One, Meg refused to divulge it.

She was twelve at the time, in terms of mortal years, and it was her first act of defiance against her Guardian. It was also the first time Elora could not control her thoughts.

When she could not bend her to her will, Elora tried to cajole her. "Such musings are frivolous and unworthy of you, child. Your time is better spent in acquiring knowledge of the powers and forces of our world. Then one day you will understand all you need to know to take your rightful position here.''

Meg knew that as far as her Guardian was concerned, the matter was settled and forgotten. But she had not forgotten. After that day, she concealed her visits to Dannelore's cottage, for she knew Elora would have disapproved. There was something the Old One feared of such curiosity, but never spoke of.

Meg had no such fear, but returned to Dannelore's cottage as often as possible, eagerly soaking up every bit of knowledge the changeling had learned.

She continued her thoughtful musings now as she moved about the small cottage, running her fingers over the carefully carved comb and marveling that mortals used it for removing the tangles from hair; picking up a petal from the table that had fallen from a flower in a pottery vessel and marveling at the fragile softness of it; skimming her fingers across the surface of a basin of water, fascinated by the feel of it and the way ripples spread from her fingers to the edges of the bowl.

Oddly, all of Dannelore's personal things—those things she had brought from the mortal world—were neatly arranged as though waiting to be gathered up and put away.

Within that glistening basin, the water rippled and expanded as images suddenly appeared in a vision of Dannelore returning along the path that led to the cottage, a brief pause as she spoke to one of the Learned Ones she passed, then her hand at the latch of the cottage door.

Gifted as she was, Dannelore had no forewarning of the presence of another. She looked up with a start.

''By the Ancient Ones, mistress!'' she exclaimed, her hand over her heart. ''You frightened me!''

''Frightened?'' Another word of which she had only limited understanding and no practical experience. There was nothing she feared.

Dannelore hastily closed the cottage door behind her, then immediately went to the window openings and drew the shutters closed.

''What are you doing here?''

This was not simple fear. The last thing Dannelore expected

or wanted was to find Meg there upon her return. The changeling was hiding something.

Dannelore tried to prevent Meg's thoughts from bonding with her own, but her power was no match. Meg's eyes widened as the secret came to her as easily as if someone beside her had told her of it.

"You're leaving!"

"Shhhh!" Dannelore motioned her to silence. "Do not speak it, do not even think it or I will be betrayed."

"They cannot know my thoughts unless I choose it," Meg pointed out. "Your secret is safe with me." She seized Dannelore's hands in hers. "Tell me everything."

But there was no need to tell it. When she gently probed, Dannelore's thoughts opened to hers like a floodgate, everything pouring out in relief at finally being able to speak of it with someone she trusted.

"You're leaving, and not coming back," Meg concluded what there was no need to probe from the changeling's thoughts.

"I cannot bear this loneliness," Dannelore's anguished thought connected with hers.

"I cannot bear to be parted from him any longer."

"But the Guardians will forbid it," Meg replied, hating herself even as she said it. Had she not broken rules in coming there? Who was she to remind Dannelore of such things?

"They cannot forbid it once it is done," Dannelore replied defiantly.

It was then, Meg sensed what she intended. "You are not going to ask them for permission to leave."

"They would not give it. They think mortals are not worthy of us, that our purpose is best served in teaching . . . and living our lives apart." Dannelore lifted her chin proudly.

"The mortal I have pledged myself to is a fine, intelligent man. He is kind and gentle, and . . ." She paused, her face filled with such radiance, tenderness, and wonder.

"What is it?" Meg insisted that Dannelore explain what she had no understanding of.

"He loves me with all his heart and soul, and with a passion that I cannot even begin to describe."

"He is a mortal," Meg reminded her. She had been lectured so countless times, but it was all she could think of. For the first time in her life, she experienced fear. She had never seen Dannelore like this before.

"In time he will grow old and die, but you will not. You will have only a short time together, then be parted forever."

Even as she spoke them, Meg knew it was the Guardian's words she spoke. Dannelore nodded.

"Yes, but I would rather have whatever time we may have together, than nothing at all."

Meg sensed there was nothing she could say that would change Dannelore's mind. And so she said simply, "When will you leave?"

"When night next becomes day in the mortal world."

"So soon?" Meg asked, suddenly aware of what the loss would mean. There would be no more afternoons spent at the cottage, learning about the life Dannelore lived in the mortal world, with all of its joy, sadness, impossibly humorous stories, or moments of quiet splendor.

"The longer I remain here, the greater the chance my plan will be discovered, for the powers of the Guardians are great. If they learn what I plan they will prevent my leaving."

Meg knew she was right. If she had so easily learned the truth, the Guardians would soon learn it as well, for Dannelore's powers were limited. She looked up, her expression intense behind crystalline blue eyes.

"Take me with you." Not a request but a simple demand. And not to be disobeyed.

Dannelore was stunned. "You do not know what you ask, mistress."

"I do know!" she insisted. "Take me with you."

"I cannot!"

"Why not?"

" 'Tis forbidden. You are an immortal. No immortal has ever gone to live in the mortal world."

"Merlin lives in the mortal world."

" 'Tis only rumor." Dannelore tried to disguise the truth,

not quite meeting Meg's gaze for she knew her mistress' powers were great.

" 'Tis no mere rumor, Dannelore, and well you know it. I have heard you speak of it with Elora."

"You eavesdropped?" Dannelore asked, aghast.

"I did not," Meg insisted. "I simply stumbled across it one afternoon when you came to see her. I cannot help it if my senses are such that I hear things others cannot."

"For shame, mistress!" Dannelore admonished.

"Great balls of fire!" Meg was losing patience. "Why does everyone treat me like a child? What difference does it make how I know it? The fact is, I know it. Do you deny it?"

"You know I cannot," Dannelore replied.

"Well then . . ."

"Merlin was sent by the Guardians," Dannelore argued. " 'Tis his destiny. 'Tis the only hope for mankind against the powers of Darkness."

"Then I shall be the hope for mankind as well," Meg announced.

Dannelore was horrified. "You do not know what you are saying."

"I know exactly what I am saying. I wish to travel into the mortal world, and I intend to do it."

" 'Tis not a place for such as you."

"What are you saying?"

Dannelore took hold of her hands. " 'Tis not a kind place, especially toward those such as you. Life can be very hard. The mortals fear such creatures as you and I. 'Tis said they have put some to death."

"What do you mean, such creatures as me? I am no different than you."

Dannelore used her limited powers to seize her and shove her before the basin of water.

"Tell me what you see reflected on the surface of the water," she demanded.

Meg could have easily wrenched free of Dannelore's grasp had she chosen, but the fact was she was pricked by a certain amount of curiosity. She glanced down at the basin and shrugged.

"I see a reflection of the inside of the cottage—table, chairs, a crack of light at the shutters, and yourself," she announced.

"What else?" the changeling insisted.

Truth. Meg was bound by it and had not the power to resist it. It defined her and others like her. It was impossible for her to lie. She should know, she had tried it on several occasions when attempting to hide some misdeed from Elora.

"I see nothing," she replied with consternation, well aware of the point Dannelore made.

"Precisely," the changeling concurred. "You have no mortal form. You are an immortal. You are not like them."

Meg shrugged. The solution seemed simple enough to her. "Then I shall transform." In her own way, she shrugged. "It cannot be any more difficult than assuming the form of a mouse or an owl."

Dannelore shook her head. " 'Tis not a game, mistress. I have heard it said 'tis very difficult, far more complicated. And dangerous."

"How could it be? 'Tis mere flesh and blood and bones."

"But there is far more to it than creating flesh and blood and bones. 'Tis hazardous, for you have no physical knowledge of such a transformation." Dannelore held her hand up and flexed her fingers.

"Simple as it is, can you do such a thing?"

"I have no need of it."

"You have need of it if you are a mortal, and yet you have no experience in such things. You will something to move with your powers and it moves." Dannelore reached for the comb which she herself had touched only a short time earlier. Dannelore lifted it with her fingers and moved it to another location.

Meg did as well, the results the same. But Dannelore shook her head.

"Witchcraft, conjurements, sorcerers, and sorceresses, the powers of darkness. Those are the least things you would be accused of. Any mortal to see such a thing would fear it, and you."

" 'Tis ignorance."

"Aye, and a great deal of it. 'Tis sad but true, ignorance rules the mortal world. Out of ignorance, you would be condemned and hanged for being a netherworld creature."

She gave Dannelore a long look. "They cannot harm me."

"Perhaps not. Though I have heard there are some who have given their lives over to the Darkness. They, too, live in the mortal world. That is not perhaps what you should fear most."

"Then what is there to fear?"

"They might not harm you, but it would not stop them from harming you through someone else—someone you cared deeply for."

Meg repeated, "They could not harm me. You forget, I do not possess such emotions. 'Tis impossible."

"And if you were to succeed in crossing over into the mortal world? What then?"

That was easy. She spoke of all the things Dannelore had told her about. "I want to experience the warmth of the sun on my face. I want to taste honey. I want to feel meadow grass beneath my feet."

"And what of the Guardians? They would know you are gone."

Meg smiled smugly. "Not until it is too late."

Dannelore shook her head. "Please understand, mistress. The decision I make is for myself, and I accept responsibility for the consequences. But I cannot take you with me."

"I could betray your plans to the Guardians," Meg threatened, though it sounded hollow even to her.

Dannelore's expression was filled with sadness, but resolute. "Then do so."

For several moments they were locked in stubborn silence, each refusing to yield. Finally, Meg could bear her friend's sadness no more.

"Oh, very well. I will not betray you," she said softly, then looked up. "Will you at least let me go with you as far as the portal? If I cannot go with you, I should like just once to glimpse the mortal world."

Dannelore hesitated. But in the end she could not refuse her young friend.

"Aye, very well. You may come. But only so far as the gate and no farther."

Meg's excitement rippled on the air. "I will meet you here when it is time to leave."

"Do not be late," Dannelore admonished her. "Or I shall go without you. The portal is only open for a few moments and I do not wish to miss it."

Meg agreed.

She returned to her chamber, but found it impossible to concentrate on her lessons on the constellations, the ancient signposts that linked their world to the heavens.

She was grateful that Cosmo and Grendel were not there, for they would surely have sensed her restlessness.

All through the evening gathering at the temple she kept her thoughts closed so that no one would know of them. Then when the agreed upon time was less than a quarter measure away, she left the temple.

When she arrived, the cottage was empty. Dannelore was waiting a short distance away, hidden in a copse of trees. The moon had begun its descent and hovered just over the horizon. Dannelore's thoughts connected with hers.

"Time grows short. We must go."

They followed the ancient path through the forest that bordered the mortal and immortal world. Countless times Meg had wandered these same paths, learning the dark and mysterious secrets of the forest, with a secret of her own—that she might one day find that hidden portal, the gateway through which others traveled between the worlds. But always she was accompanied by the Learned Ones, or Elora.

The sky began to lighten at the horizon. Soon, it would be time—those magical moments suspended between night and day.

Dannelore walked ahead, unerringly through the heavy growth of trees, and as Meg followed she realized how many times she had ventured this far in her own wanderings.

The changeling stopped before a thicket, framed on both

sides by ancient rowan trees. The ground was covered with spongy moss, thick ferns, and trailing vines that grew in tangled profusion. She swept a heavy veil of vines aside, exposing a polished black stone monolith that seemed to spring out of the ground.

"It is almost time," Dannelore said quietly.

Even as she spoke the glade filled with silver light. It gradually grew brighter as dawn rapidly drew near just beyond the horizon. A shaft of light pierced the gray veil that seemed to hang over the glade and fell upon the portal of stone. At that precise moment, Dannelore laid her hand upon the stone. It moved, swinging inward with a grating sound.

Meg had longed to find this place of stepping through the portal and escaping through it into the mortal world, intrigued by what lay beyond. But always she had been guarded and protected, prevented from exploring alone in the forest.

At a glance, it seemed little different from the world she lived in, an opening through a thicket of green much like the vines and ferns Dannelore had pushed aside. She saw the first moments of dawn exactly the same as in this place, as if the two worlds existed side by side, separated only by that stone monolith.

She felt the gentle caress of a breeze across her senses, and saw the shadow of a bird in flight, along with other sights and sounds she had heard described but never experienced before. She had only to step through . . .

"You must go back now, mistress," Dannelore reminded her. "Before the Guardians discover that you are gone."

Meg nodded. "Yes, of course." She reached out to her friend in thought and with the powers of energy she possessed.

"Thank you, for your friendship. Safe journey, and . . . happiness," she added. Even though she had no practical experience with it, still, she knew its importance to Dannelore. It was the reason the changeling was making this final journey into the mortal world.

"Thank you, for not betraying my secret." Then with one last backward glance and a parting smile, Dannelore stepped through the portal.

The light in the portal shimmered in concentric circles of brilliance that spread outward from the center, as when a stone was thrown into a pool of water, and Dannelore was gone.

For a few moments longer the portal remained open, a link between the two worlds. Then it slowly began to close . . .

Chapter Two

Return

Waves swelled across the English channel as if trying to cast the longboat back into the sea. But the rowers pulled harder, oars dipping below the churning surface in grim silent answer.

Then, as if finally surrendering the battle, the waves rose beneath the boat and carried it forward in one last thrust toward the shoreline set beneath dazzling white cliffs that rose against a slate gray sky.

Even before the wooden hull scraped the rocky beach, one of the passengers was over the side, his heavy mantle billowing from muscular shoulders as he fought his way through the cold, dragging surf.

In spite of the bitter wind and cold gray water that swirled about his ankles, he went down on both knees, digging gloved fists into the wet sand, scooping up great handfuls of it as if he were a dying man and the sand were life itself.

"Praise God," Arthur whispered, and a single word ached in his throat, "Home."

Then raising his fists to the sky he announced to the heavens as if defying the gods themselves, "I am home! My blood will wash this sand before I will leave it again!"

"Praise be, we are all home," echoed his companion as he

joined him on that lonely stretch of beach, his heavy blue mantle catching the wind like the wings of a huge majestic creature about to take flight.

One by one the others made their way to shore, until the longboat tilted over on its side, the journey ended. And one by one their gazes were drawn to those cliffs none had seen for almost fifteen years and most had despaired of ever seeing again.

Then, as if the sun gave its blessing to the end of the long voyage, it poked through the clouds, banishing the bleak gray sky, gleaming at the auburn hair of the tall warrior who led them.

The mantle swept back from wide shoulders, revealing the length of battle sword belted at his waist. His eyes were as blue as the deepening sky overhead and possessed a rare cunning and intelligence. In his handsome, chiseled features was the mark of his ancestors, both Celt and Roman. In his blood was the mark of destiny.

"What say you, Marcus Merlinus?" He turned and spoke to the young man beside him who was of an equal height. Dark hair flowed to his shoulders. His eyes were the crystalline blue found at the heart of rare gemstones. The shadows within held the secrets of the ages that belied his youth.

"I say we have only conquered this small strip of beach, milord. All of Britain yet lies before us."

Their young leader laughed, a joyous, confident sound. "Ever the wise counselor, the shield that guards my side, the caution that tempers my haste. Britain shall be one kingdom, my friend. Have you not predicted it will be so?"

"I have seen it," Merlin agreed. "But not without great sacrifice and suffering." His gaze scanned the cliffs with a faraway look, as if he saw far beyond.

"I fear no such sacrifice," the young warrior beside him spoke loudly and firmly for all those who had journeyed with him to hear.

"I welcome it, for Britain is my home. I shall not leave again." Then he turned back to gaze toward those distant gleaming cliffs.

"But first I have a need to see my family and boyhood home again." He spoke what every man felt in his heart—had felt the entire voyage and through twelve long years on pilgrimage throughout the middle kingdoms. His penetrating gaze returned to his trusted friend and counselor.

"That is, if the horses that were promised and well paid for await us."

Stirred from his thoughtful contemplations, Merlin assured him, "They will be there as promised." Then, as if sensing something more, something urgent that moved beneath his skin and whispered a vague, distant warning, he told the men, "We must go. 'Tis not safe to remain exposed out here in the open."

"It cannot be any more unsafe than a dozen places we have journeyed to," Alain de Bors, a young warrior who had traveled with them the longest, reminded them.

" 'Tis unsafe because we are here," Merlin replied, and looking at his friend, he added, "Because *you* are here. There are many who would rather keep Britain in chaos, an easy prey for her enemies. They do not wish to see Britain united, for there is strength in a common cause and they fear that strength."

"And well they should," Arthur replied. He turned to the rest of his men. "If there are any among you who wish to leave, then do so now, with my blessing and gratitude for the years we have journeyed together. I will not think less of you for it, though I have need of every strong sword I can find, and I would trust no others as I trust you. But I can well understand the need for hearth and home, for I feel it as well."

"We have pledged ourselves," Gawain, the oldest of the men, reminded him. "To Britain."

Not a single man moved toward the longboat, but by their silence all gave the answer he had hoped for and would have bet his life upon. He nodded, features taut.

"Scuttle the boat. We want none to know of our arrival. At least not yet. Then bring your weapons and keep your eyes to those cliffs."

They rolled their clothes in thick blankets and kept their swords hidden, donning the disguises of simple pilgrims returned from the Holy land. Then they rode toward a place last seen when Arthur was only a boy.

They rode for days, stopping only a few hours each night to rest the horses, avoiding small villages and hamlets lest their disguise be discovered.

There was no fire to warm them or cook their food over. They had only what they carried with them, for they dare not risk word spreading among the chieftains that Arthur had returned. So precarious was the state of all Britain, with no king possessing legitimate claim to the throne, that news of his arrival would have plunged Britain into civil war and chaos.

The past years of strife and turmoil had left the land impoverished and its people destitute. Fields lay fallow. Sheep and cattle had scattered to the hills where they roamed wild.

It was near a fortnight later when they finally crossed into the western lands and neared the fortress at Caerleon.

In the few villages they passed they witnessed firsthand the suffering the people had endured as each region fell under the rule of a different overlord who robbed the people until they had no grain to sow their crops or sheep for wool to clothe their families or food to feed them.

All of Britain lay bleeding and in chaos. Where the warlords had not been they soon would be. No hamlet or village was safe or untouched. Only the most remote outposts were beyond their reach, and only because these barren cold places offered nothing of value.

The faces of the villagers were filled with wariness and suspicion as they passed. As his men entered a hamlet and acquired the meager supplies for their journey they heard whisperings over cups of ale at a local inn:

"It will be different when Arthur returns to claim the crown, you'll see. He will crush the barbarians and bring order to the kingdom."

"Different?" Arthur roared with growing frustration when his men returned and told him what they had heard. He threw off a thick blanket and paced restlessly before the fire even though the night was bitter cold and everyone else had pulled blankets and furs tight about them.

"We have seen what is left of Britain. What is there to rule? Where are her people? How will they fight?" He shoved his hand back through his hair, his features taut with frustration and a slow, burning anger. He was like a restless panther, stalking before the gleam of the struggling fire that provided only meager warmth against the chill night air that reminded winter was not far away.

"I should have returned sooner," he agonized. "I should not have stayed away so long."

Merlin leaned back against a fallen log beside the fire. It offered some respite from the bite of the wind. One arm rested across a bent knee. He stirred the fire with a long, green stick, while his friend vented his frustration.

"It was not yet time," he quietly replied. "The power of the chieftains was too strong. They would have united the people against you and chosen one among them to be king. But their greed has been their downfall. Now they fight among themselves. The time is right for you to return and unite the people of Britain." He gestured across the small encampment where the men slept.

"You have heard what is whispered in the villages and hamlets. No one knows of our presence, yet they whisper your name with loyalty and hope. It was a promise made long ago— the king who would unite all of Britain. It is that which we have worked so long for."

Arthur stood silhouetted against the fire. It gleamed in his rich auburn hair, close-cropped against his head, and reflected in the depths of his eyes, and for a moment it seemed that he became the embodiment of the powerful lion, the image he carried upon his war shield.

Only to Merlin, his friend and counselor, did he speak his true heart and worst fears.

"The chieftains will not easily yield their claim. You have seen the people," Arthur argued. "They have suffered greatly. They have nothing left to fight with. How can I ask farmers and shepherds to follow me into battle when they have not even clothes to wear or leather boots for their feet, much less swords and armor to fight with?"

Over half his life had been devoted to Arthur. They were like brothers, and yet Merlin was often reminded that as close as they were, they were also very different. Arthur was mortal, born to fulfill his destiny as king. And it was Merlin's purpose to guide him from chaos into the light of the future that would one day become Britain out of the ashes they had found upon their return.

Time was short. Days, perhaps only a matter of hours remained for them as friends who had departed years earlier on a pilgrimage to the Holy Land in pursuit of knowledge and enlightenment, in preparation for this moment in time.

His friendship with Arthur meant more to him than anything else on this earth. For Arthur had given him something all his wondrous powers and abilities could not—a deep abiding love for his fellow man, his own humanity which was rare for one who was not of mortal flesh and blood.

But he had felt it slipping away from the first moment they set foot on the rock-strewn beach below those ancient white cliffs, and it had resonated stronger each day they traveled. That subtle change as the brotherhood of friendship took on the new roles of counselor and future king.

"You need not ask it," Merlin replied. "They will gladly take up the sword, staff—or fight with their bare hands—because you offer them hope for the future."

In the days that followed, the farther they traveled across Britain the more urgent their journey became. For even the remote west country had not escaped the strife of civil war.

"My uncle is a powerful man. Caerleon is well protected," Arthur insisted. "Lady Ygraine and my sister are safe there."

Though they had spoken of many things as the day of their arrival on the shores of Britain drew near, Merlin had not spoken of the vision he'd had only weeks earlier of Caerleon and the Lady Ygraine, Arthur's mother.

He prayed the vision was a portent of things which had not yet happened. But he could not dispel the foreboding of blood and death and danger that grew stronger with each passing day as they drew closer to Arthur's boyhood home.

Arthur drove everyone hard, but himself hardest of all, riding before his men for countless hours. Until they sat astride their exhausted mounts atop the hillside that looked down on the verdant valley at the confluence of two rivers, the towers of the fortress of Caerleon impossible to see for the clouds that passed across the moon.

Impatient after riding for so many weeks, and with Caerleon only a few meters before them, or perhaps sensing something in Merlin's silence, Arthur spurred his own warhorse on ahead.

Merlin swore at his recklessness and sent Arthur's men after him. He opened his senses as he, too, charged down the hillside, but he sensed the danger too late. Arthur and his men were too far ahead of him and riding headlong into a trap.

Arthur quickly reached the gates of Caerleon. The first of his men to follow joined him moments later, but there were too few of them to protect him as the raiders poured over the walls.

Some attacked through the shattered remains of the gates, and others closed around them from all sides. The rest of Arthur's men arrived to find themselves outnumbered and quickly surrounded.

Merlin aimed his horse through the heart of the besieged warriors, his own sword still sheathed in the leather scabbard at his saddle. As he reached Arthur's side, he clamped a powerful hand over his sword arm.

"Hold!" Merlin ordered all their men. "Stay your weapons!"

"You fool! Let go!" Arthur demanded, trying to wrench free. But his strength was no match for Merlin's.

Merlin forced his sword arm down with bone-numbing power that loosened the blade in Arthur's grasp and made his fingers tremble with weakness. He had no choice but to lower his battle sword. He was furious.

"By God! You go too far!"

"And you go surely to your death if you raise that sword!" Merlin replied.

"You are outnumbered, and they hold the lives of your men in their hands. They will cut you down before you draw a breath much less strike a blow. Have you come this far to die a fool's death?''

The raiders closed around them. The warriors—only a score of men in all—were outnumbered at least three to one by the barbarians, whose weapons were gleaming deadly bright in the pale, ghostly light of the emerging moon.

'' 'Tis not your time to die, my friend,'' Merlin continued, ''unless *you* chose to do so. Then all is lost!''

''He speaks wisely,'' one of the barbarians called out as he strode from the midst of his men.

''Are you as wise? Or are you a fool?''

The horde of barbarians parted to allow this man to pass through to where Arthur and his men sat astride their mounts, completely surrounded. A large, raw-boned hound with thick, shaggy, gray coat and eyes like yellow flames followed at the barbarian's side.

The warrior was dressed as the others in leggings and tunic meant to blend with the shades of the earth and night. His hair was worn long, to his shoulders, in a wild dark mane, and his face was painted those same colors of the earth and night, completely obscuring his features. Except for his eyes. They were clear silver-gray crystals like the heart of ice, and cold to their very depths.

War bracelets encircled each wrist, his arms protected above by wide leather bands laced taut. Leather boots encased his legs. He looked more like a creature of the night than a warrior, but that impression altered when he moved. For though he alone among his men carried no weapon, he moved like a warrior, with the lean, dangerous grace of someone who knows what it is to be both hunted and hunter. Teeth flashed in that fierce, painted expression.

''Have you returned to pick clean the bones of the dead?'' the warrior snarled. ''Perhaps there is some young girl still alive that your men have not yet raped, or a child left crawling in its murdered mother's blood.

''Perhaps your men did not steal some small trinket, or they did not scavenge some meager crust of bread!'' He boldly strode amid Arthur's warriors, his face contorted with rage.

"What is left that you did not destroy the first time?" he demanded, letting loose the rage that quivered through him and clenching the fist that was buried in the fur of the large hound, barely restraining the beast.

Arthur wrenched free of Merlin's grasp and dismounted in one vaulting movement. In spite of Merlin's warning and the fact that they were vastly outnumbered, he drew his sword and held it before him poised for battle.

He boldly advanced, ignoring the barbarians who closed around him until he was completely surrounded and cut off from his own men.

"I would ask the same of you, barbarian. I demand to know what has happened here!"

Merlin stepped between Arthur and the warrior at the same time his senses swept through the men gathered about them. All were eager for blood. But nowhere among them did he sense treachery or bloodlust that accounted for the death and destruction the young warrior spoke of.

Something dreadful had, indeed, happened at Caerleon, but he knew without doubt that these men were not responsible.

"We have only just arrived from the coast after many days journey." He spoke convincingly, letting his power work through the words.

"What has happened here?" he demanded, using that same power to ease the man's rage and suspicion. "Who are these men?"

But the warrior was not so easily manipulated, nor his suspicion so easily assuaged. He watched them warily, his sharp gaze glancing from Merlin to Arthur and back again. There was both cunning and intelligence in those cold, gray eyes— the cunning of a warrior who has met many enemies and the intelligence to live to tell of it.

"I ask the same of you, stranger," the warrior shot back at him as he advanced the last few paces that separated them to stand face to face with Arthur.

"Who comes crawling under cover of darkness to the gates

of Caerleon with battle swords and shields if not the same murderers seeking more blood?''

"I do not come crawling," Arthur fearlessly spat back at him. "I am Arthur of Caerleon! This is my home!"

The warrior's eyes narrowed to gleaming icy slivers in the dark mask of his features. He snorted with contempt.

" 'Tis well known Arthur has no use for Caerleon, nor all of Britain," he contemptuously replied.

"Arthur fled England, leaving the kingdom in chaos. While his lands and people are raped and plundered, he makes pilgrimages to Rome. When Britain's hills and valleys run with the blood of her people at the hands of barbarians, he remains safe across the ocean in princely splendor. If he were here, I would cut him down myself."

He stood before Arthur, their gazes locked in silent battle, each waiting for the other to make the first move.

"A boy was given no choice but to flee the kingdom rather than become a pawn for those who would use him, when in his heart he wanted only to remain in Britain," Arthur explained, with equal fierceness.

"I suffered every injustice and every death tenfold *because* I could not return and fight beside my people." Arthur's voice quivered with anger and the other emotions he fought to control.

"And when Britain's hills and valleys ran with the blood of her people, I would gladly have bled the earth with them. I am Arthur! This is my home! And if God wills it, I will bleed the earth now to defend it."

The warrior came closer, and even Merlin could not clearly sense his thoughts so fierce and strong were his emotions. He seized Arthur by the front of his tunic and for several moments, Merlin was certain they would draw blood.

"My family shared meals at the same table with the lord and lady of Caerleon," the warrior whispered low and threatening. "As a child I first raised a wooden sword against his young nephew and dumped him on his arse in yonder yard."

A look of comprehension slowly crossed Arthur's face even

as the warrior shoved him roughly away, his expression filled only with contempt.

Everything they'd heard of news from home, sometimes carried months by a cleric through countless villages, hamlets, and across the sea; everything that Merlin had envisioned, could not prepare them for what they found at Caerleon.

Arthur's features were haggard. Like the others, he had not slept in days in his eagerness to reach Caerleon. But it was more than fatigue that now lined his face. It was the sadness and pain of loss that was bone deep, like a wound that could never heal when he looked upon the ruins of what had once been his boyhood home.

His uncle's remains—what was left of them that had not been scavenged by wild dogs—had been buried along with the rest of the dead at Caerleon. Nearly four-score people he had once known and loved. Except for his mother, the Lady Ygraine and his half sister, Morgana. Their fate was unknown.

The walls of Caerleon bore the scars of the battle that had taken place there. Wood buildings had been looted and burned. Storerooms had been pillaged. Nothing remained but the crumbling main hall, its stone walls charred, the wooden roof open to the sky with only the ghostly skeletal remains of blackened timbers protruding at broken angles.

"You believe that I betrayed my country." Arthur's voice was thick with grief as he stood before the fire that had been lit in what remained of the large hearth.

"You could have united the people of Britain," Connor said now as they sat across the fire from each other. "But you left them to die. You betrayed your people."

The son of a Celtic nobleman and Arthur's boyhood friend, Connor bore the scars from the years of warring since Arthur had left Britain, as did his men.

There were over four score of them. There were more hidden in the distant mountains. They struck by night at marauding bands of thieves and mercenaries, then disappeared by day.

Some people believed they were not mortal men at all but

creatures of the spirit world, appearing then disappearing with the mist. They lived in the hills and forests. They hunted for their food and scavenged their weapons from the dead they left behind.

Connor and his men had discovered the dead at Caerleon several days earlier, arriving too late to save them. When they saw Arthur and his men riding toward the ruined fortress, they had been certain the murderers returned for whatever the fire had not destroyed.

"I was a boy of fifteen," Arthur tried to explain without making excuses. "Men will not follow a boy into battle, and I had many enemies. I believed that I served England better by leaving."

Connor sat cross-legged before the fire, the light of the flames gleaming in his gray eyes. "They would have followed *you.*"

"They tried to kill him," Merlin said quietly, his gaze locking with Connor's across the fire. "It is the reason we left Britain. It was not safe for him to remain. Not then."

There was a quiet certainty and conviction in the words that would not be believed otherwise.

"And now?" Connor demanded.

"I cannot change the past," Arthur said, refusing to say more of it. But it lingered in dreams of betrayal, blood, and death that came to him almost every night since.

"The future is not yet written, and I have need of every man who will join me. We were once friends, Connor. Will you join me in this fight?"

Merlin watched from across the campfire. He sensed Arthur's regret and hope intertwined. He also sensed Connor's mistrust and anger, fed by years of warring, bloodshed, and the death of too many brave warriors. As the warrior rose to his feet his men gathered their weapons and rose with him.

"You had no need of us before," Connor replied, making no attempt to disguise his contempt. "We have no need of you now. We will go on fighting as we have, without you. Welcome home, Arthur of Caerleon."

Then he turned and crossed the yard toward what remained of the main gates of Caerleon.

"Is there anything you need?" Merlin asked as Connor passed by with his men. He reached out with his senses but found nothing of the friendship that had once existed between the two young boys.

He had known Connor briefly during that last summer when two young boys were on the verge of manhood, and he'd returned to Caerleon to fulfill his destiny along with Arthur's.

His own friendship with Connor had been an uneasy one. He was the interloper, and Connor made no attempt then or now to disguise his dislike for him. But then Connor had always been fair and with a true and loyal heart, in spite of the mistrust. He had been unswervingly loyal to Arthur. He might openly challenge him in mock combat as lads often did, often besting him with wooden sword or spear. But no other was allowed to do so. Such was the loyalty of the noble-born young Connor toward the boy Arthur.

The years had changed him.

"Your men are hungry, and some have been wounded," Merlin observed with a hand at Connor's arm, attempting to bridge the chasm of time and mistrust. "Let us share what food we have over a warm fire. I have knowledge of healing and can tend their wounds."

Connor contemplated him with that wintry gray gaze, boyhood feelings not forgotten. " 'Tis said you serve the powers of Darkness."

"I serve Arthur," Merlin replied. "As always."

"That is not what one hears rumored in the hills and mountains."

"I have never had much use for rumor or speculation. 'Tis the idle chatter of fools who have nothing better to do. Come, break bread with us and share a cup of wine. 'Tis a time to heal old wounds, for much lays ahead of us all."

Connor stared down at the hand at his arm. He had heard of the conjuror's strength and powers, but he did not fear them. He looked back up at Merlin with an icy expression.

"We have fought and survived by our wits and our swords. We will continue to do so, for we have learned the only ones we can rely on are ourselves. Keep your food and your wine. We have no need of anything from you.''

Had he wished it, Merlin could have prevented them all from leaving with but a simple spellcast, but he did not. In time a spellcast wore off, and Arthur had need of men whose loyalty went soul deep.

He sensed there was nothing he could say or do that would change Connor's mind. The man's loyalty could only be won by Arthur himself, if at all. Merlin regretted it deeply, for they had need of his friendship. His hand dropped away from the warrior's arm.

Then Connor and his men were gone, disappearing over the walls and into the night as if they had never been there at all.

Arthur joined Merlin, his face etched with grim shadows. ''Is it too late? Is the kingdom lost?''

Merlin made no attempt to make things seem other than they were. The young man who stood beside him was a warrior. He had a warrior's cunning and ability to assess things as they were, not as he wished them to be. He replied with the only truth that mattered.

'' 'Tis lost only if you allow it.''

Arthur's hand closed over the hilt of the sword belted at his side as he stared after the departing warriors.

''Never!''

''What will you do?'' Simon the Wise asked as Connor and his men slipped into the deep cover of the forest just as dawn broke over the horizon.

He was as tall as Connor and equally wide of shoulder, his eyes dark and watchful. At Caerleon, he had held himself apart, silently watching, wondering what it meant now that Arthur had returned. There were many who thought him dead, or wished it.

''Do you trust him?'' he asked Connor, wondering what lay in the heart of the man he'd fought beside these last years.

''It was all a long time ago,'' Connor replied. ''I knew the heart of the boy, before he left Britain.'' His voice hardened. ''I do not know the heart of the man he has now become.''

''Will you follow him if he gathers an army against the warlords?''

''For fifteen years I have followed no man. I pledged my sword to no overlord, but waited for the day when Arthur returned to stake his claim to the throne. All these years he left Britain to her fate. I will not give my allegiance to a man I cannot respect.''

Darkness lifted in the forest. The first rays of sunlight sliced through the trees and warmed the rich, dark soil. Mist rose in pale, shimmering clouds that wrapped around thickets and stands of trees.

They had eaten only berries and stale crusts of bread the past several days, and had hunted as dawn filled the forest. But game was scarce. There was an unusual quiet in the forest that made man and animal alike wary and cautious.

Eventually a half-dozen rabbits were snared and trussed for the cookfire, but it was hardly enough to feed them all. A hawk was spotted winging overhead, but Connor stopped one of his men as he notched an arrow into his bow.

''If his hunting has been as scarce as ours he is no doubt as hungry as we. His meager flesh is not worth his death.''

They moved deeper into the forest following the spoor of a deer that had recently fed nearby. A meandering trail of neatly nipped leaves from favorite plants and low-hanging branches suggested the deer was unaware of their presence.

Deer rarely fed alone. Where there was one, there might be more. Connor signaled his men to flank wide, each man within sight of the man on either side in a human net that swept along each side of the path the deer followed.

Following the trail, they found more fresh deer spoor indicating there was more than one animal and only a short distance ahead.

Connor motioned Simon to move wide to his right as he heard the distinctive sound of an animal moving through the brush less than twenty yards ahead of them.

A deer gradually emerged from the thick cover of trees,

moving slowly as it searched the undergrowth for tender leaves and shoots.

Eventually a second deer was spotted near the first one, gradually making its way toward the bank of a nearby stream. Simon raised his bow and took aim. Connor also raised his bow. They would eat well tonight and for several nights to come.

As Connor drew back the bowstring a flock of small birds suddenly burst from a nearby thicket. The sound of their frenzied flight startled the deer. A majestic head shot up, eyes wild with alarm. As Simon released his arrow, the second deer fled through the underbrush.

With a soft curse Connor followed the second deer's frenzied flight. He heard the buck crashing through the brush, then saw the movement of muted brown amid deep forest green. He knew there wouldn't be another opportunity. He drew back the bowstring and released the arrow.

Meg could have sworn she heard someone calling to her— Grendel perhaps—for the two creatures always seemed to follow wherever she went. But she ignored it as she stepped through the stone portal to the other side.

Like ripples on the surface of a pond, waves of light shimmered around her. Sight and sound assaulted her from all around—the wild calls of birds, their sudden frenzied flight, and then other sounds. The sounds of mortals.

Amid wild shouts and the deafening sounds of voices which she'd never experienced before, Meg entered the mortal world like a newborn babe emerging from its mother's womb.

Nothing she'd learned from Dannelore prepared her for it. The sights and sounds were deafening, blinding, terrifying, and painful. And, like a newborn, she collapsed onto the floor of the forest and lay there, heart racing, blood pounding, unable to move, unable to think as she endured the first painful rush of air into lungs that had never breathed air or needed to.

She heard more sounds crashing through the forest, very close now. Emotions she'd never experienced before came at her in a rush of sensations she had no comprehension of, except one—the natural instinct of all creatures to flee, to run and hide, before those sounds and the creatures causing them were upon her.

But she was not yet accustomed to the mortal form she had taken. Stories and lessons gave her no practical knowledge of the capabilities or limitations of the mortal body. She had but one chance and that was to transform.

The deer was a natural choice. It was a transformation she had skillfully mastered as a child, and the forest was a natural refuge.

She held the crystal runes tight in her hand as she held the image of the deer in her thoughts, then imagined herself and the creature as one. Even as the transformation began, she heard the mortals fast closing in on her.

She gathered her strength as long legs took form, tucking them beneath her as the natural instinct of the deer joined with hers. In a painful, lunging movement, she leapt to her feet, willing strength and speed into long legs.

Then she was plunging through the forest, stumbling wildly through the thick cover of trees. Sunlight flashed through the heavy canopy of trees overhead. She felt the warmth of it across the deer's coat, along with exhilaration warm in her blood as she left those sounds far behind. Then a sudden stabbing pain pierced her shoulder.

It tore through flesh and sinew, glancing off bone and lodging just beneath her lung so that she could not draw a deep breath.

Pain was a new and stunning sensation. She'd never experienced anything like it before. Now she was stumbling, falling, weakness spreading through her as she tried to drive herself back to her feet.

Ahead lay the stream. She had only to cross it as she had countless times in games as a child. But this was different. She couldn't make herself take that next step no matter how much she willed it.

Her legs went out from under her. The ground was hard, jarring through her every bone, making her cry out. It was the sound of a wounded animal, terrified and in pain, the first waves of shock making it reckless, causing itself more harm as it thrashed about.

They must not find her like this. She struggled to get to her feet, but could not. Then the soft, mewling sound of a wounded animal became the faint sob of a young woman as she transformed once more.

She felt the essence of the deer leaving her, changing once more, taking on the flesh and blood of the mortal creature she had been when she first came through the portal.

She flexed her fingers. They felt strange and useless in this flesh and blood form she had now taken. She could no longer simply think of movement and experience it in the disembodied, ethereal state that had once defined who and what she was in the immortal world.

She tried to focus her thoughts and her power but felt it draining away from her, her conscious thoughts focusing instead on the new, never-before-experienced pain that throbbed through her shoulder and took her breath away.

"Did you get him?" Simon asked as he ran through the brush and caught up with Connor.

"He fell over yonder," Connor said as he moved ahead through heavy undergrowth and low-hanging branches. He was certain the arrow had struck true in that brief moment when the deer was clearly visible in perfect light.

They found the trail of blood, then heard nearby movement as the deer thrashed about wildly.

Connor hated wounding an animal. An instant kill was much better. The hound leapt on ahead, and he had to call it back for the beast would have caused the injured deer more anguish.

"Bring your knife," he called out to Simon, determined to quickly end the creature's suffering. Two thrusts across the large veins at the deer's neck and it would be over.

He continued to follow the trail of blood, the sound of thrashing close now but less frenzied. With a yelp the hound leapt ahead.

Connor ran after him, vaulting over the downed tree. He dragged the hound back. Simon was right behind him, scrambling over the tree trunk, with drawn blade.

Connor went down on one knee. He brushed aside dead leaves and broken twigs, exposing the pale curve of a bare shoulder. Then brushed aside more leaves, exposing the shaft of the arrow embedded in soft, pale flesh.

"Jesu!" Simon exclaimed as more leaves were brushed aside, revealing the fall of long golden hair matted with twigs and more leaves.

"A woman!"

Meg heard voices and felt the sudden, stunning warmth of human touch, the first she had ever experienced.

It was strangely pleasurable, even gentle, and oddly reassuring. Not at all what she had been taught to expect of mortals. She slowly opened her eyes.

Through the shock and pain, she saw the creature who bent over her. A man. But a man like none she'd ever heard described before, except in stories meant to frighten the little ones of her world.

His face was smudged with all the colors of the forest and the earth. He seemed to blend into the forest that surrounded them so that she wasn't certain she saw him at all. Except for his eyes. Not brown or blue, but the color of the sky before a storm—slate gray and cold as ice.

Instinct was something she had very little knowledge of or use for in her world. But this was not her world. It was the mortal world, and for the present she was trapped in the fragile body of a mortal human.

Caught, trapped, and unable to gather her strength and draw on her powers, instinct was all she had. And instinct told her she had nothing to fear of this mortal.

She tried to focus on the mortal's face, but her wounded body betrayed her. A strange lethargy pulled at her. Darkness swept over her.

"Who is she?" Simon asked incredulously. "What is she doing alone in the forest?"

"I do not know," Connor replied, still trying to comprehend how he could have mistaken the girl for a deer. He was certain of what he had seen and yet . . .

"But we cannot leave her here," he said grimly, well aware

that the conditions under which they traveled did not tolerate injuries, much less a gravely wounded girl.

Time and again over the past years he had been forced to leave injured men behind with whomever might care for them, or not. He and the rest of his men were always forced to move on or be caught by raiders who constantly searched for them. Their success, often their lives, depended on the grim fact that no man was allowed to slow them down. But they were in the middle of the forest. They could not leave her there to die.

She was slender, more girl than woman in the pale shoulder exposed amid the cover of leaves where she'd fallen—more woman than girl as he brushed aside more leaves and the long veil of pale gold hair and discovered that she was completely naked.

What in God's name had happened to her? To whose family did she belong? Perhaps one of their enemies? In that case she might be of value to them. Then he discovered the crystals clutched in her hand.

They were small and finely cut with figures etched into the surface of each one. They tinkled faintly when he picked them up, a fragile sound like that of tiny bells. He tucked them into a pouch at his belt.

Connor pulled his tunic over his head and wrapped it about her. He gently lifted her into his arms, taking care not to jar her shoulder with the arrow still firmly embedded in it. It would have to be removed if she was to live and be of any use to them.

He discovered she was a woman full grown, in the gentle curve of bare hip and the lush swell of full breasts that the tunic barely concealed, but so light and slender she might have been no more than a child.

She sighed so deeply that he felt it tremble through her and feared she was dead, except for the warmth of her breath that stirred against his throat as he gathered her against him.

''We will make our camp here for the night,'' Connor ordered as he carried her back through the forest, unaware that someone watched from the thick screen of trees nearby.

* * *

A branch shifted back into place.

Delicate brows knit together over soft brown eyes. Dannelore bit at her lip, torn with indecision.

She could go back through the portal and summon help, but there was no way of knowing how much time might pass while she was gone. An hour in the mortal world? A week? A month?

They might well be far away, and her mistress with them, when she returned. For she had no doubt it was indeed her mistress trapped within that mortal body and gravely wounded, unable to help herself.

Dannelore thought of the mortal man she had left the immortal world to be with, what it felt like to lie in his arms and join her body with his. He waited for her even now.

But even as she thought of him, the sounds of the departing warriors grew fainter beyond the heavy tree cover. She wrapped her mantle more tightly about her and set off after them.

Chapter Three

"The wound is deep. It has pierced the lung," old Radvald said grimly as he bent over the slender girl wrapped in Connor's tunic and a warm sheepskin.

"Your aim was true."

His braided hair had once been red, but was now streaked with gray, as were the tufts of thick brows that bristled like thick gorse over crisp blue eyes—the mark of the Norse raider who had fathered an ancestor.

His body bore the scars of blade and ax from countless battles, and the more subtle but no less painful wealed scars of hot pokers he'd been tortured with when imprisoned by a warlord who had died slowly and painfully.

It was Connor who had freed him in that long-ago raid and forever sealed the bond of friendship that went blood deep.

Connor swore softly. "Will she live?"

Radvald probed the wound with blunt fingers. Only a trace of fresh blood appeared where there should have been a great deal more.

The old warrior stood. His expression was grim.

"If the arrow is not removed the wound will fester and she

will die. To remove the arrow will cause greater damage and more bleeding. Then it will fester.''

There was no need for him to say more. Death was a grim reality they had faced many times over the years together. A warrior never recovered from such wounds, but lingered to die a slow, painful death, and usually alone for his fellow warriors could not risk capture or the possibility of death by staying with him.

''It would be better if it was ended now,'' the old warrior suggested. ''Any of your men would demand it of you. You would do no less for an animal that suffered.''

''Aye,'' Connor acknowledged. ''Any of my men, including myself.''

Radvald's expression softened, much as his own battle-scarred heart when he first saw the girl.

''I will see to it.'' He said gently. ''It will be quick, there will be no pain.'' He unsheathed his knife.

Connor clamped a hand over the old warrior's arm. ''It is my arrow. I will do it.''

Radvald nodded grimly and resheathed his knife. As Connor knelt beside the girl, he turned and left.

Since he was a lad he had been highly skilled at the hunt. His arrow usually found a quick kill. Rarely was it necessary for him to end an animal's suffering afterward.

He had hesitated only once—the first time. As he seized the deer's head and drew it back the way his father had taught him, he found himself staring into large limpid, dark eyes.

In those eyes, he saw a quiet acceptance. As if the deer understood what must then pass between them in that final moment of surrender and death, even welcomed it when its once powerful body would no longer obey its feeble commands. And for a moment it seemed as if the creature spoke to him in some language he understood only within his soul.

We have met and hunted well in the forest. Now I ask that you end my life with the same courage with which you hunted. Do it swiftly. Let my lifeblood flow back into the earth from whence all life springs, so that one day we may hunt together again.

He remembered that day as vividly as if it were now—the way the sunlight danced through the shadows, the coolness of the deep forest, the deeper cold within his heart at what needed to be done.

She lay still and silent on the pallet of furs, beneath a heavy sheepskin. The blood that seeped from the wound at her shoulder was stark against her pale skin.

He slipped an arm beneath her shoulder. Her head went back, her hair trembling in a fall of molten gold as it spilled over his arm. It was an unusual color, somewhere between the cool mist of morning light and the warmth of the midday sun. Darker gold lashes curved down over high cheekbones. Her jaw was slender, her full lips slightly parted with each ragged breath.

Barely more than a girl, yet a woman in the lush swell of full breasts, slender waist, and equally lush bottom he had held against him as he carried her back to the encampment.

How had she come to be in the forest alone and completely naked? Who was she? Someone's wife, sister, or daughter?

He thought of his mother and sisters then, gone all these winters past in the attack that had also claimed his father and brother. In all this time, one thought still haunted him and would haunt him until the day he died—he prayed they had not suffered.

He held her close, needing to comfort her as he had not been able to comfort them. Her cheek was cool beneath his. He had only to angle the blade just so. One swift movement and her suffering would quickly end.

"Forgive me," he whispered as his hand closed around the hilt of the blade.

Warmth reached deep inside Meg with each softly spoken word. It was like stepping from shadows into sunlight, like the moment when she first stepped through the stone into the mortal world, like reaching out of Darkness toward the Light.

She took a sudden breath. Dark gold lashes quivered against her cheek as her eyes opened. Her body quivered and spasmed, not in the final throes of death but like that of a wounded creature still fighting against death. She fought him, seizing the knife blade with a bare hand.

Her eyes were an intense shade of blue, unlike any color he had ever seen before, shimmering like the heart of a flame. In their depths he saw not the calm acceptance of death but a fierce will to live.

Blood spilled through her fingers where the blade cut deep so fierce was her grasp. She seemed oblivious to the pain. Instead, she stared up at him, in her eyes an almost feral look.

Her lips moved silently at first, then in ancient words for which he had no understanding.

The words might have been in Latin or ancient Celtic. So long had it been since he had spoken one, with no experience of the other that he could not be certain. And yet he instinctively understood.

"Eich le, mo chroi," he whispered over and over, words that came to him from childhood when he had comforted one of his sisters after an injury.

"You're safe, little one."

She stared up at him with that mixture of wariness and almost feral courage as he carefully pried her fingers from around the blade, his blood mingling with hers. Finally, he slipped the blade from her grasp and threw it aside.

"I will not harm you," he said gently, and repeated, "You're safe."

The fight suddenly went out of her. She wordlessly tried to mouth a response, but hadn't the strength left. Connor eased her back down onto the pallet, that fierce will hidden once more behind closed lids and dark gold lashes.

He wrapped a cloth tightly about her hand. She did not waken but lay quietly, her breathing ragged but even.

So grave was the wound from the arrow, and so much blood had she lost, that she would very likely be gone in a few hours. Yet there had been something in her eyes in that brief moment when she had looked back at him, something passionate and almost defiant, as if life itself burned within her and she would hold back death with nothing more than passion and the will to live.

"Would that all of Britain possessed such passion and courage." He brushed a strand of hair back at her forehead.

"Anyone with that much will deserves the chance to live."

The quiet of the encampment was suddenly shattered as a commotion broke out. Across the way, Simon and several men had gathered with weapons drawn. It was impossible to determine the cause for the alarm.

Connor seized the knife he had thrown aside only moments before and leapt to his feet. A quick glance assured him that his wounded captive had not awakened, so he crossed the camp in quick strides, his gaze scanning the perimeter, all senses alert to any danger.

As he approached, the circle of men suddenly parted. A slender form darted blindly from their midst. It was a woman, her hair wildly tangled and spilling from the hood of the plain brown mantle she wore.

She would have run headlong into him were it not for the tether secured about her neck. At the last moment, the tether was jerked taut, the coarse rope tightening about her neck, and tumbling her to the dirt at his feet.

She gasped and choked, trying desperately to loosen the rope with hands that were tightly bound, making it all but impossible.

"She was found lurking at the edge of camp," Simon informed him from the other end of the rope.

"Loosen the tether," Connor ordered.

"She's dangerous. She cut me with this knife." Simon held the blade aloft for all to see. It was not the sort of weapon a warrior carried, but the kind found at the table in some master's hall. Hardly a dangerous weapon, especially for an experienced warrior.

"Loosen the rope."

With a sound of disgust, Simon tossed the end of the rope into the dirt. "Be careful she doesn't cut your throat."

"With what?" Connor replied with much bemusement. "Her fingernails?"

He seized the woman by the shoulders and hauled her to her feet. Her head came up, eyes wary as she fought to breathe past the constriction of the rope about her neck.

She was not a beauty. Her features were far too plain, but there was a quiet strength in her that for a moment reminded him of the injured girl. Quickly that strength was carefully hidden behind downcast eyes and frozen silence.

He loosened the noose about her neck and removed it. Only then did she show any signs of weakness, swaying toward him as she inhaled a deep breath of air. He steadied her, but she froze at the contact, pulling back, her gaze still downcast so that he could not gauge her mood.

"What were you doing in the forest?" he demanded.

"No doubt sent by Maelgwyn," Simon suggested as he walked toward them, coiling the rope. "Or perhaps that cut-throat son of a whore, Aethelbert. Both lay claim to this forest."

When she did not respond he seized the woman by the thick of her hair, dragging her head back, wielding his knife so close that the smoothness of the blade gleamed in her expressionless eyes.

"Were you sent to learn our position and carry word of it back to your master?" he demanded. But even the threat of that blade so near her face could not extract the truth from her.

"She'll hardly be able to tell us anything if you cut her throat," Connor pointed out.

The underlying threat beneath the simple logic was not lost on Simon. Eventually, he released the woman and sheathed the knife at his belt.

"Be careful, my friend," he warned as he left to join the others, who returned to the cookfires where rabbits roasted on a spit with assorted fowl and a haunch of venison.

"You might find yourself skewered like a guinea hen on the end of your own knife."

"If she attempts it I will not bother with the rope. I will cut her throat," Connor replied as he reached for her bound wrists. His gaze met hers in silent promise as he tugged the knots from the rope and freed her.

She rubbed the angry red welts, first at one wrist then the other, all the time watching him warily.

"What is your name?" Connor demanded.

She blinked in surprise. She had not expected the simple cordiality from him. No doubt a flogging seemed more likely, or perhaps being bound to the trunk of a tree and left for the animals to gnaw at her bones—after his men had finished with her. There were times when there was more to be gained by simple diplomacy than brutal force.

"I am called Dannelore," she said haltingly.

Connor nodded. "Do you have any knowledge of healing?"

"Some, milord," she replied carefully, darting a glance about the encampment but not finding what she sought.

"I have use of you." He seized her by the arm and dragged her across the encampment.

There was no need. Dannelore would gladly have gone with him. She had no desire to risk another encounter with the one called Simon. She sensed a cruelty in that man she did not sense in this warrior, though he was the one who had wounded her mistress.

Even before she saw her mistress, Dannelore sensed her presence in that bond that connected them. But there was no answer to her silent thoughts. She prayed to the Ancient Ones she was not too late.

As they reached the far side of the encampment, Dannelore fought back her instinctive reaction at the sight of her mistress—not the disembodied, ethereal spirit of the immortal world who possessed the wondrous powers of the Light, but the flesh and blood creature she had transformed into upon entering the mortal world.

She lay still and silent on the pallet of furs, covered with a thick sheepskin. A beautiful creature—the natural transformation of her immortal form and much the same as she'd seemed in that immortal world—a creature of shimmering gold and light in the gold satin of waist-length hair that spread over the pallet and covered a pale gleaming shoulder. Then she saw the shaft of the arrow and the bloodied flesh.

Her mortal heart constricted with fear. She had lived long enough in this world to know the usual fate with such a wound. Even now, the flesh putrefied with the poisons that moved through the mortal blood that flowed through Meg's veins.

Her mistress had the power to fight the poisons, but why had she not awakened?

"It happened in the forest early this morn. The arrow rests

against the lung,'' he informed her without further explanation or excuses.

''Can you help her?''

She had been terrified that she might not be able to find her mistress, uncertain if Meg might have taken another form. Now she was terrified that having found her, Meg might die. Dannelore gathered her wits about her.

''I will do what I can,'' she replied, trying to remember the exact medicinal ingredients in the remedy for blood poisoning she'd left behind upon her return to the immortal world.

If only she had those decoctions with her now. But even the strongest herbal remedy was of little use so long as the arrow remained embedded in her mistress' shoulder, and she knew the risk of attempting to remove it. For that she had not sufficient skill.

''I must have a fire,'' she informed him, biting back the harsh edge to the words. ''A knife and clean cloths to bind the wound.''

A dark brow lifted in the miasma of green and brown markings smudged across Connor's features. She saw surprise at her sudden sharpness in those wintry gray eyes, but no reprimand or punishment followed. He nodded.

''I will see that you have what you need.'' He extended his own knife to her.

Dannelore was stunned. Only moments before he had promised to cut her throat. She hesitantly took the knife and, for a moment, wondered if he possessed the power of a changeling, for she was certain she saw her own thoughts in those quicksilver eyes.

''If you try to escape my men will be forced to go after you.''

She nodded as she took the knife. He had no way of knowing she would not have left the camp even if she could with her mistress there.

''See that she lives,'' he said gruffly as he turned to leave, and in those few words she sensed deep regret that he had been the cause of her mistress' wound. Again he surprised her.

Then he was gone, shouting orders across the encampment

for a fire to be built, water and clean cloth to be brought to her.

The knife was wet with blood. His blood, for she had seen the wound at his hand. She frowned as she set it aside wondering at the carelessness that had caused such a wound. He did not seem a man given to carelessness. Then she turned her senses to her mistress.

A fire was quickly built and water set to boil in a hammered metal pot. Dannelore cringed at seeing the strips of cloth, linen, and wool that were brought to her. She suspected most of it might have crawled there on its own given half a chance. Everything went into the simmering pot.

Several strips of cloth were hung to dry. Others were plucked from the boiling water, allowed to cool only briefly, then gently pressed against the wound at her mistress' shoulder.

Meg jerked awake, eyes suddenly wide with bewilderment, fear, and the physical pain that seared through her mortal body. She cried out, the wild sound of a wounded creature, her thoughts crying out in the ancient way when she was not able to separate herself from the physical body that trapped her.

Dannelore laid a hand gently across her forehead, connecting with her thoughts as she tried to draw on limited powers that might comfort through that simple contact.

"Do not fight this, mistress," her thoughts urged Meg. *"You have suffered a grave injury. You must rest."*

In the connection of their thoughts she sensed Meg's confusion, her overwhelmed senses as her mortal body fought against the fever that set in and the pain she had never before experienced, her bewilderment at the mortal body she now possessed.

She had no practical knowledge of mortal incarnation, having never taken that form before. Her reactions and movements were more like those of the deer she had first transformed into. She thrashed about, trying to throw off the restriction of the sheepskin and bandages, driven more by the instinct of a wounded animal than rational thought, and risked doing herself more harm.

"Nay, mistress!" Dannelore's thoughts reached out. *"You must not fight it. Trust me. I will not leave you."*

Dannelore tried to restrain her, but Meg was much stronger even wounded.

Connor heard the wild sounds. Immediately he was beside Dannelore, gently but firmly pressing the girl back down onto the pallet.

She stared at them with wild eyes, but the moment her gaze fastened on him a change came over her. Dannelore sensed it immediately. Meg quit struggling and lay back on the pallet, trembling violently, each breath a terrible effort.

The warrior gently wrapped her in the sheepskin, and soon she slept once more. Dannelore replaced the wet bandages that had now cooled with dry ones, securing them in place.

"How did you come to be alone in the forest?" Connor asked as he gently turned the girl to secure the bandage.

Dannelore chose her words carefully, saying as little as possible. "I was gathering herbals in the forest," a plausible answer for someone with healing skills. And it was the original reason she had gone into the forest the day she traveled through the portal into the immortal world.

But he was not so easily fooled. He seized her hand, turning it over in his. Dannelore sensed his thoughts and curled her fingers over the palm of her hand. There were no stains from gathering. She jerked her hand back.

"I had only just entered the forest when I came across your encampment," she quickly explained. "I thought you might be from Caerleon."

"What know you of Caerleon?"

"I am from Caerleon. I was returning there after . . . being away."

With his silence, she sensed his thoughts. She looked up, a frown drawing down her plain features. "Have you been there?"

He, too, frowned. "Aye, we came from Caerleon this morn."

An icy coldness closed around Dannelore's heart. She had not the gift of foreknowledge and so could not know of things before they happened, but in his grim thoughts she sensed that something dreadful had happened there.

"You have family at Caerleon?"

She nodded. "The Duke of Cornwall's groomsman. His name is John. We are to be wed soon." She sensed the grimness of his thoughts.

"What is it? Has something happened?"

There was no need for him to speak of it. In those grim thoughts she found her answer—the devastation he and his men had found there, the old duke's body among the dead, all the others dead or gone. And the fate of John, the groomsman, unknown.

"How long have you been gone from Caerleon?" Connor asked.

"Too long," Dannelore whispered as tears spilled down her cheeks.

The day waned, bringing with it the sharp bite of winter on the air. Cookfires burned throughout the day, the pungent smell of pine smoke mingling with the scent of roasted meat.

Connor and his men had lived the last several years off the land, sleeping under the trees and hiding out in mountain caves, always guarding against surprise attack.

Encounters with Maelgwyn and Aethelbert had made him cautious. Both men were ambitious and laid claim to the land surrounding the forest in the intervening years since Arthur had left Britain.

Aethelbert was learned. Of the two, he possessed greater skill as a tactician and field general. His army was highly organized along the system of the old Roman legions. The year before he had negotiated a pact with the northern regions for land in exchange for his support. Obviously some of those northern regions had swung their loyalty toward Maelgwyn, which undermined Aethelbert's control in the east.

Then there was Maelgwyn. Never a more murderous bastard drew breath. His ambitions were far bloodier and more treacherous. In his plan to seize the kingship of Gwynedd he had slain his older brother, though it was made to look like an accident. When their father had named another to the succession over Maelgwyn, he had had him killed. He'd then married his dead brother's wife, Berengaria, to quell the outrage of her family who were powerful rulers of Gwent.

First there were rumors that it was necessary to hold the bride at sword point for the marriage to take place. It was also rumored that Berengaria tried to take her life with a draught of poison. Then it was heard that she was chained and force-fed for her own well-being.

A son was quickly born, guaranteeing the succession. Too quickly many said, adding fuel to the rumors that Maelgwyn had raped Berengaria while his brother was still alive.

Recently there were other rumors that Maelgwyn had brought in Pict mercenaries from the north country to strengthen his army and solidify his claim to the western lands. According to those same rumors, his ambitions lay to the east as well, toward London, the historical heart, rich commercial center, and key to all Britain.

Only two things stood in his way—Aethelbert of Kent, who had already declared himself regional ruler of the eastern lands, and the old Duke of Cornwall who wielded power from Caerleon in the west.

After the attack at Caerleon only Aethelbert stood in his way, and his forces were scattered in the west, fighting pockets of insurgency that Maelgwyn had no doubt planned. A diversion that would cost Aethelbert dearly. The throne would be Maelgwyn's for the taking, plunging all of Britain into even bloodier chaos from which there might be no deliverance.

With Arthur there had been hope. He was from a noble family. His ancestors had been diplomats who had governed wisely and brought peace to Britain. The legend had begun with the circumstances of his birth—the Lady Ygraine finally conceiving after many childless years of marriage to the former Duke of Cornwall, the son born several months after the duke's death.

Lady Ygraine remarried briefly and bore a daughter, Morgana. But hope for the future of Britain lay with Arthur.

Even as an infant the rumors began that in this child was the heart and soul of the king who would one day unite all of Britain. Through boyhood, he was well educated. One of his tutors was a young man barely a few years older—Marcus Merlinus.

The two became inseparable. It was rumored by some that the tutor wielded great power over both the boy and his mother. It was further rumored by those who believed in such things that the tutor possessed unusual abilities and extraordinary powers. Some wondered, including Connor, if he had used those powers to lure Arthur from Britain.

Once they had been friends. Connor's family owned lands adjacent to those of the old Duke of Cornwall. He and Arthur were both educated at Caerleon. For a while he was also tutored by Marcus Merlinus. But his father's illness required his return to his home. When he returned to Caerleon the following fall, Arthur had changed.

In their fifteenth year Connor lost both his father and his best friend. That same year, Arthur left Caerleon on a pilgrimage to the holy lands, and beyond to Rome, with the promise that he would return before the year was out. But when the year ended Arthur had not returned.

Occasionally word was received through some traveler that he had spent the spring in Ghent, then traveled on to Rome and through parts of the Byzantine Empire. The seasons became years. Five, ten, then more, and Britain was plunged into war.

At first Connor fought for Arthur. But as the years passed, hope of Arthur's return faded. Connor felt as if he'd been betrayed.

Then he fought for his home and family, and they, too, were taken from him. And that brief and shining hope that Arthur might return was nothing more than a childhood memory buried in the past.

Camping out in the open made Connor restless and edgy. He had posted guards all along the perimeter of the camp and deep within the woods surrounding it, and he constantly prowled the encampment, a weapon always close at hand. His men were equally watchful.

The afternoon had grown colder. His breath plumed as he gave orders to one of his men to pack what provisions they could carry and be ready to leave before daybreak. Then, as it had frequently throughout the day, his gaze was drawn across the encampment to that crude shelter that had been made from a large sheepskin hide strung between sapling poles before a fire that burned steadily.

The old warrior Radvald fell into step beside him, only just returned from his watch in the forest.

"Did you see anything?"

"Others passed through the forest several days ago. I found signs of it a good distance from here. They were few in number and did not linger."

"Was it necessary to go crawling through the brush?" Connor indicated the stains on the old warrior's hands.

"The trail was easy enough to follow," Radvald answered without further comment as they reached the shelter.

When the woman Dannelore looked up expectantly, the old warrior dropped a pouch to the ground before her without explanation. She immediately scooped up the pouch, sifted through its contents of various leaves, twigs, and berries until she found what she wanted, then sprinkled these liberally into the simmer pot.

With some bemusement, Connor realized the woman had had the old warrior out leaf gathering. He squatted down beside the girl, drawing back the edge of the sheepskin.

"The poison brings the fever," Dannelore explained. "The mixture will help, but 'tis not enough. The arrow must be removed."

"Then remove it."

"My talents are limited to simple cuts, occasional boils or applying salve to a burned hand." She gravely shook her head. "This requires greater skill than mine. If I were to attempt it . . . it would kill her."

Old Radvald listened intently, crisp blue eyes watchful beneath thick brows, his mouth pulled into a sharp frown. Since Connor had brought the girl to the camp, the old warrior had never been far away and only when so ordered. Now he had been out gathering herbs to draw the poison.

"There is one who possesses such skill," Radvald said bluntly. "At Caerleon."

Dannelore's head came up sharply. "You said all were dead or run off from Caerleon."

"Not all," Radvald answered. "There is a healer there."

"No!" Connor said emphatically. "There is no one who may help us at Caerleon. We will not return there."

Dannelore sensed the immediate hostility between the war chief and the old warrior, and she sensed also an old anger that had festered for a long time like a wound that had never healed.

"We will leave at first light and find refuge in the eastern hills. A healer will be found there who may help her."

He tucked the sheepskin around her shoulder. She did not move but lay sleeping restively, her lips dry and her skin hot from the fever that raged through her body. His hand lingered at her cheek. Connor frowned at the heat of her skin that was like an inferno.

Dannelore watched with great curiosity for there was gentleness in his touch, and unspoken regret moved through his thoughts.

"I will have more wood brought," he said gruffly. "Keep the fire burning." Then he rose and left, crossing the encampment, stopping to speak with several of his men who joined him as he left the encampment.

"If all have fled, then who is the healer at Caerleon?" Dannelore asked the old warrior.

He scrubbed at the thick bristle of beard at his chin. She sensed his uneasiness at speaking out, but also sensed his concern for her mistress.

" 'Tis Merlin," he revealed. "Returned from the eastern kingdoms with Arthur."

Dannelore's hopes soared. "Merlin is at Caerleon?" It was more than she could ever have hoped for. After all these years, Merlin had returned. He possessed the power to save her mistress. She reached out to the old warrior.

"Please," she implored. "You must help me get her to Caerleon. It is her only chance."

"But Connor has forbid it. We are bound to the eastern hills."

"She will never survive the journey, and there may be none there to help her. Her only chance is to go to Caerleon." She sensed him wavering. "What difference can it make to him if she goes to Caerleon? She means nothing to him."

"He feels responsible for what happened," Radvald replied.

"All the better then to see that she has the best care. Please, Radvald." She laid a hand at his arm, using all the persuasion of her limited powers in the connection to his thoughts.

"If you wish to save her, then help us to escape."

She knew he considered it, and she might have persuaded him had a shout of alarm not gone out across the encampment.

Every warrior seized his weapon. Radvald spun about, his piercing gaze scanning the camp as others rushed toward the far side.

"Stay here!" he said gruffly. He seized the knife she had used to cut cloth for the bandages and thrust it at her. "Use this if you need to. I'll not be far away."

But as other shouts of alarm rose, he crossed the encampment and plunged into the heavy cover with several other warriors.

The attention of every man was turned toward that side of the camp, swords, spears, and knives held poised for battle. It might well be the only opportunity they would have.

Dannelore stripped away the cumbersome sheepskin and gently prodded her mistress awake. It required some effort, for the fever had dulled Meg's senses and weakened the mortal form she had taken.

Finally her eyes opened. Gradually Dannelore saw recognition in their fevered depths.

"We must leave, mistress. 'Tis not safe for us to remain here. You must help me."

Meg struggled up from the painful fog that seemed to shroud her senses. At first Dannelore's voice seemed to come from very far away. Then, gradually, she heard it more clearly along with the underlying urgency in it.

She felt strange, unable to move at first, her thoughts disconnected from her senses and the powers that had always defined her abilities. She was forced to rely on Dannelore, unable to comprehend why her movements did not obey her wishes. Then she experienced a sharp, intense sensation that radiated through her, scattering her thoughts, rendering her completely helpless.

'' 'Tis the pain,'' Dannelore said, slipping an arm beneath her shoulders and gently levering her up from the pallet of furs. She was careful not to jar Meg's shoulder with the arrow deeply embedded in it.

"You must try to stand, mistress," she encouraged, her thoughts connecting in a flow of ancient language.

Stand? Meg thought her mad. What need had she to stand? But as she tried to move with Dannelore in the old way, by merely thinking it, she found she could not. Neither could she reach out in the usual way, nor were her thoughts or senses clear. She was overwhelmed by sensations, one most powerful of all.

Her movements were jerky, halting, and uncoordinated while fever burned through her and soaked the mantle Dannelore had wrapped her in earlier. She had no knowledge of the mortal body she had transformed into, no coordination, or understanding beyond that of the creatures she had transformed into.

"What is happening?" Meg cried out in that connection of thought. *"Why am I so weak? I cannot seem to move at all."*

"It will come to you, mistress," Dannelore encouraged. *"Just as when you first learned the transformations of other creatures. Each thing learned will increase tenfold."*

"What has happened? Why can't I transform?"

"You've been injured, and I have not the skill to heal it. We must reach Caerleon. But you must help me, mistress. You must try."

Her efforts were feeble at first, hampered both by the unfamiliar mortal body she'd transformed into and the wound that drained her physical strength. Yet, she finally made it to her feet, taking uncertain hobbling steps while leaning heavily on Dannelore, each movement jarring through her shoulder with pain that made each halting step agony. Drops of blood trailed the ground as they slipped out of the encampment and into the cover of deep forest.

* * *

The body of the warrior found in the forest was rolled over. An arrow through the heart had killed him quickly. Too quickly for him to yield any information.

"I was afraid he would get away," Simon explained. "And take word of our position back to others."

"Aye," Connor acknowledged. "But we have delayed the inevitable only a few hours. Eventually they will look for him."

"Aethelbert?" Radvald speculated, for raiding parties had been seen only a day's distance from there in the past weeks.

Connor knelt beside the dead warrior, making note of the painted markings on his tunic. From his belt he took a strip of cloth found at Caerleon and drew it thoughtfully through his fingers. It bore the same obvious markings—Aethelbert's stag horn with crossed swords. Too obvious.

Aethelbert was ambitious but he was no fool, and far from his eastern territories. It could not be Aethelbert, but it might be made to seem so, for a strike deep into the heart of the western lands by someone who had pledged unity with Cornwall would be seen as an act of betrayal. Just the sort of thing another might try.

"Maelgwyn," Connor replied with certainty, leaping to his feet, his gaze scanning the forest that surrounded them. Then with a curt, "Bury him—deep so that no one will find the body," he ordered the rest of his men back to the encampment.

He frowned. Maelgwyn had grown bolder. He had to be stopped.

"The woman is gone," Radvald informed him upon his return to camp. "And the girl with her. They set off through the forest."

Connor swore under his breath at their recklessness with danger all about them. They found the fresh stain on the sheepskin, then the trail of blood that led steadily away from the encampment.

A light snow had begun to fall. If he did not follow quickly the trail would be covered by snow and darkness as light slowly faded. He took three men with him including Radvald and set off into the forest.

"You must try, mistress," Dannelore desperately implored, but even as her thoughts reached out she sensed Meg's waning strength, trapped within the injured mortal body.

Her own strength was very nearly gone from bearing her mistress' slender weight as they made their way painstakingly through the forest, following a trail she had taken months earlier when she had returned to the portal deep within the forest for what she had thought was the last time.

Those thoughts brought others—of John and his unknown fate along with the others at Caerleon. She cursed her sighted gift that it was not sufficient to tell her whether he lived or had died, then cursed it anew that it was of little help to them now.

She knew they must rest, but she feared if they stopped she might never get her mistress to move again. And now it had begun to snow, lightly at first, then more steadily.

How much further was it to Caerleon?

If she had the power of transformation she could have changed herself into a bird and flown there in less time than it took to think about it. But she had not that particular gift.

Her own powers were limited, pathetic, and sorely lacking when compared to those of her mistress. If only her mistress could have transformed or sent her thoughts afar, then help might have been summoned. But she could not, lost as she was in the mortal body and unable to draw on her powers in her weakened physical state.

At last Dannelore could go no further. She stumbled in the darkness, trying frantically to ease her mistress' fall to the hard ground.

Meg did not make a sound and at first Dannelore feared that she had died. Then she found the rapid, thready pulse at Meg's throat, but it was fleetingly reassuring. Without help, her mistress would surely die before morning. And she dare not leave her to summon help.

"Forgive me," Dannelore whispered, her tears and frustration evident. The thought that her mistress might very well die like any common mortal in the forest, her wondrous powers lost forever was more than she could bear.

The crunch of leaves beneath a foot snapped her from her misery. All senses alert, Dannelore slipped the knife from the belt at her waist. Her gaze searched the gathering darkness that steadily closed in. Then another sound drew her attention in the opposite direction.

They were upon her before she could even scream, the knife twisted from her fingers, torches suddenly appearing in an explosion of ghostly light as warriors seemed to take shape and form from the very trees that surrounded them.

Dannelore leapt to her feet and attacked the first warrior with her bare hands, biting, clawing, scratching like a wild creature as she tried to protect her mistress.

"Do not harm her!"

"Cease!" Connor snarled, cuffing her alongside the head, momentarily stunning her into submission as she fell to the ground.

"What good did you think it would do to drag her out here?"

"More good than waiting for her to die in your encampment!" Dannelore flung back at him, sensing she may have sealed both their fates with her careless words.

Chapter Four

"What news?" Arthur demanded as Gawain entered the battle-scarred hall of Caerleon and made his way to the fire that roared in the old stone hearth.

He and a handful of men had been afield since the day before, riding the countryside that surrounded Caerleon, seeking survivors who had fled into the hills, anyone who might know of the fates of Lady Ygraine and Lady Morgana.

Arthur had returned only a short while earlier, his men and horses exhausted from a similar search to the south. Their tunics and boots were caked with mud. Exhaustion showed in every face. The past hours had done little to assuage the feeling that all might well be lost.

Gawain shook his mantle, snow dusting the stone floor at his feet as he reached inside and drew out a length of fine cloth that might be worn by a highborn lady. Gawain laid the cloth down on the table, one of the few pieces of furniture that had survived intact though the surface was scarred with the deep-cut marks of someone intent on leaving his own personal sign on the destruction.

"They're alive. At least they survived the attack."

Arthur was immediately on his feet. "Where?"

" 'Tis rumored they were taken to the Abbey at Amesbury, under the protection of Constantine.''

Arthur's gaze narrowed. "Protection? By my uncle's old adversary?''

Gawain grimly nodded. "It was a word the peasants used and with great care.''

"Hostages," Merlin added with certainty.

"It seems he has been set up as regional ruler," Gawain added.

"Constantine," Arthur mused, recalling when last he had heard the name. "The southwest is his domain. It is only natural that he would throw in his lot with Aethelbert against Maelgwyn to protect his landhold.''

"Or perhaps that is what you are supposed to believe,'' Merlin suggested. "You have been gone many years. Loyalties change, and one such as Constantine will side whichever way the wind blows. If you were to strike against him, it would leave you exposed from the north.''

"And easy prey for Maelgwyn.'' Arthur saw the reasoning. "I have not the army to strike," he pointed out. "Besides, how could anyone know of my return.''

"By now all know of it," Merlin assured him. "From the moment you set foot on English soil, then by way of every hamlet and village we passed. A warrior and his men seen riding through the English countryside toward Caerleon? Who else but Arthur?''

Gawain nodded his agreement. "Those we questioned already knew of it. They spoke of nothing else. Old women pressed loaves of bread and sacks of grain upon us. Old and young men alike, even boys, pledged their loyalty. They followed us back to Caerleon.''

"Followed? Here?'' Arthur was stunned. "But to what purpose?''

"To pledge their swords and their lives to the future king,'' Merlin answered as he extended his hands toward the fire at the hearth to warm them.

"It has already begun.''

"Begun?" Arthur shot back angrily. The devastation and death at Caerleon had taken its toll.

"Look around you, my friend. What do you see? My kingdom? This burned-out hall with snow falling through the roof? Yonder graves? Caerleon, nay all of Britain lies wounded, bleeding, and starving. Maelgwyn and Aethelbert fight over the spoils like carrion, waiting only to pick each other's bones clean.

"I smell the stench of death and rot with every breath I take," Arthur continued.

"In every village and hamlet we have ridden through I see starving people and dying babies." His voice quivered with exhaustion, frustration, and anger.

"Who, then," he demanded, "is there to take up the sword and fight?"

Before anyone could answer, the main door of the hall crashed open. Every man seized his sword and battle shield.

Wind and snow swirled in through the opening, guttering the candles and smothering the meager light. The fire at the hearth danced wildly, sparks exploding on a sudden current of frigid air.

Arthur and his warriors braced for attack. But it was Merlin who advanced unarmed toward that gaping doorway steeped in dark shadows and swirling snow.

As he approached closer, his senses expanded, surrounding the ghostly images of the warriors. As Arthur and his men advanced behind him, he stayed them with an outstretched hand.

"Show yourselves."

Torches suddenly appeared as Arthur's guards closed in behind the intruders. One of the warriors walked forward, head and shoulders concealed by a heavy mantle. With a defiant gesture Merlin recognized, the hood spilled to the warrior's shoulders revealing hard-angled features, hawklike nose, and eyes as cold as winter's first storm that gusted through that doorway.

He did not carry a sword, though his men were well armed. Merlin saw the reason he carried no weapon as he shifted the slender burden he carried, the edge of sheepskin it was wrapped in falling open to reveal the pale, delicate features of a girl who looked very near death.

"You're a healer," Connor spat out. "Prove it."

Merlin glanced at the girl who lay still as death in Connor's arms. He sensed very little life in the faint, shallow heartbeat, and something else he could not quite name. He sensed much more in the warrior—anger, resentment, contempt, and the opportunity perhaps to mend the deep chasm between two men who needed each other.

"What is her injury?"

"She took an arrow in the shoulder. It pierced the lung."

At Merlin's questioning glance, Connor solemnly added, " 'Tis my arrow."

Merlin was surprised. Heartfelt honesty was the last thing he'd expected from a man who was thought to have no heart—a man who was almost as much a myth as Arthur.

Since their arrival at Caerleon they had heard many things of Connor and his men. How they lived in the hills, often disappearing for months at a time, seen again only when they struck at an enemy encampment in the dead of night like spirits of the dark world, showing no mercy, leaving his mark—the letter *A* for the house of Anglia, his lost birthright—in a prominent place so that whoever found the dead would know who had been there.

Both Maelgwyn and Aethelbert had put a price on Connor's head. Many people thought he was already dead, that it was his ghost that swept down from the hills like an avenging angel wreaking death and destruction on his enemies.

The stories made him doubt that Connor of Anglia was capable of caring for anything in this world. Certainly his own life mattered little to him. And yet he stood before Arthur, having sworn he needed nothing of them, needing him to save the life of a young girl.

"I will see what may be done," Merlin replied.

Arthur nodded. "Lady Ygraine's chamber was the only one not badly damaged. You may take her there."

When Merlin would have taken her from him, Connor said simply, "I will carry her."

Merlin nodded. "As you wish." And preceded them up the narrow stone steps to the second floor above the great hall.

Dannelore silently followed, glancing at the one who walked before them in the form of mortal flesh and blood.

Merlin had been raised as a mortal and had lived all of his life in the mortal world. She had never seen him but had heard about him from the Learned Ones.

He possessed the powers of the Light, passed down from those of his essence who had gone before him. As his sister, her mistress possessed those same powers, but Meg had remained in the immortal world. Until the day before.

She had been certain he would immediately sense the bond that connected him to her mistress. But nothing in either his expression or demeanor indicated that he had.

There were many tales of Merlin and the powers he was capable of. Dannelore had no way of knowing what his reaction would be when he learned the truth about her mistress and therefore kept her thoughts carefully hidden as they climbed the stairs.

Here the devastation was not as great as in the main hall below, although there was evidence that small fires had been started as the raiders went about their destruction.

Caerleon had once been an impressive fortress, home to the Dukes of Cornwall for many generations. It was made mostly of fieldstone and slate, buttressed with heavy timbers.

The fires had not reached the support timbers, but had smoldered out after consuming pieces of shattered furnishings, tapestries, sheepskins, fur pelts, and the singed remnants of fine clothing that she recognized the Lady Ygraine had once worn.

Even though the raiders had not been successful in destroying Caerleon, the stench of those smoldering skins and woolen garments lingered in the upper chambers and caught at the back of the throat.

Inside the lady's chamber the damage was not so severe. Dannelore had been there often, attending the Lady Ygraine. After her initial shock at the sight of the elegant tapestries torn from the walls and the chaos of overturned furnishings, she moved quickly about the chamber, gathering scattered furs and sheepskins which she arranged on the pallet.

Connor wordlessly carried Meg into the chamber and crossed to the pallet. There he gently laid her on the thick mat of furs and sheepskins. She stirred, murmuring something through fevered lips, then seemed to drift off deeply once more. He carefully eased his arm from beneath her shoulders.

Nearby, the woman Dannelore coaxed life to coals at the brazier for warmth in the icy chamber. The flames struggled and then caught, adding their golden glow to the light of the torches. Soft light played across the girl's features, and for a moment it seemed that she glowed as if the flames had found life within her.

Connor tenderly touched her cheek, fighting back the regret that was soul deep for having been the cause of this. Though she did not waken, she turned toward him as if she had felt his touch.

"See that she lives, healer," Connor said as he pushed away from the bed. It was not a request but a threat.

"I will do what I can," Merlin promised. Then he, too, left the chamber to seek fresh cloths to bind the wound and fuel to build the fire.

As he did so, Dannelore slipped over to the pallet and carefully checked the bandage at her mistress' shoulder. Meg's eyes slowly opened.

"You are safe, mistress," Dannelore assured her. "We are at Caerleon. There is someone here who will help you."

Meg had not the strength nor the ability of mortal speech. But Dannelore sensed her question in the connection of their thoughts.

" 'Tis Merlin," she replied. "He has returned with Arthur."

Meg's alarm was immediate. Dannelore sensed it and tried to reassure her.

"He is a great healer. He possesses the skills of the Ancient Ones. He will be able to remove the arrow and seal the wound."

"You do not understand," Meg told her, the thought forming

slowly and hesitantly. Now even this simple ability began to elude her.

This must be what dying feels like, she thought, losing her ability, her essence into nothingness. She fought it back, forcing her thoughts to connect with Dannelore's.

"He must not know who I am! He would force me to return and there would be serious consequences. Please, you must help me!"

"I cannot," Dannelore whispered, sensing her mistress' distress. "I have not the power. And perhaps it is best that you did return."

"No!" Meg replied with surprising strength. *"I will not return. I will not! You must obey me in this. You have the power to help me, if you join your power with mine."* She raised her hand from the pallet.

It took great effort, coordinating movement of this mortal body in which she had only recently taken form. And she was weak from loss of blood and the poison that burned through her.

"Join your hand to mine."

Dannelore pressed her hand against Meg's, palm to palm. In the connection Meg experienced a sudden flow of warmth that tingled through her fingers, down her arm and all the way through her as the power of the changeling joined with hers.

It was enough. As the heavy tapestry across the chamber opening was pushed back she performed a simple but effective spellcast, hiding her true identity from everyone including someone as powerful as Merlin.

Meg's hand fell to the pallet as she drifted once more into exhausted sleep. The connection severed, strength once more flowed through Dannelore.

"Come here, woman," Merlin called out. "I will need your help."

He had vaguely noticed the woman when the party had entered the chamber and knew she had arrived with Connor and his men. Now he realized even more about her.

"You are gifted," he observed quietly as he went about sifting a powdered mixture into a basin of water.

Dannelore looked up. "Aye, milord," she said hesitantly, holding her breath as he looked at her overlong, wondering if he sensed the spellcast. He might well be very angry, and she had no desire to experience his ire. But he smiled gently and nodded.

"Good, I will have need of your skills."

He said nothing more as he carried the basin of water to the pallet, and Dannelore let out a sigh of relief. As he drew back the edge of the sheepskin over her mistress, she was aware that the tapestry across the opening to the chamber shifted and then settled back into place.

She heard nothing, but gradually became aware that someone stood in the shadows near that opening.

"Have you come to stand guard?" Merlin asked without looking up as he began to remove the crude bandage she had made from the bits and pieces of linen and wool found in the warriors' encampment.

It was then Dannelore caught the gleam of a sword within the steeped shadows. She had not sensed the weapon, but Merlin had. There was only a moment's hesitation. When he spoke, the warrior gave no indication that Merlin's *observation* surprised him.

"I have heard you possess great skill," Connor commented, his hand tightening over the handle of the sword which stood propped before him.

"You doubt my ability," Merlin commented, again without looking up as he peeled away the layers of bandage that were caked with blood that had seeped from the wound.

"I doubt your loyalty," Connor replied bluntly.

"You believe I serve another cause."

"Yourself," came the response from the shadows. Dannelore could feel those cold gray eyes watching every move as she placed the basin closer and then handed the healer a cloth soaked in the herbal concoction to cleanse the wound.

As Merlin bent low over her mistress and listened to Meg's breathing, the tension in the chamber was like a ribbon drawn taut to the point of snapping. She kept her eyes downcast, her thoughts and energies concentrated on the task at hand.

"You believe I serve the forces of Darkness," Merlin speculated, drawing a frown from Dannelore. He was not angered by the words, merely curious. It was the warrior who was wary and untrusting, with an old anger.

"I believe you serve only yourself."

Dannelore bit at her lower lip at the words that would have made any other man draw his weapon. Yet, Merlin did not. Nor did he look up.

"Yet, you brought the girl to me."

"The choice was death."

"Ah, a choice of last resort."

"Precisely. Can you save her?"

"And assuage your guilt."

It was said without challenge or acrimony, yet Dannelore sucked in her breath for the words were dangerous enough. She sensed Connor's hand tightening over the hilt of the sword and the inner struggle not to give in to that old anger.

Unwise as it may be, he had no fear of Merlin. When it came to confrontation he would face him as a warrior, unafraid even until the moment of his destruction. But now there was something of greater value than his own life, and he refused to give in to the anger.

"I will atone for my sins before God," Connor answered simply. "Not before the Prince of Darkness."

"Then perhaps you should call on your God to heal her."

The age-old challenge between faith and the little understood powers of the universe.

It was then the warrior stepped from the shadows just inside the opening of the chamber. As he did so, he raised the gleaming sword and leveled it at Merlin's throat.

"By God's mercy we reached Caerleon in time. By God's mercy you possess a healer's skills. Or so I am told. Use your skills now, healer, or I will cut you down where you stand."

It was preposterous, of course. No mortal blow could strike Merlin down, such were his powers. Yet, for some reason he hesitated as if bowing to some greater authority, or wisdom.

"I think we must settle this one day," Merlin speculated.

"Name the day."

"But now is not the time or place," Merlin continued. Then, "Put down that sword, unless you intend to cut her shoulder from the rest of her body. For what must be done I have need of your strength."

When he hesitated, Merlin explained, "There is no magic by which I can remove the arrow. There will be much pain, far more than she has already endured. You must hold her down so that she does not cause greater damage. Once the arrow is removed, then I will mend the wound. 'Tis the only way."

Dannelore was certain Connor would refuse. But, finally, he lowered the sword. He propped it against a nearby chair and then approached the pallet.

"There." Merlin instructed him to stand at the end of the pallet. "You must hold her shoulders. Do not let her move, no matter what happens." Then he instructed Dannelore to restrain her lower body and legs.

"The arrow has pierced the lung," he concurred. "There will be only a few moments to seal the wound after the arrow is removed. It must be done quickly if she is to live." He looked directly at Connor.

"You must not question or interfere with anything you see. Is that understood?"

Connor nodded brusquely. "Get on with it, healer."

Only on one rare occasion had Dannelore seen a mortal healing. She had not the power herself, but witnessed it when a mortal dared venture through the portal into the immortal world and very nearly died because of the physical trauma of the journey. He had survived, though it had presented the Learned Ones and those who lived in their world with a unique dilemma.

They could easily have let the mortal die, but it was not their way. Therefore, it was decided that they would use their unique powers to heal him. If he survived, they would then return him to his world.

He had survived. Barely. A healing was almost as dangerous as mortal wounds, for it required the joining of bone, muscle, sinew, and flesh in ways contrary to those of the mortal world. But her mistress was not mortal.

Would Merlin sense that when the healing began? Or would the spellcast shield the knowledge from him?

As a warrior, Connor had seen many wounds. He had also seen the efforts of so-called healers to extract arrows and close various gaping injuries. He had seen men whose limbs putrefied and shriveled, the only recourse to sever the limb from the body. More often than not the wounded man preferred death to life without an arm or, worse, a leg. A man so afflicted was of no use to anyone, least of all himself.

The encounters of war left little that he had not seen. So hardened and numb had he become, he hardly saw the bodies that fell before his blade. They had become meaningless to him, empty faces who ceased to exist the moment he raised his sword. If the outcome went against him and it was his own life that was lost, then so be it.

What was it then about the accidental wounding of the girl that had so deeply affected him? What was it about her blood that he continued to feel, warm on his fingers even after he had washed it away?

Was it that he was responsible for wounding someone who had no way of defending herself? Or was it that her wounded innocence reminded him too much of his mother and sisters who had been brutally raped and murdered with no one to save them?

Connor gently placed his hands at her shoulders as the healer began. Nothing in his experience prepared him for what was to follow.

Merlin's gaze met his. "No matter what happens, you must not let her move." Connor nodded and tightened his hold over her shoulders.

She did not rouse then, so deep had the fever taken her. Not when the healer placed a strip of thick leather between her teeth to keep her from harming herself, nor when his hand closed low around the shaft of the arrow. Then he carefully placed his other hand at the base of the shaft just where it entered the shoulder.

Only Dannelore was aware of the power he summoned, sending it deep into the wound through his fingers, relaxing the flesh beneath the skin to help ease the passage of the arrow. Then with a quick nod to both Connor and Dannelore, he extracted the arrow.

Meg had been lulled by the feverish lethargy, unable to concentrate her thoughts, much less her weakened powers. She had sensed when they'd arrived at Caerleon, then had roused briefly when she'd implored Dannelore to keep her secret and create the spellcast.

Now she drifted in and out of consciousness, vaguely aware of the sounds around her. But her instincts were still those of a wounded creature. And as with a wounded creature, shock had dulled her senses. But it could not dull the pain that tore through her as the arrow was pulled from her flesh.

It was a searing pain more intense than the original wound, as damaged muscle and tendon with nerve endings exposed were brutally torn apart by the jagged arrow and splintered shaft.

She screamed, fighting her way out of the fever and unconsciousness with a strength Connor would not have thought possible so weak had she been from the loss of blood.

Her teeth gnashed at the leather strap, and her head thrashed back and forth. Her eyes were wide open, crystal blue and filled with pain. She clawed at Connor's hands and arms. She arched her back and would have done herself more harm if he had not clamped his hands down hard over her shoulders, pinning her to the furs on the pallet.

Dannelore flung herself across Meg's legs, weighting them down with her own body as the healer extracted the arrow.

And suddenly, like an arrow released from a bow, Meg collapsed upon the pallet. Her breathing was ragged and labored as the damaged lung filled with blood. More blood seeped from the wound, staining the mantle and the sheepskin. Connor shot a murderous look at Merlin. She was dying.

"Healer!" he warned on a low snarl.

"We must work quickly," Merlin replied, ignoring the warning. He ordered Dannelore, "Bring more linens." Then to Connor, a curt, "Stand away!"

"If she dies . . ."

"If you do not do as I say, she will die!" Merlin snapped. "You brought her to me. Now let me do what must be done."

The crimson stain on the sheepskin spread rapidly. Connor had never felt so helpless in all his life. He stepped back from the pallet.

As Dannelore stanched the flow of blood, Merlin removed a blue crystal from about his neck and placed it over Meg's heart. He pressed his palms together, fingers extended and closed his eyes.

When Connor would have grabbed him by the shoulder and demanded to know what foolishness he was up to, Dannelore seized him by the arm and dragged him back.

"You must not interfere!" she hissed.

Merlin breathed in deeply, closing out everything about him, the coldness of the chamber, the feeble light from the brazier and oil lamps, everything except the girl who lay before him and the power he summoned.

He turned his thoughts inward to where time and place no longer existed but all expanded across the millennia of Light, to where the life force of the power that burned within dwelled.

He let go of his awareness of everything else about him as the power grew, expanded, and moved through him. Ancient words learned long ago whispered through his senses.

The tapestry over the door opening billowed softly as if on some unseen current of air. The flames at the oil lamps suddenly quivered, then burned brighter. The fire at the brazier roared to life, its flames leaping at coals that only moments before had burned low.

As Connor started toward the pallet to put an end to it, Merlin's head went back. He glowed with golden light, and his eyes were like the hearts of two flames—brilliant blue at the center rimmed with fiery gold. The same blue as the fiery crystal that lay over her heart as if the same fire burned through both.

Merlin brushed aside the linen Dannelore had used to stanch

the flow of blood and laid his bare hand over the wound. With eyes closed he sensed the depth of the wound, saw torn tissue, shattered bone, and the deeper wound at the lung as he whispered the ancient words.

"Element of fire, spirit of light, essence of life, awaken the night.

"Fire of the soul, flame of life, as light reveals truth burn golden bright."

He drew on the power of the Ancient Ones, guiding that power through his fingers to stop the flow of blood. Guiding it deeper as he took her pain within himself, slowly sealed the damaged lung, and drew away the blood inside. Then, with great care he fused shattered bone, mended torn tissue, wove delicate muscle and fragile flesh until it was whole again.

It took enormous concentration and strength, the power burning through him and into her as he took the fever and poison within himself.

Connor stared, disbelieving, as blood disappeared beneath the healer's fingers and flesh sealed at his touch, until all that remained was a bright pink ribbon of new flesh where the wound had been.

Merlin slowly raised his head. He opened his eyes. They were once more a deep, resting blue, no longer burning with hidden fire. The crystal once more gleamed that same deep, blue color.

He sighed painfully as he sat back on bent legs and slowly pushed to his feet. Though he and Connor were of a near age, it seemed the healer had aged before Connor's eyes. He moved slowly and with great difficulty, as if he had not the strength to put one foot in front of the other. It took great effort as he sought the chair near the pallet and slumped wearily into it.

His features were haggard, and he moved painfully as if it took all his strength to breathe. His head lay against the chair back. Eyes closed, he rested for several moments. Eventually he roused, his gaze meeting Connor's.

"The bleeding is stopped, the wound is closed," he said quietly.

When Connor started to speak, Merlin raised a hand. "Not

even Arthur has seen what you have seen this night. I ask that you speak of it to no one."

He owed Merlin that much. "I am not certain what I have seen," Connor replied, disbelieving what logic refused to accept and at the same time unable to explain it otherwise. A miracle perhaps?

"I am indebted to you."

"I was counting on that."

As soon as he said it, Connor realized the clever trap that had sprung about him. Merlin knew him well. He was certain Connor would not refuse a favor asked in return for a favor given. And Connor was fairly certain he knew what that favor might be—to remain at Caerleon and join Arthur's quest.

"I consider the debt fully repaid by my agreement to say nothing of what I have seen."

Merlin's eyes glinted sharply with admiration. "I should have known you would not so easily be trapped."

"Aye, you should have."

Merlin rose from the chair, his strength restored. "Is there nothing I can say or do that will persuade you to stay?"

"You already have my answer."

Merlin yielded the argument for the moment and gave instructions to Dannelore for binding the wound with a poultice made from the herbal concoction he'd brewed.

"Will she live?" Connor asked.

Merlin looked at him with mock gravity. "I am wounded that you have so little faith in my skills," he replied, humor dancing in his eyes as he laid a hand over his heart as if mortally injured.

" 'Tis not your skill I question. I've seen proof of that. 'Tis that foul-smelling brew you concocted." Connor gestured to the basin that simmered over the brazier.

" 'Tis a curative for many things," Merlin explained. He winked at Dannelore. "Including ailments of the lower extremities. It has a most levitating effect."

Dannelore's cheeks flamed as she hastily gathered up fresh linen for the poultice. Merlin chuckled.

"Aye, she will live," he replied. "She has a strong heart and a rare spirit."

He didn't see Dannelore's sudden glance in his direction at the comment, but he sensed it and wondered what secrets the woman was keeping.

Connor approached the pallet. The girl lay still as death. Her skin was pale, almost bloodless in the soft quiver of light from the oil lamps. It was not the blue-tinged pallor of death he'd seen too many times. Instead, her skin seemed to glow as though lit from within, except for the deeper pink of the wound. A trick of the light no doubt.

He would not have believed it if he hadn't seen it, yet the arrow was removed and the horrible dying sound from the punctured lung with every breath she took had ceased.

Though it had only been a matter of moments, the wound was sealed like a wound several days old. There was no putre-faction of the flesh, merely the beginning of a scar where the arrow had pierced.

Connor brushed his fingers against her cheek. Her skin was cool instead of burning with fever. She stirred and, as if drawn by his touch, turned toward the warmth of his hand.

She did not waken but continued to sleep some deep, dreamless sleep, free from pain and fever at last, her lips lightly brushing the palm of his hand.

" 'Tis good that she lives, healer," he said gruffly.

He lingered a moment longer as if reassuring himself that she indeed lived. Then he straightened. He stepped past Merlin without so much as a word and retrieved his sword. He strode to the chamber opening and swept the tapestry aside. His cool gray gaze locked with Merlin's.

"Now I won't be forced to kill you."

Dannelore watched, horrified, wondering what Merlin would do. But he did nothing.

Merlin was thoughtful as he watched Connor leave and then continued to watch with his inner sight beyond the barrier of stone walls and stout timbers as Connor rejoined his men in the hall below.

The warrior was stubborn, strong willed, and intractable. But his heart was true and his loyalty ran blood deep. He would fight against Maelgwyn and Aethelbert to his last breath or until he was the only one left standing.

With men like him all things were possible, perhaps even a kingdom.

Chapter Five

Connor made his way along the passage to the narrow curve of stone steps that joined the second-floor chambers to the main hall below.

Prior to a few days ago, it had been over a year since he'd last been to Caerleon. Skirmishes and more urgent needs had taken him and his men through the hills into the northern territories as Maelgwyn pressed steadily southward in an effort to expand his claim.

A year ago it had been little changed from the time when he and Arthur played there as young boys in mock battles, escaped to explore the forest, and adventured along the coastal headlands.

A lifetime away, he thought at sight of scarred walls and burned-out torches that still littered the passage where fires had been set in an attempt to burn Caerleon from within.

That visit had been an uneasy one after having been gone several years before that, burdened by the loss of that childhood friendship and anger at Arthur for abandoning Caerleon, nay all of Britain in her darkest hour. But Ygraine had been unshakable in her faith in Arthur, the son she had not seen in almost fifteen years—the son who was a boy no longer by then, but a man full grown as Connor was.

"He will return," she had said with a mother's unquestioning love and devotion. "He promised, and Arthur will not break a promise to the people of Britain. You will see." Then, with that same mother's love, she had gently laid a hand on Connor's arm much as she had when he was a boy to soothe some childhood injury.

"Perhaps then you can find it in your heart to forgive him."

"And what of Britain's brave dead all these years past, dear lady?" Connor had asked. "Will forgiveness make their deaths easier to bear for those who loved them?"

"I know your loss is painful," she had replied, for that visit he had returned to find his own family murdered, in their graves unshriven.

"But it is my loss as well. Your mother was like a sister to me. She was always there for me in my darkest moments. Still, I do not blame Arthur."

Her eyes had taken on a faraway look then, and Connor wondered if she thought of that long-ago time when the old Duke of Cornwall, her husband, had been called away.

Shortly after the duke and his men had left Caerleon, one of Lady Ygraine's servants appeared at Anglia. She was near wild with hysteria and grief, claiming that Lady Ygraine had disappeared.

A search was begun. Eventually she was found wandering, dazed, in the forest near Caerleon—the same forest he and his men had hunted these days past.

She was taken to Anglia and cared for by his mother. Physically, she seemed unharmed except for a few scratches and bruises from wandering in the forest. But she seemed to have suffered some lapse of the mind. She drifted in and out of unconsciousness for several days, unable to remember anything that had happened, but plagued by recurrent dreams that woke her in the middle of the night.

Rumors began almost as soon as she arrived at Anglia. Connor was only an infant at the time, but the rumors persisted long after, whispered in hallways among servants who had been there that night when Lady Ygraine was brought to Anglia.

Some said she'd wandered away due to a weakness of the mind brought on by recurrent dreams of the duke's death in battle. Others claimed she'd been bewitched by creatures of the spirit world and lured into the forest where bizarre rituals took place. But there were others who whispered that she'd gone to meet a lover, for the Lady Ygraine was several years younger than the duke, and while the marriage seemed compatible still it was an arranged union after the death of the duke's first wife.

But Connor's mother put all rumors to rest when she insisted that the Lady Ygraine had been on her way to visit Anglia all along. The excuse was given that her cart had lost a wheel in the forest and so was merely delayed in arriving. The anxious servant was richly rewarded for her dutiful loyalty, but assured that her upset was for naught.

When the Duke of Cornwall returned shortly thereafter, Lady Ygraine seemed fully recovered from her ordeal. To all outward appearances, all seemed as it had been before. Ygraine was the devoted wife, thankful that her husband had returned safely and unharmed. Then, within only weeks of the duke's return it was learned that Lady Ygraine was with child.

Many were surprised, for during all the years of the duke's first marriage his wife had been unable to conceive. He had despaired of ever having a child. The rumor that Lady Ygraine had taken a lover in the old duke's absence began again.

But if he heard the rumors, he ignored them and preparations were made for the arrival of the Duke of Cornwall's heir. On the day the child was born, the duke proclaimed Arthur his son and heir so that all might know it, and death to any man who said otherwise.

If proof of adultery was sought in the features of the child, it was for naught, for the child favored Lady Ygraine in his blue eyes and rich auburn hair. His temperament was much like hers as well. His keen intelligence was attributed to the duke.

In time the rumors ceased altogether. Arthur was eight when

the Duke of Cornwall died. The land and fortress of Caerleon passed to the old duke's younger brother until Arthur was of an age to inherit his birthright. But when he was twelve, Arthur left Caerleon on a pilgrimage to Rome and the far eastern empires with his tutor, Marcus Merlinus, abandoning Britain to her fate.

Now, when Connor reached the main hall, Simon and his men were waiting for him. Though they were cold and soaked through, they had not joined Arthur's men before the fire at the hearth, but instead waited apart near the main entrance for his return.

Arthur rose as he caught sight of Connor and crossed the hall. Their last parting had been less than amicable, but there was neither wariness nor hostility in his demeanor as he approached. Nor was there supplication or trepidation.

His gaze was measuring, his true thoughts hidden behind an unreadable expression. He carried no sword but instead approached unarmed, either the greatest of foolishness or cunning strategy. One could never be certain where he was concerned.

"How fares the girl?" Arthur asked with what seemed to be genuine concern.

"She will live," Connor replied without elaboration.

"My counselor has vindicated himself then."

"So it would seem."

"Excellent!" Arthur exclaimed. "Now, perhaps you and your men will join us." He spread his arm wide to encompass the main hall.

"It is cold. Join us. Warm yourselves by the fire. 'Tis not a night for travel."

Many of the furnishings had been destroyed. Some of Arthur's men sat about on the stone floor, gnawing on a piece of fowl or a crust of stale bread, while others watched with guarded expressions. The main hall at Caerleon did not so much resemble a throne room for a future king as an armed military encampment.

Arthur's men were Briton and Celt, and some, like Arthur, with the blood of Roman ancestors running through their veins.

Three had left with him on that long-ago quest. Others from the middle empires had joined in along the way, forming a bond of brotherhood that had brought them back to Britain.

They were warriors all, easily recognizable by the weapons kept near at hand and the watchful glances directed at him and his men.

Arthur had always possessed the ability to draw people around him, from the pock-faced, ill-tempered cook at Caerleon when they were children to the gruff master of the hounds and the lowliest goatherd.

People were naturally drawn to him. He had an energy and unabashed enthusiasm, and the ability to make the most common of men believe that he was one of them. As a child at any given time he could be found wrestling swine in the muddy yard, chucking rocks at the dovecote with other young boys, or organizing a raid on the cook's pantry.

He was a natural-born leader who always saw his way through things, devised a truly brilliant plan of attack, and followed it with an equally brilliant plan for escape from whatever misdeed they were up to.

Other boys were unfailingly loyal to him, and girls fell for his charm like petals from spring blossoms. Such was Arthur's charisma that if a crown could have been won by sincerity and persuasive words alone, he would have been king at ten years of age.

Connor had not been immune to that charisma, but he had been wise to it. He knew Arthur as well as he knew himself—all his strong and weak points, and all the intricate workings of his mind. He saw him for what he was, a boy not unlike himself, not for what he might one day be.

He'd never hesitated in besting Arthur at chucking rocks or at swords in the play yard. And on more than one occasion when Arthur's grand scheme of the moment failed and all seemed lost, Connor saved his arse from a sound thrashing.

Out of their mutual understanding of one another had grown a mutual respect. But that was all a long time ago—*before* Arthur left England.

Connor shook his head. "We will leave now."

"The storm is full upon us," Arthur replied with a logic that had always served him well.

"It will not break before first light. Your men are hungry and tired. Come, share our fire and our food. I'm afraid there is not much, only what we brought with us. But it will be enough. And I will wager that even Maelgwyn will be warm and well fed on a night like this."

So, Connor thought, he knew about Maelgwyn. There was very little Arthur didn't know about then or now, it seemed. In the man, Connor glimpsed the clever boy who had once been his friend.

There was a logic to it that not even he could argue with. As if giving voice to that argument, the wind rattled at the burned-out doors to the main hall, held in place with timbers braced against their charred remains.

They had raced against darkness to reach Caerleon, the snow blinding them as they left the forest. Only a fool, he knew, would dare risk leaving the fortress on a night like this. They might get only a meter or two before cold overcame them, and to what purpose. Arthur was right. Wherever Maelgwyn was, he was warm and well fed, not wandering about the countryside.

He looked at his men. They were tired, hungry, and cold. Many days journey lay ahead of them if they were to make it north to join with others against a sweep by Aethelbert from the east. They said nothing as they awaited his command.

If he asked, he knew the response he would get. Simon made no pretense of his eagerness to leave. Radvald, whose wisdom he frequently sought, would have spoken in favor of taking shelter at Caerleon.

"What of our supplies?" he asked Radvald.

"Some fowl, rabbit, and a portion of deer. Enough for two days."

Two days. Not enough time to reach the mountain passes even if they hadn't taken the time to come to Caerleon.

"I say we leave tonight," Simon voiced his choice. "Now, before the storm worsens!"

Connor was no more pleased at the notion of remaining there longer than absolutely necessary. While Arthur languished at

Caerleon, Maelgwyn steadily pressed from the north and Aethelbert from the east. But he had lived as a boy in these regions and knew the foolishness of setting out afoot during a storm. There was nothing to be gained by setting out that night, but perhaps much to be lost.

He made his decision. ''We will stay the night, and leave at first light.''

They shared the food they'd hunted. Arthur's men provided bread, cheese, late summer fruit, and wine they'd procured in villages on their journey from the channel coastal region.

Connor's men mingled companionably with Arthur's men, bonded by the common brotherhood of all warriors. He did not join them but remained apart, listening to the flow of conversation from the seclusion of the shadows at the edge of the hall while he gnawed on a strip of roasted deer meat.

To his credit, Arthur did not press the issue of the friendship they'd once shared, nor his desire for Connor to join him in his quest to unite Britain.

He remained apart, in deep conversation with two men who seemed to be senior in status, studying a map of the area surrounding Caerleon and listening thoughtfully to their comments.

Conversations grew quiet as bellies were filled. Several men sought their pallets while others left to relieve themselves. Each time a man left or returned, snow swirled through the large doors as the storm worsened.

Eventually the healer returned. Connor didn't see him descend the narrow curve of steps. He just suddenly appeared out of nowhere, emerging from the shadows like a specter of the night.

His eyes narrowed as he watched Merlin cross the hall, trying to discern from his demeanor if the girl had perhaps taken a turn for the worse. He stepped carefully among the sleeping men, very near to where Connor sat.

He gave no notice that he knew Connor was there as he poured a cup of wine—contrary to the notion that he might be a spectral spirit.

"She sleeps soundly," he said unexpectedly, dispelling speculation that he had not known Connor was there.

Had Merlin seen him there in the shadows? Or were the rumors about him true—that he possessed unusual abilities, among them the ability to see things others could not and to know another's thoughts?

"She will be weak from the loss of blood," Merlin went on to explain. "But she will recover without difficulty."

Connor said nothing. If the healer expected any words of gratitude there was no outward indication of it, nor were any forthcoming.

Merlin took a sip of wine and said thoughtfully, "Your men are fine warriors. They are loyal and well disciplined. You have trained them well. Arthur could use such men in what lies ahead."

"They do not serve me. The battles we fight, we fight together."

"But someone must lead," Merlin pointed out. "It is always so. Someone of greater experience whom the others look to."

"Radvald has more experience than any other," Connor said simply.

"Yet, he defers to you in decisions." He did not seek to argue, only to understand and then perhaps persuade Connor to understand.

"It is always so. There are those who possess the ability to clearly see their way through things, to envision a course of action and the means to accomplish it, with a clear eye toward the outcome."

"There was no grand vision," Connor said bluntly, sensing the direction of the healer's thoughts.

"Maelgwyn and the others fight over the rule of Britain like hounds over a scrap of meat. Men and women were starving. Old people and children were dying. Someone had to take up the sword."

"And yet they do follow you and look to you for leadership."

Connor shrugged. "I have a better knowledge of the country. 'Tis no more than that."

He threw a shank of bone to the hound who lay watchful nearby.

"If you do nothing, you die. If you fight, you may die, but at least you will not grovel at the feet of some murdering bastard for the right to die."

"And now there is the chance for all men to choose whether they will live or die," Merlin pointed out.

Connor turned and looked at him, his gaze cold and piercing. "By following Arthur?"

"It is the reason he returned. It is his destiny."

"And the reason he left?" Connor shot back at him.

Both knew the outcome of that argument.

"He is here now. Will you not give him your support?"

"He does not need my support," Connor replied. "He is Arthur. Will men not follow blindly out of love and loyalty?"

"Will you follow Arthur?" Merlin asked, reaching out with all his power to try to understand why Connor would not join them.

"Is the man not the same as the boy who fled?" Connor asked, and in the question lay Merlin's answer.

They were at an impasse once again.

Connor knew Merlin's game—to persuade him to join with Arthur and remain at Caerleon. He had no wish to debate the matter further.

He took his leave of the healer and crossed the hall, intent on finding Radvald. He wanted his men ready to leave at first light. But as he searched for him, Simon and several of Arthur's men burst through the doors into the main hall. Every man, including Connor, reached for his weapons.

He was very near the entrance to the hall. Beside him the hound growled low in his throat. Connor stayed him with a hand at the thick ruff of fur at his neck.

Arthur's men entered the hall pushing a much shorter creature before them at the end of a tether. All were bundled in heavy wools and covered with snow.

The creature was prodded along, but whenever it stumbled or moved too slowly, one of Arthur's men poked it with a spear causing a great commotion. As they approached Connor, one of the guards jerked back on the tether, snugging it tight and forcing his captive into submission. Then with a well-placed boot heel, he shoved the creature facedown into the rushes on the floor.

Like a fish at the end of a stick, the creature squirmed and convulsed amid wild gasping and choking sounds as it clawed at the rope about its neck.

The heavy wool wrapped about the creature was matted with twigs, leaves, and gorse, and he was grunting, spitting, and scrabbling about like a wild beast. He smelled like one as well.

The creature was in fact a very short man, dressed in simple tunic and pants beneath the heavy wool. His brown hair was braided at the temples and at the fringe of bangs above clever eyes. His beard was also braided in the way of the forest people, and there was a stench about him that increased by the moment as he thawed out, suggesting that he had perhaps fallen into far more than trouble at the hands of Arthur's men.

The guard poked him again with a spear. The little man whirled, hopping back and forth from one leg to the other, waving a finger at the guard.

"Once you dare, mistake you make," he admonished threateningly. "Twice you dare, grave risk you take; thrice you dare, your neck will break!" This he indicated by snapping an imaginary piece of wood with his two hands.

As the words of the threat finally sank in, the guard raised his spear for another blow.

"Slimy little hedgehog! We'll see whose neck gets broken!"

The little man was cuffed upside the head and sent sprawling. He curled into himself and rolled, landing in a heap at Connor's feet. The hound would have leapt forward and been upon the creature if Connor hadn't ordered him back.

"Hold, Dax!"

He squatted down low and seized the little man by the scruff of the neck. The smell about the little man was dreadful. It reminded him of the beliefs of the forest people in gnomes, trolls, and other creatures of the underworld. According to those beliefs one could always recognize a troll by the stench as if they came from the bowels of the earth itself.

He hauled the creature to its feet. The little man's head came up amid a tangle of braids and matted beard. His features were like the bark of a tree, swarthy and gnarled, with sprigs of eyebrows that drooped over his eyes, fleshy jowls, and an over-large nose.

The creature smiled then—at least it seemed like a smile—giving him the look of a fool. But the eyes that gleamed beneath those shaggy brows held a cunning intelligence.

"Do not beat me, master!" the little man exclaimed, throwing his arms up for protection. "Do not beat me!"

"I do not intend to beat you," Connor informed him. "Although a good dunking in the well is tempting."

"A dunking? A dunking?" the little man squawked. "Mercy no! Mercy no! Would surely freeze, freeze would I."

He seemed to repeat everything.

"On second thought I may let the hound have you."

"Have pity, sir. Have pity. Eat me, eat me he would!" the little man wailed, dancing about wildly.

"Cease!" Connor ordered. He was beginning to think he'd been too hasty in intervening on the creature's behalf.

The little man ceased his whining and peered at him through arms crossed over his head. Dark eyes studied him intently and then gleamed with recognition.

"Ah, found you. Found you, have I," he said, slowly lowering his arms. His eyes twinkled with mischief.

"Do you not fear me, fear me?" the creature asked.

"I fear no one, little man. I have seen too much of death for that."

"Fear you death, death you fear?" he chanted.

"Only if it smells as vile as you."

The little man nodded, obviously pleased, but at what Connor had no notion.

"Should have known, known should I. True heart is rare, rare is true heart."

Drawn by the commotion, Arthur and his men approached. "What is this?"

The guards and Connor's men parted to let them pass until Arthur confronted the prisoner.

"We found this creature inside the gates," the man called Agravain explained.

Arthur studied the prisoner thoughtfully. "What is your name? Who are your people?"

The little man turned to Arthur and repeated, "What is *your* name? Who are *your* people?"

The irony of the questions, turned back on him, was not lost on Arthur. *Who was he? Who were his people?*

His reply surprised Connor.

"I am a simple warrior trying to find my way as God would grant me." He bowed his head slightly. "My name is Arthur, and I am at your service."

"Arthur is it? 'Tis Arthur!"

This seemed to impress the little man. He bowed low as well, which, considering his lack of height, almost brought his head in contact with the stones at the floor.

"I am Grendel, Grendel am I. A trader by trade, by trade a trader."

Arthur was amused. "What do you trade, trader?"

Grendel smiled wickedly. "Words for laughter, laughter for words. Perhaps a song for a maid's smile, a smile, and tricks for a crust of bread, crust of bread."

"My men are in need of laughter," Arthur replied. "Show us your tricks and we shall find a crust of bread. As for a pretty maid's smile"—he paused—"your songs will have to wait."

"Is there a pretty maid, pretty maid is there?" he asked with genuine interest, his eyes gleaming as his gaze skimmed the hall.

"Aye, perhaps," Arthur answered. "But come and warm yourself by the fire and tell us what news you have from about the countryside. Then perform a few tricks perhaps to entertain us."

This seemed to please the little man even more than the promise of bread. He bowed once more, glared at the guard who'd mistreated him, and performed his first trick—a sleight of hand that produced a squirming rabbit from the pouch that hung from his belt.

The guard was confounded while all about him laughed.

"There is nothing in his pockets, I swear. He was searched."

"Most certainly there is nothing now," one of the other men informed him as the rabbit escaped and scooted between his legs. But much to the delight of all, Grendel proved them wrong again as he reached inside the pouch and retrieved a dove which promptly escaped into the rafters overhead.

"That is meager fare, little man. We will all surely starve if you can do no better than that," Gawain remarked with a wink at his companions. "Do you not have something meatier in that pocket of yours?"

Grendel grinned, winked, then reached inside and much to everyone's humor extracted a piglet from the depths of the pouch.

"You are welcome to stay," Arthur declared. "But you might work on improving those tricks of yours. We have over three score men to feed."

"Come they will, they will come," Grendel predicted as he waddled around on little legs beside Arthur and toward the warmth of the fire.

"Who will come?" Arthur asked as he offered a skewer of meat to the trader.

"The people will come, come they will."

"What people?"

Grendel took the skewer and with great enthusiasm began to strip meat from it with sharp little teeth. As he gnawed, his gaze fastened on the warrior with the great hound at his side and narrowed with interest as the man seized a torch and left the main hall.

"Fight they will, they will fight." Grendel assured Arthur between enthusiastic smacking sounds.

Merlin joined them. He sat in the chair before the hearth, long legs stretching out before him, fingers steepled thoughtfully.

"I once knew . . . *someone*"—he chose his words carefully—"who spoke as you do."

Grendel's eyes grew wide and for a moment all smacking sounds ceased.

"Is that so, milord, milord 'tis so?"

Merlin watched him thoughtfully. "He was a bothersome little creature. I often considered stepping on him, like a bug."

Grendel swallowed hard. "You don't say, say you don't."

Merlin smiled. "Tell us more about these people you have spoken of."

"They will join Arthur, join will they," the little man said hesitantly, all his bravado of a moment before now hidden behind a watchful expression.

"They gather in the villages, in the villages they gather. Bound for Caerleon, for Caerleon bound."

It was late and the upper floors of Caerleon were cold and dark, the light from the single torch glowing across stone walls, disappearing into hollows, then reappearing again briefly to light the way ahead.

He heard the distant flutter of wings overhead as the light reached up toward the rafters. Another movement nearby along the foot of the wall drew a softly muttered curse.

"Rats."

The hound darted ahead. There was a scrabbling sound of nails and claws on stones, then sudden silence followed by a snort of satisfaction. The hound reappeared at the edge of the circle of light, the limp rat dangling from its mouth.

"I've no desire to watch you consume that wretched thing."

The hound cocked his head to one side, lips curled back in a sort of wicked smile over fangs that could tear a man apart.

"Off with you, Dax," Connor ordered, and the hound bounded past him toward the steps.

Then light from the torch pooled across the opening of the chamber. He pushed the heavy tapestry aside.

Coals glowed faintly at the brazier. Candles burned softly. The tapestry made a faint sighing sound as it fell back into place, and a figure stirred at the chair beside the pallet.

It was the woman, Dannelore. She was immediately on her feet, a watchful, guarded expression on her face.

"She has not wakened?" Connor asked.

''Nay, milord,'' she stammered. ''Most likely not for many hours,'' then hastily added, ''according to the healer.''

Connor slowly walked about the chamber, noticing the telltale signs of destruction for the first time. He also noticed that each time he moved, the woman also moved so that she was always between him and the girl, almost as if she were protecting her. Her unusual devotion puzzled Connor.

''Leave now,'' he told her abruptly.

''Milord?'' she asked, obviously stunned.

''I said, you may leave now.''

''I will stay,'' she said quietly, as if there was a choice in the matter.

''Are you not hungry?''

She blinked. ''Milord?''

''Have you had anything to eat?''

''Uh, no, milord,'' she answered hesitantly.

''There is food in the main hall, although with the arrival of our latest guest, I cannot say for how long.''

''I am not hungry.''

''You will go anyway.''

''But, milord, if she should waken . . .''

''I will tend to her.''

She was aghast. ''But you cannot—''

''Cannot?'' Connor asked. It was said so low she might not have heard it at all, except for the silken warning that needed no explanation.

''She must have more of the concoction if she wakens, and you will need more wood for the fire . . .''

A single look was enough to drive her from the chamber, the tapestry snapping back into place behind her.

When he and Arthur were lads, they had come often to this chamber. In the mornings before they were allowed to leave the hall to go adventuring as all boys did, Lady Ygraine would read to them from the ancient Latin texts that she so highly valued.

From them he learned of the ancient Romans, of battles and conquest, of the unfolding events of other cultures and kingdoms. Arthur could not wait to escape to the nearby fields or the stream for adventuring, but Connor was reluctant to leave.

He hungered for knowledge, reciting a particular word over and over in Latin until he had it perfectly. Lady Ygraine was so impressed by his ability that she gave him a small Latin text of his own. He learned it so well that it became like his first language to Arthur's consternation, and Arthur forbade him to speak it in his presence. For he was not as skilled in languages.

It was a peaceful time when he and Arthur were friends. There was nothing he wouldn't have done for Arthur. And once he believed his friend felt the same. Then Arthur left Britain.

"I'll be back," he had promised. Connor could hear the words even now as the two friends parted for what was to be the last time. Arthur was but twelve then. Connor was older by three years and near enough a man to sense that things were irrevocably changing.

"You'll see," Arthur vowed as he set off with Merlin for the Holy Land. "It won't be long, and everything will be the same as it was before between us. We'll hunt and fish, and ride, and I'll best you with a sword, for Merlin tells me I shall learn from the finest warriors in the eastern kingdoms."

With the eagerness of a child embarking on a grand adventure, Arthur had waved from the side of the ship that bore him steadily from the small harbor at Land's End. Connor watched until the boat was nothing more than a small dot on the horizon. Then Arthur disappeared completely from sight. He hadn't returned in a year or two, but after what seemed a lifetime of blood and death.

Connor placed more wood on the fire and lit another candle as the memories washed over him. Then he unsheathed his sword and propped it beside the hearth close at hand.

He welcomed the escape from the main hall filled with Arthur's ambitions and Merlin's subtle campaign to persuade him to join them.

He sat in the large chair, legs stretched before him, several layers of heavy sheepskins easing the cold at his back and the ache of tired muscles. He stared at the shining crystals that dangled from his fingers, the only possession the girl had had when he'd found her. He wondered what they meant.

He returned the crystals to the pouch at his belt. The girl had not moved since the healer had removed the arrow and bound the wound. Yet her breathing was steady and her skin was a pale pink color instead of a deathly gray pallor.

In spite of his efforts to remain awake, his eyelids soon grew heavy. Through half-closed eyes it seemed as if she was surrounded by soft, golden light, and for a moment, as Connor drifted between memories and dreams, he thought he saw another creature lying on the pallet—the deer he had hunted in the forest.

He did not know what awakened him. Perhaps it was a sound. Perhaps it was a warrior's awareness of all things around him even in sleep—even within the safety of the walls twelve feet thick surrounding him. Or perhaps it was the hunter's instinct, never knowing when he might become the hunted.

Whatever it was he was suddenly wide awake, all senses alert. He reached for his sword.

The chamber was steeped in shadows. The only light came from the brazier, where embers glowed brightly and a single candle guttered low. He tried to see through the darkness, but made out nothing beyond the feeble glow of that single candle. He listened, yet heard nothing except the steady pounding of his own heart.

He slowly reached for the candle and touched it to the wick of the oil lamp. The flame caught. Light expanded across the floor and crept up the walls of the chamber, then fell across the slender girl who stood completely naked beside the pallet.

She was pale, her skin almost bloodless in the quivering light, her blue eyes dark and luminous. Her hair spilled wildly down her back and across her shoulders, revealing more than it concealed in a glimpse of rounded breast, slender waist, and curved hip.

Her legs were long. She had shapely ankles and small feet. Her features were delicate, with almost fragile beauty. She held a hand out, as though reaching toward the warmth of the fire at the brazier. Then he realized she had actually thrust her hand into the embers.

He took a step toward her. She stiffened and looked ready to flee. He took another step, and she bolted for the door.

Her movements were awkward and clumsy. She stumbled and fell to the floor. With a curse, Connor went after her.

She pushed herself back to her feet and again lunged away from him. He caught her at the opening of the chamber, his arm closing around her waist. The sword was now cast aside. It took both hands just to prevent her escaping.

She bucked against him, trying to break his hold. When that didn't work she tried to slip from his grasp by dropping to the floor. He caught her, hauling her back against him, arms locked around her in a hold no man could have escaped.

She made desperate noises as she fought him, much like the keening sounds of a wounded animal, her waist-length hair tangling about both of them, her nails raking deep across his forearms. For someone who had been so recently injured and sickened with fever she had amazing strength.

"Cease!" he growled against her ear, holding her tight against him and lifting her clear of the floor so that she could not gain footing.

She continued to struggle, and he feared she might do herself harm. But eventually he felt the strength leave her and she slumped against him.

Her breathing was faint. Her head rolled back against his shoulder. Connor turned her and swung her up into his arms.

He carried her to the pallet and gently laid her down upon it. He covered her with sheepskins, brushing back strands of golden hair from her damp forehead and cheeks.

She didn't waken. She didn't even stir, but slept so deeply he could almost believe it had never happened. Except for the bloody marks at his arms, almost as if he'd been attacked by a wild creature.

Chapter Six

Images swept through Meg's thoughts—the terrifying journey through the portal; chaos and confusion when she'd emerged on the other side into the mortal world; the painful transformation into a creature she had no practical knowledge of; then the piercing pain at her shoulder that left her weak, defenseless, and for the first time unable to escape or help herself.

They were mingled with other images—of an encampment; her vague awareness that her thoughts and movements were oddly disjointed as if she could no longer control each thought and movement; the confusion of words and sounds she didn't understand; then another image . . . that of the fierce-looking creature who had first come upon her in the forest.

The image of the creature kept changing. One moment it took on the green and brown colors of the forest. The next it had changed, revealing the sharp-angled features of a mortal. Except for those cold eyes that had first looked back at her from the mask of many colors.

Those eyes did not change. They were still that same hard, cold color like clouds before a storm—staring at her, reaching out to her, so close she tried to look away but discovered she could not.

Those eyes were everywhere, watching her, waiting, until she feared she might be lost in that cold, gray storm. A strange, lonely, keening sound like that of a wounded animal echoed over and over through her tangled thoughts. Meg suddenly jerked awake.

A wild chaos of sensations replaced those images—the sudden rush of cold air; the unusual shaking that moved through her and wouldn't let go; the urgent, desperate sound as she dragged air into her lungs; the frantic pounding she heard and felt; the dull throb that spiraled through her, creating other sensations she had no practical knowledge of.

She had no idea where she was or what had happened beyond that encounter after stepping through the portal. She closed her eyes, trying to block out the unfamiliar discomfort that moved through her—that uneasy sensation as if everything about her was suddenly turned upside down, the shifting motion low inside that gradually swelled upward, pressing against her throat.

Instinctively, she dragged in deep gulps of cool air. Eventually everything about her seemed to right itself and the pressing sensation at her throat eased. The frantic pounding eventually slowed. She slowly opened her eyes.

Stone walls, stone floors, not unlike the stone portal she had come through. Overhead were timbers laid evenly across, not unlike the trees in the forest. It was not unlike her chamber in the village at Avalon. And nearby, close enough so that she felt its radiance, a fire burned.

Golden light, orange-blue flames. She reached out to that radiant light until the flames licked at her fingertips and burned higher. She closed her eyes and envisioned the flames, source of light, strength, and power as they glowed up the length of her arm, radiated across her skin, and then burned deep inside giving back strength and power.

When she opened her eyes the flames had receded, resting quietly once more in the metal bowl. She stared at the hand she held before her. It was finely made, with fragile bones and slender tendons beneath pale skin. She brought her other hand up and stared at the two of them.

When she touched a thumb to forefinger it created the strangest sensation—softness, warmth, strength. Then she discovered more complex movement as she reached out again and knocked a basin of water over.

Some of the contents spilled over onto her hand. It was as hot as the flames and like the flames left no mark, but filled her with a curious sense of wonder.

She tried to assimilate what she learned about the mortal world as she reached for the basin. But she was clumsy and the basin wobbled out of reach. She channeled her thoughts in the old way, levitated the bowl with ease and slowly lowered it to the surface of the table.

Wishing to explore more of her surroundings, Meg seized the sheepskin that lay across her, fingers sinking into soft wool, her awareness immediately filled with other sensations—those of softness and warmth—and vague images of someone covering her with it. She drew the sheepskin aside and attempted to stand.

Her previous transformations had been those of creatures she had learned about—a falcon, fox, and deer. The fox and the deer were four-legged creatures while the falcon had the advantage of wings. Nothing prepared her for the awkwardness of standing on two legs.

It required physical strength and balance, which she had neither of. She stumbled and fell to the floor, scraping bare skin at her hands and in other places. She lay there trembling and frustrated at her inability to master even the most simple human movement. A toddling child had more coordination.

That was how Dannelore found her, sprawled naked on the floor, eyes glistening with tears of frustration, hands clenched in fists of anger.

"By the Ancient Ones!" she exclaimed, the metal trencher she carried clattering down onto the table. She grabbed a sheepskin from the pallet and flung it across Meg's shoulders.

"What can you be thinking?" she demanded, her voice high and urgent as she snugged the fleece about Meg and helped her sit up.

Meg's senses were overwhelmed. She clasped her hands over

her ears as she was assailed with sounds and noises she'd never experienced before.

"Aye, forgive me," Dannelore communicated in the old way, her thoughts reaching out through the noise and confusion.

"I am not used to having others to speak with in the old way. I am perhaps becoming too mortal." She reached out, gently drawing Meg's hands away.

"It's just that you startled me so. Seeing you lying there like that, I thought . . ." She hesitated as Meg finally looked up.

"It's just that you were so very sick and you've been asleep so long. I feared you might have taken worse again."

Meg had no memory of this place or how she had come to be there. The last thing she clearly remembered was following Dannelore through the portal, then the sound of mortals in the forest.

"How long have I been here?"

"Four days now."

"Four days!" She had little experience with the concept of time—days, weeks, months, years did not exist in her world— but she had heard it spoken of among those who moved between the worlds and knew that four days was a considerable length of time.

"Aye, and the master has been to see you each day."

"My brother?"

Dannelore nodded. *"Each morning and each evening to check the wound at your shoulder and with strict instructions for the poultice I was to make."*

Only now did she remember the wound, her fingers lightly brushing the scar.

"Did he suspect anything?"

"He said nothing. Though I cannot be certain. He has his ways, as you do." Then Dannelore saw the raw skin at the palm of her hand.

"You must be more careful, mistress," she admonished, lapsing into spoken words. "Until you learn the way of things."

Meg reached out with her other hand and touched her fingers to Dannelore's lips.

"Teach me how to say the words."

" 'Tis a most inconvenient way of communicating,'' Dannelore warned. "And there are different languages, which I cannot understand. Sometimes, these mortals cannot even understand their own language. They yell and shout at one another, and no one can understand what the other says.''

"I want to learn,'' Meg insisted, with that same stubbornness that had brought her through the portal in the first place.

Dannelore sighed. "This will get us both into trouble,'' she muttered. " 'Tis best that you go back. Already, you very nearly got yourself killed. And there's no telling what other trouble will come down on us when it's discovered you've gone through the portal.''

Meg mimicked her perfectly, drawing her brows together in a frowning expression and expelling a heavy sigh, but the expression in her eyes glinted with mischief. She sensed a hidden thought the woman tried to keep from her.

"Do not even consider it,'' Meg warned. "If you attempt to tell my brother or cast a spell, I will be forced to transform you.''

Dannelore's startled gaze met hers. Such a threat was never to be taken lightly, but from one who possessed such powers as her young mistress it was positively frightening.

"You wouldn't.''

"I know all your thoughts,'' Meg reminded her. "And my powers return tenfold by the moment, even if I cannot yet master this mortal body.'' Meg smiled.

"It would be unwise to cross me in my weakened physical condition. I might gravely miscalculate a spellcast and change you into a mouse ...'' She thought for a moment. "Or a hedgehog perhaps. 'Tis been known to happen.''

Dannelore shook her head. "I can see there's no persuading you to go back.''

"No, there is not.''

"Then I suppose it's my responsibility to see that nothing happens to you.''

Meg smiled, unaware that it transformed her features into a rare and stunning beauty that was breathtaking and caused Dannelore to mutter dire imprecations.

"I can take care of myself," Meg assured her. *" 'Tis just that I need your help in adjusting to this transformation. Hopefully, 'tis not too dreadful a form. I would not care to have these mortals trying to hunt me down like a deer again, nor to frighten them because I am dreadful to look at. I could always change if you think it necessary."* She looked to Dannelore for advice on the matter.

Dannelore shook her head. *"I do not think it will be necessary, mistress. You will not be hunted like an animal. If anything, your features may be* too *pleasant to look upon."*

"How can that be?"

It was then Dannelore realized her mistress had absolutely no idea what she looked like.

"One thing at a time," she said, holding out her hands to Meg. *"First, you must learn to walk. 'Tis not so difficult once you get the way of it."*

"That's easy for you to say. You're not the one with these wretched marks. I don't like the feel of them at all."

"Bruises. In time they will heal," Dannelore informed her, pulling her to her feet.

The sheepskin immediately fell to the floor at Meg's feet. She stood before Dannelore in glorious, naked splendor with only the thick satin of shimmering gold hair that fell to her waist to cover anything at all.

"First we must have clothes," Dannelore muttered.

"Close?" Meg repeated experimentally.

"Aye." Dannelore nodded as she retrieved the sheepskin and secured it snugly about her mistress' shoulders.

"Keep this closed *or we'll have more trouble on our hands than Master Merlin finding out who you are."*

"You make no sense!" Meg replied with exasperation. She closed a slender hand over Dannelore's wrist, stopping her. She had already learned simple movements and instinctively assimilated them. She was learning very fast.

"I want to learn everything about the mortal world," Meg reminded her.

"Aye, and you shall," Dannelore grimly replied. *"It will come at you very fast, for there is trouble here. At least you*

*have the power to take it all in, and quickly. You must watch,
listen, and learn. I will help you as much as I can.''*

"What trouble?"

*"The fortress was attacked and Lady Ygraine and her daugh-
ter abducted. The whole countryside is at war. 'Tis the reason
Arthur and Merlin have returned—to unite the people against
their enemies.''*

But Meg sensed something more, *a sudden change* in Dannelore's thoughts and the source of that sudden change.

*"Something else has happened. Is it the one you called
John?"*

Dannelore looked up suddenly. There was such anguish in
her expression and her thoughts that it stunned Meg. She had
never sensed such powerful emotions.

Dannelore did not answer right away, but retrieved the basin
she'd brought to the chamber and very nearly dropped. She
pulled Meg into the chair before the brazier and sat opposite
with the basin cradled in her lap.

"If you are to live among the mortals you must eat." She
scooped a portion of the contents from the metal bowl with a
spoon and held it aloft.

*" 'Tis not so bad once you get used to it. Some of it is
quite good, with surprising texture and taste, although there
is precious little of that here.''*

Meg gently laid her hand over Dannelore's. *"You must tell
me what has happened.''*

Dannelore lowered the spoon to the bowl. Her shoulders
sagged. Meg sensed the powerful emotions moving through
her, emotions which had names but which she had never experienced.

"He was here. Many died in the attack, others fled." Meg's
thoughts quivered like a tightly drawn bow. *"There is no word
of him.''*

Meg instinctively felt the need to comfort Dannelore. It was
strange and a little disconcerting, this need to reach out to
another mortal who seemed so filled with pain.

"If some harm had come to him," she reasoned, *"would
you not sense it?"*

Dannelore looked up, her eyes glistening with tears and feeble hope. She nodded.

"Then he must still be alive," Meg replied. *"We must find him, and I will help. 'Tis the least I can do for all the help you have given me."*

She seized the spoon and scooped a portion of the contents from their metal container, exactly as Dannelore had done. Then, just as Dannelore had, she emptied the spoonful into her mouth. She shuddered and her delicate features twisted in an instinctive reaction.

"How have these mortals survived?" she exclaimed.

" 'Tis a question pondered by many," Dannelore admitted, pushing the bowl toward her. *"But if you are to remain in the mortal world, you must eat."*

Meg stared at the contents of the bowl and in a very mortal reaction, contemplated just exactly what she'd like to do with the contents of that bowl.

They bargained over just how much she would eat, each threatening the other with dire consequences. But she had to admit that the effect was far better than the taste. She felt stronger after swallowing a sufficient amount of the broth, although she had hidden several offending pieces of unknown substance in the folds of the cloth Dannelore had laid across her lap. At the first opportunity she flung them into the fire at the brazier.

After her mistress had eaten, Dannelore turned her attention to Meg's appearance.

"You smell," Dannelore bluntly informed her. *"It might be fine for mortals, but 'tis not fine to me. We must improve that situation immediately."*

"Smell?" Meg asked with confusion.

Dannelore seized a slender wrist and held it aloft, exposing a delicate underarm.

"Unfortunately, some of these mortals do not seem to be bothered by such things. If they had their way of things they would go about smelling like the sheep pens."

Meg had wondered about that. There did seem to be a strange essence about her. *"Do I smell like the sheep pens?"*

"Nay, you rather smell like a dead goat."

"That's not good?"

"It is not," Dannelore replied emphatically. *"But there is a cure for it."*

After her first experience eating food, Meg wasn't at all certain she wanted to find out what the cure was. She watched warily as Dannelore poured steaming water from a pot at the brazier into a shallow basin and set it before Meg at the table.

Streamers of vapor rose from the surface, then gradually ceased as the water cooled. Dannelore was about to sprinkle some sort of herbal mixture into the water, when Meg seized her by the wrist.

"What is that?" She pointed to the two images reflected on the surface of the water. One—Dannelore's reflection—she easily recognized. The other she did not.

" 'Tis your reflection," Dannelore explained.

Meg touched the surface of the water. Ripples distorted the images. Eventually the surface calmed and she saw the images clearly once more. This time she tentatively touched her own face, feeling the contact at the same time she saw it reflected on the surface of the water.

These were not the features she remembered from her dreams. Those had been strong, hard features, harsh one moment and then strangely transformed the next, all in a confusion that made no sense to her.

She stared at her eyes—not cold and gray with the storm of hidden emotions churning in their depths—but a darker color, staring back at her with curiosity.

She touched her chin, nose, forehead, and cheeks in tentative exploration. Then she glanced at Dannelore's reflection.

"I do not much care for the way I look. 'Tis too different. You have very good features. I much prefer them. I shall transform myself."

"No!" Dannelore stopped her. *"You must not."*

"Why not? I can be anything I choose."

Dannelore sat down across from her and explained. *"They have already seen you as you are. They would think it strange if you were suddenly different."* Then she added the most compelling reason of all, which she knew Meg would grasp immediately.

"Some might even grow suspicious and think you are not mortal."

Meg nodded. *"Yes, you are right. I will simply have to adjust to the way I look. But I hope I do not frighten them."*

"You do not," Dannelore assured her.

"Ohhh," Meg exclaimed as she inhaled deeply. *" 'Tis like the meadows in spring!"*

She sat in the chair before the brazier, wrapped in a thick muslin blanket, her skin above the blanket still beaded with fragrant water, her wet hair lying across one shoulder like dark molten gold.

"Now I understand."

"Aye," Dannelore confirmed. *"And you must wash frequently, or you will again smell like a dead goat."*

Meg wrinkled her nose. *"I will remember."*

The muslin blanket slipped to her waist, exposing the curve of high full breasts and slender waist. She stared down at herself and glanced over at Dannelore.

"What are these?" She touched her own breasts, watching with fascination as the nipples dimpled and hardened. While Dannelore explained the basics of human female anatomy she continued her exploration, abandoning the blanket altogether.

"And this?" With equal fascination she touched between her legs.

"I will explain that later." Dannelore crossed the chamber and pulled the muslin high about her neck. May the Ancient Ones save her. This was worse than looking after a wayward child.

"You are too fine to look at for your own good. We shall definitely have to find you something to wear. You cannot go around wrapped in muslin and sheepskins, especially with all these men about. They will get all sorts of notions into their heads."

"What sort of notions?"

Dannelore added that to the list of things her mistress must learn about.

"Now," she instructed, weaving together voice and thought, "if you are to learn the ways of mortals you must learn to speak as they speak. Listen to everything very carefully."

As she went about the chamber she continued to speak and think her thoughts at the same time so that Meg would gain an understanding of it both through the connection of their thoughts and through the sounds of the words.

"There may be a gown of Lady Ygraine's that was not burned or cut to pieces." Dannelore searched through the contents of trunks that had been scattered about the chamber.

"I would like to open the shutters," Meg said aloud, testing what she had learned. "I do not like being confined inside these walls."

"I felt the same when I first came to live in the mortal world," Dannelore explained. "But mortal bodies are frail. They build walls for protection. Listen carefully, you will hear the wind. The storm has not let up yet. Mortals would quickly die in such cold. 'Tis the reason many of the men grow restless. They wish to leave and cannot."

"Why do they wish to leave?"

"They are suspicious of Merlin and do not believe in Arthur's cause."

Dannelore found a few garments that had escaped the raiders' hasty pillaging and also located piles of torn and shredded fabric. One gown looked as if it might fit. It was made of wool in a shade of cool, pale gray—a plain color the Lady Ygraine had not been fond of and had never worn.

"Aye, this will do," Dannelore said with satisfaction and an eye toward altering the other garments which included a rich burgundy tunic with gold satin bliaud.

"They will hardly notice you for the plain color, and I'll see what can be done with the other garments. Perhaps they can be dyed—brown or black would be good."

Meg wrinkled her nose. "I do not care for the gray. 'Tis too dull. It will make me look like a mudhen. I much prefer the others if I must wear clothes at all."

"You must," Dannelore replied emphatically. "And better a mudhen than a dove for their feasting."

Her meaning was completely lost on Meg. Frowning slightly, she turned her attention to her wet hair which lay heavy and wet across her shoulders—something else that had never been a concern before.

Finally, completely exasperated and unable to explain in mortal words, she abandoned any attempt in the mortal way and blurted out, *"What is to be done with this?"*

Her hair had dried into a glorious, tumbling mass of shimmering gold waves that spilled over her shoulder and down the length of her back.

Dannelore looked up at the obvious frustration that reached her through those thoughts.

"Cut it," she muttered to herself without thinking. "Perhaps then they will not take notice of you."

It seemed a reasonable solution to Meg. She seized the carving knife from the table and was about to cut off all her golden tresses when Dannelore stopped her.

"I will have to be more careful with my words until you become more familiar in the way mortals speak."

She took the knife from Meg and explained, " 'Tis not seemly for a woman to cut her hair. They would think you wrong headed if you cut it off, or worse—a witch or spellcaster." She sighed with growing concern.

"We shall just have to find a way to cover your hair. A hood perhaps."

With an impish smile Meg mimicked her deep sigh. "You worry too much."

"And you worry not enough!" Dannelore warned. "If Master Merlin discovers what you've done . . ."

"We shall have to make certain he does not," Meg informed her.

Her ability to assimilate was amazing. It seemed to increase with each new thing she learned, and she was hungry for knowledge of the mortal world. Through the morning her ability to speak steadily improved as long as it pertained to matters

Dannelore was familiar with. The rest would have to come of its own as she interacted with others.

"What about my other abilities?" Meg asked. "Are they different in the mortal world?"

"They are the same as before," Dannelore assured her. " 'Tis only that everything else around you is quite different. These mortals do not understand our ways. You must be very careful how you use your abilities."

Meg understood the need for secrecy, but she couldn't resist a bit of experimentation, just to make certain she hadn't lost her touch. While Dannelore turned her attention to the gray gown, Meg concentrated on the basin of water that sat on the table.

"There," Dannelore announced a few minutes later, holding the gown up for inspection. "I am not well skilled with a needle. You shall have to try it on to see the exact fit." When Meg didn't immediately respond, she looked up.

"Is there something amiss? Do you feel unwell, mistress?"

"I feel quite well," Meg assured her, laughter bubbling into her throat.

Dannelore stared at her curiously, wondering what had caused such good humor. Then she realized Meg's attention was focused on a location over her head. She followed the direction of her gaze and looked up. The basin of water hovered directly above her, suspended in air. Her eyes widened.

Dannelore had heard enough stories of her mistress' lessons in levitation to know she was in serious jeopardy of being thoroughly doused.

"Careful, mistress," she admonished. "You must concentrate. Lower the bowl back to the table."

"I am concentrating," Meg replied through her laughter, whooping with delight at Dannelore's expression as the bowl wobbled precariously.

"Mistress!" Dannelore's voice rose several octaves in warning. She attempted to step from beneath the bowl, but it moved with her. When she attempted to escape in another direction, it followed.

"What if someone should see?" Dannelore scolded, suspecting far more was amiss than poor skills.

"I would know if anyone approached. We are quite safe."

Dannelore felt anything but safe. She tried another tactic. "You should not tire yourself, mistress."

"I do not feel tired at all. I have rested long enough," Meg responded as she sent the bowl scurrying after the changeling. Dannelore stopped abruptly and reversed directions. The bowl also reversed, tipping just enough to spill a few drops of water on her head. Dannelore shrieked. Deciding on a different course of action, she tried reaching for the bowl, which just escaped her grasp.

Meg clapped her hands together, focusing her power in yet another direction. The shutters flew open. To her delight snow swirled into the chamber in a glittering, twinkling cloud.

"You are right. My powers are not diminished at all, and there are so many more wondrous things to explore in the mortal world."

While she delighted in the splendor of her first experience with snow, she sensed Dannelore focusing her own powers into a spellcast. Her simple spell was powerless against Meg's.

She sent the bowl in a new direction, whipping it around behind the woman, playfully tapping her on the backside.

Dannelore was indignant. "That is enough! You go too far, mistress!"

"Not nearly far enough."

While Dannelore frantically tried to close the shutters though still under persistent attack from the bowl, Meg turned her thoughts in a new direction.

"Nay!" Dannelore pleaded. "Not the gown!"

Meg's experience with needlework was even more lacking than the changeling's. But she needed no experience for what she had in mind. Concentrating a portion of her attention on the gown, she sent it aloft like a pennant being hoisted atop a pole.

As if it had taken on a life of its own the gown whipped about the chamber over their heads in ridiculous poses with its sleeves waving, skirts flying. Then it swept low in an attack on Dannelore. Under siege from both the bowl of water, the gown, and the snow that swirled in through the open shutters, the poor woman was beside herself.

Out of desperation, Dannelore threatened, "If you do not cease, I will tell Master Merlin everything myself!"

That got Meg's attention. The bowl came to a halt in midair. Overhead, the gown ceased its frantic flight.

"And how will you explain your part in my escape?"

"I took no part in your escape from Avalon," Dannelore replied indignantly. "I did not even know of it until the warriors came upon you in the forest."

"You are to guard against any others going through the portal." Meg reminded her of the long-standing law of their world.

"Therefore it can only be assumed that you aided my escape. It will not go well for you when that is discovered."

"You cannot tell a lie," Dannelore reminded her.

"No, but I can be most convincing with the truth."

Abruptly, Meg's attention was drawn in another direction.

"Someone is coming. My brother!" She saw the satisfied look that crossed the changeling's face.

In a final act of defiance, Meg sent a burst of power aloft. As Merlin swept the tapestry aside and stepped through the opening to the chamber, the bowl overturned, dousing Dannelore with water, and threads exploded from the seams of the gown.

Sleeves and pieces of fabric drifted to the floor, landing at Merlin's feet. In her frantic attempt to escape a dousing, Dannelore slipped on the wet stones of the floor and landed on her bottom. Her hair was drenched, sagging low over her forehead, and drooping into her eyes.

Merlin's gaze swept the chamber, the scattered pieces of the gown, the open shutters with snow swirling in, and Dannelore's sodden appearance.

"Is something amiss, Mistress Dannelore?" he asked.

She pushed the sodden mass of hair back from her forehead. Her gaze narrowed on Meg who sat innocently before the brazier like a convalescing patient, a woolen blanket clutched about her trembling shoulders as she tried to muffle her laughter.

For a moment Meg was certain Dannelore would tell him everything. She knew she deserved it, but she couldn't help herself.

"Nay, milord," Dannelore finally muttered. "There is naught amiss. I but slipped on the wet stones."

Merlin looked from one to the other. Meg sensed his probing thoughts, but she kept her own well hidden and the spellcast she'd set when they'd first arrived at Caerleon kept her secret safe.

He picked up the pieces of fabric and helped Dannelore to her feet. "You must take greater care, mistress." Then he stepped past her and closed the shutters.

"Yes, milord."

"You would not wish to injure yourself or sicken from the cold. Most find it advisable not to go about mopping the floors during a storm and with the shutters open."

That almost did it. Dannelore's mouth dropped open, then snapped shut. Meg sensed it took all her will not to tell him everything.

"Mistress Dannelore has not been herself," Meg hastily intervened, and then had a sudden ingenious thought. "She is deeply concerned about someone who once lived here. There has been no word of him since the attack."

That ended any plan Dannelore had to tell him. If Merlin learned of Meg's escape, it would also be discovered that Dannelore had left Avalon. Both would be forced to return and Dannelore might never learn the fate of the mortal she searched for.

"Many are missing," Merlin replied. "What is his name? I will see what may be learned of his fate."

"John," Dannelore replied. "He was groomsman to the Duke of Cornwall."

He nodded. "He may have fled into the hills with the others. Almost daily they return now that Arthur is at Caerleon. Perhaps someone has some word of him."

"Thank you, milord. I am most grateful."

Merlin turned his attention to Meg. He was pleased with the progress of the wound.

"You are most fortunate; the arrow did not pierce the heart," he said as he gently probed the wound at her shoulder.

"Are you feeling stronger this afternoon?"

To Meg's bemusement, Dannelore answered tersely, "Much stronger, milord. She must not overdo. She might have a relapse." By her tone of voice it was likely Dannelore might be the cause of that *relapse*.

He seemed to sense the woman's vexation and perhaps sensed that Meg had some part in the chaos he'd walked into when he first entered the chamber.

"What is your name?" Merlin asked, turning his amused attention back to her.

Her thoughts froze. Her name. She could not tell a lie. What, she wondered, did Merlin know about *her?* She could not probe his thoughts without exposing her own. She sensed Dannelore's panic.

"I am called Meg."

"I know someone by that name," he replied. "It was a very long time ago. She was hardly more than an infant." He looked up and studied her thoughtfully.

"She had the bluest eyes. Very much like yours."

Dannelore ceased breathing altogether. Meg, too, held her breath, focusing her power to keep his thoughts from hers.

Then he smiled, his attention returning to the wound at her shoulder.

"I had hoped you would be much improved by now. The wound closed easily enough, but one can never tell about these things. And I am not one to accept failure."

"I am most grateful that you do not," Meg replied. Behind him, she heard Dannelore finally take a breath.

Throughout the examination Meg studied him. She had heard countless stories about him. Of his tutoring by the Ancient Ones; his ordeal in the Great Unknown; of his transformation, born as a mortal but with the wisdom of the ages in his blood; of his encounters with the powers of Darkness; and of his bond with Arthur who might one day be king if he succeeded in uniting all of Britain.

He was both legend and myth, at the same time more than and not at all what she had expected from stories she had heard about him.

He applied a healing balm to her scraped palm. Beneath it was an old scar, a knife wound she did not remember. His touch was soothing and gentle, with a radiant warmth that seeped through her skin into her very bones.

It was that same healing power that had sealed the wound at her shoulder and saved her life. Though she possessed many of the same powers as Merlin, she had never had occasion to use that particular power.

He was kind, not at all the fierce, sorcerer-warrior she'd heard whispered about with both awe and trepidation in the immortal world—a force to be respected and feared. She did not think he seemed so frightening at all.

He was most pleasant to look at when compared with other mortals she had seen since stepping through the portal. His hair was dark and fell to his shoulders in gleaming waves. He wore a full beard, closely cropped. It molded a strong jaw and finely curved mouth. His nose was long and straight, his dark brows drawn together in concentration over piercing blue eyes.

Though their features were dissimilar with her light hair and fine features, there were other similarities. She wrinkled her nose in speculation, having not paid much attention when looking at her reflection. She hoped it was not as long.

But their eyes—therein lay a striking resemblance she had noticed immediately, and she wondered if he was aware of it as well.

"What is it, mistress, that you find so fascinating that you must stare at me?" he asked without looking up. It was then Meg realized she'd unwisely dropped her guard for a moment. He had sensed her staring at him.

Behind him, she caught sight of Dannelore's warning look. Her thoughts connected with Meg's.

"Be careful what you say!"

"I was thinking you don't resemble a fire-breathing dragon

with horrible teeth at all,'' Meg truthfully replied. Dannelore's eyes rolled back in her head.

Merlin coughed sharply, looking up at her with both amusement and bemusement.

''Who told you such a thing?''

Again she caught sight of Dannelore's frantic expression. She smiled with amusement.

'' 'Tis widely heard. There are many stories about Merlin the Enlightened One.''

He looked at her quizzically. ''Now that is a name I have not heard in a very long time. What else did you hear?''

''That you have the ability to pull things out of thin air.'' Behind him, Dannelore rolled her eyes.

''Such as rabbits out of a pocket?'' he suggested, thinking of Grendel's sleight-of-hand trick.

''Yes.''

''Please continue,'' he said with growing amusement.

'' 'Tis said you have the power to call upon the forces of nature with a single thought.''

''Most interesting. What else?''

''Transformation, of course,'' she added.

''Ah, yes. The fire-breathing dragon.''

''With horrible teeth to tear foolish mortals apart.''

''Of course.'' It was all he could do to keep from grinning at her.

''If I could do all these things, does it not seem reasonable that I would halt this dreadful storm so that we are not snowbound.''

''I suppose.''

''And as for rabbits in the pocket''—he turned the pocket of his tunic inside out to prove it was empty—''as you can see I have none.''

''Don't forget the dragon.''

He nodded. ''The dragon. I assure you if I had such power I would be sorely tested not to use it.'' He leaned close to whisper, ''There are many foolish mortals within these walls.''

''You do not seem much disposed toward breathing fire,'' she concluded.

"Not recently," he replied, his mouth curving in a deep smile. "I've been told it can be quite hazardous."

She smiled inwardly. She discovered that she liked him very much. He had cleverly replied to each of her theories about The Enchanter, while denying nothing and telling no lies.

"What of yourself, mistress? How did you come to be in the forest alone?"

The question caught her off guard. Without looking up she sensed Dannelore's latest panic. Could she be as clever?

"I remember very little before arriving at Caerleon," she replied. "Vague images, things I try to remember but cannot."

"What of Maelgwyn?" It was a simple enough question, but it was a trap. She sensed it immediately and knew he probed her thoughts for the truth.

"I had never heard his name before coming to Caerleon."

"Did you see anyone in the forest, other than the warrior who found you?"

"Nay, milord."

"Perhaps you will remember more in time."

"Perhaps."

He lightly stroked the palm of her hand. She immediately experienced a deep, penetrating warmth. When she looked down the injury was almost completely gone.

"I think you will live," he declared with satisfaction. "Perhaps you would care to join us at the evening meal."

"I would like that very much," Meg replied enthusiastically.

"She must rest," Dannelore insisted. "Perhaps on the morrow or the day after."

"Or course," Merlin agreed. "When you are fully recovered will be soon enough. A hall filled with warriors is hardly appropriate company for a young lady. Perhaps then we can discuss your adventures in the forest further."

It was on the tip of Meg's tongue to tell both of them what they could do with their notions of young ladies, when Dannelore stepped between them.

"You are looking quite pale, my dear," she told Meg. "I will fix you a refreshing tisane."

"I will visit later to check the bandage and see that the

wound does not fester,'' Merlin told them. He bowed slightly and then left.

''I am considering preparing you a fine poison!'' Meg fumed. ''Why did you send him away? I enjoy his company. He is most challenging.''

''You play foolish games.'' Dannelore wagged a finger at her. ''You will trip yourself up if you continue. 'Tis best to stay away from Merlin. You are not as clever as you think, and he is more clever than you think. He will see through the spellcast.''

Meg laughed. ''You have so little faith. You must trust me.''

''Trust you? Aye, and we'll both find ourselves cast into the netherworld.''

''Perhaps you are right,'' Meg conceded. ''I may have acted unwisely.''

Dannelore watched her through narrowed eyes. ''What new game is this?''

''No game. I simply realize the error of my ways. I will be more careful in the future.''

Dannelore laid a hand at her forehead. ''Are you feeling unwell?''

''A bit weak perhaps,'' Meg confessed.

''Aye, well and no wonder. Carrying on as you have, flying things about the room, risking being discovered. What would you have done if he'd walked in a moment sooner?''

Probably emptied the basin over his *head.* It was what she wanted to say, but didn't.

''Sit and rest before the fire,'' Dannelore instructed. ''I've had a pottage simmering since early morn in the kitchen below. It will be a sight better than dried deer meat for a change— tough as tree bark that is. Then we'll see about mending the gray gown. You can't go about naked.''

Meg had no desire to sit or rest. Since she was someone who had never been confined, stone walls made her feel trapped. She wanted to explore. Her gaze fell on the blue tunic.

The fabric was soft and silky, taking on the warmth of her skin as she held it against her. And she much preferred the blue color of the tunic, the burgundy of the other gown.

She put on the gown first, then the tunic and bliaud, lacing it down the side the same as Dannelore's. The garments fit well enough, the bliaud lacing taut at the waist, the sleeves of the gown fitted at the arms and the hem brushing her bare feet. The tunic was worn loose over all and provided additional warmth. What she had first thought cumbersome and unnecessary did seem to have a purpose.

She caught her reflection in the basin, startled by what she saw. The rich colors shimmered on the surface of the water, the blue of the tunic matching the color of her eyes, and her hair shimmered like a golden waterfall over her shoulder.

Since she had no experience in such matters, she could not judge whether that was good or bad, she knew only that the colors of the clothes pleased her far more than the gray gown had. Then she turned her attention to exploring.

The chamber had once belonged to Lady Ygraine. Remnants of tapestries that had once adorned the walls still hung there. Several wooden chests had been overturned, their contents strewn across the floor.

Dannelore had tried to establish some order. The chairs had been righted and set before a table. Light was provided by the fire at the brazier and several oil lamps that blazed brightly. Along the walls, in niches, were small statues, a metal ewer, and several personal items.

The walls and floors were made of the same square-cut fieldstone as the rest of Caerleon, with cross beams overhead. A heavy tapestry hung across the opening.

Her gaze fixed on that opening. A guard stood in the passage just beyond. Not to guard against her escape, Dannelore had explained, but to guard against others who might come in.

Meg didn't quite understand the logic of that, nor see the reason for it. But none had entered the chamber except Dannelore and Merlin.

If only she could leave the chamber for a little while, Meg thought, her fingers skimming across the surface of the stones at the wall—and return before Dannelore was any the wiser.

She drummed her fingers against a stone, then stared as she

continued to lightly drum on it. Her fingers did not drum on the surface of the stone but sank into it!

Meg flattened her hand against the wall and pressed lightly. It was not the stone that moved, but her hand. It moved through the stone.

Dannelore said her abilities were the same as before. It was the world around her that was different. She must simply adjust to that difference. Focusing her power, she thrust her hand into the stone. It passed through easily.

She pulled her hand back and slowly smiled. Dannelore would not be at all pleased. Then she focused her power once more, concentrating all of her energy into her hand as she pressed it against the stone at the wall.

Deep within her, where the power of the Light burned, the transformation slowly began. It was not easy. She was not yet used to this mortal body.

She took a deep breath, imagined herself changing even as she felt the rough texture of the stone through her skin, the sharp coldness that melted away at her touch, her own essence transforming, molding to the tiny spaces and fissures made centuries ago when the stone first formed.

Then the wall surrounded her. At first it resisted, the dark coldness trying to cast her back, but like the powerful light from which it had been born a millennia ago, she warmed the stone, burning bright, reaching for the other side.

Chapter Seven

"Four days!" Connor swore as he leaned over a map spread before him on the small prayer table in the chapel adjacent to the main hall.

"Will this cursed storm never end?"

Throughout Caerleon his men occupied themselves as best they could, tending to various wounds, repairing or replacing lost weapons from among the few carelessly left behind after the attack, mending tunics and boots, scrounging for food, blankets, fleece skins, anything that might be needed and could be carried at a moment's notice.

In spite of the fact that Arthur was the master of Caerleon by birthright, he posted his own guards at the towers and the battlements alongside Arthur's. Arthur had been gone a long time whereas Connor knew Maelgwyn too well. He left nothing to chance.

" 'Tis as if the weather conspires against us," Simon expressed his own frustration, "while Maelgwyn steadily closes around us."

"He is no fool," Connor replied, knowing full well what he spoke of. "There is no need for him to risk his men in this weather. He has the men and resources to wait out the storm.

He will hole up in the hills, saving both for a strike against us. It will go the better for him if he can catch us languishing here at Caerleon.''

He rubbed his left shoulder, a reflexive instinct in response to imaginary pain. Real pain had ceased long ago, assuaged in part by the retribution in blood he'd taken through the years. But it wasn't enough. This was a deeper pain that never went away but focused around the memory of his own capture and torture at the hands of Maelgwyn.

That he could have born easily enough. He was a warrior, and the life of a warrior had taught him to detach himself from the pain of torture or wounds. But Maelgwyn had added an interesting element to Connor's torture.

He supervised it personally, taking particular delight in the smell of burning flesh as he drove a red-hot poker deep into Connor's shoulder as his victim hung upside down, suspended helplessly like an animal waiting to be gutted, his wrists bound by thick ropes so that the harder he instinctively fought against the pain, the more damage to muscles and tendons drawn to the point of snapping.

Maelgwyn's goal had been to slowly cripple Connor with torture in the hope of driving him mad, all the while describing exactly how he'd tortured Connor's family before they had died. He might have succeeded if not for Radvald, who had more cunning, determination, and reckless stubbornness than was wise for any ten men.

He had entered Maelgwyn's encampment with only three men, wearing the tunics and leggings of four of Maelgwyn's warriors previously sent out to guard the perimeter of the encampment.

Eventually he made his way to where Connor hung suspended, burned and bleeding, the ground beneath him puddled with vomit as he was tortured.

''Eh boy! Are ye alive?'' Radvald gruffly demanded. ''Or are ye nothin' more than crow bait?''

''Alive enough to curse you for not getting here sooner, old man,'' Connor responded from his upside-down position.

''We had a bit o' business to tend to first,'' Radvald replied, keeping careful watch lest they draw attention. "Four of Maelgwyn's men cooling in yon trees. I'd hoped for Maelgwyn himself."

"He's mine," Connor swore. "As soon as I get down from here."

"That's the spirit, lad. Do you think you can walk?"

"Not trussed like a partridge. Get me down!"

"Soon enough. Getting down is one thing, getting out of camp is another. I've brought only a handful of men. We'll have to fight our way out, once they know what we're up to."

"Get me down, now!"

"Easy lad. With so few, it must be done carefully. I've others waiting beyond the encampment." He slipped a knife inside Connor's boot.

The other three men had fanned out, positioning themselves in a strategic half-circle around Connor and close to Maelgwyn's men who warmed themselves around the very same fire that had heated the poker used to torture Connor. At a nodded signal from one of his men, Radvald swiftly sliced first through the set of ropes at one of Connor's wrists then the ropes at the other.

A cry had gone up nearby as Radvald was seen cutting him loose, but it died as quickly as the man's throat was cut. Then the encampment erupted in chaos.

The feeling gradually flowed back into Connor's numbed hands and fingers, but he made an easy target. In spite of the number of hours he'd hung there, stripped to the waist, hanging like a trussed game bird, the loss of blood from the wound had been minimal. Such was the nature of Maelgwyn's preferred method of torture that while the poker burned through flesh and muscle it also cauterized the wound—a benevolent form of torture and mutilation.

But as the blood flowed back into his numbed hands and fingers, searing pain also returned. He could just imagine the slow torture Maelgwyn would inflict if he failed to escape now.

Strengthened by that thought and the burning desire to see Maelgwyn at the end of a sword begging for his life, Connor found the strength to lever his upper body upward so that he could reach the knife inside his boot.

While Radvald and his men wreaked havoc within, those outside the encampment rained arrows down on Maelgwyn's unsuspecting men.

One well-aimed arrow cleanly severed the rope that suspended him by the ankles. Connor landed on the ground with a sickening thud that jarred through his injured shoulder.

He clenched his teeth against the pain and fought back the nausea that swelled into his throat. Rolling as he hit the ground, he lunged to unsteady feet, seized the nearest warrior and cut his throat. He shoved the man away from him and lunged at the next man, aware that Radvald fought beside him.

They quickly cut their way to the edge of the encampment and fled with the others. They'd been on the run ever since, living off the land, striking in sudden attacks without warning, then disappearing just as quickly. Fighting Arthur's fight against Maelgwyn and Aethelbert.

Ghost Warriors the people called them because of their painted faces and muted brown tunics, blending in, watching, waiting, then disappearing like ancient spirits. But now the Ghost Warriors were trapped at Caerleon by the weather, unable to disappear.

The map detailed with painstaking accuracy the surrounding valley, the forest, and the distant hills toward Dumonia in the north—ancient kingdom of the Welsh and Maelgwyn's stronghold.

All across the map were dozens of marks, the locations of encounters with Maelgwyn over the past year. Their encounter four days ago at the Caledon Forest was the most recent.

Connor raked his hands back through his hair with equal measures of frustration and helplessness. He felt like a caged animal. He threw down the piece of charcoal he'd used to mark the locations.

"I'll be up on the battlements," he told Simon with an abruptness that cut off any suggestion of joining him there.

At the second-floor passage he passed the guard outside Lady Ygraine's chamber. The guard, one of Arthur's men, acknowledged him with a perfunctory nod in the pulsing light from a nearby torch at the wall.

Connor continued down the adjacent passage, finally taking the steps that led to the battlements, two and three at a time, remembering the last time he'd been at Caerleon with Arthur when they were fuzz-cheeked lads. Boys one moment, men the next, no longer friends.

At the end of the passage a stout door opened onto the battlements, a series of stonework posts built behind a half-wall that rimmed the top of the four walls of the rectangular stone fortress.

The Dukes of Cornwall had not reigned for over six generations by accident. They'd learned that constant vigilance was a key to holding their power, and this fortress had offered both protection and vigilance. Until a fortnight ago.

There was no torch at the door that led to the battlements, plunging the passage into half-light that quivered between darkness and shadow.

In spite of the poor light he saw the movement in the shadows, his hand instinctively closing around the handle of the short-bladed knife that he'd worn since Maelgwyn's lesson in torture.

Another step closer as the shadow approached and the blade eased from the belt of his pants, gleaming dully in the half-light within the passage.

"Ho there, boy!" a voice called out from the surrounding shadows. "Stay that blade, you might get hurt."

Radvald stepped into the meager light, the gleam of the torches glinting in watchful eyes and in the russet hues of his beard.

"By the Father, old man!" Connor swore softly. "I could have gutted you like a cod before you took another step."

"Not if I'd gutted you first," Radvald shot back at him, humor twinkling in his eyes. "You made enough noise coming up that passage."

"Only the dead could have heard me," Connor flung back. "And you almost joined them."

"Ha!" Radvald shouted with laughter. "You can't kill me, boy. Don't you know that? I'm protected by Odin himself."

"You're a blasphemous old man. Your god cannot protect you."

"And yours can?" Radvald snorted. "Best see about them boots yer wearin'. Sounded like a herd of sheep. Could have heard you a furlong away."

Connor nodded. "You've been up on the battlements?"

"Aye, near froze my arse off."

"No change then?"

"Change enough," Radvald growled. "There's no snow." His gruff voice was laced with cynicism. "Now, it's raining down ice enough to blind both man and beast. Reminds me of my boyhood home ... reminds me of why I left to go adventurin' with my uncles all those years ago. I hate the damn cold."

Connor shook his head. "A Viking who hates the cold?"

Radvald shrugged. "Aye, it's the reason we left the damned place."

Among his men none had so canny an instinct for the weather as the Norseman who'd spent his childhood years raiding the North Sea lanes with his uncles before being lost over the side in a storm.

Cast adrift near the eastern coast of Britain, he'd managed to survive by cunning and strength. A free man who owed fealty to no other, he'd given his loyalty to Connor's father after the Duke of Monmouth intervened when the Norseman had gotten himself into a bit of trouble and was about to be hanged.

It had to do with a mongrel dog the Norseman had found being beaten to death. He'd intervened and it had nearly cost him his own life. Radvald and the mongrel both lived, however, and joined the household of the duke.

An odd friendship formed between the free Norseman and the old duke, bound by a mongrel hound that turned out to be a cunning hunting dog. Connor's boyhood memories of his father and Radvald always began and ended with the old duke's standing inquiry of his master at the hounds: "How is the hound?"

And Radvald's answer, "Ready for the hunt."

It was an odd conversation that defined their friendship—the hound was symbolic of all the hounds that had come after the first one, including the present gray hound, Dax. And the words were a bond between the younger and the older warrior, their meaning always understood with no explanations necessary.

"How is the hound this afternoon?" Connor asked.

Radvald grinned, his teeth flashing in the shadows. "Not yet ready for the hunt. Perhaps by morning."

A possible break in the weather by morning. Connor nodded.

"Warm yourself by the fire," he told Radvald. "I don't want your old bones locking up on you just when I need your war ax to protect my back."

Radvald guffawed. "I can still take you two falls out of three, boy. Just give me some of that hearty brew, and we'll make it three for three."

Connor shook his head as the old warrior disappeared down the passage at a powerful lope that defied the years—and the scars that covered his body.

There was no point continuing up to the battlements. Connor turned and was about to start back down the passage after Radvald when he suddenly stopped.

"I know you're there," he called out.

Meg bit at her lower lip as she hung back in the darkness of the passage. If she kept very still, perhaps he would think he was mistaken.

"You may as well show yourself." He waited.

No hope there. She silently wondered if he was gifted, so careful had she been when she'd stepped through the wall. Eventually, Meg moved from the shadows at the corner that had concealed her from Radvald into the dimly lit passage.

Connor made no attempt to hide his surprise. She was the last one he'd expected to find hiding out in the passage. One of the servant girls who'd arrived recently from a neighboring village possibly, perhaps even the woman Dannelore, but not this slender girl who had so recently lain gravely wounded from his arrow.

Though he'd been informed that she recovered steadily and

the woman, Dannelore, was confident of her recovery, he'd been less certain. But there was little evidence of the wasting fever that had set in. The deathly pallor was gone, her eyes were clear, and she seemed hardly discomforted either by the wound or the loss of blood.

"What are you doing here?" he said, making no attempt to disguise his surprise or his displeasure at finding her there.

Her blue eyes shimmered like the heart of a flame, and her hair was like the gold of a flame, alive, vibrant as it spilled around her shoulders, begging a man's hand.

Meg was not yet familiar with the direct way in which mortals spoke, their abruptness and spontaneity, their speaking out instinctively and without thinking—something that was uncharacteristic in her world where every action was guided by thought.

For lack of a more appropriate response, she blurted out, "What are *you* doing here?"

Her reply caught him off guard, as did her smile. These were not exactly the responses he'd expected. Whether from his men or others he encountered, he was used to being obeyed and responded to appropriately, not questioned in return.

"How did you get past the guard?"

"I walked."

"He did not try to stop you?"

She answered with complete honesty. "He did not see me."

"I shall have to discuss that with him."

"You're displeased."

"The guard was instructed to remain outside the chamber at all times to prevent anyone from entering."

"Then he performed his duty," she replied. "No one entered the chamber except for Dannelore and Master Merlin."

Rather than argue with her, Connor informed her, "I will escort you back to it."

"I will not go," she informed him.

He slowly turned, his head angling around so he might stare at her. Meg sensed that she had responded incorrectly and frantically sought an appropriate response.

"What I mean is, I do not wish to return to my chamber.

Surely you can understand. I have been there over four days.''
She sensed his refusal and searched for something else that
might convince him.

"I do not like walls."

Her voice had gone very quiet.

"They are cold and confining. I much prefer ..." She
searched for something he would understand.

"The forest?" he suggested.

"Yes, exactly."

"Is that why you were in the forest? You had escaped and
were hiding out?"

"Something very much like that."

He accepted that for now as he took her hand in his and laid
it over his arm. She was dressed in a rich blue gown with a
burgundy tunic laced tight at the curve of her small waist, the
sleeves of the gown emphasizing her slender arms.

The blue of the gown reflected in the deep blue of her eyes—
eyes filled with fiery light. He felt her pull back at the contact
of his hand. His fingers closed over hers.

"Tell me, do you always go about without any shoes?" he
asked as he led her down the steps of the passage to the second-
floor landing.

She could have pulled free if she wanted too. She did not.
After the first stunning warmth of his hand, she discovered she
liked his touch very much. It was like being touched by the
sun—warm, languid, gentle, at the same time strangely stirring.

She glanced down at her bare feet, frowning softly. Shoes
were not something she was familiar with, and she hadn't given
them any thought.

He answered his own question. "We'll see what can be done
about that. You'll catch your death of the ague if you run
around like that."

She had no reference for *ague* or any notion why it would
be flying around loose, though death was not an unknown
concept. It was merely something she'd never had to deal with.

They stopped at the second-floor landing. The guard looked
up in brief acknowledgment. Then his face mottled with color
when he saw her, and a red flush rose steadily up his neck.

Meg had no reference for embarrassment or chagrin and so had no understanding of it. But she did sense the guard's extreme discomfort and knew it had to do with her escape.

There was only the slightest acknowledgment, but she sensed both men's thoughts. The warrior, Connor, was not about to let this go. No longer needed at his post, his expression grim, the guard followed them down the stairs to the main hall below.

As Connor led her to the entrance to the main hall, Meg was burning with a question she had to ask.

"How did you know I was in the passage?" Perhaps he was gifted after all.

"I smelled you."

She pulled her hand from his. Her expression was grave, her soft, full mouth curved like an upside-down bow.

"What is it?"

Large blue eyes filled with a somber expression stared back at him.

"Do I smell like a dead goat?"

His shoulders shook with silent laughter which he attempted to disguise behind a sudden cough. His fingers tightened over her hand.

"I assure you, you do not."

"You are certain?" she asked with grave concern.

Even with her brow wrinkled with worry and her mouth curving into an anxious frown, she was a most ravishing creature.

"Most certain."

At the bottom-floor landing light from a half-dozen torches at the entrance to the main hall fell across her delicate features.

"Then you do not find me offensive?" There was visible relief in her vivid blue eyes, along with curiosity.

"I do not," Connor replied. Her honesty and bluntness were refreshing compared to the behavior of other women such as Arthur's half sister, Lady Morgana. It had been a number of years since he'd last seen Morgana. It had been a wearisome experience.

"Good. I would not like to smell like one. I don't think it

would be very pleasant. They do not smell very agreeable when they are alive.''

As she followed him down the spiral of stairs, his hands closed over hers, she commented, "I do not find you offensive either. You do not look or smell at all like a dung heap.''

Her unaffected honesty made it difficult to be offended. Still, it took him a moment to recover, mostly from chuckling. He stopped and turned to look at her. She was so very innocent and beguiling.

"A dung heap?" He struggled with laughter and incredulity. Living off the land was not easy, particularly when it came to matters of appearance or keeping oneself clean. But his appearance had never caused him to be lacking for the attentions of a woman.

"Yes, like in the forest with your face painted.''

It was then he realized what she spoke of. "Sometimes it is necessary to disguise one's features. I hope I did not frighten you.''

"No, but it did make me wonder. After all, I was warned.''

"Warned?" His curiosity sharpened. "About encountering warriors in the forest?''

"Anyone at all.'' She leaned forward and added discreetly. "I was told they smell quite badly.''

"Who told you this?''

They had been having such a pleasant conversation, she almost blurted out that it was Cosmo who had told her. She had even gotten him to laugh and had discovered that it was a very nice sound. It transformed him completely. The lines eased about his mouth and eyes, his mouth curved in a most pleasant expression, and those eyes did not seem so cold or forbidding.

Quite the contrary, she discovered hidden depths that sparkled with flecks of golden light. But it was the sound of his voice that fascinated her. It was rich with laughter and warm with other hidden emotions she had no experience with but longed to discover.

"A friend told me," she finally answered. "But he had a

very unpleasant experience which was probably his own fault. He has a very quarrelsome nature.''

''You are outspoken, aren't you,'' Connor remarked.

Her answer was completely guileless. ''I do not know how to be otherwise. Does it offend you?''

''Not at all,'' he assured her.

She shrugged her slender shoulders. '' 'Tis just as well. I cannot lie anyway.''

His laughter echoed off the stone walls as they reached the bottom landing at the main hall.

Meg's senses were assaulted by the sights and sounds of near a full four score of men who now encamped at Caerleon. She was fascinated by the boisterous conversations and light-hearted banter amid the noise and clatter of the evening meal as tankards and platters were set out upon the table. But the focus of her fascination was the healer, Merlin, and the man who sat with him in deep conversation. Arthur of Caerleon.

Then she felt Dannelore's presence. The changeling saw them from across the hall where she helped serve the evening meal. The metal pitcher she was holding thudded down on the table where Arthur and Merlin sat, the contents sloshing over the side. She crossed the hall, her expression pale and tight. There was no need for words as her thoughts frantically reached out to Meg.

''What can you be thinking? You should not be here!''

And as she reached Meg, '' 'Tis good to see you up and about, but you must not tire yourself. You would not want to cause yourself harm.''

The last was said with particular emphasis which Meg chose to ignore. She tossed her head defiantly and answered sweetly.

''Thank you for your concern. But I am not at all tired. I find confinement particularly wearing.'' And in the connection of their shared thoughts, *''I have no intention of returning to that chamber!''*

''Mistress, please . . . !'' But any further plea or warning was cut off as they were joined by both Arthur and Merlin.

''Did I hear laughter, my friend?'' Arthur asked congenially.

"It would seem this young lady has accomplished what no one else could achieve, as well as bringing you to the hall."

It was as if day turned to night. Meg sensed the conflict between the two men immediately, and saw it in the icy coldness in Connor's eyes. His reply was not threatening, nor was it congenial.

"I find her company and her honesty refreshing."

Arthur sensed it too, yet his smile never wavered. "Then perhaps you can persuade her to join us for the evening meal, provided my counselor declares her to be sufficiently recovered. I would not wish to jeopardize your health, mistress."

Meg sensed Connor's wariness, and felt it in the touch of his hand supporting her arm. But there was no time to search his thoughts. In her brother's presence she needed all her own thoughts and her powers carefully controlled.

Merlin took her hand, his fingers lightly enfolding hers. In that touch his powers reached deep inside, moving through her, until she felt a gently searching warmth at her shoulder.

It was dangerous and intriguing, confronting the brother she had never known, using her own powers to keep his at bay, concealing herself, eluding his thoughts like moving the pieces on an imaginary chessboard.

If he sensed anything, he gave no indication of it, but instead patted her hand gently.

"She seems much recovered."

"Owing no doubt to your skills, friend," Arthur commended him. Then he turned to Meg.

"Join us then." And much louder for all to hear. "I promise, my men will be on their best behavior."

"You will outsmart yourself!" Dannelore warned in the connection of their thoughts. *"What will you do when Master Merlin learns the truth?"*

"I do not intend for him to learn the truth," she replied, then added, *"and perhaps I will be able to learn something about John."*

Dannelore finally conceded, but she was not happy about it.

Connor had no choice but to accompany her. He would not have entrusted her to Arthur or any of his men.

The noise first experienced when she came down the steps was nothing compared to the noise that surrounded them at the table. Several of Connor's men moved to make room for them. She was seated next to Radvald on the long bench, Connor sat at her other side.

The food was spartan but adequate, and included the pottage Dannelore had spoken of, a thick, steaming concoction with pieces of food floating in it which were mostly unidentifiable. The pottage was ladled into deep trenchers and wood bowls and then scooped hungrily with crusts of hot bread.

"It's good enough," Radvald assured her. "Long as it isn't crawlin'."

Those around them laughed with good humor, she suspected at her expense. Meg eyed the trencher of pottage warily. She wasn't at all certain about this and wondered just what she'd gotten herself into.

"What do I do if it does crawl?" she asked.

"Kill it!" he announced to hoots of wild laughter. Taking him at his word, she seized the knife from his belt before he could prevent it and held it ready to do battle.

"Ho, Radvald!" one of the men hooted. "Be careful she doesn't kill you first."

The old warrior eyed her warily. "That's a sharp blade, miss."

"Good, then it will be easy to kill whatever is in that bowl."

"I'm certain Mistress Dannelore has killed everything twice over," Connor said. "You won't have any need for the knife."

She eyed the pottage with great skepticism, then finally handed the knife over.

"Since I no longer have a weapon, you'll have to do it."

Connor suppressed a smile. "If anything moves in that bowl, you have my word that I will slay it."

"Thank you, sir."

The steamy aroma wasn't offensive. In fact it had a rather pleasant, herbal essence which was familiar to her. But she didn't like the looks of those unknown chunks bobbing about. And she wasn't at all certain about the mechanics of scooping with crusts of bread. Although the whole thing didn't seem to present much of a problem to Radvald or any of Arthur's men.

They scooped and stuffed the sodden mixture into their mouths with much smacking and licking of lips, in between bits of conversation, comments which brought looks in her direction and great hoots of laughter. Needless to say, a good portion of the pottage found its way down their sleeves and onto the fronts of their tunics. Whatever dribbled down their fingers, they licked clean for lack of a cloth to wipe them.

Connor did not eat, but sat watching those about him with careful, guarded eyes, much changed from the man who had laughed so easily before.

"Why do you dislike Arthur?" She saw surprise flash in those cold gray eyes and wondered if he would deny it. Surely such an attitude was not a wise one in their present company. But he did not deny it.

"I knew Arthur when we were boys," he replied. "That was a long time ago. He changed. I no longer know him."

"And you have not changed?" she asked. Determined to experience as much of the mortal world as possible, she attempted to scoop some of the pottage with a crust of bread only to have a chunk of food and the bread sink into the bowl.

"You think I should not be so critical."

"I think you should not be so hasty to judge."

Connor cut off another crust of bread. Brushing her hand aside, he scooped up a chunk of meat and thick gravy. He held it for her.

She wrapped her fingers around his hand and gingerly nibbled at the sodden bread, like a trusting creature with no reason to fear the hand that feeds it. Her teeth were small and even, her fingers slender and fragile around his hand.

"It's good!" she exclaimed.

Her surprise was so genuine and sincere that he couldn't help but smile. Everything seemed new to her, as if experienced for the first time with the wonder and innocence of a child.

"You should not be so hasty to judge," he repeated. In her enthusiasm gravy dribbled down her chin. He reached out and scooped it with his finger.

She caught his hand and licked his finger with a delicate flick of her tongue just as she had seen the others do. His skin was faintly salty, surprisingly smooth and rough at the same time.

It was all about texture—his skin against hers where her fingers closed over his hand, the taste of him, rough and gentle against her lips—confusing for someone who had never touched or been touched.

She sensed his reaction, although she had no experience with such things and no idea what it meant or even what it was. She only knew what she felt in the connection of her hand within his, the sudden tensing of every muscle as if preparing for battle, and the sudden heat that burned through him.

Everything was so new to her and not as easy as she had expected. Had she angered him in some way? She pulled her hand from his.

"I did not mean to offend you."

"You did not offend me."

"You're angry with me."

"I am not angry."

"If I have not offended you, then what is it? Tell me so that I may prevent it in the future."

"It's just that . . ."

She sensed him struggling to find the words to explain.

"It's been a very long time since I felt the touch of a woman."

"Is that bad? Or is it my touch that you do not like?" she suggested with complete candor. "I didn't do it right?"

Connor swore softly. She had an unusual way of putting things.

"You did it right."

"And that's bad? If it's good, how can it be bad?" She shook her head.

"I don't understand at all." She scooped another piece of bread into the bowl. "You'll have to explain this to me."

He wasn't certain he understood it himself.

Arthur was a charming host. He'd learned much of Eastern ways and delighted Connor's men with stories of the Eastern empires. Connor had no interest in such stories. He wanted to be gone from Caerleon. She wasn't certain why that thought disturbed her.

She sensed his restlessness and the cause. "The storm is almost over," she assured him. "Soon you will be able to leave Caerleon."

"I hope you are right, mistress," Radvald replied good-naturedly, unaware that anything unusual had taken place. "He is like a caged animal with the wind howling outside these walls. I fear the storm may soon be preferable to the beast."

"The weather will lift on the morrow," she assured them all since it seemed so important. She had never seen snow and was looking forward to her first encounter.

Connor looked at her speculatively. She felt that scrutiny and realized she had perhaps made a grave error in what seemed a simple prediction at the time.

"You seem most certain about the weather, mistress," Arthur commented over his tankard of ale. Humor glinted in his eyes as he exchanged a look with Merlin. Only a few hours earlier his counselor had made that same prediction, but with a certainty that came from his unusual powers of perception.

"How do you know it will be tomorrow?"

She felt the speculative gazes of all fastened on her, including Merlin's. He watched her with open curiosity and more. She sensed his probing thoughts and kept her own carefully guarded.

From the shadows behind her, where Dannelore had been hovering ever since Meg had entered the hall and joined Arthur and his men, the changeling warned, *"Be careful, mistress. Master Merlin will see through any deception."*

But before she could reply, Radvald unwittingly came to her rescue.

"It takes no great skill or knowledge," the old warrior replied with good humor, in no small part due to the second tankard of brew that he'd emptied and now set onto the table with a loud thud, wiping his mouth with the back of his sleeve.

"I can feel it in my bones. Just as I felt it days ago. And my bones are never wrong."

"Aye, never wrong, with all their loud creaking and complaining," a young warrior teased beside him, much to the delight of the others who broke out in wild hoots and guffaws of laughter. All of it at old Radvald's expense.

"Have yer bit of fun, young mongrels," Radvald replied. "But I can still take any three of you. Even with these creaking old bones!"

All about them conversation returned to normal, the weather momentarily forgotten with colorful stories, improbable tales of the warriors' adventures both in Britain and afar, and attempts on the part of the younger warriors to prove their prowess as they challenged Radvald to contests of arm wrestling.

Meg sensed Dannelore's silent relief and admonition.

"Now you see how careful you must be! Let us leave before there is another encounter."

But Meg refused. She was fascinated by things she had never before seen or experienced. Everything was new to her, and she embraced all with the enthusiasm of a child. Dannelore finally ceased her admonitions, but continued to hover nearby in the shadows.

Meg opened her senses and let them flow about the hall, learning much from overheard conversations—the concern of all for the days that lay ahead, uncertainty in what Arthur and his men had found upon their arrival at Caerleon, the eagerness of Connor's men to leave. Dreams, ambitions, hopes, old adversaries and new, all woven into a tapestry of laughter, intrigue, and even danger.

She sensed it all, learning much of those around her, particularly Arthur. He had returned to his childhood home filled with a sense of purpose and duty, bound by a boyhood legacy, only to find his home in ruins, his family's fate unknown, and a cold welcome from an old friend who was friend no longer.

She understood the issues of that lost friendship but not the emotions that lay behind them. That would come eventually with a better understanding of these mortals.

Yet in both men she sensed similar thoughts and emotions in the loss that both felt, though she suspected neither would easily admit to that. It was fascinating to her that for all their outward and outspoken differences, they were very much alike.

Did either of them sense it? Did that in some way add to their estrangement?

Radvald acquitted himself quite well against the younger warriors. He reminded Meg of a large, playful cat, much like Nicodemus, content to toy with the warriors much like a cat with a mouse, laughing heartily at their attempts to best him at arm wrestling, yet thoroughly capable of showing his claws when the situation warranted it. But also like a cat, he was straightforward in his attack, even at arm wrestling, patiently waiting for his prey to wear himself out, then pouncing in for the kill.

Not so the warrior called Simon the Wise—Simon the Dangerous to her way of thinking.

He was handsome with lean features, more like a wolf with watchful dark eyes and a predatory demeanor—watching, stalking, circling. And she was the prey. Meg sensed it in those eyes that constantly watched, like the hungry wolf's, waiting for the smallest mistake.

"Tell us," Simon said, those eyes fixed on her, "what were you doing in the forest? A young lady, alone? Who are your people?"

She had sensed the question in Connor's thoughts, but he had not asked it. Now he too waited speculatively for her response. Behind her, she sensed Dannelore's sudden, silent warning.

"I have no memory of anything before I was found," she replied, returning to the answer she had given before. "Only vague images."

"But surely you have family. They will be most concerned about your safety."

She answered truthfully. "I have no memory of my family. If there were others there, I do not recall."

"One of Maelgwyn's men was found near our encampment," Simon pointed out. "Where there is one there are more."

She needed no gift of inner sight to explain his meaning. He was certain she had been sent by Maelgwyn.

"I do not know the man you speak of."

It had grown quiet in the hall once more, except for Radvald's pleasure of the ale he downed to quench his thirst after his exertions. Both Arthur and Merlin listened with interest.

"Yet you have just said you remembered nothing. Therefore, you may have become separated from Maelgwyn and simply not remember it—or chose not to remember." A satisfied look gleamed in Simon's eyes.

She did not know what she had done to earn this man's enmity, but she had. He deliberately sought to trip her up and expose her as none of the others had. Not even Merlin with his abilities to sense what others could not. No, not Merlin. He was waiting for someone else to do it. Dannelore had been right about being careful. It was only that she had not realized the true source of the danger.

Meg skillfully moved within his thoughts. There she saw the dark corners of ambition and ruthlessness that made a mockery of his name, Simon the Wise. And she wondered if Connor knew the depths of that ambition and ruthlessness. With a certainty, she knew that if he had been the first to reach her in the forest, she would have been killed.

Like the mist at dawn, she surrounded his thoughts, using her power to confuse, disorient, and befuddle his own memory of things. Then, like that mist, she carefully withdrew, holding his thoughts within her own.

"I am not familiar with matters of war," she replied, still controlling his thoughts and his memory. "But from what I have heard of Maelgwyn, if he had been in the forest you would not be alive."

She sensed his instinct to argue, accuse, and trap her. But the struggle was brief and no match for her. He shook his head as if trying to cast off the confusion, but could not. In the end he could do nothing but accept her explanation.

"You are right of course, mistress."

She accepted his apology with a soft smile, a valuable lesson learned. There were dangers here that even Dannelore with her knowledge of mortals had not anticipated.

Connor had been listening attentively. She felt his thoughts, the speculation, and something she was not prepared for, his admiration.

"Simon is a skilled warrior, but there are times when he is perhaps hasty in his judgment."

"And what of your judgment?" she asked. She sensed it now as she had sensed it in the forest. She had nothing to fear of this mortal. But she didn't merely want to hear it in his thoughts, she wanted to hear him say it.

"I am more cautious in my judgment."

Meg smiled inwardly. He was cautious in all things. She felt a tugging at her elbow. Her first thought was that it was Dannelore with some additional words of caution. But when she turned around it was not Dannelore who pulled at her sleeve.

"I understand you have been ill. May I offer my wishes for your complete recovery, mistress. A rose perhaps, as fair as you are beautiful."

Meg was forced to adjust her line of sight downward by at least two feet to find the source of the compliment—a small, gnomelike creature who barely reached her shoulder as she sat at the table.

He was dressed in a coarsely woven tunic and breeches, with leather leggings wrapped about his stubby legs. His face was encircled by a scrubby beard. He had a pug nose and bushy eyebrows above eyes that were very familiar in their twinkling with humor and mischief.

He bowed low from the waist, hand extended with the delicate rose. "My name is Grendel. I am a trader by trade, by trade a trader."

Meg almost burst out laughing. A trader of what? she wanted to ask. Clothes? She hoped so, for his were ridiculous. Mischief? No doubt. By the Ancient Ones how had he gotten here?

"I have wandered far," he replied, and she knew he had heard her thoughts. "A most perilous journey, through *rocks* and *deep forest*. Then I was caught in a storm."

She bit her cheek to keep from laughing out loud as she took the rose. "It must have been most difficult for you."

"Aye, it was. I am not accustomed to such journeys, and all because of a beautiful young maid . . . much like yourself."

"A young maid?" Radvald guffawed. "More likely it was her father who turned you out, little man. Yer prospects are a wee bit *short*."

Grendel glared at her, but all she could do was join in their laughter. Even Connor seemed amused by the little man's declarations of lost love.

In the connection of their thoughts she sensed the coming tirade and cut him off.

"Thank you for your concern, Grendel. I assure you I am quite well. *And I am not at all ready to return!*"

If Grendel was disappointed he gave no outward sign of it. "Perhaps I can show you some of my tricks, mistress," he suggested.

She smiled her gratitude. "I would like that very much."

"But do not try any of your tricks on me, Grendel," she silently warned, remembering his distaste for mortals, *"or I will change you into one of these people."*

Throughout the rest of the evening, both Grendel and Dannelore were constant companions. While Dannelore preferred to hover in the shadows, Grendel entertained Arthur's men with his rhyming insults, stories, and sleight-of-hand tricks.

It was much later when Arthur's guards burst through the doors of the main hall escorting a dozen, soaked men who were bundled to their eyes and seemed near frozen. Under threat from those guards one of the men advanced unafraid toward the fire at the hearth, dropping pieces of ice in his wake.

While all waited he warmed himself before the fire. Eventually he removed the heavy woolen hood and fleece mantle. He was a young man, of an age near Connor and Arthur. Meg immediately sensed Connor's reaction. He knew this man.

"I am Geoffrey of Exmoor. My men and I have come to join Arthur."

"Geoffrey of Exmoor," Arthur repeated the name as he rose from his chair and slowly rounded the table. Meg sensed his recognition as well.

No words were exchanged. None seemed to be necessary. Perhaps, Meg speculated, there was an understanding which mortals somehow comprehended. She found that most interesting.

"If you will have us," Geoffrey added. The two men stood only a small distance apart. They were of an even height, although Geoffrey of Exmoor was built more lightly with a wiry, tensile strength. His men waited expectantly, surrounded by Arthur's guards. Everyone waited expectantly.

Finally Arthur reached out, clasping Geoffrey of Exmoor at the shoulders.

"It has been a long time."

"It has."

"Yes, I will have you and your men," Arthur told him enthusiastically. Then he turned to them. "Welcome. You are all welcome." And turning back to Geoffrey. "Come sit with us. There is much to talk about."

Geoffrey joined Arthur and Merlin while his men surrounded the fire, warming themselves, dispelling Meg's first impression of great frozen creatures. All were warriors, armed with swords, axes, and bows.

"There are more," Geoffrey was heard to say. "They will come once word spreads."

"Exmoor is far. How is it you heard before others?"

"From a merchantman who put to port," Geoffrey replied over mulled wine. "He spoke of a princely fellow who put to shore from a longboat several weeks past with a score of followers. By his description I knew it could be no other. By God, we've waited an eternity."

"We have all waited an eternity," Arthur replied.

Eventually they settled into conversation about Maelgwyn. Dannelore brought food from the kitchen, and Geoffrey and his men ate, telling Arthur and Merlin what they knew of Maelgwyn and his army.

"His attack on Caerleon was symbolic," Geoffrey concluded. "By destroying Caerleon, it was his intent to destroy any hope that you might return to lead an army against him." He looked about the great hall.

"How many have joined?"

"Only those you see here. You are among the first. I pray there will be more."

Geoffrey's gaze scanned the hall. "By the saints!" he exclaimed as he rose from his chair and approached Connor. Connor rose to greet him.

They clasped arms, and in the fierceness of the embrace Meg sensed a genuine affection. Geoffrey grinned as they drew apart.

"You have joined as well."

"I have not," Connor replied, and Geoffrey's smile faded.

"But you are here."

"Only by misfortune of weather. As soon as the weather clears we will be gone."

"But you cannot mean that! We have waited for this day!"

"I leave on the morrow."

Geoffrey's smile faded completely. "Then nothing has changed."

"Nothing has changed. I will not risk the lives of my men for a coward's cause."

"I had hoped you might feel differently. We need Arthur," Geoffrey argued.

"We need a man we can trust. A man who will not abandon us in our hour of need." Connor's voice was as cold as the expression in his gray eyes. "I see no such man in this hall. Certainly not Arthur."

Chapter Eight

The shutters were thrown open, and Meg sat at the stone window ledge, legs tucked beneath her, face raised to the warmth of the sun that spilled through the opening.

Just as she had predicted, the weather had cleared. Clouds banked at the far horizon over the distant hills, and the sky was an amazing shade of blue.

All of it was quite amazing to her—the warmth of the sun and the vivid colors of both sky and landscape below—seen through mortal eyes and felt against her skin, every part of it a new experience that fascinated her.

She touched her cheek, amazed at the warmth there—a new experience for one who had spent most of her existence in disembodied form.

It recalled the previous evening when she had touched Connor—the texture of his skin against hers, the taste of him on her tongue.

From the yard below came sounds of Arthur's men as they left the main hall. They had stirred at first light and not ceased since. Arthur prepared to go to the abbey.

"Tell me about Lady Ygraine," Meg said thoughtfully from her perch at the window.

"She is a most gentle lady," Dannelore answered as she rolled fleece skins and stored them in the corner. She then replenished oil at the lamps and in general set order to the room.

"But a sad lady," she added on a thoughtful note. "You can see it in her eyes."

"Sad? For what reason?" Meg still found mortal emotions difficult to understand. She seized every opportunity to learn more about them.

"I only came to Caerleon a short while ago," the changeling explained. "Most of what I know I heard from others who had been with her for many years. The old duke died some time ago—the Lady Morgana's father."

"And Arthur's father as well," Meg added.

"Some say different." Dannelore then explained the story she'd heard among the serving girls, of the time before Arthur's birth when Lady Ygraine disappeared for a time.

"Disappeared? Where?"

" 'Tis not known. Some say she was abducted, for the Duke of Cornwall was a powerful man and would have paid handsomely for her return. But a ransom was never demanded."

"And what did others believe?"

"Others believed she was not abducted at all, but had met with a secret lover."

"Lover." Meg mulled that over a bit while she tried to assimilate the other aspects of the story.

" 'Tis said she visited with Lady Anne for a time. Others say the Lady of Monmouth gave her shelter.

"Aye," Dannelore read her thoughts. "Home of the warrior who found you in the forest. He and Arthur were raised together as boys, as close as brothers some say."

Meg tucked that bit of information away. What, she wondered, had caused the estrangement between the friends?

"What happened when the Duke of Cornwall returned?"

"Lady Ygraine came back to Caerleon. Shortly after that it was announced she was to have a child. 'Tis said that Arthur is not the child of the old duke at all, but the child of another.

Yet the old duke recognized him as his son and refused to tolerate speculation otherwise.

" 'Tis said,'' Dannelore continued, pausing in her folding and straightening, ''that the Ancient Ones had a hand in it. And 'tis reason Master Merlin was sent into the mortal world to be counselor to Arthur.''

''Why is Lady Ygraine sad? It would seem a great honor to be mother to a future king.''

''She was quite young when she wed the Duke of Cornwall after his first wife died. It was an arranged marriage.'' Dannelore then explained about arranged marriages.

''I cannot see why two people cannot be together if they wish to,'' Meg philosophized.

''I agree,'' Dannelore said wistfully.

There was a great deal of activity in the yard below. In addition to the preparations being made for the journey to the Abbey at Amesbury, more people had arrived throughout the morning now that the weather had cleared.

There were mostly men, young and old, even boys, and a few women. They were dressed in simple clothes—leggings, tunics, and woolen shirts. Some carried weapons, others arrived with only the clothes on their backs. They had come to join Arthur.

Meg leaned far out the window, her thoughts flying afar like a falcon. She could almost feel the lift of the wind beneath her wings.

''Oh, no,'' Dannelore exclaimed, seizing her by the shoulder and hauling her back from the window. The shutters were closed and barred.

''All we need is for someone to see you transform. Already there is talk.''

Meg turned from her perch at the ledge. ''What talk?''

''That you were sent by Maelgwyn.''

Meg snorted with irritation, knowing full well the source. ''Simon. I cannot imagine why he is called Simon the Wise.''

''The doubt is there,'' Dannelore warned, ''and these mortals are suspicious creatures. You must not give them any reason to doubt that you are other than what you say you are.''

Until I can persuade you to return to Avalon, Dannelore silently thought to herself.

Meg smiled to herself at the woman's musings. "Tell me about Lady Morgana," she said as she stood on the window ledge practicing her balance on two feet.

Dannelore busied herself, removing ash from the brazier, unaware of the balancing act that went on behind her. It was several moments before she replied, and Meg sensed her choosing the words carefully.

"Lady Morgana is very beautiful. She is also very . . ."

Meg sensed the word she preferred to use. "Vain?"

Dannelore stood up, hand on hip, contemplating the proper response. "Vain is a strong word."

Meg turned back in the other direction and tiptoed carefully along the ledge. "Willful, mean-spirited, conniving, deceitful . . ."

Dannelore whirled around. "You are reading my thoughts!" Then she saw Meg, perched on the narrow ledge at the window like a delicate butterfly about to take flight or a fledgling sparrow about to pitch headfirst from the nest. She shrieked with alarm.

Teetering precariously on the ledge, Meg was never in serious danger of falling. Preventing it simply required a little concentration, and some levitation, on her part, and she would have alighted safely on the floor. But she looked up. Connor stood framed in the doorway of the chamber.

Her concentration broken, she teetered precariously on the edge of disaster. She had not the coordination or the skill to save herself without her powers. Unable to use them lest she give herself away, she tumbled from the window ledge.

For the second time in her life, she felt completely helpless. And for the second time, Connor was there. He caught her with one arm about her waist and the other under her knees.

"Do you always go about leaping from windows, mistress?" he muttered.

The disapproval in his voice matched the expression on his face. But it was another one of those subtleties of mortal emotions that Meg was not yet familiar with.

"I usually open them first."

Her reply was so matter-of-fact it momentarily halted his tirade. When he recovered, it was all he could do to keep a straight face as he carried her to the chair and deposited her in it.

"The next time you decide to go walking on ledges you might consider growing a pair of wings first," was the most effective reprimand he could think of.

Over his shoulder, Meg exchanged a bemused look with Dannelore, who rolled her eyes.

"I do not have need of wings when you are there to catch me," Meg replied with that same matter-of-factness.

"I will not be there the next time," Connor replied, easing his arm from beneath her legs.

"I have great faith in you," Meg replied. "You have been there every time I needed you."

His expression tightened. She sensed he struggled with some problem that deeply vexed him. She did not dare connect her thoughts to his at the risk of divulging her ability, and so instead attempted to understand in the mortal way Dannelore had explained to her.

Connor cut a sharp glance to Dannelore. "Leave us."

There was an uneasiness in his tone that unsettled even Meg with her lack of experience in such things. Uncertain whether she should leave or stay, the changeling cast a questioning glance at Meg.

"Mistress?" Dannelore asked uncertainly in the connection of their thoughts.

Meg sensed her uneasiness. She, too, had never seen the warrior in such a mood. He seemed greatly displeased about something, but it was impossible to discern if she was the cause of it.

"It will be all right," she assured the changeling. *"Please do as he asks."*

Dannelore gathered up a basket of mending and, with a curious if concerned glance, left the chamber.

"Do not eavesdrop!" Meg silently remonstrated when she sensed the woman in the shadows just outside the chamber.

With an undignified comment that brought a faint smile to

Meg's lips, the changeling stiffly marched down the passage and descended the stairs to the main hall.

Connor squatted before the chair, his gray wintry gaze boring into hers as if he perhaps sought to connect his thoughts to hers as he struggled with words he somehow found difficult to say.

"I am leaving Caerleon."

"Yes, I know. Arthur and the others make ready to leave as well."

He realized she assumed he left with Arthur and the others, and he saw no reason to explain. He frowned, wrestling with uncertainty about that decision and equally uncertain why it bothered him. He saw his course clearly, and clearly he could not join with Arthur. There was too much between them.

"You are feeling well this morn?"

"Aye, very well," Meg replied with bemusement, sensing without the need of her powers that he had not precisely come to inquire about her health.

"I am much stronger all the time. Much thanks to Merlin's healing skills." That brought a frown, and she realized—not for the first time—that there was no great love lost between the two. Something in the past lay between the warrior and the healer, some difficulty which Connor of Monmouth could not forgive.

"I am pleased. I had hoped for your full recovery." He paused again, choosing his words thoughtfully. "It was my arrow that struck you down in the forest."

"Yes, I know."

She replied with such candor, and absolutely no condemnation, that it took him by surprise.

"You were aware of it?"

"Yes." She realized she should perhaps not have revealed it. After all, she had been delirious with fever for many days and unconscious before that according to Dannelore. She would have had no way of knowing it.

"Dannelore told me," she hastily added. He seemed to accept that explanation.

"And you bear me no ill will because of it?"

Meg was confused. "Should I?"

"Any man I know would have. It could easily have cost your life."

That was not even relevant under the circumstances, but he had no way of knowing. He was obviously greatly distressed by it, and she sought some way to assuage his guilt. If only she were better adapted to mortal emotions and ways of dealing with them.

"But it did not."

She laid her hand lightly over his exactly as she had seen Dannelore comfort the injured among his men as she tended their wounds.

It was a simple gesture but seemed to bring ease to others. What she did not anticipate was the comfort touching him brought her. Like the previous evening when she had licked the spilled gravy from his fingers. She realized afterward that she had erred somehow, but there was no mistake in the pleasurable feelings it brought. Like now.

His hand was scarred where she laid hers, and in those scars she sensed the pain of each one exactly as it was when it was new, as well as the fierce warrior's spirit that accompanied each one—a warrior true of heart, with honor, courage, and loyalty that ran blood deep.

"It might easily have been another I encountered that day in the forest," she continued, knowing there had been others. What might her fate have been if they had found her first?

"So you see, I owe you my life."

Connor shook his head. There was some truth in what she said, but he knew full well where responsibility lay and he accepted it even if she did not.

Her touch was like the warm breath of spring upon a cold spirit. She made him feel alive when he was certain his soul had been dead for a millennia so many had he killed, so easy had it become to take another life in the name of revenge and think nothing of it. But her touch made him think of other things, of lost days, lost friendships, lost dreams. He turned his hand so that it cradled hers.

Her hand was small and slender, pale and soft, lost within

his large, callused warrior's hand that for so long had known nothing but the handle of a sword. Yet there was strength there. He felt it in the tender warmth as her fingers tightened over his, moving through him and somehow touching some place deep inside that he had thought frozen and dead.

His gaze met hers—blue as deep as a man's soul, and an inner fire like the wildest heart.

Meg sensed he struggled with some deep inner conflict and longed to open her thoughts to his so that she might know what it was. But she dare not.

"You are safe here," he finally said, looking down at her hand where it lay in his, trusting yet strong, giving back that strength in a simple touch.

Then, as if he suddenly arrived at some decision, he turned her hand in his. He reached inside his tunic and retrieved something he carried there. He opened his fingers over her cupped palm. There was a faint tinkling sound as the crystals spilled into her hand.

Meg's eyes widened with pleasure. "I thought I had lost them when . . ." She had been about to say when she came through the portal. She quickly caught herself, and instead added, "In the forest."

It eased his guilt somewhat to see how it pleased her to have the crystals back.

"They were all I found," he explained, recalling that he had found her completely naked. Not only did she have no other possessions, she had no clothes.

Needing some means other than meager mortal emotions by which to understand him, Meg allowed herself a glimpse at his thoughts. She saw how he had first seen her and saw as well what he had barely admitted to himself—the tangled feelings of guilt and regret, and some other strange emotions that she experienced just as he had experienced them—a longing ache of need deep inside that pulsed with each beat of her heart.

Like an eavesdropper who had seen something she had not wanted and did not understand, Meg quickly retreated from his thoughts and emotions.

"It pleases you to have them?"

"Yes," Meg assured him. "Thank you for their return."

"I did not recognize the symbols," he confessed, lightly brushing his fingers across the crystals. They had lain cold within his tunic the past days, but were now warmed by her touch.

"They are very old," she explained. "They have been in my family a very long time." She stopped, realizing her blunder. She supposedly had no memory of her family.

"At least, I believe so. They look very old."

It was as near the truth, with a few omissions, as she dared tell him. He nodded, apparently satisfied. Still, he seemed to struggle with something more left unsaid.

"You will promise not to go walking about on ledges."

The next time she found herself on a ledge she would use the powers she'd been born with instead of her mortal abilities which were still sorely lacking.

"I promise, and you must take care as well," she told him with a mock serious expression. "I would not want you falling off ledges."

She had meant it to be humorous. He was anything but amused. His frown deepened, altering his expression. Somehow she'd angered him. The look in his eyes changed as well, from cool gray to winter's darkest storm. He pulled her against him.

He slipped a hand behind her neck. His other hand slipped back through her hair. Before she could utter a sound, before she could even think, he angled her head back with those powerful hands and covered her mouth with his.

She felt the anger in his fingers as they pressed into her scalp and in his lips as he forced hers apart. Then, on a deep groan the anger was gone, replaced by something far more powerful. She felt it in the heat of his mouth, then tasted it in the sweet fire of the tongue stroking hers.

Meg was stunned. Nothing prepared her. She had no time to think. There was only sensation, the feel of his mouth against hers, sweet, wild, and hot.

Power. She had none. She could not have ended it or pulled away if she'd tried.

Possession. She felt herself consumed by something she'd never experienced before.

Surrender. Helpless as when he'd first found her in the forest, all she could do was surrender to him.

Her hands came up instinctively to push him away, but instead she held on, terrified of what was happening, terrified to let go.

It was violent, terrifying, and stunning. And it ended as suddenly as it began when Connor held her away from him.

He was as stunned as she was. She could see it in his eyes, the expression on his face, and she heard it in his voice when he swore softly as she touched his lips.

She didn't understand the meaning of those hard words, but she recognized the sound he made when he spoke them. It was the same sound he'd made when he kissed her, somewhere between agony and helplessness.

Just as he had, she slipped her hand behind his neck and pulled him close. Then, just as he had kissed her, she kissed him. Tentatively at first, her lips bruised and swollen against his, then more deeply as they slowly parted and her tongue touched his.

On a sound that seemed as if it were torn from some place deep inside him, Connor pushed her away from him. He stood without a word, and then he was gone.

Eventually, she sensed Dannelore's return and the concern in her unspoken thoughts as the changeling entered the chamber and found Meg alone.

"Is anything amiss? Are you all right?"

Meg turned away so that Dannelore could not see her face. "There is naught amiss," she assured her, but when she touched her tongue to her lips she could still taste him. Deep inside she could still feel the heat that had ignited with that kiss.

Arthur's men prepared for the journey to the Abbey at Amesbury to gain the release of Lady Ygraine and Lady Morgana. They secured provisions and weapons at their saddles and in scabbards secured at their backs. Skins of water were brought. Blankets and fleece skins were rolled and tied down. A distance apart in the far corner of the yard, as though separated by an invisible wall, Connor's men also prepared to leave.

"Is there nothing I can say that will change your mind?" Geoffrey asked his friend as they stood together in the yard. Connor jerked tight the strings on a rolled fleece.

"You know my feelings," he replied as he stuffed the fleece inside a leather bag that already contained rations of food. As he straightened, he cast a glance at the second-floor windows at the main hall, then glanced away.

"I had hoped to change them," Geoffrey admitted with a faint smile. "You're wrong about Arthur, you know."

"I don't see it that way."

"Isn't it proof enough that he came back. Look around you at the men who have already come to join him."

"And what of the men who died needlessly at the hands of Maelgwyn and Aethelbert these years past while he waited abroad?" Connor flung back at him.

"I do not pretend to know the reasons that kept him away," Geoffrey confessed. "But I trust in his word that it was necessary."

"That is the conjuror speaking," Connor corrected him. "And how far can you trust a man who some say isn't a man at all but the spawn of the devil?"

"Those are the stories of superstitious old women and small children who believe in dragons," Geoffrey argued. "Now is what is important. Arthur is here, and I believe he is the one to unite all of Britain. The people believe it too or they would not have come."

"I wish I could say something that would persuade you not to go," Connor replied. "He has been away too long. He does not know Maelgwyn as we do. He is not ready for this. Perhaps never will be. I fear what awaits you, my friend."

"All the more reason we need every good man with us at Amesbury! Join us, Connor. You have fought the long fight. As you say, you above all know Maelgwyn's mind and heart for you have faced him often enough in battle. Arthur needs you.''

Connor snorted with contempt. ''It does not look as if he needs anyone except the conjuror. I would not be at all surprised if he has not called on a spell to turn Maelgwyn's warriors into mice.''

Frustration weighted Geoffrey's reply. ''The conflict between you is an old one. I cannot resolve it for you. I had only hoped that you might set it aside for a greater cause.

''So, this is good-bye.''

Connor nodded. ''I will take up Maelgwyn's trail in the forest. With the weather clearing he will be on the move.'' He clasped his friend about the shoulders in a brotherly embrace.

''Watch your back, my friend.''

''And you.''

The gates were opened and Arthur rode out with his men, Merlin beside him at the head of the mounted warriors. The others followed afoot.

''What are your orders?'' Simon asked as he joined Connor. He cast a wary glance after the departing warriors.

Connor tucked away the map he'd made. He cinched the leather pack closed and shouldered it, settling the weight between his shoulder blades.

''Shepston by nightfall,'' he replied. ''Then we'll pick up the trail of Maelgwyn's raiders in the forest at first light.'' He whistled to the long-legged hound and followed him through the gate at Caerleon, on a course due east toward the distant hills.

They set a steady pace and approached Shepston by midafternoon. The village was set into the curve of the Tye River, surrounded by rolling hills. It was a tiny enclave of thatched huts that squatted in a sheltered turn of the river. The surrounding hillside was scattered with rocks, some of them taller than a man, and ill-suited for planting crops. But sheep didn't mind rocks. They grazed on the hillsides and grew fat with thick, woolly coats.

The people of Shepston had escaped murder and plunder at the hands of Maelgwyn's raiders by cunning and tenacity. Their flocks were scattered among the hills. Anything of value—food, fleece skins, metal utensils, weapons, or whatever might be bartered—was thought to be safely hidden, possibly in the ancient stone fields with their strange stone circles where not even Maelgwyn's raiders would dare go.

In spite of their impoverished existence, a warm meal could always be found there, along with a tankard of ale and a warm girl. Connor adjusted the heavy leather pack with its sacks of grain. The grain would be used to buy food and perhaps some information, for the proprietor of the local inn was an enterprising man.

The hound caught a scent and bounded on ahead. He quickly returned, uneasy and restless as he reached Connor's side.

"What is it, Dax?"

In one quick, fluid motion, Connor eased the pack to the ground and the sword from the scabbard at his back. His men did the same. He gave a hand signal, and they silently followed the course of the river into Shepston. As they rounded the bend in the river, the hound began to growl uneasily.

Old Radvald's eyes narrowed as he lifted his face to the wind which had turned sharp and cold as the sun angled down toward the horizon.

"The air has the smell of death in it. That's what the hound smelled."

Connor smelled it as well, that unmistakable stench of rotting flesh.

"Aye," he said low, and with another signal sent half of his men up the embankment to the hillock that overlooked Shepston. Better to see from high ground what you walked into than to discover it after you walked into it.

He took the other half of his men and split them again, sending several across the shallow river while he cautiously advanced toward the village along the river access.

Connor's senses sharpened. All about them the countryside was still as death. Not a creature stirred below or bird called overhead in the late afternoon sky. No sheep dotted the hillsides. No voices were heard, no cookfire smoke spiraled from smoke-holes in thatched roofs.

Across the river a portion of his men advanced, spread out along the course of the river so that the whole of them could not be taken by surprise. On the hill that overlooked the village others from his force were silhouetted against the fading light. A hand signal communicated that nothing was seen.

They entered the first hut, known to be occupied by a shepherd and his son. It was dark inside with no evening fire lit, and the stench was almost unbearable.

"Filthy, stinking shepherds!" Radvald spat. "Ha' they taken to slaughterin' sheep in their huts?"

"Torch!" Connor ordered. "That's not the stench of slaughtered sheep we smell."

A tinder was struck. It sparked and fire caught at a tightly twisted sheaf of straw. One of his men held it aloft.

"Jesu!" the man swore, and almost dropped the straw torch.

"Hold that flame steady, boy!" Radvald snarled as he found a tallow candle and righted it in the metal dish. He seized the straw and lit the candle. As the flame flickered and then caught, light gradually filled the small hut and revealed the slaughter inside.

Father and son had been brutally tortured. They had been tied to chairs, their hands bound behind them, their legs bound at the ankles. Their eyes had been gouged out and then their tongues had been cut off. Their throats had been cut and their severed tongues stuffed into the gaping wound.

"Why would anyone do such a thing?" the young warrior asked. His skin was several shades lighter than his usual ruddy complexion.

"It's a warning," Radvald translated the gruesome message. "About giving information to the enemy."

"What enemy? These people had no enemies."

"Maelgwyn," Connor said softly. He looked across at the young warrior who seemed about to be sick.

They'd seen many atrocities in the years they'd fought together, all in the course of war. But nothing like this. This was brutality for the sake of brutality.

"Tell the others what we found, then join Simon on the hill

above.'' And remembering Geoffrey's parting warning, ''Look to your backs.''

They cut the shepherd and his son loose and covered them with fleece skins. Outside the hut they were informed of similar atrocities in the other huts. No one had been left alive. Not even the innkeeper, who was known to sell ale and his daughter to whoever offered coin or trade whether it was Maelgwyn's warriors or Aethelbert's.

The village was small, a half-dozen huts all within a hundred yards. Connor squatted in the muddied dirt.

''Something is all wrong here.'' He rose suddenly and slowly began to walk through the village, ordering his men to stay well back at the perimeter. Only Radvald, wise and cunning, went with him.

His narrowed gaze scanned the muddied ground before each of the huts as they passed by, before them saw the markings of prints clearly made in the mud thick with clay.

''There was a purpose to all of this.''

''What purpose?'' Radvald asked. ''Besides bloodlust that would make my Viking ancestors quail in their boots.''

Connor squatted low outside one hut and gestured to a set of prints. ''Tell me what you see.''

''Boot marks. Many of them.''

''Any distinguishing marks?''

''Eh, what are you talking about?'' He looked closer, eyes narrowed against the fading light.

''A notch in the heel of one boot.''

''Aye, and in this set uneven marks.''

''An injury?''

Connor nodded. ''Now, over here.'' He indicated another area heavily trod with boot marks.

''The notched heel and the uneven pair, made several times.''

''And it is the same at each hut we passed.''

''How many men then?''

''No more than a dozen, but made to seem as if there were four times that number,'' Connor replied with certainty. ''And leading from the village toward the hills and the Amesbury Forest.''

"As you knew you would find them," Radvald concluded. "A dozen or four times that number, we will find them."

Connor did not reply but continued to thoughtfully study those marks.

"Why go to all the trouble to disguise their numbers?" he mused.

Radvald shrugged. "They knew we would follow eventually. They wanted us to think they are more than they are."

"We know for certain the number of raiders we followed through the forest," Connor reminded him. "We had enough encounters with them. We were outnumbered."

"And fought them back each time. Perhaps more died from their wounds."

Connor shook his head. "No, that is not what has happened. They wish us to think that they have all fled back into the forest, but 'tis only a handful—the marks we found were made by no more than a dozen."

"Where are the others?"

Connor's gaze sharpened as he rose and called out to one of his men to take a half-dozen others and search for tracks that led away from the village in the opposite direction.

The rest of the villagers were tended to while his men searched. One of his men stepped from the last hut as the searchers returned.

"What news?" Connor demanded.

"We found tracks several hundred meters east of the village."

"How many?"

"At least two score."

"You're certain?"

The warrior nodded. "No two were the same. They traveled light and fast, no more than a half-day ahead."

Connor nodded. "Those bodies had been there no more than a half-day."

"What are you thinkin'?" Radvald asked.

"A handful of Maelgwyn's raiders are headed for the Cadmon Forest."

"And the others? For Caerleon?"

Connor shook his head. "What they seek is not at Caerleon." His gaze met Radvald's. His lips flattened into a grim expression.

"Arthur is not at Caerleon."

Radvald nodded. "Constantine throws in his lot with Maelgwyn. The devout bishop and the heathen butcher." He stated the obvious, "Arthur will be outnumbered, with no warning of what awaits him."

"Aye, and Geoffrey and his men as well." Connor snorted with disgust. Simon had joined them and awaited orders to set off for the forest.

"What will you do?" Radvald asked.

Connor did not answer for a very long time. He stared across the village, his eyes as cold as the dead.

"We leave for the Abbey," Connor spat out, making no attempt to hide his bitterness at that decision.

"The Abbey?" Simon looked from one to the other with surprise. "When Maelgwyn's men escape to the forest? Have you thrown your lot in with Arthur after all?"

Connor cut him a sharp glance, but said nothing. They were all tired. They would be more tired still before this night was through.

"We do not go to join Arthur. We go to save a friend."

As for the village and the dead, he ordered his men, "Burn it!"

Dannelore watched her mistress with a thoughtful expression. Since the day before Meg had been quiet and withdrawn, her thoughts closed. Through the night she had paced restlessly, unable to sleep. Now it was nearly dawn. The changeling went to put more wood on the fire at the brazier.

"You will not speak of it?"

"There is nothing to speak of," Meg replied as she spread the ancient crystals before her in the glow of an oil lamp.

Dannelore glanced over her shoulder and saw the shimmering pieces, each differently marked. Only the gifted ones saw the messages foretold in the crystals as they were laid out at random. She had never possessed such ability.

Meg glided her fingers over each crystal, letting the power flow through her fingertips. Light glowed deep within the heart of each one, growing in intensity as she touched it, whispering a message in ancient words that flowed through her.

She saw the cross of the god the mortals worshipped, the shimmer of an ancient sword, and cold gray eyes staring back at her from the depths of the crystal.

"They have followed Arthur, and they are all in danger," she whispered as she brushed her fingers over another crystal.

"What do you see?"

Suddenly, Meg cried out. She jerked her hand back.

"What is it?" Dannelore anxiously asked. "By the Ancient Ones! You've cut yourself." She grabbed a linen cloth and blotted at the blood that dripped from Meg's fingers. But when she removed the cloth there was no cut. Still, drops of blood formed at the tips of Meg's fingers and spilled onto the crystals.

"I do not understand," Dannelore said as she again tried to stop the bleeding.

"It is all right," Meg consoled her. "It has nearly stopped now."

Dannelore looked at her with confusion. "But there was no cut."

Meg clasped her trembling hands together. "No, there was no cut. The blood came from the vision in the crystals."

Dannelore looked at the crystals spread before her mistress.

"What did you see?" she whispered.

Meg looked up. "Death."

Her hands shook as she paced the chamber. She clasped them together to stop the trembling. Scrying visions in mortal form was new to her. She was only just learning to use her powers through her mortal abilities.

"But surely the bishop will release Lady Ygraine and Lady Morgana."

"He will not release them," Meg said with certainty.

She gathered a thick fleece tight about her shoulders, trying to warm herself against a sudden coldness deep inside, as if she had glimpsed something more. What it was she couldn't say, for nothing else had taken form. But something was there. Something that peered at her from the edges of her vision.

"He does not hold them for their protection," she explained to Dannelore. "He holds them for ransom."

"Ransom?" Dannelore incredulously looked about her. "There is nothing of value left at Caerleon to pay a ransom, only crumbling stone walls."

"He seeks far more," Meg said with certainty. "He wants Arthur, and he will kill anyone who stands in his way."

Dannelore went back to stirring the fire at the brazier. "Merlin will protect Arthur. There is nothing to be concerned about." She threw several small pieces of wood onto the coals.

"I will fix you an herbal tisane," she continued. "It will help you sleep. You must rest. You are only just recovered from your wound."

The changeling poked at the coals, feeding more pieces of pungent bark and straw into the embers. They caught, the flames greedily consuming the straw and licking about the small pieces of wood. She fed larger pieces until the fire burned brightly. But still she shivered in spite of the steadily burning fire.

"By the Ancient Ones," she muttered. "I swear it grows colder in here by the moment. 'Tis as if there is a window open." She bent down to pick up a bigger piece of wood for the fire. It was then she caught a glimpse of the open window.

The bar had been removed. One of the shutters stood open. It was freezing cold, and a cloud of mist seemed to hang suspended at the ledge. Then, as if stirred by some unseen current of air, it disappeared over the edge.

Dannelore ran to the window opening. It was dawn. The sky was a soft pearlescent gray. The sun was just beginning to rise at the horizon, a sliver of blood red color that glowed like a distant flame, and streamers of pale golden mist rose in the cold morning air.

Chapter Nine

"This is madness!" Simon made no attempt to hide his contempt. "You risk our lives for Arthur?"

"Not for Arthur," Connor assured him. "But neither will I abandon a friend and allow him to go to his death needlessly. And you forget," he reminded him, "Geoffrey saved your life on more than one occasion."

"Aye," Simon acknowledged. "And I've always thought him to be sound of mind. But throwing in his lot with Arthur is madness."

Connor did not answer. He finished filling the skin of water and tied it off.

"And if I chose not to follow?" Simon demanded.

Connor wordlessly rose to his feet.

"I would regret the loss," he said with sincerity. "Still, every man here has always known he can go his own way if he so chooses." He shouldered the skin.

"Best keep moving," he said, as he crossed the stream where it narrowed. The moon had disappeared, and the sky had begun to grow lighter. The going would be easier once the sun came up. But there was the possibility that Arthur was already at Amesbury. They had to make up for lost time.

Radvald's eyes narrowed as he studied Connor. But Connor said nothing. He turned and broke into a ground-eating lope. One by one his men followed. All except Simon.

"You know we'll likely pay for this with our lives, old man," Simon said.

The Norseman shrugged. "Perhaps, as will many of them. I believe that is why we are called warriors." Then he turned and disappeared down the trail after the others.

Simon made a disgusted sound as he cinched his battle sword tight in the scabbard at his back. Then he shouldered his water skin. He was the last to cross the stream and follow down the trail.

"We found guards here, here, and here." Agravain indicated spots on the map drawn in the dirt around which Arthur and the others gathered.

It had taken them two days to reach the Abbey at Amesbury, traveling into the early evening each day and making cold camps for the night, for over half of them were afoot.

Earlier, Agravain and two others had ridden out and approached Amesbury under cover of darkness. The first light of dawn was just beginning to show through the thick cover of trees when they returned.

"The tower is also guarded and this outer wall."

"Total number of guards?" Arthur asked.

"A dozen by our count, plus these men positioned afield."

"What were you able to learn?" he asked one of the men who'd gone into the nearby village upon their arrival the previous evening.

"The bishop has taken all the men to the abbey to serve him, and he demanded loyalty from their families on threat of their lives. At least a full two score from the village and surrounding area."

"That might be useful when the time comes," Arthur thoughtfully replied. "You've done well. Rest and feed yourselves."

When they had gone, he continued to contemplate the map.

"You heard?" he asked of Merlin who stood some distance apart and leaned against the gnarled trunk of an old oak, his arms crossed over his chest.

"Aye," Merlin acknowledged. "And there are an unknown number of men loyal to the bishop inside the abbey."

Arthur nodded grimly. "At the very least we are outnumbered. At the extreme the odds are unknown."

"What is your plan?"

"To negotiate for the release of Lady Ygraine and my sister."

"And if that fails?"

Arthur rose, twisting the stick he'd drawn the map with.

"In all probability it will fail," he realistically acknowledged. "I remember Constantine well. He is not known for using words where a sword will work just as well. And his power has grown considerably." He snapped the stick in his fingers.

"What some men will do in the name of God!" he said contemptuously. He turned and stared down at the map that lay between them.

"We must get inside the abbey. We have not the men nor the weapons for a prolonged siege."

Merlin nodded his agreement. "Yet it is risky to hand Constantine the very thing he seeks by walking into the abbey."

"Aye, that is why not all of us will go." Arthur indicated the map and the outer breastworks. "Most will remain behind and gain entrance here." He indicated the location at the back wall.

"There is an escape door here near the edge of the forest. I remember it from occasions when Lady Ygraine would visit Bishop Alexander in the days before Constantine. When she met with the bishop I wandered the abbey and discovered the passage." He chuckled at the memory.

"On one occasion my mother's guards found me high in a tree deep within the forest. I had watched their approach from the abbey and swooped down on them with a small sword the duke had given me, ready to do battle. It didn't occur to me that I was outnumbered." The smile faded.

"Now we are again outnumbered."

"I will be at your side when you enter the abbey," Merlin said without room for question or argument. "And what of our escape?"

"The same way we go in," Arthur said. "I will not leave without Lady Ygraine and Lady Morgana." His expression was grim. "If I am to lead my people against Maelgwyn and others like him, let it begin here."

"And if we fail?" Merlin asked.

"Tell me what you see, counselor?"

"I see blood and death."

"Do you see my death?"

In all the years they'd been together, in all the campaigns, and battles on foreign soil, with all the questions asked over the better part of a lifetime, Arthur had never asked that one question.

"Do not ask that," Merlin solemnly said. He turned to join the others in preparation for the confrontation at the abbey, but Arthur stopped him with a hand at his arm.

"Do you see my death?" he persisted.

Merlin had seen all of it once, the entire future laid out like a road upon which a journey must be started and ended. Along that road shrouded in the mists of time he had glimpsed encounters with others, men who would join them, the cause greater than anything they could imagine, struggle, hardship, and yes— death. At least death as Arthur understood it. But not eternal death. For Merlin and those who were like him understood what lay beyond. For they had been created in that beyond where there was no such thing as death.

"The path of your life extends far ahead, my friend, beyond Amesbury Abbey." That much he would tell him. And the rest? Perhaps it was possible to change the future.

"Good," Arthur said, his previous humor restored. "I was not ready to die anyway. After all, I have yet to build my kingdom."

Preparations were made, plans were set. A full score of men were to wait at the edge of the trees, dispersed several yards apart, their weapons at the ready. Between them, positioned in sparse cover, tunics and weapons were visible to make it appear that a much larger force waited for Arthur's return.

Geoffrey and a full score of men, minus their tunics, were to cut through the forest behind the abbey and gain entrance by that monk's door. A handful of men, including Merlin, were to accompany Arthur to the front gates of the abbey.

When Geoffrey and his men had been gone a suitable amount of time to be in position at the monk's hole, Arthur and his men rode out under the banner of the House of Cornwall and with weapons in their scabbards. They were ordered to halt by the guard at the top of the gate who wore the tunic of the religious order of Bishop Constantine.

"I have come to call on Lady Ygraine, Duchess of Cornwall," Arthur called out, making no mention of Caerleon or the destruction found there.

"Who calls on the Lady Ygraine?" the guard called out.

Arthur and Merlin exchanged a look. There was no attempt to deny her presence at the abbey.

"Her son, Arthur of Cornwall," he called out, keeping tight rein on his nervous mount while the banners of Cornwall fluttered overhead in the frigid morning air.

Merlin kept a watchful eye on the abbey tower. The guard disappeared and another took his place. Several moments passed. They began to think they would be refused entry. Then the first guard returned.

He ordered them to dismount and leave their weapons. Weapons were not seemly in God's house. Arthur and Merlin exchanged another glance. So few in number, stripped of their weapons, they would be easy prey for Constantine. And if the good bishop also imprisoned Arthur of Caerleon, his power would be complete.

"Do as he asks," Arthur told his men.

"I do not like this," Agravain said under his breath as he dismounted, laying his sword across his saddle.

"Nor I," Arthur confessed as he did the same. Then with a wink at his men he concealed a long knife up the sleeve of his tunic. The others did likewise.

One man was to remain with the horses. He was given orders

to join with the others at the edge of the forest at the first sign of trouble. Then Arthur and Merlin walked toward the gate of Amesbury Abbey.

Metal grated against metal as the heavy gate was swung open. They walked inside, the gate closing behind them.

Each man was wary and alert, eyes scanning the small enclosed courtyard, the entrance of the abbey hall, and the upper tower windows. They were completely surrounded by men who wore the bishop's insignia across the fronts of their tunics and carried swords in scabbards at their belts.

"Pious looking, aren't they?" Merlin quipped low under his breath as they took stock of their situation. "Strange the things men do in the name of religion." Their conversation was cut short as they were greeted by a bald-headed man in flowing robes displaying that same insignia and wearing a gold cross about his neck.

He introduced himself. "I am Brother Tomas. I have been asked to take you to His Eminence, the Bishop."

"Will the Lady Ygraine be there as well?" Arthur asked. "I hope my mother is well?"

There was no response. Brother Tomas turned and walked toward the abbey hall. More guards appeared on the walls above them.

"Are we surrounded?" Arthur asked in a low voice.

"Completely," Merlin replied. They had no choice but to follow.

"What about alternative routes of escape?"

"I'm working on it."

The abbey hall looked much the same as Arthur remembered it, spartan, with stone walls, earthen floors, and a central hearth where a fire burned in a feeble effort to ward off the bone-aching chill that was ever-present in stone halls.

What was not the same was the raised dais at the far end, the high-backed chair much like a throne on which Bishop Constantine sat, imperiously awaiting their arrival. Or at least it seemed he awaited their arrival. Until they realized there were several others in the abbey hall, waiting for an audience with his eminence.

It seemed the bishop was holding court, dispensing justice as he saw it on those who had trespassed in some form or another. It was like the open senate at Rome. The accused trespassers were allowed to speak on their own behalf and present their defense. But it was a mock trial, for no matter their argument against the offense they were accused of, the verdicts handed down by Constantine were all the same— guilty. And the punishment dispensed with equanimity—death.

It was all for their benefit, Merlin realized. The extended wait like that of nameless peasants, to speak their cause; the humiliation that someone of Arthur's status and noble birth was forced to endure; the certainty of the fates of all those who preceded them a harbinger of what was to come; the uncertainty over the fates of those who had brought them here. And the bishop was the grand puppet master, pulling all the strings from his throne.

Merlin opened his senses and sent them afar into every corner of the abbey, seeking out enemies, deceptions, and lies. Lady Ygraine and Lady Morgana were there. But something was wrong. Very wrong.

"Be careful what you say," he cautioned Arthur as the last unfortunate supplicant was led away. "Remember, it was not Lady Ygraine's capture he sought, but yours."

"What of Geoffrey?"

"He is inside the abbey," he said with certainty. Then the bishop was greeting Arthur.

"Come forward, Arthur of Caerleon," he said, like a king bestowing favors. And then, as if he did not already know the reason, "What brings you to Amesbury?"

At that moment a morning mist purled over the walls of Amesbury Abbey. The guards were completely unaware that anything was amiss, that in spite of their constant vigil, someone slipped past them completely unnoticed—a disembodied spirit of sunlight and mist that entered the abbey in spite of stoutly barred doors and thick stone walls.

On a current of air that briefly stirred the flames at the torches at the walls, Meg slipped inside the abbey hall. And there, concealed by shadows and the power of transformation, she found Arthur and Merlin. She silently watched from the shadows as they approached a man in elegant flowing white robes—the Bishop Constantine, no doubt.

Her experience with mortal beliefs and religion was somewhat limited. But she understood the basic concept, not unlike the reverence and respect given the Ancient Ones. By what she had heard at Caerleon, the Bishop Constantine was such a man. Why then, she wondered, the need for so many armed warriors?

Arthur and his men were completely surrounded, outnumbered, and unarmed. Yet he confronted the bishop unafraid, with dignity, charisma, and a certain bearing of unmistakable power even in the presence of such overwhelming odds. The bishop was also aware of it and of the undeniable effect on his men. His words were silken, even paternalistic, but beneath them seethed an unspoken rage and deadly ambition.

"I am most grateful for your hospitality toward the Lady Ygraine," Arthur began diplomatically, with far too much calm for a man completely outnumbered.

"I have come to escort her and Lady Morgana back to Caerleon now that the danger there has past."

"Your gratitude is noted, however, it is my belief that Lady Ygraine will be much safer in my care, and she has spoken most seriously of her intention to take the veil."

"All the more reason then for her to return to Caerleon for a time, to make certain of her choice," Arthur responded. "Since it is a most serious matter."

"There is no need for her to consider it further. The lady is quite certain I assure you. She has already taken her first instruction as a new postulant."

Meg emerged from the shadows, moving among them without their being aware of it. She sensed Arthur's growing impatience, yet nothing by either word or gesture betrayed it.

"All the more reason then that I should see her. Her people are most concerned for her safety and good health. They have always been very loyal to Lady Ygraine." Only now was a slight edge heard in the words.

"With the entire countryside at war, it would seem a matter

of good diplomacy to calm their fears and concerns since Caerleon lies so near to Amesbury."

The bishop's eyes narrowed, the only outward indication of his true feelings. He made a dismissive gesture with his hand.

"I will have her write a missive to them, assuring them of her well-being and her choice in the matter."

"Ah, if that were only possible," Arthur rejoined, spreading his hands wide as though helpless in the matter. "But, you see, the people of Caerleon are not educated. They cannot read."

"Ah, yes, ignorant peasants!" the bishop acknowledged, making no attempt to disguise his contempt.

She sensed Arthur's anger. Sensed, too, that it was precisely what the bishop wanted. She reacted instinctively, opening her thoughts to him.

"Do not give in to your anger! 'Tis what he wants. He will use it against you!" And immediately realized the mistake she'd made.

She'd very nearly betrayed herself. Arthur had heard her thoughts, but Merlin had heard them as well. He glanced around, his gaze narrowing as he searched the abbey hall. Meg immediately cloaked herself in a spellcast, as easily as if an invisible wall protected her from his probing thoughts.

"Uneducated, but not ignorant," Arthur replied to the bishop. "They have asked that I speak with her on their behalf. There are matters of grave importance which only she might know."

The bishop was clearly not pleased. He seemed deeply disturbed, but she could not tell if it was in reaction to Arthur's comment or if it was possibly something else. Had he sensed her thoughts as well?

He was not gifted in the ancient ways. She would have sensed it immediately if he were a kindred spirit. Did he perhaps possess the dark powers?

She had heard stories of such creatures, long ago banished from the world of mankind by the powers of the Light. They were supposed to exist only in legend and myth, creatures of darkness and evil that might have ruled the universe a millennia ago had they not been driven into the vast unknown. They were not even spoken of by the Learned Ones. Their very existence was not even acknowledged. Yet at one time they had existed.

It was said that a creature of the light would be immediately aware of that darkness of evil if it were present, for they were complete opposites and their powers sought to consume and destroy the powers of the Light. She sensed none of that in the bishop. But he was hiding something.

Her senses were drawn to the circular winding stairs that led from the abbey hall up into the tower.

Lady Ygraine was there, she sensed it and turned her powers inward, transforming once more, moving unnoticed through the guards in the abbey hall.

The tower contained only two chambers. A small one at the first landing and a larger one at the very top of the winding stairs. It was at the smaller chamber that she sensed the presence of Lady Ygraine.

Strange, she thought. For so many guards below, there were none here. She listened carefully, reaching out with her senses. She sensed the presence of two humans, but there was something strange and disconcerting that confused her. Uncertain what she would find inside the small chamber, she did not open the door but instead slipped through it.

Emerging on the other side she was aware of two things: Moving through wood doors was definitely easier than moving through stone walls, although she was certain it would come much easier to her with practice. The other thing she was aware of was that it was unbearably cold in the chamber.

It was sparsely furnished, to the point of being almost barren. There was no hearth or brazier for warmth. Nor were there any of the other usual amenities she had discovered in the mortal world. There was only the narrow, raised pallet in the center of the chamber and two enormous candles set in tall metal candle holders at one end.

She slowly approached the pallet. A woman lay there.

She was slender and fine boned, an elegant creature who lay in peaceful repose. Her lashes were long and dark, and rested against her pale cheeks, hinting at youthful beauty that still lingered in spite of the delicate lines at her eyes and mouth.

Her hair was unbound and lay spread about her shoulders. It was rich auburn with silver wisps that framed her face. In those features, Meg recognized a resemblance to the lady's son.

There was an inherent elegance in the curves of her high cheekbones and her long, slender neck that belied the simple worsted woolen gown she wore. As if only fine satins and mescaline silk might have once touched her skin. Her nose was slender and long, over a full mouth curved in a faint smile as if she knew secrets that she lay dreaming of. One hand lay across her breast, the other at her side.

Meg reached out with her thoughts, but there was no answer. Then she reached out and touched Lady Ygraine's hand. She immediately jerked her own back.

There was no warmth of human life as when Connor had touched her, nor even that felt in the changeling's touch. Meg frowned in confusion. She sensed this was Lady Ygraine. She saw the resemblance to Arthur in the lady's features. Yet she would not waken, and her skin was cold as ice.

Meg sensed someone at the chamber door and had barely enough time to slip into the shadows as the door opened. A slender young woman stood framed by the glow of light from the torches outside the chamber. Then she entered, for a moment surrounded by darkness as she closed the door behind her.

She entered the pool of light that surrounded the pallet, staring down at the woman who lay there. She slowly rounded the pallet until she was standing beside it, still staring down at the woman who silently lay upon it.

"He is here, Mother," she said, her voice quivering somewhere between sorrow and laughter. "After all these years, Arthur has returned. But he's too late isn't he, Mother?" Her voice changed cadences, rose and fell, in ways Meg had never heard before.

"Your precious son? The chosen one? Ruler of all Britain?" the young woman speculated. "I fear not. Even now, Arthur may be slain in the hall below." Her voice caught then, in a strange sound that might have been one of sorrow. Suddenly she whirled around.

"Who's there?" she demanded, the light of the candles

quivering across her features. She was beautiful, with raven black hair, pale skin, liquid dark eyes, and bore a faint resemblance to the lady on the pallet. Meg knew this must be the Lady Morgana, Arthur's sister.

"Is someone there?" Morgana seized a candle from the holder and slowly rounded the end of the pallet, holding it before her so that the light from the candle reached across the chamber into the shadows.

She found nothing, nor when she turned and shined the candle in another direction, or another. But, as she turned back to the pallet and returned the candle to the holder, she felt the brush of cool air against her cheek as if someone had just walked past her.

In the hall below, the bishop's voice was edged with anger.

"Lady Ygraine is in seclusion."

"You may tell her that I have come to see her," Arthur replied.

"I'm afraid that is impossible."

"I'm afraid I must insist," Arthur responded. "I demand to see Lady Ygraine."

The bishop's eyes hardened. He slowly smiled. All about the room, Meg sensed tension suddenly drawn to the breaking point.

"You may demand nothing." He gave a signal and guards started to move in on Arthur and his men. They drew the weapons concealed in their tunics and faced the bishop's force.

When a guard lunged at Merlin with his broadsword he was greeted by a blow to the midsection, followed by another bone-shattering one to the face.

The guard staggered backward, blood spurting from his nose. Merlin seized his sword, tossed it to Arthur, and turned to meet the next attacker.

Meg had never seen a battle—fighting and bloodshed. It was shocking and terrifying. Arthur and his men were greatly outnumbered, and she feared for the outcome.

Unseen by mortal eyes it was easy for her to move among them. When one of Constantine's warriors lunged toward her, she concentrated her energy and sent him bowling over backwards. When another fell and lost his sword, she again concentrated her energy and sent the sword sliding across the dirt floor and into the hands of one of Arthur's men. But even with her powers and Merlin's they could not hold out for long.

Arthur fought fiercely and with surprising confidence. Far too confident, she thought, for someone who was so greatly outnumbered. Then she sensed the reason for that confidence in flashes of insight—more of his men had gained entry to the abbey.

But something was wrong. She opened her senses and sent her thoughts throughout the abbey. She sensed Arthur's warriors and knew they had met resistance where they attempted to enter the abbey.

She swept through the chapel, the flames of torches guttering in her wake. On a single thought she sensed the concealed door behind the altar. It stood ajar and a silent warning skittered along her senses. As she swept into the passage she heard more sounds of battle ahead.

The passage descended several steps, then leveled off. The light of torches quivered at the walls. As she continued down the passage the sounds of embattled warriors drew closer.

It was an all-out siege. She recognized the warriors from Caerleon. They had attempted to gain entrance to the abbey by way of the monk's door and had run headlong into a score of Constantine's warriors.

The warriors of Caerleon were outnumbered. Several were dead. They could not hope to hold on for long. Without help, Arthur and his men were doomed.

For the first time in her life Meg felt helpless. She had only her powers, and they seemed so insignificant in comparison to the fierce fighting of the warriors.

She had only her powers . . .

Meg turned her thoughts inward, drawing on the powers of the Light, transforming into a single quivering flame that suddenly burst into a searing inferno as she swept toward Constantine's warriors.

They were oblivious to anything but the battle before them. Then the firestorm exploded among them. There were screams and cries of alarm. The embattled warriors separated, suddenly terrified and fearful for their lives.

Fire swept through the passage, gliding along the walls, a burst of golden light that reached to the ceiling, curling, undulating like a blue serpent at the heart of the inferno along the passage floor.

Constantine's warriors scattered in all directions and in the snapping, crackling of the flames, many thought they heard the sound of soft laughter.

Meg burst into the sunlight at the end of the passage in a shower of golden mist, transformed once more as she swept past the men of Caerleon.

She had given them time, though it was precious little. Constantine's warriors would soon recover and take up the battle again.

Inside the abbey, Merlin's power protected Arthur and the others. But even as she sensed it, she sensed, too, the blow that Merlin did not see.

She saw it clearly like a vision in crystal runes. The bishop had taken up a sword and joined his men. His sword caught Merlin from the side, opening a ribbon of flesh that angled from his back across his ribs.

Merlin was stunned. She sensed his surprise and the pain that seared through him cold as ice. The blow staggered him. He very nearly went to his knees but fought back.

Beyond the abbey, she saw what Arthur could not see and perhaps even Merlin was not aware of. The rest of Arthur's men swarmed the gates of the abbey, but could not breach them. If they could not, all those inside would die.

Connor and his men followed the sounds of battle as they reached the edge of the forest. It knifed through the frigid air, sending flocks of winter birds from the trees in the forest, making a knot of dread coil deep in his gut as they swarmed through the forest.

Smoke spiraled above the abbey. Arthur's warriors vainly attempted to storm the gates. But neither Arthur nor Geoffrey was among them. Connor gave orders to his men. Ropes with metal hooks were uncoiled, their only hope of breaching those walls. Then, with swords and battle axes drawn, they joined the battle.

The fighting was fierce at the gates. High above on the walls, Constantine's men let loose a volley of arrows and stones. As Connor's men joined the fight, a half-dozen metal hooks attached to ropes were sent sailing over the top of the walls.

Three were immediately cut, sending climbers back into the melee below. Two more of his men made it to the top, both fought fiercely before falling wounded below. The sixth fought his way over the top. Others followed and fighting continued along the tops of those walls. Then the gates suddenly swung open. With a loud war cry, Connor and his men charged into the abbey.

They cut their way through to the abbey hall. Connor fought to his right and then his left, shoved one man aside, then ran another through with his sword.

"Behind you!" The warning was urgent.

Connor instinctively shifted and whirled around to block an unseen attack. As he fought one of Constantine's men he was aware of another warrior who fought at his back.

When another attack came at his left, the warrior deflected the sword, pushed the attacker back, and ran him through. As an unexpected blow staggered the other warrior back, Connor shifted again, whirled around and ran his attacker through. Three more of Constantine's men came at them and together they took them down. When two attacked Connor at the same time, the other warrior recklessly taunted one, separating them. As the battle took up at Connor's back, he concentrated on the other attacker. Whoever the warrior was, he fought fearlessly.

As his opponent lagged and made mistakes, Connor side-stepped a lunge that came too slowly, went down on one knee and brought the sword up, opening the attacker from belly to throat. He shoved the dead warrior away from him. As he pushed to his feet, he stared into the painted face mask of the unknown warrior who had fought so bravely at his back, and saved his life.

Connor did not recognize him. He did not wear the white and red colors of the bishop's warriors, neither was he one of Arthur's men.

He was tall and slim, with a lean strength and a power in his stance and the way he held a broadsword that suggested he would be a worthy opponent. His tunic, leggings, and shield were made of leather, much the same as those worn by Connor's men. Unusual markings were painted across his face, making it impossible to discern his features, but the sword he held was unlike any Connor had ever seen. It gleamed like blue fire.

"I owe you my life," Connor said.

"As I owe mine to you," the warrior replied.

Before Connor could say anything more or ask the warrior his name, he lifted that gleaming sword in silent salute. Then he turned and disappeared through the embattled warriors. There was no time to consider the encounter further as Connor turned and fought his way toward Arthur.

Where are the others? Connor thought, searching the embattled warriors. Neither Geoffrey nor his men were among them.

"Go to the chapel."

Connor heard the words as clearly as if someone stood at his shoulder and spoke them. But when he spun around, no one was near enough to be heard over the chaos of the fighting.

There was no time to question where it had come from. Connor spun back around. He took a dozen men with him as they cut their way through to the chapel.

He knew the monk's passage well. He and Arthur had played there often, escaping into the dark, musty passage that led to the forest to avoid long hours of afternoon prayers when Lady Ygraine visited the abbey.

He and his men easily found the open door behind the altar and charged down the passage. They met Constantine's men where the monk's door opened into the forest. There the course of the battle changed as his men joined Geoffrey's and they closed around the bishop's warriors.

As the battle shifted and the last of Constantine's men laid down his weapons, a lone warrior was seen silhouetted against the light of torches at the other end of the passage. When the battle finally ended, he raised his sword in final salute, then turned and disappeared.

Dannelore sensed a presence the moment she walked into the darkened chamber at Caerleon. She seized a burning stick from the fire at the brazier and lit a nearby candle. It sputtered briefly then caught, light spreading across the chamber as the flame grew.

She saw nothing at first. Then, as the flame grew steady, she saw a form huddled near the window opening at the wall. The shutter above stood open.

As she drew closer with the candle she saw the curve of shoulders, the fall of brilliant gold hair, and slender arms tightly wrapped about an equally slender silhouette.

"Praise be to the Ancient Ones," Dannelore fervently exclaimed on a sharp expulsion of air. "You've returned and you're safe." She went to her mistress then, setting the candle on the nearby table.

Meg's head was bowed, waves of golden hair sweeping forward to conceal her features, and her shoulders shook. Dannelore sensed the anguish of her thoughts.

"Dear child," she whispered. "What's happened?" For she could not discern it from Meg's thoughts, so tormented were they and filled with pain that it terrified the changeling.

Meg raised her head. Her brilliant blue eyes were haunted with shadows, and tears streamed her cheeks.

Dannelore gasped. For she had never seen such agony and soul-deep pain. Surely no immortal creature had ever experienced those emotions. Fear stabbed through the changeling's heart.

"What is it? Where have you been? What have you seen?"

Meg fought to speak past the tightness in her throat but could not. Nor could she form the thoughts to describe what she had experienced at Amesbury Abbey.

When she had come through the portal into the mortal world she had wanted to experience life and everything she'd heard stories about. She'd imagined countless times how it would be.

But nothing she had imagined prepared her for what she'd seen and experienced at Amesbury—the fierce fighting, the desperate struggle, the hatred, the blood, and the sounds of the dying.

Today she had learned there was another part of life— death—and she had been part of it. Now it was a part of her, the images forever sealed within her memory and etched upon her soul.

Meg felt as if she might shatter. She tightened her arms as if trying to hold herself together.

"Never speak of it again," she whispered. "Never."

Chapter Ten

The victory at Amesbury was a hollow one. As word eventually reached Caerleon, it was learned Lady Ygraine was dead.

Dannelore was deeply grieved. In her time at Caerleon she had been companion to Ygraine and had a fondness for the gentle lady. But Arthur's was the deeper more profound grief. After so many years he had returned to find his home destroyed and now this loss.

Within days of the battle at Amesbury the first of Arthur's men returned. There had been losses, and many had been injured. The people of Caerleon, who continued to arrive almost daily even in bad weather, helped prepare for the wounded.

Every capable pair of hands was put to work. Several of the women had some experience in setting bones and stitching wounds. Bandages were readied, muslin cloth was set to boiling, and what medicinal herbs could be found with winter hard upon them were gathered.

Among the men a smithy set up his forge and began making iron-tipped arrows and hammering out the metal for swords and spears. Carts arrived with crops harvested earlier in the fall to feed the growing population of Caerleon, along with sheep and wooly headed cattle which would need winter forage.

A makeshift stable was built to shelter the animals. Repairs were made in all the outbuildings of Caerleon. Crude huts sprang up within the protection of the walls. Every piece of wood and bundle of straw was scrounged to make thatch roofs and doors to hold back the winter cold.

Meg worked alongside everyone else. She cut endless lengths of cloth for binding wounds, prepared thread for closing wounds, spent long hours over the simmer pot as linens were readied, and took it upon herself to stockpile, sort, and label all the medicinal herbs that were gathered, along with providing instructions for their proper uses.

She had never used written words before, but it came quickly to her with help provided by a monk who had recently joined them at Caerleon. She listened intently as Dannelore explained about the preparation of medicinal concoctions and their uses, and wrote everything down in a journal.

"Keep your mind on what you're doing," Dannelore cautioned. "The wrong mixture for the wrong ailment could be fatal. Learning healing ways is a serious responsibility."

And Meg took it very seriously.

She had not seen Merlin or Connor since that fateful encounter at Amesbury. She knew they were alive, but more than that she did not know. There had been too much to do at Caerleon, and she dare not leave.

Nor could she risk using her powers. She had already risked too much. Even now she could not be certain Connor had not recognized her. There had been a moment in the midst of battle when she'd sensed a flash of instinct, that moment when he had looked at her and thought he knew her.

Then it was gone, lost in the heat of the fierce battle that had followed. Would he remember? she wondered. Would he even return to Caerleon? Or would he take up pursuit of Maelgwyn's army?

"Aye, that's it," Dannelore remarked as she found her in the herbal. "That should be enough dragon herb to have them all wetting their pants."

Startled from her thoughts, Meg looked up and realized the mistake she'd very nearly made, scooping the dragon's herb into an earthenware jar with a label for an herb used to make tea for alleviating fever.

"If the fever doesn't kill them, losing all that water will!" Dannelore commented dryly. "Now you must check all of it again to make certain the mixtures are correct."

"I'm sorry," Meg apologized as she poured the contents into a jar labeled Dragon Herb.

Dannelore frowned. It was not like her mistress to be wrong about anything, much less apologize.

"I made plenty of mistakes of my own when I was learning the proper mixtures," she said with a gentler voice. "These mortals are not strong creatures. I do not understand how they have survived this long. It must be stubbornness."

"Aye, perhaps," Meg said thoughtfully, recalling the way Connor had fought at the abbey. "Though some are stronger than others."

Dannelore looked over at her. There was something in her voice that suggested she was not thinking of reactions to poorly mixed herbs.

"Aye, some," she agreed. "Like my John. He is very strong. It comes from working with those great four-legged beasties the old duke used to keep. Fine animals they were. John used to take great pride in keepin' them so fine for the duke."

Meg laid down the ladle she had been scooping herbs with. She heard the familiar wistfulness in Dannelore's voice. It was always there when she spoke of him.

"Perhaps he was at the abbey with Lady Ygraine," she suggested, uncertain of the man's fate for she had not seen him at the abbey.

"Aye, perhaps," Dannelore replied, and said nothing more. Just as she had said nothing when word was first received of the victory at Amesbury. There had been no word of survivors, only of Lady Ygraine's death.

"They're here! Arthur is here!" young Tristan ran into the herbal, yelling at the top of his lungs.

He was one of many refugees who had arrived at Caerleon, to join Arthur. He was an orphan. His parents had been killed the previous winter in a raid by Aethelbert. Since then he'd been living off the land and what handouts he could beggar from others. He was all of ten years old and, what he lacked in size he made up for in enthusiasm.

Tristan had soulful dark eyes that often revealed a young boy's pain and silken dark hair that sculpted a too-narrow face with a sad mouth, straight nose, and sooty dark lashes. The tunic he wore had been *borrowed* and was much too big for him. It was uncertain that he would ever grow into it because of the fevers that often raged through him.

He has an angel's face, the monk had said with that prophetic sigh of sadness of one who knows when another has not long to live. Meg refused to accept that Tristan would not survive. There was too much life in those eyes which at the moment glinted mischievously as he spotted the peppermint sweets she wrapped. He had a particular fondness for them.

Right on his heels was Grendel. They were of an even height, if uneven temperaments. Grendel had been assigned to keep an eye on Tristan because he was the only one small enough to fit into the hiding places the boy was fond of squeezing into.

"I intend to offer him my sword," Tristan said matter-of-factly. "Arthur will have need of all good warriors when he sets out after Maelgwyn." His hand darted out for a peppermint sweet.

"Good," Grendel reminded him as he slapped the boy's hand, "is the important word. The important word is *good.*" He grinned.

Sharp as a needle, Tristan eyed the small creature thoughtfully. Hardly knowing who, or what, he was dealing with, he replied, "I will be a good warrior . . . The best warrior! And I will be *tall.*"

Grendel's eyes narrowed. " 'Tis another *short* comment. Another short comment it is."

"Cease!" Dannelore ordered, raising her voice to an octave none had ever heard before. All three looked at her with amazement.

"That's better!" she announced. "Off with you!" She turned on Tristan. "And put that wee broadsword away before I lay it across your backside!"

Not wishing to experience her wrath, Grendel tried to make himself as small as possible and attempted to sneak out unnoticed with the boy.

"You!" Dannelore seized him by the collar. "Make yourself useful. We'll need more wood. There's scarce enough of it as it is. And you," she turned on Meg.

At the door Grendel peered curiously, wondering what the changeling seriously considered for her. She was walking a very fine line between authority and disaster, considering what Meg was capable of. Tristan peered over his shoulder.

"Finish labeling the jars and then join me in the main hall. We must make a place for the injured." There was an edge of anxiety in her voice.

"By the Ancient Ones I have no idea where we'll put everyone with the roof leakin', all the wood buildings burnt to the ground, and people comin' out our ears."

She swept out of the small room in a flurry of activity, oblivious to the two who hid in the shadows at the entrance.

"Ah," Tristan grumbled. "She didn't even threaten her. What was that all about?"

"Wisdom," Grendel replied. "Come my wee fellow, we've wood to gather."

"Mistress Dannelore said nothing about me gatherin' wood!" Tristan protested.

"Didn't she now? She didn't?" Grendel pondered, rubbing one hand across his bearded chin while he seized the boy with the other.

"No!" Tristan stubbornly insisted. His protest ended on a choke of childish fury as the little man twisted his fist in the neck of the boy's tunic, cutting off all further protest, not to mention air.

"What say you about gathering wood? About gatherin' wood, say you?"

Eventually Tristan responded with a muffled sound and a furious nod.

"That's better. Better it is," Grendel said with satisfaction as he hobbled down the passage in that odd gait of his, dragging the protesting Tristan along behind him.

"Now who is the tallest? The tallest who is? Hmmmm?"

Meg quickly capped off the jars, yanked off the cloth tied about her waist, and headed for the main hall.

Dannelore was there. The doors of the main hall had been opened. Beyond the steps, they could see the front gates of Caerleon, newly mended, which also stood open as Arthur and his men returned.

"You wanted to experience life," Dannelore told her. "Aye, well then, this is part of it. You have no idea what you're in for, mistress."

But Meg did know. She knew exactly. She had seen the fighting, the blood, and the death. There was a sudden tightness in her throat, and her fingers grasped the folds of her gown as she watched and waited with a new emotion, hope that replaced fear.

Arthur and his men were the first to arrive, astride their warhorses. He dismounted but did not immediately come into the great hall. Instead he remained with his men, seeing to the wounded, assisting one of his warriors to dismount, then with one arm about his waist, helping the wounded man into the hall.

Dannelore quickly directed them into the main hall where a roaring fire had been kept burning, fresh bandages were piled upon a table along with the healing herbs Meg had prepared, and pallets had been laid out.

Merlin followed, assisting another warrior, Agravain. Though he seemed fit enough, she saw the deep frown and beads of perspiration on her brother's face. She slipped an arm about Agravain's waist at his other side and guided his arm about her shoulder, relieving some of the weight from Merlin.

Agravain was not as badly injured as some of the others and refused to lie on one of the pallets. Instead, he agreed to have his wounds tended by one of the village women. Meg turned to Merlin.

He had stood apart, leaning against the nearby wall. It took no particular powers to discern that he was in deep pain. It showed all over his face.

"You've been injured."

He immediately straightened and, as Agravain was tended to, turned to leave the hall.

" 'Tis nothing."

" 'Tis more than nothing, milord counselor," she said with rising concern that the injury should still plague him when he possessed such marvelous healing powers.

"The wound still seeps."

His head came up sharply, those striking blue eyes so like her own pinning her. "How do you know that?"

She smiled. She gestured to his tunic. "Blood stains your tunic. Will you let me look at it?"

He shook his head wearily. " 'Tis nothing. There are others far more seriously wounded. Perhaps later." And then he left, returning to the yard outside the main hall to help the others.

"Stubborn," she muttered, and with a faint smile, "Seems to be a family trait."

Others were brought in and their wounds attended. Meg found herself directing them in an orderly fashion—the more seriously wounded to the pallets closer to the fire, where there was abundant hot water and sufficient light to dress wounds; the less severely injured to the pallets that lined the walls, where they were made comfortable until they could be seen to. Then she heard a familiar sound—the long, yowling bark of the gray hound.

"Dax!" she exclaimed, kneeling down as the hound bounded toward her. It was a greeting of kindred spirits, those who have lived and experienced the animal world of which he was so clearly king in intelligence, pride, and brutal strength. That brutal strength almost bowled her over due to Dax's enthusiasm, but she held on, sinking her hands into his thick gray coat.

Where is he? she wondered, a strange lightness welling inside her, along with the fierce beating of her mortal heart.

He is near, for you would not venture far from his side.

Then she heard his voice as he called for the hound.

"Ho! Dax! Where are you?"

Now she saw him, silhouetted against the pale gray of the late afternoon light at the doorway. His face was bathed in shadows. She could not see his expression, but she could feel his eyes on her and sensed emotions that filled her with other strange emotions.

He entered the hall as others pushed past him, nodding in acknowledgment in that way of men who have fought together and lived to talk of it. He slowly strode toward her.

"Dax!" he commanded in a low voice, and the hound reluctantly left her side.

Meg slowly stood, her hands suddenly useless at her sides, fidgeting and twisting as if they had a mind of their own. She buried them in the folds of her gown.

"You are well, mistress?" Connor asked.

Startled, Meg stared at him. It seemed preposterous that he should ask such a thing of her after what he had been through. Had he sensed something more than she'd originally thought? Did he suspect the identity of the warrior who had fought at his side?

No, it was impossible. He could not know. It was only the usual greeting between two people.

"I am very well, milord," she replied, averting her gaze from his searching one.

From behind him, at the entrance to the hall, there was a woman's sudden outcry that drew their attention. It was Dannelore. She pushed through the injured warriors who streamed into the hall and flew into the arms of a man so smudged and stained with blood and the filth of battle that it was almost impossible to discern his features.

Her excitement almost staggered the wounded fighter who leaned on another for support, and he would have gone down if he hadn't wrapped his arms about the changeling. She had enough strength for two as she buried her face in the curve of his neck and clung to him. Then, in the midst of the hall, with scores of people moving about them, they kissed.

In spite of his injuries there was nothing tentative or gentle about the kiss. It was passionate, the man holding Dannelore's face between massive, bloodied hands that trembled, devouring her as if she was the sweetest drink and he was a man dying of thirst.

Tears streamed down Dannelore's cheeks. In spite of his

injuries there was no gentleness in her, but a recklessness and openness of passion that Meg would not have thought her capable of.

Her hands lay over his, holding onto him, taking him in, her response equally passionate as with eyes closed she seemed to breathe him in, then changed the angle of the kiss and deepened it. With the tears were faint sobs and urgent sounds of both pleasure and yearning. Sounds that tugged at something deep inside Meg as she watched. Something deep, primal, and wholly mortal that echoed the kiss days ago when Connor had left Caerleon.

The ache of the memory that had lain wrapped in fear tightened deep inside.

"John," she murmured with certainty, glancing away from them when it became unbearable to watch them any longer. "She has longed for word of him. I had hoped he might be at Amesbury."

"He and others from Caerleon fought bravely. Our losses would have been greater if not for them. Lady Ygraine is dead," he added somberly.

"Yes, I know," she replied, and then hastily added, "We received word of it before your return."

She reached for his hand which was wrapped with a bloodied cloth.

"You have been injured!"

Her touch moved through him, a gentle warmth that slipped past the bandage, taking away the cold, pain, and weariness of the past several days. His fingers curled over hers, holding onto the warmth and gentleness.

" 'Tis nothing," he said, reluctantly pulling from her slender grasp. "There are others in far greater need."

She realized that indeed there were as Arthur finally entered the main hall, one of his men leaning heavily on his shoulder. Moving to the man's other side, Connor helped support him with a strong arm about the waist.

"Bring him," Meg said as she moved ahead of them, directing them through the wounded who now lay on pallets lined up across the floor. The man was severely wounded and would need tending first.

There were no more pallets near the fire so she quickly made one, stripping the thick fleece from about her own shoulders and spreading it across the fresh straw that covered the earthen floor.

"You will be cold, mistress," the injured man protested, his face a bloodied mask from a head wound.

"The fire will warm me." She smiled, surprised at his concern for her when he was so clearly suffering.

These mortals never failed to surprise her. They were not the simple, unfeeling, foolish creatures she had been led to believe. Although—she thought of Cosmo—this one did smell quite foul from the grit and grime of battle, not to mention the putrefaction of the wound. But his concern for her made it seem insignificant.

He grimaced with pain as Arthur and Connor laid him on the pallet. He had other wounds more grievous, she quickly discerned with a simple touch, the knowledge moving through her with a faint echo of memory of the battle he had fought. She stole away the memory and the pain as her thoughts connected with his. At least this much she could do. His eyes closed and he drifted into dreamless, painless sleep.

"Mistress?"

She heard the note of concern in Arthur's voice. It touched her deeply, for she would not have expected it.

"He sleeps," she assured him. "Hope that he will continue to do so while his wounds are mended."

"Will he live?"

She did not possess the power of life or death. In her world neither existed. But here it defined these mortals. Time was an enemy. Time carried them from life to that moment of death and then they were gone, their mortal bodies merely shells that in time wasted away to nothingness, the essence of their being once more part of the light.

She remembered the touch of Ygraine's hand at Caerleon, robbed of warmth and life, her essence no longer felt within her mortal body, the beating of her heart forever silenced. It was the first time Meg had touched death, sensed the darkness and finality of it. And she had drawn back in surprise and sadness at the loss. Transformed into a mortal creature, she felt mortal emotions.

She cast off the unwanted emotions—the unwanted awareness of the fragility of mortal life.

"He will live," she said with grim determination, and she would do all in her power to make certain of it.

A confrontation at the entrance to the main hall drew their attention. A slender young woman regally stood amidst the chaos, silhouetted against the light of the torches.

"That can be done later," she said to one of the women who stood in confusion, her arms piled high with bandages. "You will come with me. I am cold and hungry. A fire must be built in my chamber and food brought."

The young woman was dressed in a mud-stained blue gown and tunic. Her long dark hair was pulled back and plaited in a thick braid that fell over one shoulder.

"Do you understand me?" she demanded of the woman who had been given specific instructions to deliver the bandages and so hesitated. The young woman's voice rose several octaves, along with the serving woman's distress.

"Is everyone here ignorant?" the younger woman demanded, loud enough for all to hear.

"Thank you for your kindness, mistress," Arthur said as he rose and crossed the hall to where the young woman stood in growing agitation.

It was then the woman stepped into the light of those torches and Meg recognized her—the young woman she had seen at Amesbury—Morgana, Arthur's half sister who had been abducted with the Lady Ygraine when Caerleon was attacked by Constantine.

She had no more time to contemplate Arthur's sister as she turned to the task at hand.

Connor squatted beside the pallet. He watched as she calmly pried away the warrior's bloodied tunic, her slender fingers gentle as they eased away bandages caked with more blood, grime, and bits of flesh. She didn't cringe or grow pale but instead possessed a calmness that seemed to flow through her fingers, calming the man who lay there.

Light from the fire at the hearth spun through a tendril of pale gold hair that escaped the braid that lay over her shoulder and played across delicate features and tipped the dark gold of her downcast lashes as she concentrated on the task before her.

He had thought to never see her again when he left Caerleon. But every step that carried him away, the stronger became the memory of the slender naked creature he'd found in the forest, wounded by his own arrow; of the countless times he'd stolen into her chamber at Caerleon and watched her sleeping, praying she would live; of the feel of her skin when they'd parted, like warm satin beneath his hand, her hair like gold silk where it fell over his arm; of the startled sound she made and the look in her eyes when he'd kissed her.

There had been no fear in those shimmering blue depths, but instead a glow of warmth like the heart of a flame that suddenly became an inferno as the flame burned wild and hot.

And the taste of her. Like sun-drenched honey, filling his senses and memory with sweet fire.

He didn't ever want to leave her again.

The thought stunned him, like the first contact in the first battle he'd ever fought, jarring through him bone-deep. There had been too many leavings, too many deaths, too much loss in his life.

He stood suddenly, the feelings unwelcome, his voice gruff. "Is there anything you need?"

She heard the gruffness edged with anger and looked up. "More water, and wood for the fire. We will need a great deal of it."

"You'll have it. Is there anything else?"

"You must have that hand looked at," she reminded him. "Or the wound will fester."

"Later."

Meg heard the coolness in his voice that matched the color of those slate gray eyes and frowned, wondering at the sudden change in him.

He turned and made his way through the pallets laid end to

end across the floor, calling loudly for the hound as he left the hall. With good-natured enthusiasm and obviously ignoring his master's suddenly foul temper, the hound bounded ahead of him and out through the door of the main hall.

And they said mortal women were changeable and unpredictable!

Meg had never experienced anything like the next hours at Caerleon. It was difficult to believe that Arthur and his men had been victorious at Amesbury. The wounds needing to be stitched and bandaged seemed endless.

She worked alongside Dannelore and the other women, moving from pallet to pallet, closing wounds, applying poultices, tearing cloth for more bandages.

Merlin tirelessly worked along with them, refusing to have his own wound tended too, insisting that he could care for it himself.

When a bone needed mending, his touch eased broken ends back into place. When bleeding could not be stopped, he closed a wound. When pain was unbearable, he closed the warrior's mind to it. And when death was inevitable, he sat beside the fallen warrior, easing that final journey from life.

It was late. Sometime past she vaguely remembered the evening meal had been served. Then, the rest of Arthur's and Connor's men joined the injured, laying out their pallets on the earthen floor of the main hall for it was too cold to sleep in the yard outside.

The fire blazed at the hearth and several braziers had been lit about the large hall, adding their warmth for those who slept there. Over the snoring of sleeping men there was an occasional moan from one of the wounded who was quickly tended by one of the women.

Dannelore had tended John's wounds, which were not serious, and then had gone with him to the pantry to find something to eat, for there was little left of the deer meat stew they'd prepared in anticipation of Arthur's return.

Lady Morgana had not been pleased about the condition she

had found her chamber in upon her return. It was the same as when she had left after the attack by Constantine's men; there had been no time to clean it before her arrival.

She refused to sleep in it, claiming it unfit for a pigsty, and chose instead the larger chamber that had once belonged to Lady Ygraine. She then insisted that one of the village women clean it and provide fresh straw for her pallet.

When she was informed that there was none due to the fact that it had all been used in the main hall below, her furious response was heard throughout the hall. Then she discovered that the door had not been replaced across the threshold. The poor village woman sought out Meg, wringing her hands.

"What am I to do? Nothing pleases her. She says a tapestry across the opening is not enough protection with so many men about."

Meg failed to see the reason for alarm. "Tell her that if the room does not please her, she may sleep down here."

The poor woman looked at her aghast. Old Radvald who had sought her out for some salve for a burn coughed loudly. He didn't seem nearly so ill disposed as amused.

"I cannot tell her that!"

Meg had shrugged. "Very well then. She can sleep in the stables. It offers comfort and privacy. And she can close the door."

The woman obviously thought Meg had lost all reason, but she didn't argue the matter further. Meg had no idea what she told Lady Morgana, but she quickly returned with a smile of gratitude.

"She told me to get out. Thank you, mistress."

Sometime later, Arthur also returned downstairs and promptly poured himself a healthy draught of ale.

"Near two hundred men at Caerleon and half again as many people from the countryside. We have not enough food, blankets, or wood to warm them, and I have not one one-hundredth the problems with them I have with one woman. God help us all," he muttered. "I should have let Constantine have her!"

Then his gaze had fallen on Meg. "Do you perhaps have something that has a calming effect?"

"Lavender," she replied. "Perhaps she would like lavender tea."

"It would probably take a hogshead of tea to soothe her," he replied, pouring himself another draught of stout ale. "If I don't kill her first. I had forgotten how difficult my sister can be."

Arthur now sat dozing in a nearby chair, several minor wounds bandaged, his hand resting over the sword propped by his side. Exhaustion lined his face. The tankard of ale was empty.

Meg was not aware that Merlin had drawn close and watched as she secured another bandage over yet another wound.

"You have a healer's touch," Merlin said thoughtfully, speaking low so as not to disturb those who slept nearby. He took her hand between his, cradling it.

"Such a gift is rare."

She hastily drew her hand from his, afraid of what he might sense in the simple contact.

"My skills are nothing compared to yours. A simple touch, a clean bandage, a poultice to draw the poison. Nothing more."

"I suspect far more than that, mistress," he replied, and she waited, holding her breath, wondering if he had sensed something, if she had somehow given herself away.

"Perhaps it is your woman's touch," he suggested. "I suspect Arthur's men respond more readily to it than to mine."

She slowly let out the breath she had been holding and laughed with equal amounts of humor and relief.

"A foolish notion, milord."

"Not at all foolish. I can see it in their faces when they look upon you. Such beauty is rare, and accompanied by a gentle spirit, even more rare. Where were you raised, mistress?"

" 'Tis not important where I was raised. What I mean is that such things are not important to me. Therefore, I assume I was raised not to put much stock in such things."

"I thought perhaps you had remembered how you came to be in the forest."

She felt him watching her. He would sense any attempt to evade the truth, therefore she carefully closed her thoughts to him and raised her gaze to meet his.

"Perhaps I will remember more in time."

"Perhaps," he speculated.

"Do you think such things as beauty are important?"

"I have never considered it, mistress. I prefer to avoid matters of the heart."

She looked at him curiously. "Why would you wish to do that?" She thought of the reunion between Dannelore and John. Dannelore had been so happy she had cried. "They bring such happiness."

He made a dismissive gesture. "Such things are not for someone such as I."

Now she was very curious. "Why is that?" She sensed him evading the real truth with carefully chosen words. Not a lie, merely the omission of the whole truth.

"My duties to Arthur are more important than anything. Nothing else matters."

"But I think perhaps we cannot choose whether or not we will love someone," Meg suggested. "It seems to me that it just happens." She had already discovered that mortal emotions were very unpredictable.

"I will not allow it to happen," he answered. "If one is careful, it can be avoided."

"The same as being injured in a battle?" she inquired with the simple logic that the ability should apply to the one and the other.

"You have a sharp tongue, mistress."

She frowned, not at all certain how a tongue could be sharp. She shrugged. "I merely speak the truth. If you can avoid one, you should be able to avoid the other."

Merlin smiled. "You are quite logical, mistress. And quite right." He frowned. "I should have been able to avoid it."

"But since you did not, will you at least let me tend your wound?" she asked. He shook his head.

" 'Tis not a serious matter. It bruised my pride more than my skin." He winked at her. "A lesson well learned—always watch out for the man at your back, even when you think he is not there.''

If he only knew, she thought. For she had been a warrior with him, but had been unable to save him from the wound. She smiled, glad for the time she was able to share with this brother she had never known. She did not think him so fearsome. She quite liked him.

"I will try to remember."

She gathered remnants of linen cloth and the basin of herbal water. Fortunately most of the injuries were not too serious—minor cuts that would heal quickly; a few cracked ribs and bruised heads. She stepped over sleeping men as she crossed the hall, careful not to wake them.

She had not seen Dannelore in several hours and set off in search of her. She headed for the pantry where extra linens and herbs were kept.

Among those sleeping were some of the women and girls who had helped with the wounded. One woman slept beside a man, a small boy tucked between them. As Meg passed other sleeping forms, a heavy fleece was suddenly pulled over two snuggled bodies.

The passage between the main hall and the kitchens was dimly lit. There was only the meager illumination of a single torch which sent light quivering on invisible currents of air across the stone walls.

As she approached the pantry she heard faint sounds. As she drew closer she realized they were voices. Dannelore's and John's.

Meg sensed something that made her hesitate, a wildness and urgency that reached out from the shadows.

She heard Dannelore's soft entreaties and John's whispered responses. Then, in the powerful connection of their thoughts, she *saw* the images within the darkened shadows of the pantry—the sudden haste with which clothes were pushed aside, the trembling of his hand as it closed over Dannelore's breast, her soft sigh in response, the rasp of leather ties being loosened followed by a sudden expectancy that weighted the very air around them, the sudden shiver of cold air against bare skin.

Then they suddenly came together, their bodies straining with urgency.

Because she was not mortal, Meg had no experience of such things. She had only the connection of her thoughts to Dannelore's and the deeper understanding that she had stumbled upon something intensely private.

Nor had she the sensibility to be embarrassed about it, merely curious and absolutely certain that no matter how urgent and desperate those sounds, Dannelore did not wish to be rescued from whatever calamitous situation was about to befall her.

"I do not think I will ever understand mortals," she whispered as she quickly fled past the pantry and headed for the kitchens.

The kitchens were near enough to the main hall for meals to be prepared and delivered while still warm. Two large stone hearths filled one wall. A large long table filled the center of the main kitchen with a long bench on the far side. An odd assortment of utensils, carving knives, bowls, platters, and trenchers was stacked on the table. Huge cook pots simmered on fires that had been banked low in preparation for the morning meal. As she entered the kitchen Meg saw a movement along the wall. The creature was four-legged instead of two legged.

"Dax," she called out softly, and the large hound lumbered over to her, tail wagging in greeting. He immediately nudged his nose into her hand.

"How are you?" she exclaimed, gently clasping his large head between her hands, her fingers digging into thick fur and kneading thick neck muscles. The hound angled his neck for better access to her fingers, leaning into her, and groaning with pleasure.

"Worthless beast!" Connor muttered as he came up behind the animal and saw that his fearless companion had been reduced to quivering helplessness by a mere slip of a girl.

"The last man who attempted that almost lost a hand."

"I am not a man," she logically replied, continuing to scratch Dax's neck.

"I had noticed."

She looked up. There was something in his voice. Something

rough and husky and reminiscent of that day when he left Caerleon.

He grunted. "He won't be fit for hunting rabbits or squirrels when you get through with him."

"We could use a few rabbits and squirrels for the stew pot," she said with equal logic, turning the hound's head to one side and frowning at a cut in front of one ear.

"He's been injured."

Connor shrugged as he found several rib bones on a platter and seized one. He sat on a stool near the wall, gnawing thoughtfully, his long legs stretched out before him.

"Many times over. 'Tis the nature of the beasts. It will heal."

"It will heal faster with proper care." She applied a smear of salve made of crushed comfrey. The hound stood quietly while she applied it, then licked her hand.

"You see," she told Connor. "He appreciates it."

"He is an animal. He knows nothing of appreciation. He knows food, water, and a warm place to sleep on a cold night. Nothing more."

She looked at Dax. "We will have to be patient with him," she explained to the hound which cocked its head to one side as if listening.

"After all, humans are such foolish creatures."

"Foolish?" Connor replied with a snort as he gnawed on a rib bone. "Compared to a hound?"

Meg looked up. "Aye, foolish. Who else but a man would go about with a wound that festers and risk losing a hand or arm to poison?"

She seized the bone and threw it to Dax. As the hound fell to the floor and began gnawing, she inspected Connor's wound in the quivering light of the fire at the hearth.

"What do you think, my friend?" She looked to Dax for confirmation.

As if in response, the hound lifted his head and whined softly.

"Yes, I am quite sure of it," Meg agreed as if they had discussed the matter at great length.

"He is most arrogant."

"Arrogant?" Connor exclaimed. "It had nothing to do with arrogance. There were matters that needed attending to. I had to see to my men. Fortifications had to be made, guards posted. The victory at Amesbury comes at a price. Maelgwyn will soon learn of it and strike even harder at the south lands to establish his claim."

"And you will be most impressive wielding a sword with a stump instead of a hand," Meg replied as she removed the crude bandage he'd hastily wrapped about his hand and inspected the wound. "Perhaps we can strap it to your arm, like the wooden leg one of the villagers wears."

"Perhaps you concern yourself where you should not."

Not the least intimidated, she merely grinned at the warning note in his voice.

"Perhaps," she continued, not about to let him have the last word, "I should let it fester until it smells like an old dead goat."

She probed the wound to see if it festered. He instinctively jerked at the pain.

"One hand," he warned, "would be more than enough to silence a bothersome magpie!"

"Only if you can catch it," she retorted.

"Easily done," he replied.

She gasped as his other hand slipped beneath her chin, strong fingers angling it up so that her gaze met his. Just as it was that day he left Caerleon, his hand was warm, burning through her where he touched. And just as on that day, burning places he did not touch.

The skin at his thumb was callused and scraped at the curve of her bottom lip as he stroked it back and forth, creating a rough heat that immediately brought back the memory of that kiss the morning he had left Caerleon; and as on that morning the gesture pulled at something deep inside her.

"Your hand," she haltingly reminded him, her voice barely more than a whisper.

He did not answer, nor did he release her. Gone was the playfulness of a moment before. Gone, too, was the amusement and easy banter.

His face was a taut mask that concealed his emotions. Even without the use of her powers, she sensed his conflict, and felt it in the hand that trembled as he held her.

"I will not hurt you," she assured him. "You may ask any of the others. They did not find my skills lacking or my care of them disagreeable."

"Is that what you think?" he asked. "That I fear the pain?"

"What else is there, milord?" she asked with bewilderment. "You did not fear Constantine, nor do you fear Maelgwyn. I think you do not even fear death."

"Aye," he responded, "not even death. But you—"

"Me, milord? What is there to fear of me?"

He did not answer. "Do your bandaging, mistress, before I begin to smell like a dead goat."

She worked carefully and quickly, afraid his temperament might change again as quickly as it had before. She bent over his hand, carefully cleaning the wound. Then she applied a healing salve and covered it with a thick piece of linen to protect against further injury.

"Your laughter," he said as she worked over his hand. "And your honesty," he continued. "You do not disguise your thoughts in carefully chosen words that have double meanings."

She looked up and frowned. She had absolutely no notion what he was talking about.

"Milord?"

"You are completely without guile or ambition."

"You make no sense," she said as she wrapped a length of linen over the bandage. "It seems to me those qualities are greatly admired. And in great abundance."

He laughed as he settled back against the wall behind him while she worked over his hand.

"Your ability to forgive."

She knew he spoke of the accident in the forest. " 'Tis a small thing. But little enough of it I think in this world." Her gaze met his for a moment as understanding passed between them.

"And you are not afraid to speak your mind."

"Why not? What is there to fear?"

"There are those who would be killed for being so bold and those who would kill others for such boldness."

"I am not afraid of anything," she answered with complete guilelessness, simply because she did not know how to be afraid.

Their gazes met. "You should be," he said softly.

She finished tying off the bandage, and he flexed his hand. The wrap was tight enough to ensure the bandage stayed firmly in place but not so tight as to restrict movement.

"What payment do you demand for your work?" he asked, continuing to flex his hand.

Payment? How ridiculous, she thought. "There is nothing I need."

"Nothing at all? A piece of fine cloth perhaps for a new gown. A warm fleece perhaps to replace the one you gave away. A length of ribbon for your hair, or perhaps a trinket from the smithy. I am told he is highly skilled with silver and gold."

"I have no need for such things. As for keeping warm, what I wear will be sufficient. 'Tis more than many others have."

"There must be something," he said, humor returning to his voice. She knew he teased, yet sensed that if she named something he would give it to her.

"A kiss, milord."

He did not reply, but instead turned away. She did not connect her thoughts to his. She was afraid of what she would find there.

"You find me repulsive," she concluded, uncertain why she felt so devastated. She thought of Lady Morgana. "Perhaps I am not tall enough, or my figure fine enough? Perhaps, I have offended you in some way?"

His gaze snapped back to hers, dark and ominous as a winter storm, that quicksilver mood changing once more.

"I do not find you loathsome," he snapped. "You have not offended me."

"There must be something wrong with me," she said, trying to understand. There was nothing logical about this at all. He had kissed her once. He did not find her offensive, yet he was obviously determined not to kiss her again.

"There is nothing wrong with you," he assured her. "Quite the contrary. You are most pleasing to look at. You are intelligent and witty." He swore again, his voice low and rough. "You make me want to laugh and cry. You are perfect."

"Then kiss me," she replied, seeing absolutely no logic or reason for his reluctance. "That is the payment I demand."

Chapter Eleven

"For someone who is not afraid, you take great risks."

"I see no risk. 'Tis a small thing I ask."

"Have you asked the same of others you tended this afternoon?"

How ridiculous, she thought. And what reason did he have to be angry with her? A trinket or cloth for a gown would have cost him a goodly sum. A kiss cost him nothing.

"No," she replied with a shrug. "They did not ask."

"Did not ask?" Connor didn't know whether to laugh or scream.

He was certain she was telling the truth, but she had the most maddening way of simplifying everything. He felt like strangling her.

"Besides"—she shrugged—"I did not wish them to kiss me."

"And you wish me to kiss you?"

She wondered if he had trouble hearing. "I have said so, haven't I?"

"Aye," Connor said slowly. "But I think you do not understand what you ask."

She looked at him with those shimmering blue eyes that quivered like the heart of a flame.

"I understand perfectly well," she replied with matter-of-factness. As if they were discussing some herbal cure, the cost of a hogshead of ale, or the weather. " 'Tis a simple enough thing I ask."

The simplest things had been known to cause war or the downfall of empires, he thought to himself.

She presented herself with that same matter-of-factness she always demonstrated. "I am ready when you are."

He smothered the urge to grin. She looked as if she were waiting for someone to hand her a stack of fresh bandages or a basket of eggs.

"You're certain?"

"Yes, very certain. You can kiss me now."

The thought that he needed permission was very entertaining.

"You will have to come closer."

She nodded as she saw the logic of that and approached until she was standing before him with no more than a hand's breadth between them.

"Closer," he ordered and was rewarded with a flash of irritation in those shimmering blue eyes.

"I cannot. Your legs block the way," she replied.

He spread them, guiding her between so that she stood very close.

"I would like it to be a good one," she insisted.

He bit back laughter, struggling to keep a sober expression. "I will try to make the experience worth your time." By God, she had a way of dispelling his worst mood.

"Not like the first one either. I would like a different kiss this time," she informed him.

After the kiss she had seen between Dannelore and John she suspected there were different types of kisses. And while his first kiss had been very pleasurable, it had been far too brief. After all, she had a great deal to learn about such things.

"I will see what I can do," he replied with mock seriousness.

"Thank you. I appreciate that."

"Be quiet."

She blinked with surprise. "I beg your pardon?" They didn't seem to be getting off to a very good start.

"I cannot kiss you when you are talking," he explained, using some of her own logic.

"Oh. Yes, I see. You are quite right. I will not say another word."

"And you will have to come closer," Connor said, slowly pulling her closer between his legs.

She did not resist, but watched him expectantly, like a student waiting for her tutor to begin her lesson. And this was going to be a lesson she would not forget. There were some things she should be afraid of, and he had every intention of showing her just what a few of these were.

As if he'd given the matter a great deal of thought, he announced, "Your hair is not right either."

She touched a hand to the thick braid that hung over her shoulder, a perplexed expression curving her sensual mouth into a frown that somehow had the effect of making her all the more desirable.

"What is wrong with my hair?" She couldn't see what her hair had to do with it.

"Ah, ah, ah," he warned, wagging a finger at her, and reminded her, "Not a word."

Her lovely mouth snapped shut, twisting into an enticing pout. For someone so logical, opinionated, and headstrong, saying nothing at all required an extreme exercise in self-control. It was all he could do to keep from grinning at her. Connor decided this was going to be a very enjoyable experience indeed.

He lifted the thick braid from her shoulder and untied the yarn at the end. He loosened the silken ribbons of hair, combing his fingers through until it lay in shimmering golden waves across her shoulders.

She carefully watched everything he did as if she were going to be questioned upon it later. At one point she started to say something—a question no doubt—but remembered his instructions and promptly closed her mouth.

Connor's hands stroked back through her hair. It was like

warm satin, rich and heavy in his fingers, silken waves of pure gold that wrapped about them. He brought his hands back to frame her face.

"You must do everything I say."

She nodded in response, still watching him with rapt attention and complete concentration.

"You must relax," he began, making small circular motions at the tendons at the back of her neck.

"Close your eyes," he commanded, his voice now very low as he continued to stroke her neck.

"Think of the wind in the trees, and water tumbling over rocks." His fingers skimmed over her cheeks as he cradled her face in his hands.

"Think of warm summer sun on your skin." He bent over her. "On your eyelids." He lightly brushed his lips across her eyelids.

"Feel it on your cheeks." He brushed his lips across her cheek. Then he slowly angled her head back. There was no resistance.

"Feel it here." His lips skimmed her jaw.

"Here." Skimmed the corner of her mouth.

His voice was barely more than a whisper. "Here." And his lips skimmed the other corner of her mouth as her hands pressed against the front of his tunic.

"Here." He stroked the fullness of that lower lip with his tongue. Her lips parted on a startled sound of pleasure. He lightly stroked the curve of her upper lip, lingering at the small whorl of flesh at the very center.

"Here." He brushed his mouth across hers. And pleasure became a soft moan of desire as her fingers curled into soft leather.

"And here." He slowly lowered his mouth to hers.

Sweet fire. It danced across her senses. Then he caressed her lips apart and invaded every part of her.

There had been no tenderness in that first kiss, only a sort of desperate wildness edged with anger. This kiss was different, unlike anything she had ever experienced.

Fire in her blood. It burned along each nerve ending, dark

and wild, as his tongue skimmed her teeth, tasting her in startling ways. And the hunger awakened.

Her breath hitched. Soft sounds. Longing sounds as he took her mouth again, forced her lips apart, and slipped inside.

It was not enough, not near enough. Not when his tongue stroked hers. Not when he retreated to nibble at her bottom lip, the beard at his chin lightly scraping her skin. Not even when her head went back and she felt that mouth glide down her throat.

He tasted her. Every curve, the angle of bone above the bodice of her gown, each silken hollow of flesh beneath. Then he brought his hands up, stroking the sides of her breasts through the wool of her gown.

He scraped his thumb across the front of her bodice and the peak of flesh that hardened there. Then his mouth followed, nipping at her through the fabric until she was wet.

"This is what you should fear," he whispered.

Those strong warrior's hands held her, gliding down her back, slipping over her bottom, knifing his body into the cleft of hers.

Her breasts rose and fell on each shuddering breath. Her pale skin was marked where the roughness of his beard had scraped. Her mouth was softly swollen.

In the dimly lit chamber with only the light from a single oil lamp and the air redolent with desire, the twin pools of her eyes were dark and mysterious like deepest sapphires.

She slipped a hand behind his neck, her fingers curling in the thick waves of dark hair that spilled over the collar of his tunic. Those gray eyes were flinty, watchful; his every muscle tensed.

Her fingers twisted in the thick mane of his hair. Her body arched to meet his, breasts pressing against the front of his tunic, hips molded against his, the soft heat of her body against the rigid shaft of flesh that strained between them as she angled his head down and brushed her mouth across his.

He made a startled sound.

"You must be quiet," she insisted and felt the sudden expulsion of air against her lips, heard his softly muttered curse.

"You must relax."

Tension throbbed through him like the warning of a coming storm.

"Close your eyes."

"Meg . . ."

"Close your eyes." On another curse he closed them.

"Here," she whispered as her lips parted beneath his.

Her fingers twisted in his hair, her nails dug into the soft leather that covered his shoulder. She deepened the kiss.

And here, her body cried out as she touched him the way he had touched her. Hands skimming over the hard planes and surfaces of his body, each rigid muscle, each corded tendon, the ridge of each sharp cheekbone, the bristle of thick lashes. And could not seem to touch him enough.

She tasted him the way he had tasted her. The scrape of beard at his jaw, the frown at the corner of his mouth, the heat of his lips. And could not taste him enough.

This was what she had sensed between Dannelore and John. The need, the longing, the hunger that ached deep inside. And so much more. Not a simple thing at all.

She slowly ended the kiss and pushed away from him. It was a moment before she recovered her senses.

"Thank you."

Connor was still struggling to recover.

"Thank you?" he said incredulously, still attempting to draw his first breath.

It was the first time a maid had ever thanked him. Usually it was the other way around. He stared at her incredulously.

She nodded. "It was very different from the first time. And most pleasant."

Pleasant?

"Good eventide, milord." She turned and left the pantry as if she'd been doing nothing more important than sampling fresh picked berries or a pie warm from the oven.

Pleasant?

Connor was finally able to draw a full breath, and he expelled it on a sharp burst of laughter. And he had thought to teach her a lesson!

Over the next several days all but the most seriously wounded recovered sufficiently to rejoin their fellow warriors. Several of Connor's men were among the more seriously injured and were not yet well enough to leave Caerleon. But he made no secret that he intended to leave as soon as they had recovered.

It was late afternoon, several days after their return. A new storm had set in, forcing all to seek shelter within the walls and main hall of Caerleon. Arthur seized the opportunity to form a council with his men and others who had fought at Amesbury. They sat about a scarred round table, where Arthur insisted they all had a right to speak their minds and offer an opinion.

Connor reluctantly joined them at the round table, but did not join in the conversation. He had no intention of joining Arthur's council, but sat quietly, listening to others who spoke.

"If not for that explosion in the monk's passage," Geoffrey said, "we would all have died. It caught Constantine's men by surprise. Many of them did not make it out. Many thanks, my friend."

Meg looked up from the bandage she was changing and glanced over at Connor.

Connor frowned. "It was none of my doing. It was over by the time my men and I arrived."

"But we still would have been hard pressed if you had not come," Geoffrey added.

"We would all have been hard pressed if one of your men had not opened those gates," one of Connor's men commented.

Meg finished tying off the bandage and gathered the remaining linen and the basin of water.

"I would like to take the credit," Agravain replied, "but in truth, it was not our doing either." He glanced around the table. "By the time our last man reached the top of the walls, the gates were already open. We assumed it was someone inside the abbey." Others nodded their agreement, but no one seemed to know who had opened the gates.

Meg continued to listen discreetly as she stopped to adjust a bandage or replace a dressing. The other women worked around her, serving cups of ale and wine.

Dannelore's gaze met hers. They had not spoken of what had happened at Amesbury, yet she sensed the woman's unspoken questions.

" 'Tis fortunate that your man fought so well at your back," Agravain told Connor, recalling the warrior he had seen in the midst of battle.

"But I have not seen him since our return. I hope he was not gravely wounded. I would fight beside such a warrior anytime."

"Nor have I seen him," Connor replied. His speculative gaze met Meg's. "I assumed he fought for Arthur."

Arthur frowned. "I know of no such warrior. Perhaps he was originally from Caerleon and was taken prisoner with the others."

"In full armor and battle sword?" Agravain questioned. "More the fool Constantine to allow a man to keep his weapon."

"The warrior was not from Caerleon."

Merlin sat quietly at the table, near to the warmth of the fire at the hearth. It helped ease the ache of coldness that had been with him since receiving a wound at Amesbury.

"Perhaps he fought alone."

"No warrior fights alone," One of Arthur's men replied. " 'Tis a death wish. 'Tis more likely that he has lost a great deal at the hands of Constantine and joins us like the others who have arrived at Caerleon. Surely he will eventually declare himself and join us."

"What say you?" Merlin turned to Connor. "You fought beside this warrior. What did this man look like?"

Connor's gaze was still fastened on Meg. He preferred the memory of that *pleasant* kiss in her eyes to speculation over an unknown warrior who had not been seen since the battle.

The gaze that calmly met his held no memory of that kiss. Yet it was there. He saw it in the way her hand trembled faintly as she replaced yet another bandage, and he smiled inwardly.

"There was no time to take notice," he admitted. "I saw him clearly only once, at the passage behind the altar in the chapel."

His gaze returned to Meg, to the way she moved, her slender

body beneath the soft wool of the gown; remembering the feel of her through the fabric and the taste of her.

"He was tall and lean, yet strong. He bested three of Constantine's men while fighting at my side. But I could not see his features clearly for the helm that covered his head."

"Surely there is something more you remember," Agravain speculated. "Such a warrior would not easily be forgotten."

Connor continued watching her—the way she gently smiled at one of the wounded men, the crystal blue of her eyes as light reflected from the fire at the hearth and seemed to hold the flame in those blue depths, the angle of her head as she bent to catch a word.

"He did not follow into the passage," Connor recalled, his gaze narrowing thoughtfully, "but raised his sword and saluted, then returned to the battle."

"I saw him as well," another of Arthur's warriors commented. "But he did not return. I assumed he had followed your men."

"What do you know of this warrior, mistress?" Connor asked.

Her startled gaze met his.

"Perhaps you have seen him among the wounded," he suggested as he silently speculated about the sudden wariness in her eyes. Then it was gone, making him wonder if he had seen it there at all.

Meg chose her words carefully. "I have not seen the warrior you speak of," she replied. "He is not among the wounded."

"It seems he has disappeared," Agravain concluded.

"Whoever he is, we are deeply indebted to him," Arthur added. "I can only hope that he will join our cause. I would not care to face him in battle."

Others concurred and Meg hastily returned to tending the wounded. But as she moved among them, she could feel Connor watching her.

Arthur and his men spoke of other things then. Of the surprising numbers of Constantine's warriors, among them some who were not monks at all but obviously Maelgwyn's men whom Connor had followed from the Caledon Forest; of the despicable conditions the people taken prisoner at Caerleon had endured; the torture chambers that made all shudder to think of being imprisoned in them, and the tragedy of Lady Ygraine's death from some wasting sickness only days before they reached Caerleon.

"Constantine!" the warrior called Gawain spat contemptuously. "To think that such cruelty cloaked itself in holy robes. And practiced such unholy acts as we found in that hidden chamber."

Meg listened intently, for it was the first she had heard it spoken of and in her brief time at Amesbury she had sensed nothing of such a place.

"The dark arts, demonology." Another who had seen it spoke almost in a whisper as if in fear of calling for those same demons by speaking of them.

"We saw the altar where that devil worhipped the darkness and the symbol of his own destruction—the sign of evil." Several about the table made the sign of the cross to protect themselves against such evil.

"Constantine is dead," Arthur reminded them. "And his evil with him. We must now turn our thoughts to Maelgwyn. My counselor is right. He will soon learn what has happened here if he has not already. By imprisoning Lady Ygraine and Lady Morgana he controlled the south, strengthening his position against any claim from Aethelbert. That is now gone. He must have the south or be driven back to Gwynedd. He will return. And we must be prepared to meet the challenge."

"We must have a strategy to defend against Maelgwyn," another, called Bedevere, concluded. "Fortifications must be made."

Arthur silently listened to them all. As they continued to discuss the massive fortifications that must be constructed at Caerleon in order to withstand an attack from Maelgwyn, Connor felt Arthur watching him intently.

"You have not yet spoken," Arthur said, his gaze narrowed thoughtfully.

Connor shook his head. "These men are your warriors. 'Tis not my place to speak."

"You have met Maelgwyn in battle. You still bear the scars of that encounter. I value your thoughts on this matter."

Arthur saw the hand that tightened about the tankard before Connor. He spoke of old wounds, deeper than the scars of the flesh. He knew it was likely possible Connor of Anglesey would throw the contents in his face and the consequences be damned.

But he also knew the boy the man had once been—a boy of courage, honor, loyalty. It was that loyalty to Geoffrey that had brought him to Amesbury and had altered the course of the battle that might well have ended with their defeat. Once he had known that same loyalty. He prayed there was something of it left now. If not to him, then perhaps to the other men who would follow him against Maelgwyn.

"What would you do if you led an army against Maelgwyn?" All about the round table fell quiet, waiting for his response.

"To defend a pile of rocks is to die upon them, like a sacrifice upon Constantine's unholy altar," Connor replied, biting off each word.

Bedevere sprang to his feet, drawing his sword. "Your contempt for Arthur is well known. But, by God, you go too far with your insults and your blasphemy! It ends here!"

Connor did not respond, did not so much as acknowledge Bedevere's challenge with even the slightest change of expression or reaction, except the cold gray of those wintry eyes that could easily have frozen the warrior to the ground where he stood.

"Only a fool would make a stand at Caerleon," Connor replied, taking a long sip of wine from the tankard. " 'Tis exactly what Maelgwyn expects." That wintry gaze met Bedevere's. "By all means, give him what he expects. As for me, I would defend nothing."

"Aye," Bedevere snorted with contempt. "Nor give your loyalty to any man!"

The warrior walked on dangerous ground and all about the table knew it.

"Enough!" Arthur intervened, and when Bedevere would have spoken again, added, "This man sits at my council table by my invitation, as do you all. If you challenge that, Sir Bedevere, then you challenge me.''

The warrior knew he'd gone too far. He sheathed his sword and returned to the table. Arthur turned to Connor.

''What would you do to stop Maelgwyn?''

''Attack,'' Connor replied simply. ''Attack before he expects it. Find his encampment in the mountains and destroy it.''

''The weather . . . ?'' one of Arthur's men asked.

'' 'Tis as much an enemy to Maelgwyn. You have the advantage in knowing the land while he is a stranger. The only way to trap the beast is to seek out its den, not wait for it to attack at your door. Draw him out, then close the snare around him.''

The discussion continued until it was necessary to light more oil lamps at the tables and the torches at the walls. The fire at the hearth was built high against the evening cold that permeated stone walls and earthen floors, and the smoke from the cookfires in the kitchens permeated the air.

''Join us for the evening meal, mistress,'' Arthur invited Meg. ''I grow weary of looking at these bearded faces across the supper table. 'Tis enough to ruin any man's appetite. And I grow weary of talks of battles and campaigns. I find a woman's sweet voice preferable to these grunting oafs. And your presence will guarantee good manners and improved eating habits.'' His comments met with grunts of dismay and comments of denial.

Connor awaited her answer with great interest. Since their encounter several days earlier, she had been kept busy with the other women. He had missed her maddening logic and her directness. He had missed laughter. He had missed her. And there was the little matter of payback for that last encounter.

Meg was acutely aware that all those gathered at the round table awaited her answer. Including Connor who seemed to wait with particular interest.

They'd had almost no contact over the past few days, and she could not gauge his mood. Nor did she dare connect her thoughts to his and risk her brother's awareness of it. But if the expression on his face—that sharp gray gaze and the eager, predatory look like that of a wolf stalking its next meal—was any indication of his mood, she would have to be very careful if she accepted Arthur's invitation.

It would be safer to take her meals with the other women as she had since the warriors returned from Amesbury. Tending the wounded had made it easy since they worked together. Meals were often taken among the wounded when there was the opportunity to rest for a few minutes. But with so few wounded left in the main hall and sufficient hands to meet their needs, this excuse would have seemed exactly that—an excuse.

She had no doubt Arthur—and Connor—would see right through it. And she had no intention of letting Connor believe that he disturbed her in the least.

Dannelore had quietly come up beside her and laid a warning hand on her arm. If she had dared risk opening her thoughts to the woman she knew what she would find there—the warning not to risk too much with Merlin so near.

"Thank you, milord," she accepted Arthur's invitation. Her gaze met Connor's briefly, then returned to Arthur's. "I would find that most enjoyable."

"Done," Arthur announced. He then put his men on notice. "You must all be on your best behavior this evening."

"What are you doing?" Dannelore whispered frantically, grabbing at her arm. "You risk too much. Merlin will surely discover who you are!"

"He will not," Meg replied with far more confidence than certainty. "We have had several encounters and he suspects nothing. Do you have so little faith in my abilities that you think I cannot keep the truth from him?"

" 'Tis not your abilities that concern me, but his. His powers are great. If he should learn who you are . . . These are dangerous times. If what they said about Constantine is true . . . You have already interfered in matters you should not have when you went to Amesbury."

"If I had not gone to Amesbury they might all have died, including your John," Meg pointed out. "I still cannot understand why my brother was powerless there." She shook her head.

"You worry needlessly. I will be careful. And besides, I did not come here to hide out in the kitchen or pantry. I cannot learn about the mortal world by hiding among sacks of grain and barrels of dried apples. These things do not carry on very interesting conversations.''

''You prefer conversations with Connor of Anglesey?'' the changeling suggested.

Meg thought of their last ''conversation'' and couldn't help smiling. But she knew the woman's game. She needed no gift of sight or special sense to know the direction of Dannelore's question.

She handed the last of the bandages to one of the other women. Then she removed the bloodstained apron and also handed it over.

''I must wash my hands and find a more suitable gown.'' She picked at the loose, coarse woolen robe that one of the women had given her, a good choice for working among the wounded. It was stained with blood from changing bandages. ''I find conversations with anyone more enlightening than sacks of grain and dried fruit. Even the hound, Dax, has more to say.''

She wore the gown Dannelore had given her when she'd first arrived at Caerleon. It had been washed and the color was far more pleasing than sack cloth. For shoes she wore a pair of Dannelore's much-worn leather slippers.

Though she was not susceptible to bouts of infirmity such as the ague from which mortals suffered, the slippers offered some protection from the cold of the earthen floor of the main hall and the roughness of the stone steps.

After Lady Morgana's return to Caerleon, she and Dannelore had moved to the smaller chamber at the far end of the upstairs passage. The changeling had despaired that it could ever be habitable, for it had suffered a great deal.

The walls had been blackened with soot from fires that had been set. Most of the furnishings had been destroyed in those fires. The tapestries hung in singed tatters, and oil from over-turned lamps coated everything with greasy blackened grime. At least the shutters and door were intact, which had seemed strange to Meg when the door to Lady Ygraine's chamber had been shattered from its hinges.

After the initial cleaning of the chamber, when they'd worn down two brushes and it seemed there was even more soot and grime on the walls than when they'd started, Dannelore had despaired that the chamber would ever be habitable again.

She had gone back to the kitchens for more hot water, more brushes, and an abundant supply of fresh straw with the hope of soaking up some of the oily grime.

When she returned she found the walls restored to their former cleanliness and the floor of the chamber rid of the oily residue. A faint pungence of fragrant pine smoke lingered in the air, and the stones at the walls and floor were warm to the touch. She looked at Meg with growing suspicion. Before she could say a word of reproval, Meg held up a hand.

"Do not lecture me," she told Dannelore. "There are some things in this mortal world which simply are not worth the effort, and this was one of them. I decided my way was much easier."

Her first suspicions confirmed, Dannelore's eyes widened. "You set fire to the entire chamber?"

Meg shrugged. "It seemed the thing to do—finish what Constantine's men began. The oil burned very nicely and everything is now clean."

Dannelore shook her head with amazement at the intensity of such a fire that had burned everything clean. "What if you had been discovered?"

Meg shrugged again. "I would simply pass it off to my poor skills at building a fire in the brazier. It was just a small fire."

"May the Ancient Ones protect us from drunks and fools," Dannelore muttered.

"I beg your pardon?"

"You must be more careful."

"I will try, but I simply cannot see the reason for doing something the hard way when it may be done more simply."

Dannelore threw up her hands in frustration, then gathered the water and brushes and carried them back downstairs.

Over all, Meg was quite pleased with the chamber. She had

sprinkled dried herbs amongst the straw at the floor to ward off the usual crawling pests that seemed to be everywhere inside Caerleon, and had added pine boughs which dispelled the last of the smoky smell.

Since the furnishings had all been lost in the original fire she had made pallets for herself and Dannelore of warm fleece spread over grain sacks filled with more straw and sweet herbs.

A fire burned at the brazier and oil lamps filled with pine oil added a pungent fragrance to the air in the small chamber.

Meg washed from a small basin and finished plaiting her hair in a thick braid. Last she donned the slender belt of shining crystals which created faint musical sounds with the movement of the fabric when she walked.

She had no means for judging her appearance, it would just have to be sufficient. At least she was clean and did not smell like a dead goat.

She'd had that particular experience a few days earlier when she'd ventured with Grendel among the inhabitants who occupied the huts and cottages inside the walls of Caerleon fortress in search of more of the precious medicinal herbs needed for the wounded.

A goatherd had discovered a dead goat among his herd. The animal had been dead for some time, caught outside the shelter during the last storm and frozen to death. When the weather had warmed the goatherd had found the carcass but had not had time to remove it.

With his usual gift for subtleties, Grendel had drawn her attention to the overripe beast, which was hardly necessary due to the stench.

"Dead goat!" he commented, reminding her of his opinion of mortals while holding his nose as they passed by. Afterward, fearful that she might have indeed begun to smell like one, Meg had taken to washing regularly and to the liberal use of fragrant herbs.

"At least I do not smell like one," she reassured herself. Nothing reassured her about her appearance, since all she had to go on was her reflection in the small basin of water.

It quivered, the clear water, redolent with the fragrance of sweet herbs, suddenly growing dark and murky as she looked closer. She touched her finger to the surface and saw stirring clouds of visions in the shallow depths.

"Grendel says yer to eat with Master Arthur tonight," young Tristan announced as he charged into the chamber unannounced, like a miniature whirlwind barely touching the ground in his excitement and creating small disasters wherever he happened to be as Dannelore had assured her was the way of all small boys.

His disaster on this occasion was very nearly upsetting the basin. Water sloshed over the sides as the table wobbled unsteadily.

"I'm sorry," Tristan apologized, a stricken expression on his small face at the latest disaster he'd very nearly caused.

Meg caught the basin before it tipped over, preventing the contents from washing over the sides and setting the large bowl upon the steadier surface of a low stone shelf. But as the sloshing ceased and the water calmed, the swirling visions were gone.

"It's all right," Meg assured him, uncertain of what she had seen, even more uncertain as to why she had seen it.

"There's no harm done."

"You won't say anything?" His voice rose several notches with his growing alarm. "If Master Connor learns of it, he will think I am nothing but an addlepated clot. He'll refuse to show me the proper use of a sword." A tear quivered at the lashes of one eye.

Meg knelt before Tristan. It was all she could do to smother back laughter as she gently wiped away the single tear. Such a strange sensation—these tears. Something else she must learn more about. Along with children—small mortals—who were forever getting themselves into mischief. Little bundles of energy and recklessness who one day grew into fierce warriors. Somehow it was difficult imagining Connor had ever been a child like Tristan.

"Who called you such a thing?" she asked, taking his small hands in hers.

"Grendel. He also said I was a clumsy toad."

The pot calling the kettle black, as Dannelore would say. She suspected it had more to do with the fact that his clothes were far too big for him, the legs of his pants flopping over the ends of his toes.

The problem was that the damage had already been done. Tristan believed that he was an addlepated clot and clumsy as a toad.

"Open your hand," she told him.

Small fingers slowly unfolded over a grimy palm.

"I'm going to give you something."

"What is it?"

"It's magic," she explained, and opened her hand over his. A small black rock, smooth as glass dropped into his hand.

"If you rub it very hard and concentrate, you will be brave, strong, and surefooted."

"Not a clumsy toad anymore?"

She gave him a long look. "Have you ever seen a clumsy toad?"

He thought about that for a minute, then shook his head. "They never stay in one place long enough."

"That's exactly right. They're forever hopping all over the place. Not clumsy at all."

"Was Grendel teasing me?"

She nodded. "It seems so."

"Can I keep the rock?"

It wasn't magic, of course. She couldn't give him that. The power was something one was born with. But a small boy sorely in need of confidence needed a little magic to believe in.

"You may keep it. But it must be our secret."

He nodded enthusiastically. "I won't tell anyone. Not even Master Connor."

She stopped him as he headed for the door, just short of another disaster as his pantlegs tangled with his feet.

"Let's get these out of your way," she suggested.

She had only the yarn she'd used to bind her hair. She untied it. Cutting the yarn in two, she tied each length about a rolled, hitched-up pantleg as a precaution against further disasters.

"You don't have a ribbon for your hair," he protested with heartbreaking gallantry, those mossy green eyes darkly fringed with sooty lashes and tipped with tears. How many girls would lose their hearts to him? she wondered. And without either a father or mother to care for him and tell him of such things.

"It doesn't matter," she assured him.

She shook her hair free of the cumbersome plait, grateful that she didn't have one and couldn't bind it as Dannelore insisted she must.

With much ceremony, as if they were at the court of some king, he bowed low over his rolled pantlegs, the glossy stone tucked safely in the pouch at his belt. Then he extended a small grubby hand.

"Are you ready, mistress?"

She smothered back laughter at the sight they no doubt made—her much-altered gown, worn slippers, and hair flying about in wild abandon, escorted by a child with rolled pantlegs, smudged face, and dirt in more places than she cared to consider.

She replied with mock seriousness and great ceremony, "Arthur and his warriors of the round table await, milord."

Then she gave him a wink and a dazzling smile as she took his small hand in hers.

Chapter Twelve

Connor heard her laughter as they came down the stairs.

She and the boy, Tristan, were still laughing over some private joke as he escorted her into the main hall as if she were a grand lady at some powerful king's court.

Connor felt a sharp pang inside, for he knew what it was to feel the radiance of her smile and the soft music of her laughter; and he envied the boy of ten years with his tunic hanging to his knees, his pantlegs tied about his ankles, a smudged face, and eyes turned in adoration on the vision of beauty at his side.

"Mistress Meg, you brighten even this dingy hall with your radiance," Arthur complimented in greeting.

She swallowed her laughter then, and Connor saw her roll her eyes at young Tristan. Like two children who'd been caught at some prank.

The evening meal was surprisingly pleasant. The food was plain and simple—roast deer and partridge with vegetables and stewed apples, prepared with pungent herbs and pine nuts. What the repast lacked in variety was made up for with imagination as Arthur's men, in high spirits, told about foods they'd encountered in their travels in the middle eastern kingdoms. Some of the names—couscous, roast yak—were imaginative, while others which translated into goat stomach, eyeball stew, and shimlava or sheep testes left little to the imagination or the appetite.

There was an abundance of ale and mead, which Connor's men put to good use, and sufficient wine for Arthur's men. They were all in high spirits, though well mannered, which Connor attributed to Meg's presence as he enjoyed it from across the table.

Men sat on benches at both sides of long tables, set to form a large U in the center of the hall. Connor's men sat side by side with Arthur's in an easy comradery that came from having fought together at Amesbury. He had declined Arthur's invitation to sit at his other side, preferring to be where he could observe those who sat across from him.

The hound, Dax, had abandoned him, having fallen under Meg's spell as easily as his men and the boy, Tristan. The beast could presently be found at her feet, drawn by that special gift she seemed to possess for making all creatures fall at her feet.

Another, he noticed, observed her as well. Merlin sat quietly at Arthur's other side, listening intently to the conversation that flowed about him, those piercing eyes that seemed to see everything narrowed in thoughtful speculation.

The wound Merlin had received at Amesbury still bothered him. It was noticeable in the drawn look on his face and the stiffness with which he moved, as if holding himself against the pain. But, like the others, he said nothing of the discomfort.

Merlin had not hung back, letting others join in the fight as Constantine had at first, but had fought in the thick of battle as fiercely as anyone and with admirable skill. He had not been afraid to bloody himself or anyone else, and had earned Connor's grudging respect.

In the flow of boisterous conversations usually found amongst men, Meg's musical laughter was like sunlight in the smoky gloom of the hall as she listened to stories told by both his men and Arthur's. It was a welcome contrast to the aftermath of the battle and the sadness of many over the death of Lady Ygraine.

The latest story was about one of his own men, Thomas,

and their under-cover-of-darkness venture into a village well known to them.

Thomas had immediately gone to the hut of a particular young girl he'd visited before. Before dawn when Connor and the others had arrived to drag him reluctantly from her bed, Thomas discovered that the woman in his bed was not the girl, but her mother.

The woman was not at all bothered by the mistake, in fact quite well pleased by it. Her daughter was not, and the incident almost had a bloody ending as the girl took after both Thomas and her mother with a cleaver.

The girl was eventually mollified when Thomas gave her a pretty trinket and bedded her as well. But the next time Connor and his men visited the village, Thomas found both women eagerly waiting for him and both demanding his attention. He couldn't choose one without bringing down the wrath of the other.

Meg listened with wide-eyed fascination. "What did he do?"

"He was hard pressed to make the right decision." Old Radvald continued the story with much rolling of the eyes and great exaggeration.

"They were like a couple of she-cats, claws bared and ready to set upon him no matter what choice he made. So he made the only choice he could. He refused both women and returned to the forest to wait for our return. He was convinced that a night spent on the hard, cold ground was preferable to the aggravation from the two."

"I would have bedded 'em both!" another warrior proclaimed. "Please 'em both and have 'em purring over you. But the lad didn't have it in him!"

"Aye," another agreed. "But you do, Alston. Yer full o' it!"

Meg understood most of what was said, although some of the finer points eluded her. She laughed as she imagined two women taking after Thomas with a meat cleaver. It was all the more humorous because Thomas was a very unseemly fellow.

He was short and compact, with thick banded arms and legs,

flat nose, squinty eyes, and a lopsided grin that made him look more like a troll.

" 'Tis hard to think of them fightin' over him." Old Radvald snorted. "He's not much to look at, that's for certain. And a woman likes a man who is fine to look at." He pushed back the sleeve of his tunic and flexed his muscles to the laughter of all the younger men.

"It's not the size," another rejoined. "It's what you do with it."

"Aye," another agreed, rolling his eyes. "And Thomas has good shoulders."

Connor shook his head. He'd heard the story too many times. He got more pleasure out of watching Meg's reaction. She expressed laughter, then thoughtfulness, and then laughter again.

"That's the way of it," another agreed. "You've got to get yer shoulders into it and they'll be right pleased with you every time."

"You must forgive them," Connor told her. "They rarely have the opportunity to eat at a table in company other than their own, and they've forgotten their manners."

She laughed, not the least affronted by their colorful, lewd comments. They reminded her of Grendel and Cosmo in their more colorful moments.

"I suspect only half of it is true."

Connor smiled, captivated by her. "Less than half."

"And what stories might be told about you?" she asked with a teasing smile that curved her mouth and sparkled at her eyes in ways that reminded him of the maid he'd encountered in the pantry days earlier.

"Are there no young girls or their mothers left behind broken-hearted?"

Connor shook his head. "No one."

"There was one young lady at Chilton," one of his men reminded him, then added, "But it was doomed from the beginning."

Another of his men added his agreement. "Aye, he was prettier than she was."

Meg gave him a long, considering look. She could see it when, in moments like that one, the frown lines smoothed about his mouth and disappeared between the thrust of those slanting brows.

The fierce warrior's expression had eased with wine and humorous conversation, revealing someone she had only glimpsed before—a handsome young man who could turn the head of any young lady or her mother.

Even those eyes, cold enough to turn one's soul to ice, seemed different as she found him watching her. Still distant and cool but in constantly changing shades of gray that intrigued rather than frightened.

"And the one," another of his men joined in the telling, "whose father was a smithy. Connor had most serious need of his skills to mend his blade."

"Aye, for certain 'twas in sore need of repair when she got through with him!"

His men laughed, surprising her that they would dare make jests at his expense.

She had come to understand their humor and knew the comments had been at his expense. But nothing in either his expression or tone indicated any reaction except for the cool gleam in his eyes.

"As you will be in sore need of repair when I get through with you," he replied with an equally cool smile, very much like the grin of the wolf when it bares its fangs.

The raucous laughter of both his men and Arthur's filled the hall, and Meg was fascinated by yet another aspect of these mortals—the strength found in comradery evidenced in a loyalty that ran blood-deep and yet found in the ability to laugh with one another as well as at one another.

"I see my brother entertains like a newly crowned king at court."

A woman's voice was heard amid the laughter, for a moment silencing further conversation as the attention of all was drawn toward the stone steps at one side of the main hall.

Lady Morgana of Caerleon stood in regal splendor, her gaze

sweeping the hall, a faint smile curving her lips as if she'd made a jest that had somehow eluded everyone else.

That gaze missed nothing, and from her place at Arthur's left, Meg immediately found herself the object of intense curiosity which she returned with equal measure.

Arthur's sister had been in seclusion since her return to Caerleon, overcome with grief over the death of her mother Lady Ygraine and still suffering from her imprisonment at the hands of Constantine.

Her meals were sent up to her, with the food barely picked at or returned untouched. A young servant girl who had returned with her from Amesbury attended to her needs, much to the relief of Dannelore who had been kept busy tending the needs of the wounded and organizing the kitchens, pressed into serving meals for the considerable number of men who now occupied Caerleon.

Lady Morgana was slender and of medium height, her striking features which bore a strong resemblance to her brother's somehow all the more striking because of the black tunic she wore over a gown of the same color.

But the resemblance ended there. Where Arthur's coloring favored Lady Ygraine's in the red-gold shade of his hair and his light blue eyes, Lady Morgana's hair was dark as midnight satin, drawn back from pale features and secured beneath a silver circlet and black headdress.

The overall effect emphasized the angle of the cheekbones beneath her pale skin and the slant of dark eyes that reminded Meg of a watchful cat.

Arthur stood and greeted her. ''Welcome, sister. I am pleased to see that you have sufficiently recovered from your ordeal to join us.''

Her presence surprised everyone. Or not quite everyone, Meg realized, as she glanced at Connor.

He watched with detached bemusement as Lady Morgana slowly crossed the hall amid curious and openly admiring glances from Arthur's men, the young servant girl silently hovering in her wake like a dutiful shadow.

She approached the table where Arthur sat with a cool, speculative expression for each of those who also sat there. With barely a nod toward her brother, her gaze fixed longest, and narrowed slightly, on Merlin.

To outward appearances it was a speculative look tinged with a moment of confusion as though she could not recall who he was. But Meg sensed emotions that peeked from behind the artful guise of temporary confusion—a thinly veiled hostility that for a moment lay naked and exposed in the sudden darkening of Morgana's cat eyes.

"Ah, yes," she said as if suddenly remembering. "Marcus Merlinus, the companion and tutor—counselor my brother now calls you, I believe."

Meg watched her brother with avid interest. If Merlin sensed anything behind the simple greeting, he gave nothing away by either word or expression as he courteously acknowledged her.

"Good eventide, Lady Morgana."

A smile curved her lips, but never reached her eyes. "You take away the boy and return the man to rule over Britain. There are some who believed my brother would not return."

Did Meg hear something more in the soft silk of her reply? Incredulity? Doubt? Perhaps even anger?

"Or perhaps hoped it," Merlin replied.

Morgana inclined her head in acknowledgment. "There are many who will see their ambitions thwarted by his return."

"Join us, sister," Arthur invited. "Your presence is most welcome."

Two of Arthur's warriors rose and offered their places at the table. Morgana's gaze moved with frank and open admiration over Agravain, Alston, and Bedevere, then widened with less than admiration as it fell on Meg, seated beside Arthur.

"What is this, brother?" she asked with faint amusement. "Spoils of war?"

"Mistress Meg is a guest at Caerleon," Arthur explained, frowning slightly. "She was set upon in the forest, no doubt by the same barbarians who took you and our mother prisoner. Connor and his men found her."

Her gaze shifted appreciatively to Connor. "You do not offer your place, milord?'' Morgana asked, her mouth curving in a flirtatious smile.

"You already have more than you can occupy,'' Connor pointed out. "And from here I can offer protection to our guest.''

"Protection?'' Morgana inquired with incredulity. "From whom?''

Yes, Meg wondered, her gaze narrowing. From whom? She certainly didn't feel threatened by anyone.

"From you, Morgana. You may sheath your claws. You have nothing to fear. In fact, you may very well owe her your life. She is a healer.''

Morgana laughed then, a rich, throaty sound. "You always were able to lift me from the worst mood, Connor. If only you had been here when Caerleon was attacked.''

He nodded his agreement. "The Duke of Cornwall was a noble man. I valued his friendship.''

A trencher of food was placed before Morgana by her servant. She looked at it with lifted brow.

"Bring me something else. 'Tis what you have brought me the last two days.''

"There is nothing else,'' Arthur explained. " 'Tis the same that we have all eaten—and grateful for it with all of England embattled and starving.''

"Take it away,'' she ordered the girl, then, lifting a metal goblet of wine, toasted him, "Your kingdom awaits, brother.''

Connor's gaze sharpened. He had known Morgana all his life. She was highborn, intelligent, and beautiful. She was also willful and spoiled, the youngest child of the old Duke of Cornwall and his second wife, Lady Ygraine.

She had been born in Arthur's shadow, the son the old Duke had always hoped for. But when Arthur left Caerleon with Merlin, Morgana became the favored child.

As the years passed and many, including the old Duke came to believe Arthur would never return, Morgana was considered the heir to Caerleon, a rich bride price for the man who would wed her.

An alliance by marriage between Caerleon and Anglesey

would have consolidated the western lands and provided a united strength against Maelgwyn. Connor's father had favored such an alliance. But it was his brother, Damon, older by two years and heir to Anglesey on whose behalf the betrothal was offered.

His memories of Morgana were those of childhood, when she was a toddling child and he had been friends with Arthur. She was no longer a child the summer her betrothal to his brother was announced—that summer when Connor was but twenty and had finally earned his sword, when the sun burned especially hot, and when Morgana cast her eyes his way, not his brother's.

Connor was the second son, the hellion, for whom life was always a game, but he worshipped his older brother. It was because of Damon he'd finally focused his talents and strengths, choosing to take up the sword. Damon was the thinker, the steady son, the one whom the people of Anglesey looked to when his father became ill.

Connor would never have betrayed Damon, and Morgana knew that. When he rebuffed her flirtations she deceived him.

That last summer it was young Constance whose bed he warmed. Constance, one of his mother's servant girls, with her silky skin and earthy smell.

She had brown hair, luminous brown eyes, and a wanton spirit. He was fourteen when she first tumbled into his bed, of a same age but with far more experience, and claiming she had lost her way back to his mother's chambers—on the far side of Anglesey hall. She regularly lost her way after that.

Connor bedded her well and often in those first throes of what he was certain must be love, but his father later pointed out was merely a healthy lust.

He was very fond of Constance and eventually set her up with a small cottage of her own where they could be together. It was to her cottage he went after receiving a message from her upon his return to Anglesey after several weeks in the north country.

Even before he entered the cottage he had a full cockstand just thinking of her eager hands and mouth. It was dark inside, but he thought nothing of it as those eager hands reached for him.

He was fairly bursting from his clothes and took her in the doorway of the cottage first, entering her fast and hard with only one thought—to ease his aching flesh.

The second time, he took her on the straw pallet and then he tried to be more mindful of her wants and needs. But she was wild beneath him, taking them both over the edge even before that first kiss—the kiss that immediately told him the woman beneath him was not Constance.

He was furious when he discovered Morgana's deception. All he could think was that he'd betrayed his brother. It did little to mollify his anger to know that Morgana had been no virgin.

He was determined to tell his brother the truth and then leave Anglesey. Morgana begged him to understand, she insisted that she loved him. Perhaps sensing that he might never return, she pleaded with him not to go, insisting that she would tell Damon. She reasoned that no one need ever know.

"But I will know!"

Within only days Maelgwyn had struck from the north in the first wave of his brutal campaign to crush resistance in the western lands.

Connor's father and brother died in the attack. Anglesey eventually fell and was sacked, help arriving too late from Caerleon.

Connor was taken prisoner by Maelgwyn. He was tortured and left for dead. Eventually he returned to Anglesey and discovered that his mother and sisters were also dead. Old Radvald found him and took him to Caerleon where he eventually recovered.

Lady Ygraine cared for him, insisting that it was the least she could do in return for everything his mother had once done for her.

Morgana was there as well, sitting at his bedside, alternating between prayers for forgiveness if only he would live and excuses why none of it was her fault.

Eventually he recovered. Morgana was just as beautiful,

perhaps more so than before. But he was not the same man who had once bedded her. He was scarred and cynical and had no more illusions. In some ways he saw things too clearly.

As conversation once more flowed about the table, Morgana's gaze returned to Meg.

"Do you speak, girl?" she asked. "Or merely gawk at your betters?"

Lady Morgana reminded her of Cosmo when he was in one of his petulant moods and attempting to draw attention to himself. And she was confused. She had no concept of one person being better than another. Perhaps more knowledgeable or better skilled. But not better. It seemed a ridiculous question to ask.

"I can speak very well, thank you," Meg politely assured her. "But in truth I do not see anyone who is better."

Connor smiled behind the hand propped at his chin. Arthur hid a grin behind his mug of wine. Even Merlin had a difficult time keeping a straight face.

Meg was aware that Dannelore had suddenly appeared and stood close at her elbow. She could almost hear the woman's thoughts as a restraining hand was laid on her shoulder in silent warning.

Be careful, the gesture seemed to say, although Meg had absolutely no idea of what she'd done or of the reason to take care.

Color rushed to Morgana's cheeks and blazed at her eyes. "What a saucy little tart you've found, dear brother," she exclaimed. "And here I had given up hope of your return, much less with a mistress."

An audible silence fell over the table. Several seated about it shifted uneasily, and Meg found herself the center of embarrassed attention.

"You misunderstand, sister," Arthur was quick to reply.

But before he could elaborate further, Connor explained, "Meg is under my protection."

"I see," Morgana's reaction was a faint narrowing of her dark eyes even though her mouth curved in a smile.

"And warms your bed as well? I had not thought you to

care for such attachments. But you should be careful, it seems she has found *my* place at my brother's table much to her liking. You may soon find your bed has grown cold.''

Behind her, Meg heard Dannelore's sudden indrawn breath and felt a hand at her elbow in urgent restraint. But Meg chose to ignore both the changeling's distress and the restraint.

Her experience with mortals was admittedly limited. Nothing she'd experienced prepared her for a confrontation with Morgana. She was not certain about the meaning of warming Connor's bed, but she understood anger. And it was obvious that Arthur's sister was angry with her and made no attempt to disguise it.

It was there in the sharpness of her every word in spite of her smile and in the sharpness at her eyes—a contradiction Meg found most disconcerting.

''I did not realize it was yours,'' she replied. ''But you may have it back. I am through with it.''

She wasn't at all certain what she'd said that was so humorous, but everyone suddenly was having a very difficult time keeping a straight face. Everyone except Lady Morgana. At the moment she looked as if she'd just swallowed something offensive, except that she hadn't touched her food at all.

''Good heavens, Connor. The child is absolutely unruly,'' Morgana exclaimed. ''You must teach her manners.''

Manners? Lady Morgana had to be the most ill-mannered creature Meg had ever encountered! Crude and vile as they were, trolls had better manners! She had the notion to turn Lady Morgana into a troll.

Much experienced in warfare, Connor knew the makings of a battle when he saw one. He rounded the table and slipped a hand beneath Meg's arm and hauled her to her feet.

''Leaving so soon?'' Morgana inquired, the sharpness of her words giving the lie to the smile at her lips.

''Are you so eager to have her in your bed again?''

''I thought I would attempt to teach her some manners,'' Connor replied evenly.

Meg's gaze snapped to his. Images of slimy, oozing swamp creatures filled her thoughts as he pulled her away from the table. But she had neither the time nor the opportunity to carry out that thought as he escorted her from the table and across the hall.

Connor pulled her into the passage at the edge of the hall and pushed her up against the wall, his hands flattened against the stones at either side of her head, preventing escape.

She braced for the anger. One word, she thought. If he says just one word in defense of that thin-lipped shrew I will turn him into a toad.

Then, she realized he wasn't angry at all. He was laughing! Laughter rolled from him, rocked his shoulders, and brought tears to his eyes as he shook his head from side to side with disbelief.

"By God, you are wonderful!"

She stared at him incredulously. A moment earlier he'd looked as if he would separate her head from her shoulders. He leaned forward resting his forehead against hers, laughter rumbling through him.

Eventually it subsided. But it was still there in those gray eyes that shimmered from winter cool to summer heat. Then his hands were slipping through her hair, cradling her face.

"Wonderful," he whispered.

And before she could draw another breath, he was kissing her.

Deeply, wildly, that heat moving through her blood and burning her soul. And she was kissing him back, angling her mouth against his, allowing him to taste all of her as she tasted him. A kiss that whispered across her lips in tender stroking words that knew no language but it's own. And with eyes closed, Meg let his kiss take her. Into falling, drifting places like midnight dreams. A spiral of sensation that carried her into a world of awakening splendor.

It was a long time before she was able to breathe again. He seemed to have similar difficulties as he leaned against the cool stones, his cheek low beside hers.

"Do you wish for me to warm your bed?" she asked.

Laughter was gone as he pushed away from the wall, and

her. He did not answer but turned away as if he had not heard or had not wanted to hear.

"Do you?" she asked.

He looked at her then—surrounded by a cloud of golden hair that tumbled to her waist—at her willowy slenderness, the high breasts pressing against the soft fabric of her gown, remembering the way he'd found her in the forest. And those eyes, like brilliant sapphires that burned into a man's soul.

"Any man would wish it." Then he seized her by the wrist.

It seemed likely the only answer she was going to get, for he pulled her back into the crowded hall with its noise, crude jokes, laughter, and shouted wagers as the night's entertainment began.

She did not understand. She wanted to know what Morgana meant by it. And she wanted to know his answer, not someone else's.

As they reached the table where some of his men were already setting up a game, she pulled back, refusing to go any further, demanding an answer. *His* answer.

"Do *you* wish it?"

Connor turned. He knew nothing about her. She might be the daughter, or wife, of one of Maelgwyn's chieftains. A lie would have been better for both of them. But he told her the truth.

"Aye," he said. "From the first moment I saw you, and every moment since."

Chapter Thirteen

Meg stood atop the wall above the gatehouse at Caerleon. It was bitter cold, the sun glimpsed briefly through ominous clouds that gathered. They would have snow before nightfall.

She wore only a thin woolen shift but she was not cold, even as another blast of frigid air swept over the wall, whipping her hair about her head and shoulders.

Dannelore found her there as Meg knew she would, just as she had with increasing frequency the past five days since Arthur and his men had ridden out of Caerleon.

Word had come that Maelgwyn himself had struck in the river lands east of Caerleon, attacking the strongholds of those who had once been loyal to the Duke of Cornwall.

They could not hope to hold out for long against him with Aethelbert's mercenaries at their backs. And so Arthur and his army had ridden out to join them. To the surprise of many, including Arthur, Connor had ridden with him.

Several of his men still recovered from wounds received at Amesbury and were not strong enough to leave. It would have been cowardly to remain behind with the wounded. For those like Radvald who knew him well, the move came as no surprise. But he let each man make his own decision. In the end all chose to go with him. Even Simon, who had argued the loudest against joining Arthur. Each day since, Dannelore had found her mistress here, her gaze fixed on that far horizon.

In that way that connected them, Meg sensed her presence even before she approached.

"How is my brother?"

Merlin was still plagued by the wound he had received at Amesbury and had not gone with Arthur. Though he said nothing of the wound, it had festered and weakened him, leaving him barely able to sit a horse.

He and Arthur had met the night before Arthur's departure. Plans were made. After their departure he had retreated to the small chamber near the chapel once occupied by the resident monk at Caerleon, to rest and meditate.

"He is no worse," Dannelore replied. "But the fever persists. I do not understand it. The others recover, but he does not."

"And his own healing powers?" Meg asked. "Does he refuse to use his own skills?"

"Men, bah!" Dannelore snorted. "They are terrible patients. And I suspect healers as patients are the worst. They think they know everything. I finally persuaded him to take some of my special tea." She frowned. "Still, I am worried. It is not like him to be taken ill. He has never suffered an injury or illness before."

Meg turned. "Perhaps I should see him."

Dannelore shook her head. "He is resting now. Later perhaps, although I do not know what good it will do. The forthcoming battle worries him. 'Tis the first time he and Arthur have been apart since their return. There is much danger. But it comforted him to know that Connor rode with Arthur." She watched Meg carefully for any outward reaction.

Meg nodded, her thoughts also on one who rode with Arthur. "The battle has not yet begun," she said with a faraway look in her eyes as if she saw it all, as indeed she had in her dreams. "But it will begin soon."

That morning she had risen before dawn, awakened by those dreams. She had seen events unfolding as clearly as if she rode beside Arthur.

She had traveled through those dreams until she found the one she sought, drawn by his touch, the remembered feel of him, and she had entered his dreams, slipping into his thoughts, touching him as he had touched her.

Even now the memory of it filled her with an ache of longing she had never experienced before. She wrapped her arms tightly about herself as if she could hold onto that longing, for even that was better than emptiness.

She had wanted to go with them as she had at Amesbury. It would have been easy, and no one among Arthur's men would have been the wiser. Those at Caerleon would not have given her sudden disappearance any thought, for Dannelore could see to their needs.

No doubt Morgana would have been delighted, for she made no attempt to disguise her dislike of Meg. But with Merlin at Caerleon Meg dare not leave, for he would surely become suspicious. She prayed they would all be safe—she prayed Connor would be safe. But she knew the realities of war. She had seen them at Amesbury—the brutality, blood, and death.

Her arms tightened as that longing ache deep inside twisted into fear.

"Your thoughts betray you, mistress," Dannelore said softly. " 'Tis dangerous and well you know it, these feelings you share—mortal feelings. You must not allow it," she cautioned. But her warning seemed to fall on deaf ears, for Meg did not listen. She approached closer until she stood beside Meg.

"You are not like these mortals. 'Tis only a transformation, an illusion. The emotions are an illusion."

"They are real," Meg replied. "I have never felt anything like them before. You above all know what I feel. You gave up everything to come back to the mortal world."

"I am half mortal, but you are not. You are an immortal. The way lies differently for you. Above all, you must not allow yourself to feel these things. You do not know what you are doing."

"I know exactly what I am doing," Meg replied. " 'Tis the reason I came through the portal. I wanted to feel alive!"

"You must return before it is too late!"

Meg shook her head. "I cannot. Not yet."

"Later may be too late!"

Meg held up a hand and for the first time Dannelore sensed the force of the power that moved through her, more radiant than a thousand suns. And for the first time, it was directed at the changeling.

"You are my friend," Meg whispered. "You cared for me when I was injured. You have taught me many things. And I am deeply grateful. But do not overstep yourself."

It was a gentle warning, but a warning nonetheless and one Dannelore dare not ignore. The power of the chosen ones was to be feared and respected.

"And do not think to betray me to my brother," Meg added.

"I gave my word," Dannelore sadly replied. "I will keep it."

The waiting seemed interminable. Eventually, as Meg knew it would, the weather worsened and she was forced to retreat inside the fortress walls. But the gathering storm within Caerleon was almost as fierce as the storm that gathered outside— a storm called Morgana.

Nothing pleased her. She criticized the plain food everyone was forced to eat, the lack of sufficient fuel for either oil lamps or the braziers used to heat the smaller chambers, and the generally crowded conditions inside Caerleon with the wounded who still convalesced and increased the population.

She repeatedly sent the staff of servants she'd commandeered out into the village that had sprung up within the walls of Caerleon in search of food more suitable to her tastes, wood for her own personal use, and whatever else could be found that might make her more comfortable, no matter the hardship it created for others.

But there was little wood to be found, and the food the villagers ate was no better than that of those who resided in the main hall. The lack of sufficient wood forced Morgana to remain in the main hall most hours of the day, where she complained bitterly about everything, including the fact that her brother was not there so she might complain to him.

By the third day the wounded had left the main hall, preferring the shelter of the stables, the recently repaired armory, or a peasant hut rather than being forced to endure her unpleasant company.

Those who remained were ready to break up what remained of the furnishings at Caerleon in order to provide wood for her chamber just to be rid of her.

Grendel's irrepressible good humor was sorely tested. Morgana abhorred "little people" as she called them, openly referring to them as disgusting, sneaky little thieves. She was convinced Grendel was responsible for the disappearance of a partridge she'd had set aside for herself.

John and two young boys hunted daily. On the last day before the storm they'd chanced upon a flock of partridge scratching for seeds under the mantle of snow just beyond the gates of Caerleon. They'd brought down several with their bows, and the woman who had taken over as cook had planned a meal of roast partridge—the first meat they'd eaten in days.

When the partridge Morgana had confiscated for herself disappeared she flew into a rage, accusing Grendel of taking the bird. When John informed her that he was the one who had taken the partridge and at present it was roasting with the others, the meat to be distributed fairly among all, she vowed to have his head roasting on a spit right along with Grendel's for she was certain the little man was guilty of countless other crimes.

Young Tristan became even more of a shadow. Before entering the main hall, he looked for Meg, avoiding any possible notice by Morgana who was more inclined to cuff his ear for general purposes or to ban him entirely from the hall for no good reason except to do it—and usually just before the evening meal, preventing him from eating.

Tristan had been appointed apprentice gamekeeper since Morgana insisted that everyone earn their keep. He had a sharp eye and a keen mind, and learned quickly from John about forest animals. He often left Caerleon on his own—no one could blame him—returning with several rabbits he'd snared or birds he'd come upon.

Even Dannelore who knew Lady Morgana from her previous service to Lady Ygraine and who had the patience of the Ancient

Ones, soon tired of the woman's constant complaining and spitefulness.

"A healthy dose of pennyroyal liberally sprinkled over her food would ease her mood," Dannelore snapped one evening when Morgana incessantly complained about the rabbit stew which they'd eaten for several days. The hunting had been poor, and Tristan had been unable to find anything else.

"It would most likely kill her," Meg pointed out. "At the very least it would put her into a deep sleep."

"Either way we would not have to listen to her complaints," the changeling replied. "She is like a petulant child, whining all the time—the food is not right, it is too cold; her chamber is too drafty."

Grendel nodded. "If she closed her mouth it would not be so drafty. I think you should cast a spell on her. Transform her, into something vile and foul smelling." He thoughtfully tapped a finger against the side of his head.

"Say perhaps a worm." His eyes narrowed with pleasure. "Yes, a worm. Then see how she likes being picked on—by every bird that comes along. 'Twould serve her right."

Meg shook her head even though she agreed with him. "I dare not. Weak as he is, my brother might become suspicious."

"He would do it if he were forced to share her company," Grendel said, convinced of it. "He would turn her into a stone or a piece of firewood, since she is so fond of it."

There was a loud crash followed by a furious outburst from Morgana.

"What is it now?" Dannelore exclaimed, and set aside the healing concoction she had been mixing for poultices for the wounded. Meg had agreed to take them into the village, for few of the wounded remained inside the main hall.

"I will go," Meg informed her, making a bleak face. "It is my turn."

"May the Ancient Ones protect and keep you," Grendel said with mock seriousness, like a priest giving his blessing to a warrior about to go into battle.

The latest disaster was a spilled apple flummery which one of the young serving girls, Tilda, accidentally dropped. Terrified, she'd tried frantically to scoop it back into the bowl only to have Morgana rail at her all the more.

"I will not eat what has spilled on the floor, you brainless twit. Bring me another and be quick about it!"

With tears streaming down her cheeks, a bad burn on her hand from the steaming flummery, the young girl did not even see Meg until she practically collided with her in the passage between the hall and the kitchens.

Through blubbering tears and hiccups Tilda tried to explain that it was not her fault. The poor thing was near hysterical, and Meg could only imagine the next disaster that would befall the girl if she did not keep her wits about her.

She steadied Tilda with a gentle hand, then with her thoughts, calming her, taking away the fear and hysteria.

"I did not mean to spill it, mistress."

"I know," Meg assured her. The girl was not much younger than herself.

"She insists on a new bowl." Tilda's voice hitched on a hiccup. "But what am I to do? 'Tis the last of the flummery."

Meg put an arm about the girl's shoulders as they returned to the main kitchen. She reached for a bowl from the shelf.

"If Lady Morgana insists on a new bowl, then she shall have it." And she poured the contents from one bowl into the other. The girl's eyes widened at the deception, then crinkled with laughter.

"Oh, mistress, you are a sly one."

"I am merely doing exactly as Lady Morgana wishes." She turned the girl and aimed her back in the direction of the main hall. "I am certain she will enjoy it thoroughly."

And Morgana did, exclaiming over the dessert the cook had prepared. "Why, 'tis the best I have ever tasted."

While Meg and Tilda hid in the shadows and smothered back laughter until their sides ached and tears streamed down their cheeks.

Since Dannelore was the only one who had any patience with Morgana, more often than not it was Meg who took Merlin his meals.

"Are you not afraid of him?" Tilda asked, her eyes wide

with fear. " 'Tis said he changes young girls into mice and little boys into ferrets."

If she only knew . . .

"Well," Meg rationalized, "young Tristan seems safe enough." Then she twitched her nose playfully and Tilda's eyes grew even wider.

"Ohhh, do be careful, mistress. Cook has an awfully large cat."

Merlin stirred as she arrived with his meal. He had been sitting at a table reading some ancient text left by the old monk at Caerleon and had dozed off. He smiled kindly as he waved the food away.

"Please take it away. I am certain there are others who would enjoy it far more than I."

"You must eat," Meg coaxed, feeling that tightening of apprehension she experienced whenever she saw him. He had grown thin and his strength seemed to be less each day in spite of the healing tonics Dannelore prepared.

"I will prepare you something else," she offered.

"And have Morgana screeching at you over it?" he replied, catching her eye. "I am well aware of Morgana's faults. She always was a petulant child. Contrary to fine wine, she has not improved with the years."

Meg laughed. Such close contact with Merlin was always dangerous. She had to constantly guard against his probing her thoughts lest he discover the truth. But she found she much enjoyed his company.

"Come," he invited. "Do not leave so quickly. I enjoy your company."

She took a chair near his. "Only if you will allow me to check your wound."

"You are most persistent."

She nodded. "I am often reminded of that." He finally relented, sitting back in his chair as she checked the wound at his side. It had healed well enough, but the skin was tender to the touch, causing him to draw in his breath. And there was the weakness that never went away but only seemed to worsen.

"Your touch is gentle," he commented. "You have the gift of a true healer."

She smiled at the compliment. "I have been told I have much to learn," she said without thinking.

"There is much you can learn from Dannelore. Perhaps you might be willing to learn more?"

She looked up at him. "Perhaps." It was difficult to keep her thoughts guarded. She found she wanted to open them to him, to blend their thoughts and experience the knowledge he had acquired. But she dare not.

"What of you, mistress?" he asked as she set the trencher at the edge of the brazier to keep the food warm. Unbeknownst to Morgana a steady supply of wood kept the fire going throughout the day and night so that he was allowed to stay in the relative comfort of the monk's chamber, rather than endure the drafty cold of the main hall which never seemed to be warm enough no matter how warm the fire.

"Have you remembered anything before your injury in the forest?"

She chose her words carefully. "There are times when I think something will come to me—bits and pieces of memory. Then it is gone. Dannelore has assured me it will return eventually."

He laid a hand gently over hers. "I could help you remember."

The contact was startling. She immediately felt the warmth of energy that moved through him and reached out to her, like a kindred spirit.

Did he feel it as well?

She quickly removed her hand from his.

"Please take no offense, milord. But I would be afraid."

He gave no indication that he had sensed anything in that brief contact.

"Afraid?" he replied incredulously. "What is there to be afraid of?"

"I have heard," she said most seriously, "that you have the power to turn one's head to mush."

He chuckled. "Only if it was mush to begin with. In your

case, I do not think there would be any cause for concern. You are a very clever girl. More clever than you let on.''

Her gaze snapped to his. Had he perhaps sensed something after all?

''Who else has been able to put Morgana in her place?'' he continued, his blue gaze watching her thoughtfully.

''And with much gratitude.'' He smiled gently.

She slowly let out the breath she'd been holding.

'' 'Tis not where I would like to put her.''

Merlin settled back in his chair, wincing at the pain each movement caused him.

''Morgana can be . . .'' He searched for the word and finally settled for a diplomatic one. ''. . . difficult at times.''

''It is beyond me how brother and sister can be so different,'' Meg confessed.

''They were raised by different hands,'' Merlin explained. ''Arthur was already a strong young lad when Morgana was born. She was doted on by the old Duke of Cornwall . . .'' Again he seemed to search for the more diplomatic explanation.

''Because she and not Arthur was his child?''

''You have heard the old stories.''

'' 'Tis difficult not to hear them with so many people arriving at Caerleon each day,'' she confessed, and added what she'd also heard, '' 'Tis said Arthur was sired by another.''

What she did not say was that it was also said there were magical forces at work—that another, chosen by the Ancient Ones, had seduced Lady Ygraine and fathered Arthur.

His sharp gaze pinned hers. She could feel the probing of his unspoken thoughts and carefully guarded them.

''The stuff of rumors and legends.'' He made a dismissive gesture. ''Arthur is a man, not some mystical creature conjured from the mists. But a man with a destiny that must be fulfilled.''

True, she thought with a secretive smile. But there was one who was a mystical creature *conjured* from the mists. And he sat before her.

''And you will see that he does.''

He shrugged as if it was no great thing. ''I will do my small part.''

She decided she liked her brother very much.

An easy comradery settled between them. He told her of the years he and Arthur had spent in the eastern kingdoms, his destiny to serve Arthur, and Arthur's own destiny on a distant battlefield.

She reached for a goblet of wine to hand to him. As he spoke it suddenly slipped from her fingers, the contents spilling across the floor of the chamber.

Over and over again, she saw it happen. And like the voices of the Ancient Ones whispering through dreams, she sensed when it began—the unfolding of events—and glimpsed the stirring images beyond the walls of Caerleon like clouds gathering before a storm—the moment when the first sword was raised, the first blow struck, and blood spilling onto the earth on a distant battlefield beneath the light of the last full moon. Like wine spilled from a goblet.

It had grown silent once more in the chamber. The fire guttered at the brazier as it fought the cold, sounding like the muttering of voices. Merlin was unaware of her thoughts. She was grateful for that. Still he knew when the battle had started.

"It has begun," he said prophetically.

Outside the monk's chamber Morgana hesitated, her hand at the latch. She heard the murmur of a soft voice and then Merlin's reply, and quickly drew her hand back, her fingers curling into a knotted fist. As silently as she had approached, she slipped back into the shadows.

Arthur's army crossed the Severn into Somerset. Five days from Caerleon they joined Sir Balan of Montrose.

His army had been scattered by Maelgwyn and dismissed as no longer a threat in Maelgwyn's sweep toward Silchester and the small force there led by Gilbert of Marhaus. Without help Marhaus could not hope to hold Silchester. He would be decimated and Silchester, a vital trade center, ripe for the taking.

Battle-weary and beleaguered, Sir Balan shook his head when told that Arthur of Caerleon was encamped nearby with his army and wished to meet with him.

"Arthur is dead," he replied. "Slain at Amesbury by Constantine."

"The reports of my death are greatly exaggerated," responded Arthur as he edged his warhorse through the gathered warriors and swung down from the saddle. They had followed those rumors, no doubt spread by Maelgwyn, all the way from Caerleon.

"Arthur of Caerleon?" young Sir Balan asked incredulously.

Arthur nodded, with growing amusement. "The last time I checked."

"How may I know for certain?" Balan asked, still unable to believe that the army now massed on his perimeter was Arthur's.

Arthur pulled off his gauntlet and thrust his fisted hand toward the young warrior.

"As a boy I received that scar while playing with a sword I should not have taken. It belonged to Sir Guilford of Montrose. He did not punish me, but instead made me promise that the next time I set foot in Somerset it would be to join with Somerset in uniting the kingdom."

Young Balan recognized the scar. He was a number of years younger than Arthur and remembered the story. It had been told often by his father over the years.

"It was this sword you took," he told Arthur. "My father's sword. You do not join with Somerset, milord. 'Tis Somerset that joins with you." Though he'd been wounded and it caused him great pain, he went down on one knee and lowered his head.

"I pledge my sword to you, Arthur of Caerleon."

"Stand," Arthur gently replied, humbled by the young warrior's words. And when it seemed the young warrior's strength was spent, he slipped a hand beneath his arm and supported him.

"We fight together," he told Balan. "Side by side." He looked around. "Sir Guilford?"

"Dead three years past, at the battle at Simford."

Arthur nodded. "He was a good man. I shall never forget him."

"Aye, he was," Balan agreed.

"What say we avenge Sir Guilford?"

Balan nodded. "I would like that very much."

"Then tell me what you can of Maelgwyn's army."

After they had spoken, Arthur asked Connor to join his war council, for there were plans to be made.

" 'Tis not my place," Connor replied. "I will stay with my men."

The old enmity was still there. That much had not changed. And after all these weeks Arthur still knew no way to bridge it. He did not appeal to the friend, but instead appealed to the warrior.

"Balan has only met Maelgwyn in battle once, caught by surprise, and he barely survived while you have had several encounters," Arthur pointed out. "I do not intend to make the same mistake. We know his strength and his position. I need to know the mind of the man. The way he thinks, how he directs his war generals, his tactics. There is no one more qualified to tell me this. And I do not believe after all these years that you came to Somerset to allow your men to be slaughtered by Maelgwyn."

Connor studied Arthur with narrowed gaze. Eventually he nodded.

"Maelgwyn's greatest strength lies in the numbers of his warriors. Their weapons are crude but effective. They are ruthless. There is no code of honor among them. They strike head-on in a massive, overwhelming blow, killing everyone in their path. Sir Balan and his men survived by accident. They fragmented and scattered."

"And the reason you have survived all these years?" Arthur bluntly asked.

Connor allowed a faint smile. Much as he hated to admit it, there was no denying the truth.

"A long time ago I learned the mind of the man. The way he thinks, how he directs his war generals, and his tactics. To beat Maelgwyn you have to become Maelgwyn." Then he added, "You do have one advantage."

"What is that?"

Connor nodded. "You have horses, Maelgwyn does not."

"Good." Arthur had found a break in the ice. "And here I thought the situation was completely hopeless."

"Not completely," Connor replied.

Battle plans were made. Balan's reinforced army was to form an open-field assault at Maelgwyn's back, timed to coordinate with Maelgwyn's attack on Marhaus. The balance of Arthur's army, joined by Connor and his men, was to split into two forces, one sweeping in from the north, the other from south of the main battle. Then close like a rope being tightened about the throat of the wolf. It all depended on Marhaus—unaware of the presence of Arthur's army and with no way to get word to him—holding the eastern line of the battle.

Arthur gave orders for his men to prepare to march. Young Balan stopped him. Because of his injuries it had been determined that his men would join under Arthur's command.

"I will not be left behind," he insisted. "I belong with my men."

Arthur nodded. "Can you sit a horse?"

It was settled. Arthur was to take command of the northern advance, while Connor was given command of the southern advance, both forces composed of warriors afoot and astride.

They found Maelgwyn's army an hour to the east, encamped on the border of Somerset to await the coming dawn and the battle with Marhaus.

"He is certain of victory," Connor said as they saw the distant campfires.

"How do you know this?"

"Maelgwyn has been known to attack at night, striking while his adversary sleeps."

"And their guard is down," Arthur concluded.

Connor nodded. Their gazes met in a oneness of thought they had once shared as boys testing their cunning and strength against boyhood adversaries on mock battlefields. Arthur's eyes gleamed.

"We now have two advantages. Pass the word. We will use Maelgwyn's tactics against him—we attack under cover of darkness."

Like a storm that strikes without warning Arthur's army swept down on the encampment. But even though they had the advantage of surprise, the fighting was fierce. As Connor knew only too well, Maelgwyn's hordes were ruthless warriors. Personal loss meant nothing. They did not fight for a cause or something they believed in. They fought for blood.

Arthur's strategy gave them that second critical advantage. Geoffrey's men plunged into the heart of the encampment while Arthur and Connor each led additional attacks from the flank positions and closed the noose.

The encampment was engulfed with small fires that quickly spread, providing light to the embattled warriors and at the same time creating an eerie tableau beneath the midnight sky. The night was ablaze with fire, filled with the screams of the dying, and blood.

Like a sword, Connor cleaved through resistance at the southern flank, he and his men cutting their way through to the center of the encampment as Arthur did likewise from the northern flank. And amid the chaos and death they heard additional battle cries as Marhaus' men, no doubt seeing the light of fire on the horizon, swept in from the east, tightening the rope.

He vaulted from the back of his horse, slashing to his left and taking down one warrior, then quickly spun to the right and ran another through. He did not stop but kept moving, hacking his way through to the center of the encampment with but one thought—Maelgwyn!

Time and again he was attacked, and each time he drove his attacker back, meeting blow for blow with a brutal relentlessness, driven by that one thought, past the point of fatigue, past numbness, like a mindless barbarian. Not for cause or belief, but for blood.

Then, as he reached the center of the encampment, he and Arthur were fighting side by side, surrounded by embattled warriors.

There were times it was almost impossible to tell who were enemies and who were their own men. In the chaos of battle, they tripped over the bodies of the fallen, fought back to their feet, and in the melee searched for some glimpse of Maelgwyn.

Then, as the fighting intensified, he and Arthur fought back-to-back as they had countless times as lads in mock battle, each protecting the other while they met the attack head-on.

An opening gaped through the throng of enemies that had suddenly surged around them and Connor yelled at Arthur, "Get out! I can hold them!"

"And leave all the glory to you?" Arthur shouted. "Not bloody likely!"

He took down another warrior, turned to meet the next blow, and saw the sword suddenly thrust at Connor's blind side. He lunged and brought his sword up.

With that instinct of all warriors who have fought in battle, Connor heard that sudden movement of air—a sword slicing through it—and glimpsed his own death. Then he heard the sound of steel against steel followed by a deathly scream. He spun around.

In that way that time sometimes seems to stand still for just a moment, moving out of itself, framing itself in frozen images, Connor saw the fallen warrior with sword clutched in hand, knew that he looked at what could have been his own death, and then saw the tip of Arthur's sword buried in the man's chest. At great risk to himself, Arthur had saved his life.

Their gazes met. Not as they were at that moment, but as they had been, when countless times as boys they had met each other's gaze on some pretend battlefield, fearless, with true hearts, and the bond of friendship stronger than blood.

Stronger than the empty years between then and now, stronger than all the doubt, loss, and anger. And in that moment, with the blood of their enemy staining their tunics, they were as simple as two boys who had once stood together before destiny intervened, with swords raised to the sky, and pledged their lives to one another. As simple as one life risked for another.

"If you've nothing better to do," Radvald snarled from somewhere nearby, "you might help remove this tree that has fallen on me."

The tree was a giant of a warrior whom the old Viking

had finally taken down only to find himself pinned under the towering giant's body.

As the battle at last waned about them, Arthur and Connor rolled the giant from atop the Viking, and then each extended a hand to him.

"I'm not an invalid," Radvald grumbled as he ignored their offer of assistance. Slowly and with great effort, he finally stood.

He glared down at the fallen giant. "Cursed barbarian," he spat out.

Arthur and Connor exchanged amused glances.

"I feared he had you there for a moment," Connor replied.

"Bah!" the Viking exclaimed. He looked around with a fierce expression.

"Don't tell me the fightin' is over. I was just gettin' my second wind."

"Best to save it," Arthur advised him. "For Maelgwyn."

None among Arthur's warriors had encountered him in the fighting at the center of the encampment. Nor was he found among the dead or wounded along the perimeter, or anywhere throughout the Somerset countryside in the days that followed.

The darkness which had given Arthur the advantage of surprise in the initial attack had also provided escape for the wolf.

"He has disappeared like the devil in darkness," Arthur said days later as he sat astride his horse beside Connor. They'd searched the countryside and found no sign of Maelgwyn. He sensed his friend's anger and frustration at the loss.

"There will be another day."

"I do not want another day!" Connor replied. "I want Maelgwyn's head on a pike this day."

"I understand your anger, my friend. But while we chase the wolf, Caerleon is unguarded. Our men are exhausted. The wounded must be tended. Best to gather our strength and fight another day."

Connor knew he was right. "He was almost within our grasp." The words were edged with frustration.

"And will be again, I promise you. Until now, Maelgwyn

has murdered, sacked, and plundered at will. But we have wounded the wolf and he crawls back to his den.''

"Aye," Connor acknowledged, knowing that Arthur spoke the truth and wisely. There would be another time, another place.

The tension eased between his shoulders, just as the old animosities had eased between them since that moment on the battlefield when Arthur had set aside destiny and placed himself in great danger to save a friend's life.

He was weary of the fighting, blood, and death. They chased their tails looking for Maelgwyn. There would be another day, but as he had many times over in the past days he found his thoughts turning away from the blood and death and turning toward the softness of a golden vision that had moved through his thoughts and dreams since leaving Caerleon—that last moment when parting.

She had not tried to persuade him against going, nor had she spoken of her fears. She had simply said, "I will be waiting for you."

"Aye," he repeated. " 'Tis time to go home."

If any had seen her, they would have sworn she flew down the steps to the main hall below, with only one thought and heedless of any danger.

"Where are you going?" a voice snapped, suddenly halting her flight across the hall.

Morgana.

There had been a break in the weather the past few days, and Morgana had ventured with increasing frequency from her chamber to bedevil everyone at Caerleon with her endless whining, criticism, and orders.

"Arthur has returned," she replied, refusing to allow Morgana to ruin another day.

"Returned? But that is impossible. I would be the first to know of it."

Meg realized the grave mistake she'd made. "I only just

learned of it.'' And without exactly telling a lie, ''One of the boys returned from hunting in the forest . . .''

She did not finish the thought. In so far as it went, it was the truth. Tristan and two other boys had returned from hunting only a short while earlier. But they had had no word of Arthur. No one knew of it. Except Meg. She had seen it in the ancient crystals.

She saw the suspicious look on Morgana's face, but did not give her the chance to question her further. She turned and fled out the doors of the hall. As she reached the steps, the guards at the top of the wall called down that riders approached. Then it was announced that it was Arthur.

The inhabitants of Caerleon poured out of their huts and climbed atop roofs and posts in their eagerness to welcome Arthur and his men as they slowly rode through the gates.

The warriors' tunics were caked with mud, grime, and the blood of battle. Many were not recognizable for the dirt and sweat that covered their faces. Some slumped wearily in their saddles while others walked, supporting the wounded or carrying them on litters. But on the faces of all were expressions of victory.

Arthur rode slightly ahead of them, and at his right rode Connor.

Morgana saw him, and her expression softened and grew eager, a smile of open sensuality curving her mouth as she waited for Connor to arrive with her brother at the entrance to the main hall.

Meg did not see her as she eagerly ran down the steps of the main hall, where she encountered Dannelore and John. The changeling tried to stop her with a hand at her arm. Their thoughts connected, and in that connection Dannelore saw what she had feared for weeks.

''You must not! You do not know what you are doing.''

Meg gently removed her fingers from her sleeve.

''I know exactly what I am doing.''

She turned and crossed the yard, moving through the jubilant warriors until she reached Connor's horse.

He reached down and she took his hand. He lifted her into

the saddle before him. His gaze met hers and in its gray depths she saw the weariness of battle and the misery of death.

His hand slipped through her hair, tenderly touching her cheek, and in that touch of flesh covered with sweat, grime, and blood, she felt him let go of the weariness and misery and reach for something more. As the people of Caerleon swarmed around Arthur and his men in celebration, Connor turned his horse toward those open gates.

She did not ask where he was taking her. It did not matter.

Chapter Fourteen

The sun was perched low on the horizon when they finally stopped on a hill overlooking a lake. The sky deepened to gray as twilight came on, and mist rose from the surface of the lake like ghosts gathering on some ancient battlefield. And behind that ghostly army loomed the castle they defended—ancient stone and timber walls, dark, abandoned, and fallen to ruin.

Nothing was said as Connor guided the horse down the hill and across the snowy landscape that surrounded the lake. As they drew closer, ancient walls loomed dark and forbidding in stark contrast to the pristine mantle of snow that lay over the land like a white robe worn by a fallen king.

The gates stood open. No guards announced their arrival. There was only the mournful sound of the wind as it lifted the tattered remnants of a banner and sent a shutter slapping back upon its hinges, and from somewhere nearby come the sound of water lapping against a stone wall.

Connor dismounted and tethered the horse. Then he reached for her, easing her down beside him.

At a glance Meg saw the remains of stables, animal pens, dovecote, smokehouse, and kitchens.

"What is this place?"

"It was my home."

There was something in his voice. Both a fierceness and a sadness as if something was torn from deep inside him. And in the fading light the expression on his face revealed both that sadness and fierceness.

Home.

It was a word that had no meaning for her. Raised as she had been by the counsel of elders and the Learned Ones, she had been nurtured in a world that mirrored the mortal world but for all intents and purposes had no walls, no boundaries, no ties to place or home. No emotional history of a place called home. Her world simply existed. She had simply existed.

But in her time at Caerleon, listening to Arthur speak of his own memories, and his hopes and dreams for Britain and the future, she had a vague sense of what it was that bound mortals to a particular place.

It was the history of a place—the events of childhood and growing up, of family, hopes, and dreams—that defined each mortal life whether a person was highborn or low.

It was that sense of belonging to something and it belonging to you, whether it was only in memory or a physical place that you returned to. It was, she realized, what defined the mortal heart and soul, what they loved, fought for, and died for.

She heard all those things in his voice as clearly as if he'd given words to them. A sadness of longing for what once was, and had been lost.

His hand closed over hers.

The main hall was built in the old Roman style with wide steps, a portico, and columns that supported a second-story balcony. It was at the second story that a broken shutter hung askew, swinging precariously.

The front entrance was of wood, the battered and scarred opening giving evidence of the fierce fighting that had found its way past the gates and up the steps. Over time the timbers of the massive wood door had warped and though it hung from only one huge metal hinge, it was stuck fast in the opening.

Connor leaned his shoulder into the door and pushed. The

wood creaked and groaned, then finally gave way, scraping open across stained and broken flagstones.

The destruction did not stop at the entrance. Those who lived here had not yielded even when the enemy breached the door, but had fought to the last, giving no quarter, no surrender.

Meg sensed it even without the light of a candle or oil lamp to reveal the chaos of broken furnishings, torn tapestries, scattered utensils, a child's cradle turned on its side, a small yarn and straw figure cruelly stomped under a boot heel, and the blood that had stained the stones.

She saw it as he had seen it on a day years before, and felt the agony of what he had found. Then light pooled softly from the stub of a candle.

He set the candle into a notch in a stone at the fireplace and began building a fire. When the flames had caught he began feeding in larger pieces of wood, remnants of those tapestries, the broken pieces of a chair, anything that would burn.

" 'Tis a wonder you survived the ride from Caerleon so bad is the stench about me," Connor murmured low.

"Not quite as bad as a goat," she replied. But he did not smile in return.

"I have the smell of death about me. Even after all these years, I can still smell it." He abruptly rose to his feet. "Do not let the fire go out," he said, then spun on his heel and left.

She fed more wood onto the fire. She also found an oil lamp and more candles in a niche in the wall and lit them. Light spread throughout the large chamber.

Few of the original furnishings had survived intact. Many of the broken pieces had been burned in the large fireplace long ago, perhaps by some people trying to warm themselves on a night very much like this one.

Only one tapestry survived, dusty and sagging from neglect like a faded old woman. The utensils—fine spoons, ladles, and knives made of pewter—had disappeared as had the cradle, perhaps hidden or stolen. But the doll made of yarn and straw had survived, kicked forlornly into a corner where it had been overlooked or simply passed over as unimportant.

Meg sensed it there, hidden, waiting to be found, perhaps waiting for a child's hand to hold it once more.

She found it under a pile of debris. The yarn hair had once been plaited into a thick braid. It was now matted and dirty. The blue gown was torn, the imprint of a boot heel on it still visible after all these years. It wore a broken expression. The features of the face had been stitched onto muslin. But part of the stitches at the mouth were missing. What had once been a smile was now only half a smile, a forlorn expression.

She had seen young girls at Caerleon playing with figures very much like this, only none so finely made nor the cloth so rich. This had once been a child's toy.

"It belonged to my brother's daughter, Dalenn."

Meg spun around. She had not realized that he'd returned. He'd stripped off the leather tunic and muslin shirt. He was bare to the waist, beads of water glistening at his hair and across his shoulders. The sight of him without his shirt, dressed only in tight, clinging breeches and soft leather boots stunned her.

He was finely made, his body a contrast of lean, flat surfaces and bulging curves, sharp planes and hard angles, and taut golden skin webbed with pale scars. The scars only made her want to touch him all the more. To feel their ridges and valleys with a healer's touch, and in the touching to learn him and the cost that had been paid with each one.

He slowly walked toward her and took the doll, turning it over in his hands. In spite of the iciness of the water as it dripped on her hand his skin was warm.

"She was only four. My nephew was only a few weeks old when they came." He paused, closing his eyes as he remembered.

"My father had taken precautions against Maelgwyn. More guards were posted at the walls and more warriors were armed within the walls. But in the end it made no difference.

"I was told afterward that they attacked at night under cover of darkness, when my family was inside at the evening meal. A tactic Maelgwyn has a particular fondness for." His face hardened. "His orders were to spare no man, woman, or child.

And they did not. I escaped only because I was not here that night."

"But in truth, you did not escape," Meg said softly, sensing the guilt that had burned through him since that long-ago night. "There are different kinds of death."

He dried the frigid droplets from his skin with his shirt.

"We knew the danger. It was the reason my father had me take my men into the countryside to search for Maelgwyn."

"You did as your father asked," she pointed out. "You could not have known otherwise." But how she wished that she had known him then, for she would have been able to tell him what was to come, to have spared him this pain.

Connor snorted. "It was my duty. I was searching for Maelgwyn, never realizing where he had struck until I returned."

"Not unlike Arthur's duty when he left Britain," she said, laying a hand gently at his arm.

His gaze was thoughtful as it met hers. "Perhaps." He threw more wood on the fire.

The light from the fire at the hearth played across the scarred walls. Still thoughtful, he quietly said, "I should have been here."

"And died with them. How would that have served your family?"

The anger went out of his voice. "I know my father would not have wished my death, but I have always felt that . . ."

"That there was something you could have done to save them," she finished for him. "You could not. You would have died with them."

"I know that here." He pointed to his head.

"But not in your heart."

"Aye. And now all that is left are these scarred, crumbling walls, and the blood."

She shook her head. "You are wrong," she said softly as she slowly walked about the large room, touching a scarred table, running her fingers across the stones at the wall, letting her senses expand until she touched the essence of those who had once lived there.

Their spirits reached out to her, not from the horror and

violence of their deaths but from the lives they'd lived and the love they'd shared—a foolish argument between brothers, a child's laughter, a quick embrace between young lovers, a lingering embrace between old lovers.

"This was a place of happiness and love," she said as she returned to where he stood and ran her fingers across the stones there, images of laughter and love moving through her senses. Her gaze met his as she imagined how it had been before that night of death.

"You remember one painful moment of loss. Is it not better to remember a lifetime of happiness?"

He shook his head, ever at a loss to understand her logic and wisdom.

"Aye, and in the darkest moments it was all that sustained me."

He laid a hand against her cheek. She felt the coolness from the water he'd bathed in, and also a gentle warmth.

" 'Tis all I have to offer—crumbling walls and fallow fields. Nothing more."

"I do not want titles or land," she answered softly, sensing that with her answer some invisible line was crossed between what was and what would be.

"I want you."

His rough warrior's hands slipped back through her hair, through her senses in a way that was inescapable since he'd first touched her weeks ago and sealed both their fates.

His fingers trembled against her skin, and Meg lost herself in his kiss. He tasted of cold night air, icy water that beaded his skin and skimmed her lips, then heat as the kiss deepened, his tongue slipping between to steal her breath away.

Her slender hands came up, uncertain, hesitant, trembling as the kiss ended. She knew what passed between a man and woman. More than once in her time at Caerleon she had come upon a couple in a secluded corner or dimly lit passage as they urgently came together amid sounds that spoke their own language.

In the chamber she shared with Dannelore she was aware

that John often slipped into the bed on the far side, the one that Dannelore had made from straw and animal skins.

At those times Meg lay there silently in the darkness, trying not to listen but unable to block out the urgent whispers and the even more urgent swishes of clothing being hastily removed, followed by a sudden gasp and then the sound of their joining, equally urgent and fierce, until it ended and they lay spent until the early hours just before dawn when John left again.

As first light finally came, she and Dannelore said nothing of what had passed. But in her heart Meg longed to know more. She wanted to experience what mortals did when they came together in such a way. She wanted to feel what it was that seemed to grow stronger with each time, like a hunger that had been awakened.

She had tasted that hunger with Connor's kisses. Each time, it left an ache of longing deep inside that never went away but hid there, part of her now, a needing to feel that contact again, a needing of him. But she had nothing to draw on, no experience in such things, only the need.

"I don't know what to do," she whispered, overwhelmed by these mortal emotions, by uncertainty. Overwhelmed by the need.

"What do you want?" Connor gently asked. He saw the confusion and uncertainty in her eyes, the brilliant blue suddenly filled with shadows of doubt.

"I want to touch you."

Connor inhaled sharply. It was one of those moments when she made him want to laugh and cry. There was nothing shy or hesitant about her. There was only honesty.

"Then touch me," he replied, his voice low and intense.

Her fingers trembled faintly as she reached out, lightly tracing the hard ridge of muscle at his chest.

"Your skin is so warm," she whispered with awe. How was it possible when there was barely any heat from the fire?

Her exploration did not stop there. She ran her fingers up across the curve of taut, hard muscle to his shoulder. There she lightly ran her fingers over the deeply gouged scar that contorted the muscle and exposed the ridge of tendon. She

traced each web of broken flesh, each whorl of twisted muscle
with a healer's touch and a lover's caress.

Through that connection, she felt the pain he had suffered
and endured, and sensed the brutality that had inflicted it—not
a wound of battle but a wound of torture, and tears filled her
eyes.

"Do not weep for me," he whispered. "Anything but that."

Her gaze met his. She understood. The words came from
pain and pride. The scars on his body were who he was, no
more no less. And understanding that pain, pride, and the man,
she tenderly brushed her lips across that scarred flesh.

She heard his sudden drawn breath, felt the sudden tensing
of his flesh, and tasted the heat that suddenly burned like an
inferno beneath her lips.

Had she caused him pain?

He was tightly coiled as if ready for battle. His hands were
clenched at his sides. Yet he did nothing to stop her. Instead,
he stood perfectly still, his chest rising and falling on each
ragged breath as she continued to touch him. Down the length
of those well-muscled arms, those powerful hands that had held
her with such care and tenderness, then across the taut flatness
of his belly.

"Dear God!" he whispered, but whether it was a curse or
a plea for help she did not know, as her lips followed where
her fingers led.

Need.

Following that slender dark ribbon that rose from his breeches
and fanned out across the hard planes and curves of his chest
in a light dusting of dark hair that whorled about taut male
nipples.

Hunger.

"Meg." Neither a curse nor a plea for help, but a tender
warning as her lips again followed where her fingers led, each
taste making her eager for the next.

Then her hand slipped about his neck as she angled him
down for her kiss. Not a tentative kiss, but one filled with both
hunger and need.

It took every ounce of self-control he possessed, his hands

rigid at his sides, touching her only with his mouth, letting her explorations take them both to dangerous places.

It would be worth it, he vowed. Worth every agonizing moment when all he wanted to do was lose himself in the searing, healing heat of her body, to feel her trembling, restless, and needy beneath him, to feel the desire awaken in her body as it now awakened in her kiss.

Her breath whispered against his lips in a soft startled sound. Her blue eyes were wide, dark, shimmering with heat. Each breath shuddered out of her lungs. Still he kept his hands at his sides.

''Now you must let me touch you.''

She did not protest. Not when he lightly brushed the backs of his fingers across the ridge of bone above the neck of her gown. Not when his fingers moved lower, lightly stroking the curve of her breast through the bodice of her gown. Nor when he slowly pulled the bow from the laces of her gown. But she continued watching him with those dark eyes.

He eased the gown from her shoulders, exposing pale, silken skin and the darker pink of newly healed flesh where his arrow had entered. Then as she had done he brushed his lips across that seam of flesh, remembering the pain and agony he'd caused her, trying to take away the memory of it with a kiss.

He heard the sound she made. Not a sound of pain but a startled sound, the discovery of pleasure. He edged the gown lower, exposing the curve of a breast, and his mouth followed, tasting her. He eased the gown lower still, his lips following, and her breathing came in short, choppy sounds. He tugged the gown lower, and she ceased breathing altogether. Then he tasted her as she had tasted him.

Lightly at first, experimentally, tracing that delicately puckered flesh that beaded and hardened with each tender stroke until it was wet and glistening. And still she had not breathed. Then, gently, he suckled her into his mouth. And the air quivered out of her lungs in a faint, desperate sound.

Meg felt as if she were being torn apart by the sensations that swirled through her. Physical sensations and chaotic emotions that all collided at that place where he touched her, pulling her into the wet heat of his mouth.

Everything she'd learned fled in a heartbeat. She had no practical experience to guide her. Of everything she'd learned about the mortal world, nothing prepared her for this. Not even her powers, nor the gifts she'd been born with. She had only mortal instinct to guide her and no experience there. Only what she felt.

With only those newfound instincts to guide her, she slipped her hands through his hair, holding him to her, offering him everything she was.

Her head went back, eyes closed, lips parted on a breathless sound that was all wonder and pure pleasure. Nothing she'd ever experienced was like this. None of her wondrous powers, no creature transformation, conjurement, nor illusion.

It was pure sensation—the taste of him, the feel of him, the scent that permeated the air, the soft, stirring sounds as he whispered against her skin, and the sight of those powerful hands, gently stroking and caressing—all of her senses becoming one sensation—him.

Connor slipped an arm beneath her knees and picked her up. She made no protest, but there was doubt in the dark pools of her eyes as he laid her back upon the bed of furs.

"Are you afraid?"

She shook her head, the soft gold of her hair shimmering about her shoulders. " 'Tis only that . . ."

"You do not know what to do?" He stroked her cheek then stroked his mouth against hers.

"I know the way of it," she said with that openness that was so inherently a part of her. "I have seen your men with the girls at Caerleon. But they know what to do, it seems to come naturally for them. I wish to do it right."

Connor fought back laughter as he lay beside her, propped up on one elbow. He could have told her that it came naturally to them because they'd done it many times before with little care for whom it was with. Instead, he smiled tenderly and brushed a wisp of hair back from her forehead.

"You need have no fear, little one. You will do it right. I am the one who is afraid I may not do it right."

Her eyes widened, soft brows drawing together into a frown. "But how can that be? I've heard the stories your men tell. You've had much practice."

Again, he fought back the urge to laugh. Not at her, but with sheer pleasure. She had absolutely no idea how desirable she was, that combination of curiosity and innocence mixed with openness and simple logic, how unaffected she was beside him in naked splendor covered only by that fall of magnificent golden hair that revealed far more than it concealed in the dusky nipple that peeked from among gold satin strands.

How to answer? How to explain that while he'd found pleasure with other women, it had only been momentary and then easily forgotten. It had never been important to him if they were pleasured. It had never mattered before.

"I want to be gentle," he said softy. "I want to take away the fear. I want to give you pleasure."

She did not understand how he could have doubts. But they were there just the same.

"You have always been gentle, even though I did not always want you to be," she replied with that same candor. "I have never been afraid of you." She laid a hand against his cheek. "Not even in the forest." Her voice was husky as her mouth stroked his.

His hands closed over hers as she pulled him down to her on the pallet of furs. He angled them up over her head, pinning them into the soft fur as his mouth closed over hers. Then he kept them pinned as his mouth glided over her, retracing the path he'd taken before—the sharp angle of bone at her shoulder, the soft hollow beneath, across the swell of her breast, then slowly lower.

Her breath locked in her lungs in breathless anticipation, then escaped on a sound of pleasure as his tongue stroked, teased, and tormented her. And when she lay wet and panting beneath him, he tormented her more in tiny nibbling ways that made her arch her back and twist beneath him, straining against the restraint at her wrists, her breath convulsing in jerky, pleading sounds. And still he tormented her.

Moving lower, his hands gliding down over her arms, refusing to release her as his mouth found other pleasure places—the sensitive place where her flesh tingled and rippled across her ribs, then lower, dipping into the soft plain of her belly, and lower yet to dip into the cleft of her navel.

She no longer struggled to free herself, but sank her fingers into the thick fur overhead, holding on as he moved lower, tasting every inch of her—the bone at her hip, the slope beneath, then nipping at the inside of her thigh in small, tender bites—his hands gliding down over her body, touching every place he tasted, igniting a fire until she was flushed with heat, the air burned in her lungs, and blood pulsed wildly in her veins.

Her head was thrown back, the magnificent gold of her hair spread across the furs like a radiant sunburst. Her eyes were closed, her body throbbed. Then he traced a wet path across her lower belly and she cried out, a desperate, sobbing, begging sound.

The taste of her burned through him—innocence, sweetness, awakening desire. It was not enough, not nearly enough. His hands closed over her hips, angling them up so that her slender legs splayed over his shoulders. Then he tasted all of her.

She cried out and surrendered to pleasure. Her nails dug into his arms, her hips arched against the heat of his mouth. Waves of pure sensation engulfed her, swept her over the edge, then shattered her.

Nothing in her existence, nothing Dannelore had taught her, no well-learned lessons, not even the powers she'd been born with, prepared her for it. That single moment when everything else ceased to exist, when the ache deep inside was obliterated by wave after wave of pleasure.

Her body still shuddering, she reached for him, skimming the leather breeches from his hips, touching him, learning him, tasting him—the pleasure sound he made as her mouth opened beneath his; the sound of surprise as her teeth grazed his nipple; the sound of desire as her mouth skimmed lower; then the sound of need, a soft curse that broke from his lips and caressed hers as he wrestled her back down onto the furs.

She was like warm satin, sliding through his hands, whispering through his senses, a shimmer of gold color, wet heat as his fingers found her, fierce strength as her body arched with pleasure, shivering need as he slipped between her thighs, breathless wonder as his flesh pressed against her softness, then awakening passion as he moved inside her.

Hands clasped over her head, fingers laced, and her eyes darkened. Her lips parted softly on a wordless sound even as her body parted softly, giving him everything, holding nothing back, learning from him, learning him, in the tightness of his body snugged deep within hers.

It was a strength and a power she'd never known. It soared within her, more powerful and wondrous than anything she had imagined, anything she had ever been or ever would be.

Her slender fingers tightened over his, holding on to him, holding him, lost in the wonder of his body moving within her, then found in the wonder of moving with him.

There was no sense of time, no sense of place. There was only here and now, and the need to possess and be possessed, to touch and be touched, to burn and be burned in the heat of their bodies.

"Who are you?" he whispered against the taut peak of her breast.

She gasped with pleasure. "You know who I am."

"Aye, I know who you are," he replied, his voice low and harsh. "You make me laugh when I want to curse the world. You make me see beauty where there is only ugliness. You make me see life when all around there is only death. I know who you are." His hands tightened over hers as he moved deep inside her, and his mouth found hers.

"You are the other half of my soul."

The fire at the hearth was a thousand fires that burned inside her. The light that glowed across the walls was the light of a thousand suns.

It drenched him, poured over him until it glowed golden at

the tips of his hair, gleamed across his glistening body, and turned the cool gray of his eyes to molten ice.

And then the sun burst, exploding inside them in deep shuddering spasms that tore them apart, shattered them, destroying what they had been, creating what they would be.

"There was nothing for you to be concerned about," she assured him, when she was finally able to catch her breath again. "You did very well."

She felt the gentle rumble of laughter move through his chest as he rolled over and took her with him, so that she was sprawled on top of him.

"I am pleased that you approve." The warm gleam in his eyes belied his sarcasm. Then that gleam sharpened, reminding her of a grinning wolf, just before it devours its prey.

"But do I sense a hint of disappointment?"

"No!" she enthusiastically assured him. Then added, " 'Tis only that . . ." She bit at her lower lip as if not quite certain how to say it.

He seized her by the chin and forced her to look at him, warm fingers causing tiny ripples of pleasure even in that simple contact.

"Only what?"

" 'Tis only that I wondered if there were not other ways it might be done."

"Other ways?" Connor laughed, out loud this time, until tears ran down his cheeks and he almost dislodged her.

He was still chuckling as he held her firmly in place. "Where did you get such a notion?"

She replied with a shrug of a lovely naked shoulder and her usual candor. "At Caerleon."

"From eavesdropping in darkened corners."

"I was not eavesdropping," she informed him, her eyes flashing with indignation.

" 'Tis a little difficult not to notice when it's going on in plain sight, or in the room beside you. Dannelore and John are not very quiet."

"Noisy are they?" he quipped, trying very hard not to laugh

at her. She was so very serious and thoughtful as if she'd given the matter a great deal of thought.

"Aye, noisy as two squirrels up a tree."

"As noisy as all that?"

She nodded. "All sorts of strange sounds."

His hands closed over her arms as he rolled again, taking her with him, his mouth nuzzling her breast. She gasped with startled pleasure.

"Were any of the sounds like that?" he asked.

Her reply was a breathless, "Perhaps."

His body nuzzled the slippery cleft of her body and she exhaled on a soft moan.

"Or like that?"

She nodded. He moved his hips against hers and the soft moan became a more needy sound.

"Or that?"

She no longer remembered what they had been discussing. Or cared as need became a fierce sound low at her throat.

"Aye."

Laughter was gone from his voice. His hands trembled with other emotions as they stopped the restless movement of her hips.

"Let me show you all the other ways," he whispered as he entered her in one long, savage thrust.

Chapter Fifteen

The weather which had imprisoned them at Caerleon became their ally, conspirator, and guardian. Each morning when they rose to a new snowfall was another day they could not yet return, another day they stole for themselves.

They stayed at Monmouth over a fortnight, closed away in a snowbound world with much of the countryside impassable. But they were not alone. Their companions were the mice that now claimed Monmouth as their own, a curmudgeonly cat who resembled an overweight hedgehog but kept the population under control, and Thaddeus who resembled a scarecrow.

He was tall, lanky, and loose-boned. His tunic and breeches hung on his bony frame and seemed as if they would fall off with each step. His gray hair stuck out at odd angles like silver straw, and he was forever falling over his feet. Precisely like a scarecrow might if it suddenly became mortal. But he was also a conjuror of enormous talents, particularly when it came to scavenging firewood and food.

Thaddeus had once served Connor's father and his father before him when he was just a boy. Connor explained that for the longest time many thought him to be simple-minded for he did not speak.

He was limited in many physical ways, including a clubfoot, which accounted for his shuffling, loose-limbed gait. But it was discovered that what he lacked in physical abilities he more than made up for with his keen intellect, especially with letters and numbers.

He'd learned to read and write, and was devoted to Connor's father. The Duke of Monmouth made Thaddeus keeper of the stores at Monmouth over many others, and the soundness of that decision had been proved many times over for the holdings at Monmouth grew to be some of the richest in all Britain.

It was a position Thaddeus still held with great pride. If not for his skills at procuring almost everything from a decanter of wine to eggs, bread cakes, and fresh game as if from thin air, they might have been forced to return to Caerleon.

Thaddeus first appeared late on their first day at Monmouth. It had rained an icy sleet all night and it continued to grow colder with the promise of snow before nightfall.

Connor had taken advantage of a break in the freezing downpour to hunt in the overgrown orchards that were now home to hundreds of birds, squirrels, and a variety of other creatures.

Meg remained behind, for she had no boots or warm covering to protect against the freezing cold. Connor had been gone for several hours. She kept the fire going as he had told her, but it would not be long before the wood they had would be gone.

She set off into other parts of the house to find more. But her search was less than fruitful. She found only the splintered remains of wood furnishings that had suffered the fate of those found in the duke's hall.

She carried these back to the central hall, only to find a substantial number of huge logs stacked by the hearth. Several had already been added to the fire. The logs hissed, and smoke rolled up through the smoke-hole as flames burned away snow and ice, and found pockets of pine tar. She assumed Connor had returned. But it was not his presence she sensed in the room.

"I know you're there," she called out, unafraid, for she sensed no danger. "You may as well come out."

It was then Thaddeus stepped from the shadows at the opening of the hallway she'd discovered earlier led to the kitchens of Monmouth.

It had once been a massive stone structure with many rooms, and she had gone in search of something they might eat; perhaps some wheat or barley which might be ground into flour for cakes, or dried fruits which had been carefully put away in earthen jars, for the orchards and fields of Monmouth had once produced sufficient crops to support not only Connor's family but the many families who dwelled nearby and traded in wool, fresh meats, game birds, and fish.

But she discovered the mice had been very efficient. Grain sacks had been eaten through, their contents long ago consumed. Whatever else had once filled the storerooms at Monmouth had either been carried off or destroyed, except for a few dusty casks which contained wine.

Her own hunger was forgotten when she first saw Thaddeus. He was so lanky, with sunken cheeks and thin bony hands that her discomfort seemed inconsequential.

"Is there something I may get for you?" she asked, thinking that perhaps he was taken ill.

"Not frightened."

"Of course not," she replied. "What is there to be afraid of? You mean me no harm." It was then Meg realized the grave error she'd made. He had not spoken at all. She had responded to his thoughts.

His own surprise was just as great. *"You are one of the gifted ones!"*

She had blundered badly. How could she have been caught unaware?

"We have no food," she said apologetically in an attempt to disguise her mistake. "But you are welcome to what water we have."

"We have food now," Connor replied as he returned, startling her. So unsettled was she over her foolish mistake that she had not heard him return.

"Who are you talking to?" Then he looked up. The expression on his face went from guarded to stunned surprise, then jubilation as he saw just who it was.

''By God!'' he exclaimed, casting aside the brace of rabbits he'd snared.

He crossed the room in long strides and threw his arms about their gaunt visitor with so much enthusiasm she was certain the poor man's bones would shatter.

''I thought you were dead!'' Connor declared, holding the man at arm's length. His voice caught slightly. ''By God, I thought you were all dead.

''Come,'' he invited. ''Sit by the fire. You must tell me everything.''

Introductions were made. It was then Meg learned the esteemed position Thaddeus had once held in Connor's household. She would not have thought it possible, but the old man's demeanor changed markedly. Something that very closely resembled a smile turned the corners of his mouth and gleamed in his eyes whenever he looked at Connor.

They communicated in a language of hand signals, and Connor translated, explaining for her. But no explanation was necessary. She heard the man's story in his thoughts as clearly as if it were spoken—how he and the other servants had fought . . . alongside Connor's father and brother when the attack came, the death and devastation that followed, and when all seemed hopeless how Connor's father had sent Thaddeus from Monmouth to find Connor and warn him about Maelgwyn.

But he had not been able to find Connor, even though he'd followed his course for months, losing him in the forest, hearing of him again months later in another location, finally returning to what was left of Monmouth only to discover that he'd missed Connor by a matter of days.

Others had survived and fled into the countryside, taking refuge in remote camps and villages. But Thaddeus remained at Monmouth, steadfast in his duty and the belief that one day Connor would return.

He bore the scars his loyalty had cost him in a long-healed wound that had very nearly laid open the side of his head and had left him sightless in one eye. But he saw well enough with the eye that remained, watching Meg with avid interest.

''Thaddeus and some of the others live in servants' chambers near the kitchens," Connor explained. "They gradually returned after the attack and have lived here ever since."

Her startled gaze met his. "They have been here all along? Yester eve when . . . ?" Her cheeks flamed at the thought of what they must have seen while she and Connor made love.

"Noisy as two squirrels up a tree," he commented, barely able to suppress a grin.

Her mortification—a mortal emotion of which she would not have thought herself capable—was complete. She turned to the fire, an excuse if she needed one for the sudden color in her cheeks, and poked at a log that hardly needed poking.

"But it seems," Connor continued, "they have not ventured into this part of the house in a long time. It is large and drafty, and difficult to keep warm."

"Aye, most certainly drafty!" Meg muttered. "With the flapping of too much chatter!"

She thrust the metal poker at the log, sending a burst of sparks up the smoke-hole while Connor tried, and failed, to smother his laughter.

"I will see to these rabbits." He smirked. "My stomach is pressing against my backbone." But before he could retrieve them, Thaddeus seized them and, with a gentle shake of his head, carried them off to the kitchens.

"I must see if I may help," Meg said, leaving Connor to his smirking at her expense. She was eager to speak with Thaddeus about his discovery of her ability.

She need not have worried.

She found him in the kitchen, the rabbits all laid out for skinning. She knew he was aware that she'd followed him. He did not look up but set about preparing the rabbits.

"You need have no concern, mistress."

Meg sensed his gentle, reassuring thoughts.

"I am of the forest people. Ours is an ancient belief. We who believe in those such as yourself, offer only honor and respect."

Dannelore had told her of such people, whose beliefs were older than any other among the people of Britain. They believed in the powers of earth, wind, and fire.

For thousands of years they revered those among them with abilities such as hers, most often changelings who possessed the ability of thought, along with other abilities such as those of the healers or the seers whose visions foretold the future.

Many of them still lived very primitive lives, eking out an existence in the forest and remote places, carving their ancient symbols in the trunks of trees and erecting stone monoliths, and often being forced into hiding.

The greatest irony was that the religion of the mortals, which taught tolerance and mercy, showed neither to those who did not believe in it.

Thaddeus reached inside his tunic and retrieved a medallion which hung from a thin strip of leather about his neck. The medallion, made of stone, was oblong and polished satin-smooth. Ancient symbols were carved across the front and back of the stone. They matched the symbols of the crystal runes she had carried through the portal.

With a gentle smile, he assured her, *"Your secret is safe."*

Every day thereafter there was sufficient food; fresh game, baked maslin cakes, boiled eggs, cheeses, and fruit tarts prepared by one of the women who had returned to Monmouth under Thaddeus' watchful eye.

Except for Thaddeus, they rarely saw anyone else. Those who had returned kept to themselves in another part of the house. But that first afternoon she decided she and Connor could no longer sleep before the large hearth in the main room.

"What are you afraid of?" Connor asked when she insisted that he and Thaddeus carry the cumbersome tapestry up to the second-floor chamber, which was the only one that still had a door intact.

After Thaddeus had left, she explained, "I do not wish an audience when we are sleeping."

"Sleeping? What is there to see when we are sleeping?" he asked with maddening innocence. "You will have to explain it to me," he said, coming up behind her.

"You know very well what I speak of," she replied, laying out the thick fleece skins across the tapestry which had now become their bed.

"Then perhaps you will show me."

There was something in his voice that should have warned her, and something more in the heat of his hands as they closed over her breasts and he pulled her back against him.

"Connor . . . ! Someone will see . . . !"

"The door is closed," he whispered against the side of her neck. "There is no one to see."

Her nipples hardened and a dull ache began low inside her.

" 'Tis not possible," she whispered, sounding somewhere between surprise and certainty.

"What is not possible?"

Her head went back against his shoulder as her hands closed over his and her back arched as he gently squeezed her nipples and his mouth skimmed her shoulder above the gown.

"What is not possible?" he asked again.

"The heat," she whispered on a broken sound as her eyes drifted shut. Then she cried out softly as his teeth gently sank in at her neck. Sighed when the ties of her gown spilled through his fingers and he skimmed the gown past her hips. Burned as his hands found bare flesh.

"The aching." As his mouth skimmed down her back.

"The wanting." As his tongue traced her spine and his hands stroked her hips.

"The need." As he gently pulled her to her knees on the soft skins and then pulled her back against him and she felt the startling contact of bare skin against bare skin.

Her hands went back, seeking, needing to touch, finding him; sleek, smooth, and hard.

His hands circled over her breasts, and swept down, finding her, soft, silken, wet. Then thrusting inside her. Her head went back against his shoulder, and she moaned softly at the tender invasion.

Her body found the rhythm, her hips moving against his touch. But it was not enough, not nearly enough as her hands clasped his thighs and she whispered his name on a sound that was needy, wanting, and burned through him.

He took her back against him, his hands gliding over slick, throbbing flesh, then slipping between to torture her. She grew restless, her body reaching out for release from the aching, the wanting, the needing.

His lips caressed her shoulder as his fingers caressed her. His mouth found hers as his flesh found her. His tongue stroked between her waiting lips as he stroked inside her.

It was startling, stunning, and all pleasure as he entered her slowly, in rhythm with his kiss, his hands finding that rhythm at her breasts and then gliding low to torture her where his body claimed hers.

He held her imprisoned by that need and the wanting of him, unlike anything she had ever known. It burned through her blood as he burned her flesh. It moved in her soul as he moved inside her in a claiming that was sweet and hot.

Then he laid her over his arm, yanked her hips up, and thrust deep inside her.

She cried out as he found the ache within her and obliterated it, whispered huskily as his hands stroked low where her sleek flesh gloved his, and wept as he stroked her to a shattering climax and then joined her.

Afterward, Connor gathered her against him, pulling the warm fleece skins over them. Meg closed her eyes, absorbing the feel of him as if she could take him inside her as she did when they made love. It was only now, afterward, when Dannelore's parting warning and her own doubts crowded in, that she was forced to confront the grave step she'd taken.

To live among the mortals and learn from them was one thing. But to lie with a mortal, to open her heart, to learn his emotions and experience her own for the first time was not only unwise, it was dangerous.

Their lives were worlds apart. He was mortal, she was not, and neither could change that. He was bound by honor, pride, and loyalties that went blood deep. She was more deeply bound to her world, for she was the very essence of the power and light of that world, a creature who had escaped for a time and taken on mortal form.

She saw, felt, and experienced everything he saw, felt, and experienced. But her destiny lay with eternity. His was bound by the mortal world.

She had committed the greatest transgression, certain in her eagerness and naivete that when she had experienced life in the mortal world, all she had to do was return to her own. But nothing was as she had expected it. She had not anticipated the depth of the human emotions she had acquired . . . nor the possible consequences.

She levered herself up on arms braced across his chest. Those cool gray eyes looked back at her with a sated calm that found an echo within her. A peacefulness that she hated to destroy but must.

"What is it?" he asked, stroking a finger along the curve of her cheek. "Did you find me somehow lacking?"

She shook her head. "Nay and that is what concerns me."

"This is the first time I've ever been criticized for pleasing a maid."

" 'Tis not the pleasing that concerns me," she said, pushing away from him, trying to form the words just so, for she was aware that she was often too direct, too candid, and she instinctively sensed this might be a time for great care.

"Then what is it?" He rolled after her, gently seizing her by the wrist. "Did I hurt you?"

Impossible for her to lie. She shook her head again. "Nay," she whispered huskily with remembered pleasure. "It was most wonderful."

Amusement glinted in Connor's eyes. He smoothed a lock of hair back from her forehead.

"I suspect this is the moment when a young maid worries about her lost virtue." Amusement, because long before he ever bedded her, Connor knew he would never let her go.

She frowned at him, and surprised him. "Virtue lies within a person's heart. 'Tis not something that can be lost or taken."

"I agree."

And Connor found that he did. He realized now that it would not have mattered to him if she had lain with another man—husband or lover. The matter would have been if another man laid claim to her heart.

"Then if not your lost virtue, what is it that troubles you?"

She chose her words carefully.

"I know there are precautions that can be taken."

"Precautions? Against what?"

"A child."

His voice tightened as his fingers tightened about her wrist. "Is that what you're afraid of? That you might conceive a child?" There was pain there, laced with anger.

"It's been known to happen," she replied hesitantly, knowing that she'd angered him by the cold look in his eyes, hating herself for it.

He swung up, an arm braced on a bent knee as he sat beside her, his every muscle tense, the expression on his face hard, his eyes glacial.

"Do you believe me to be so much the fool, or so lacking in experience, that I did not think of it?" he demanded, then answered his own question, stunning her.

"Aye, I thought of it." His voice changed then, softening on a sound that reached into her heart, "And prayed for it."

"I do not understand." And for the first time in her life, with all her powers and abilities, she did not. It was madness.

"You know nothing about me, my family, where I come from." She tried desperately to make him understand, saying words he'd already said to himself.

"I may be promised to another . . ." She struggled to find the words. "There may come a day when I must leave this place."

"No."

It was as simple as that one small word.

"Connor, please . . ."

"No!"

He seized her by the shoulders and forced her back down onto the pallet of skins. He held her face between his hands as if he could force her to understand the words by pressing them into her brain.

"I have lost too much. My family, my home, my pride and honor. I will not lose more. Not again. Not this house, not these lands." His hands bruised and his mouth was urgent.

"I will not lose *you*." His tongue plunged into her mouth,

and she moaned as desire flooded through her with a quickening need.

She wanted to deny him. She wanted to tell him that he was powerless, that nothing he could say or do would change her fate. She wanted to deny the heat of his body as he stroked away each protest. She wanted to deny the answering heat of her own body. But she could not.

It *was* madness. A madness that claimed her soul, and she welcomed it as she welcomed him, opening to him, taking him deep inside her in a joining that was primal, searing, surrendering . . . surrendering her fate to a mortal she loved more than life itself.

She refused to think about the time when the weather would change and they would be forced to return to Caerleon, when Connor would once again take his place beside Arthur in a war that was not yet won, when she must eventually face her destiny. Instead, she hoarded time, holding on to it with both hands, savoring each moment with him.

She often awoke in the middle of the night, stirred from uncertain dreams. Even in sleep Connor protected her, pulling her into the sheltering safety of his body, wrapping her in a cocoon of warmth and love, then rousing from sleep to fill her with heat and passion.

Their days were filled with discovery, sharing, and laughter. She had never experienced such openness, such depth of emotion, such tenderness or playfulness. It seemed she had never been a child, all her time consumed with lessons to prepare her for the destiny that awaited her.

By day he taught her how to be a child. But by night he taught her how to be a woman.

"I am going outside," Meg announced as if handing down a royal proclamation.

"I cannot—will not—stay within these walls one moment longer."

They were in the upper-floor chamber where they spent most

of their days and nights, for it was much easier to warm the smaller private chamber than the hall below.

Connor sat before the fire tightening the string in the longbow he used for hunting.

"Did you hear what I said?" she demanded. He finally looked up.

"It would be difficult not to hear." He leaned forward as if sharing a secret. "Especially since we are the only two people in the room."

She was radiantly, gloriously beautiful with her cheeks aglow from the warmth of the fire. Light from the flames caught in the golden waves of hair that tumbled to her waist like rich satin as she stood before him, hands planted on hips and looking very much like some wanton wench who very badly needed tumbling in some meadow. Except that it was the dead of winter and the nearest meadow was buried under several feet of snow.

He had sensed her restlessness and felt it as well. It matched his own. But for other reasons. How long might it take, he wondered, for the two of them to reach the coast and then cross the channel to one of the southern kingdoms where they might lose themselves and never be found?

He longed for it, to simply disappear with her, to live out their lives in another place far away . . . far from here.

And that was the dilemma. He could not bear the thought of leaving this land, this place where the blood of his ancestors had bled into the ground, this Britain he had sworn to protect.

Nor could he face the possibility of losing her. And so he, too, put up imaginary walls of clouds and snow, and reasons not to return, against the day when there would be no more snow and no more reasons that he could give her or himself.

It had stopped snowing a few hours earlier and he'd considered hunting, even though Thaddeus and his people provided more than enough food for them. He needed time to think on what was to be done when they did return, when the war eventually ended, when her memory returned. But every moment away from her was a moment nearer that time, and he had put it off, spending the time mending the bow.

He set the bow aside.

"All right, but you cannot go out dressed like that."

She turned the skirt of the gown this way and that, inspecting it. It was finely made of a soft wool, and one of the women had said the color—a light blue—was very becoming to her.

She had a number of gowns now, added from those once worn by his brother's wife and two provided by the women who served Thaddeus.

"What is wrong with my gown?"

"There is nothing wrong with it. It is most becoming. I especially like the front." He gave her an appreciative look.

The bodice of the gown swept low, exposing the creamy swell of her breasts above a row of laces which often came undone at the coaxing of his ingenious fingers—and at the most inconvenient moments.

" 'Tis the matter of your shoes."

"I have no shoes."

"Precisely. Which is why I asked Thaddeus for these." From among the thick pile of furs that had been neatly rolled and set aside he produced a pair of boots.

They were finely made, sized to fit small feet, and lined with fleece.

"They are lovely," she exclaimed as she seized the boots and put them on, but the lacings proved far too complicated. He brushed her hands aside.

"I do not know how you have managed to survive this long. For someone who knows so much, it amazes me how little you know about such simple things."

She smiled as he efficiently laced the boots. "I have no time for such things. Besides, you do it much better."

He looked up. He highly suspected he'd been outfoxed. "Better is it?" he said in a low dangerous tone she should have paid better attention to as his fingers snaked up around her knee and then skimmed her thigh.

She squealed with outrage and danced away from him. "Oh, no. If we stay here now, we will never get outside today."

"Would that be so terrible?" He reached for her again, only to have his hands close over air instead of around a lovely waist.

"Not terrible," she conceded. "Merely untimely. There will be time later." Then she danced toward him, luxuriating in the feel of the fleece boots, and slipped an arm about his neck.

"It may take us hours." She teasingly skimmed her lips across his.

"Hours?"

She smiled. "Days."

He set her from him. "Then we'd best hurry."

He had another surprise for her, a long woolen mantle lined in fleece which he wrapped around her, discarding the thin woolen shawl she'd carried from Caerleon.

And with a wicked grin, he declared, "I want you warm when we return from our walk."

They walked along the low outer wall of Monmouth. Here the snow had been trampled down by the animals Thaddeus' people had brought with them and was not deep.

The clouds parted, bunching up against the distant hills and for a time the sun shone through with a tentative, elusive warmth as if to say, This will not last, enjoy it while you can. And they did, strolling along the wall to the edge of the orchards where Connor had hunted and then turning where the wall opened onto a kirkyard filled with ancient carved stones.

They stopped there before the newest stones, seven in all. Connor's parents, his sisters, and his brother and his family. The names of the two children were carved on one stone with a Latin inscription.

Connor knelt before the stones and bowed his head. Meg sensed that this was something deep and private and stood apart as he whispered prayers to his god. Then he made the sign of the cross, touching his forehead, each shoulder, and lastly his lips. He stood eventually, his thoughts known only to himself.

"You are not a believer?" he said quietly, startling her.

She searched for an appropriate answer. "I believe that such things are private, known only in a person's heart."

"Perhaps you believe as Thaddeus believes," he suggested, unaware how close he came to the truth, a truth he obviously gave no credence.

"The forest people believe in the powers of the sky and the earth."

She nodded. " 'Tis a very ancient belief that predates Christianity."

"There is only one true God," he replied.

"A tolerant, benevolent god who brings death to helpless women and children," she countered, for there had been no mercy for those who had died under Maelgwyn's sword . . . there had been no mercy for his family.

He looked at her thoughtfully. "Perhaps you believe in the god of the forest."

"Is not your god the god of all things, including the forest?"

"Aye, that is what I believe." He looked out across those upright stones. "What I must believe."

That was perhaps the greater truth, and she could not take it from him. Instead, she pushed it back, tucking it away in that far-off time and place that she refused to think of—the day when they must leave this place.

Connor insisted on checking the rabbit snares he'd set in the orchard. Meg went with him, exploring while he checked the traps.

The first snowball hit him squarely in the back. The second in the back of the head. There was no time to aim a third one, as he whirled around and charged toward her.

There was the snow that pulled at her boots. Then the boots themselves which she was not used to. Warm as they were, they were also clumsy and cumbersome, especially for someone used to moving by swifter means. Then there was the hem of her gown which tangled about her ankles, the heavy mantle which made escape impossible.

He caught her as easily as that one-eyed, curmudgeonly cat snared mice, dragging her down, and pouncing on her.

She kicked and squirmed in an attempt to get away, but like those mice soon lay breathless and panting beneath him.

"You did deliberately hit me with those snowballs," he accused.

She gave him a withering glare and remarked candidly, "They didn't suddenly sprout wings and fly."

"You will of course be punished," he calmly announced.

Her eyes narrowed. "While holding me down? How brave of you, Sir Warrior!"

"Of course," he admitted. "I'm no fool."

He pinned her knees with his leg while his hands found the opening of the mantle and promptly began tickling her.

"You are the lowest dog!" Meg squealed with laughter, momentarily unable to think of anything else to call him. Eventually she thought of something, and with good reason as he tickled her with far more seriousness.

"Lower than a dog!" she shrieked while trying to escape. "Lower than scum!"

She twisted and turned, but only managed to ensnare herself more.

"You'll have to do better than that," Connor replied, seeking new places to torment her.

She laughed wildly, her cheeks ablaze. "Lower than goat droppings!"

"That does it!" Connor announced with mock anger. "There will be no mercy now." And he found those new places to torture her as his hands skimmed up her thighs taking the hem of her gown with them.

"You're never cold," he marveled, amazed at her ability to stay so warm when all about them was frozen.

"Connor, no!" she gasped. "You cannot mean to . . ." Her laughter of moments before was swallowed on an awakening shudder as his hands found even warmer places.

"Can't I?" he growled against her throat.

"Someone will see!"

"What will they see?"

"Us!"

"If they do, then I will carve out their eyes."

Laughter bubbled back into her throat because she knew it was a hollow promise.

"What will become of poor Thaddeus? He is already short one eye." And then in a stern voice, "You must wait, milord."

"Why must I? I assure you I am quite ready."

He moved his hips against hers, and to her stunned surprise

she discovered that he'd removed the barriers of their clothes as his warm flesh nestled against hers. He was indeed ready.

"It is now *later*." He reminded her of their conversation before they'd left the chamber and of their agreed upon *appointment*.

"I meant *much later*." But her body betrayed her, welcoming him, gliding over him.

"That was not the agreement," he said huskily.

Her breath hitched, a soft, needy sound. "You are ruthless, milord."

"Always," he whispered against her lips as her sleek flesh enfolded him.

"Have mercy, milord."

"Never."

It was some time later when they returned to Monmouth hall, covered with snow like children, their clothes wet inside and out. And like children their faces were aglow, Connor could not keep from grabbing for her, and Meg could not keep from giggling.

They were met at the entrance by a stoical Thaddeus. They'd received word. Connor was needed at Caerleon. There were rumors that Maelgwyn and Aethelbert had united against Arthur. Even now Arthur was making plans for war.

Meg was stunned. She had hoped for more time in the foolish belief that perhaps they need never return. Now there was no more time.

Connor nodded, giving Thaddeus instructions for the provisions they would need for the following morning.

They did not take their supper with Thaddeus and the others in the kitchens, but instead had food brought to the chamber they had shared after that first night.

They spoke little, each retreating into their own thoughts. A fire burned at the brazier. The chamber was warm, the shutters closed against the storm which had rolled in after they'd returned from their walk, a drizzling rain which would not delay their departure but only added to the overall gloom and misery.

Meg sat on the pallet of furs before the fire and untied the yarn from the end of her hair. Then she felt warm fingers brush against hers as Connor seized the thick plait and began loosening the strands for her.

"The first time I saw you, your hair was loose about your shoulders." He leaned forward in the chair and slowly fanned the loose waves across her shoulder as Meg sat perfectly still.

"I thought I must be dreaming, that nothing could be so beautiful, so fine." He swept the thick curtain of her hair forward over her other shoulder.

"I feared I might never see anything so fine ever again." He cradled the heavy satin of her hair. His voice had gone low in his throat at the memory. "And I could not bear the thought of it."

Meg launched herself into his arms. They went around her in a fierce embrace, squeezing the air from her lungs. He buried his face in her hair.

"We will return," he vowed into the softness of her hair. "I will bring you back, and we will be wed. I promise you."

She silenced him with a hand against his mouth.

"No promises," she whispered, needing with all her heart to hear them, needing with all her heart to make those same promises to him and knowing she could not.

Her fingers trembled against his lips. She trembled in his arms. Her mouth trembled against his as she brought him down for her kiss.

"Tonight is all I ask."

Shadows quivered as a gust of air stirred the flames at the brazier. A shadow separated from the others, hesitated for a moment at the edge of the pallet, then slipped beneath thick fleece.

Her lover was not asleep. He struck with the instinct of a warrior and the speed of a demon as he seized her, rolled her onto her back, and pinned her into the thick fleece.

"Where have you been?" Jealousy glittered at his eyes and dripped from each word.

"Do you think you can keep me waiting like some obedient

hound for whatever spare crumbs you finally decide to throw my way?''

She was no match for his strength, but he was no match for her cunning.

''Obedient, I think, as long as the crumbs are called *wealth* and *power!*'' she reminded him. ''Now, take your hands off me.''

He shoved her away from him and rolled to his feet, anger etched in each angle and plane of his body as he strode naked to the table and splashed wine into a wooden goblet.

Morgana did not go after him. Not yet. After all, it was part of the hunt. And she did so like the hunt. And the capture. Most of all the capture.

She slowly rose from the pallet, her long dark hair draped about her body, but revealing a pale shoulder, a curve of hip, a length of thigh, a dusky nipple as she eventually joined him beside the table.

''I've been to see a man about the future,'' she told him, reaching for the goblet, her eyes gleaming darkly over the rim as she drank.

''You've been to see the conjuror,'' he accused. ''I can smell it on you. The herbs and leaves that witch brews for him. 'Tis the smell of ungodly things. I will have none of it!''

''Are you so certain?'' she asked.

He was certain of nothing, especially not her. Perhaps that was what had kept him coming back.

''Not this time.''

He heard the hesitation in his voice and knew she heard it too. She seemed to know everything. Even that Maelgwyn would join with Aethelbert against Arthur.

She slowly walked toward him and reached out. He watched her carefully. In the weeks since he'd first bedded her, he'd learned that she could be unpredictable. But instead of reaching for him as she usually did, she began stroking herself.

He watched through narrowed eyes, wondering at this new game of hers. Then she stunned him by skimming her tongue over one of her fingers, her gaze never leaving his. She made a low sound in her throat as she tasted herself. Then, her eyes widened as if with a sudden thought, she extended a slender hand toward him.

"Would you like a taste?" The thrill of the hunt soared through her veins.

"Damn you!" He refused to take her hand, refused that slick sweet nectar she offered, even as his flesh became engorged and stood up against his belly.

"Taste it."

And it was as if he could taste her, dark, sweet, forbidden, that taste just at his lips so that he instinctively drew his tongue across them. It wasn't possible, and yet he would've sworn he could taste her.

"Now," she whispered. And he seized her wrist, in a bone-crushing grasp that made her cry out. Then he did taste her, slowly, savoring the sweetness. But it was not enough, just as she knew it would not be.

He swore again as his gaze met hers, and he reached for her. He kissed her, fast, hard, and deep, trying to punish her, but he was the one who was punished. He could not seem to get enough of her.

There was no gentleness in him when he picked her up and threw her back down onto the pallet. No gentleness as he pinned her pale, slender legs. None when he sank his teeth into a pale breast or when he thrust inside her, fast, hard, and deep.

Morgana cried out with pleasure, her back arching with the thrill of conquest as he stabbed into her again and again.

She sensed when the moment of climax was near, and clung to him. Felt his body spasm and dug her nails in deep.

The conquest of Simon the Wise was complete.

Chapter Sixteen

They left Monmouth at first light. The rider who'd brought the message from Arthur, one of Connor's men, accompanied them.

Rain turned to ice by midmorning and made the journey slow, miserable, and treacherous. The road they'd traveled only a fortnight earlier had become a maze of ruts and sinkholes, making it difficult for the horses to keep their footing. Eventually they abandoned the road altogether and cut cross-country on a course Connor had traveled frequently as a child.

Meg rode before Connor in the wide saddle. It was an uncomfortable mode of travel, and even held in place by his arms and wrapped within the mantle he'd given her, she fought constantly to keep from being dislodged from atop the beast and tumbled into the mud.

By the time they stopped at midday to rest the horses, she was ready to take a broad axe to the beast except she was certain she didn't have the strength to lift one.

Then she discovered there were things far worse than being tumbled onto her backside in the mud. In fact, a mud bath was probably just what she needed to ease the soreness that had set in, making it almost impossible to walk. When Connor lifted her down from the horse she would have fallen if he hadn't caught her.

"It takes getting used to," he sympathized, holding her close until the feeling returned to her legs.

"I do not think I care to get used to it," she retorted. "I think the beast has earned a meal of star thistle when we get back to Caerleon. I vow he found every hole in the road."

Connor chuckled, laughter rumbling through his chest as he held her against him. For all the uncertainty of what lay ahead of them, the one blessed certainty was her ability to make him laugh when things were most miserable.

"I will recommend it to the groomsman."

"No need to bother," she replied. "I will feed it to him, myself. And what is that dreadful smell?"

She seemed a little steadier on her feet, and Connor steered her away from the horse and the warm cloud that had enveloped them before she recovered enough to do the poor beast real harm.

"Another fine characteristic of horses," he explained.

" 'Tis a wonder they have survived at all."

They ate a cold meal of maslin cakes, dried meat, and hard-cooked eggs washed down with a skin of wine that Thaddeus had packed for them. She had grown fond of him in her brief time at Monmouth. Just before they departed he had seized her hand, blinking back emotion at his one good eye.

"I had despaired that the young master would ever return to Monmouth," he had confided. *"His heart was so filled with anger, pain, and the hunger for revenge. You have brought him back to us. May the Ancient Ones keep you in their care, young mistress, until you return."*

Meg thanked him, stunned by his kindness. There had been a connection in his simple touch, the bond of ancient belief and something more that made her wonder if he suspected the truth about her.

It was the greatest irony that in this strange and foreign world that was not her own, she felt a warmth of kinship she had never experienced in her own world. She suspected it had to do with her newly acquired emotions.

After they ate, she and Connor walked a ways apart from the horses so that she might have some privacy. She had discovered that being jarred atop a horse for several hours created a dire need to relieve herself—another minor inconvenience of being transformed as a mortal.

On the whole though, she had to admit that the advantages outweighed the disadvantages. Especially when it came to things like newly found friendships, the warmth of a fire on a cold winter night, the intoxicating taste of mulled wine warming her blood, or those last lingering moments just before dawn when she reached for Connor that last morning together and lost herself in the shattering need to join her body with his yet again.

There was no doubt that was a far superior advantage!

"I would speak with you, Meg," he said when she emerged from a secluded place behind a hawthorn bush, observing the usual rules of propriety which mortals seemed so consumed with in some things and so lacking in others.

There was a seriousness in his voice that had not been there before, not even when they'd first returned from their play in the snow and found Arthur's message waiting for them. Afterward he had tried to lighten their last few hours together by keeping her preoccupied with other more delightful things.

Her gaze met his—solemn gray, the inky dark centers making it seem even more solemn. He had removed his heavy leather gloves and now reached for her, drawing her down onto a fallen tree trunk.

"I had hoped for more time," Connor quietly explained. "But now there is very little, and there are things we must speak of."

"Very well," she replied, uneasy at his sudden solemnity, trying to hold on to the earlier humor.

"You are probably fond of the horse," she went on, needing humor for what awaited them at Caerleon. "Therefore, I will not insist that the beast be made into a stew."

"Meg . . ."

"But I absolutely draw the line at ever crawling atop the creature after today."

"Be quiet!"

He had never raised his voice to her. It was something new, and she sensed new, underlying emotions, along with fierce determination. Whatever he had to say, he would not be deterred.

"We cannot know what lies ahead. I have renewed my pledge to Arthur. My duty as a warrior lies with him."

She said nothing, but laced her fingers through his.

"Monmouth lies in ruins. There is no one to rebuild it. There are only a handful to work the land. I have only my sword, my shield, and my name to offer. And this." He freed his hand from hers and removed a ring from his third finger.

She had seen it before. It was simply made of pounded silver, inscribed with Latin words and the emblem of a stag horn. It had never left his hand. Until this moment. He took hold of her hand once more.

"My father possessed many fine things, gold and jewels acquired by his father and passed down. But of all the things he possessed he valued this ring above all else. It has been given by every Duke of Monmouth to the woman chosen to be his wife. My father gave it to my mother, and I give it to you."

She tried to pull her hand from his, but he held fast, slipping the ring over her first finger.

"With this ring you are protected by my sword, my shield, all that I hold sacred." He closed his hand over hers.

This was what Dannelore had warned her of. This was what she could not foresee when she had left Caerleon with him. This was the tender trap she could not escape except with the truth.

And that she could not do, for she could not bear to see the look in his eyes when he learned who and what she was.

It was near nightfall when they reached Caerleon. They entered through a small side gate as darkness settled over the fortress and torches appeared at the watchtowers. John greeted them and had their horses taken to the stables.

"Dannelore will be relieved that you have returned," John said.

In the unspoken Meg sensed far more that went unsaid.

"Has something happened?" Even as she asked, she opened her thoughts and senses for some indication of what disturbed the man. But she could find no cause for it, except perhaps one. She experienced a sudden apprehension.

"Is Master Merlin worse?"

"Nay, no worse," John replied. "But the wounds he received at Amesbury still have not healed properly. It sorely vexes Dannelore. He eats little and hardly sleeps, and since receiving word that Aethelbert joins Maelgwyn against Arthur, he has worked himself near to exhaustion. She is deeply concerned for him."

Meg frowned. She and her brother were not like mortals who were plagued with illnesses and suffered from lingering injuries. Their powers protected them, and with his healing abilities, she could not understand why the wounds still lingered.

The trip from Monmouth had been long and tiring, and the day had steadily grown colder. Rain had turned to sleet which held the promise of snow before morning. The relative warmth of the main hall at Caerleon should have seemed welcoming, but Meg instinctively shivered as if some coldness of foreboding passed like a shadow across her senses.

The hound, Dax, who had accompanied them to Monmouth, seemed to sense it as well. Not even the inviting scent of food could entice him further. He hung back beside the large doors of the hall, eager to escape. At the first opportunity, he slunk out the door, preferring the icy wind outside to the icy feeling within.

How strange, Meg thought, for the hound was never far from Connor's side.

In spite of the grave news Arthur had received that Aethelbert now joined Maelgwyn, the usual noise and raucous conversations greeted them as they entered the hall. The evening meal had been served, and with so many now in residence at Caerleon, their arrival was not immediately made known.

She scanned the hall for sight of her brother, but could not find him. He was not at his usual place at Arthur's table. That place was now occupied by Arthur's sister, Morgana. Nor was he at any of the other tables.

Several of Connor's men who sat at tables nearby called out greetings. Word of their arrival spread quickly, and Meg's gaze locked with Morgana's.

In those dark eyes she saw a coldness of hatred Arthur's sister made no attempt to disguise. Meg instinctively shivered as if a cold hand had touched her soul and wished they could have remained at Monmouth.

"Come," Connor said. "Let us join the others. A draught of wine will ease the cold of the journey." His warm hand closed over her icy ones. He was unaware of the icy glare directed at them.

Unable to rid herself of the sudden uneasiness, Meg shook her head. "I must find Dannelore. Perhaps there is a curative she has not thought of that might be made for Master Merlin."

"Surely it can wait," he suggested. "We have only just returned."

"No! It cannot!" She bit back the sharpness in her voice, uncertain of what it was that made her uneasy.

But he had heard it. "Is something amiss? Are you unwell?"

Another had also heard it. Simon the Wise frowned as he joined them, bringing news that Arthur wished to meet with Connor.

He spoke in whispered tones, drowned out to everyone else by the sounds from the hall. Everyone except Meg. She heard each word as clearly as if he had spoken them to her, so heightened was her sense of hearing.

It had not been deliberate. She had no reason or need to eavesdrop on conversations between Connor and his men, yet she could not help it. It was an instinctive reaction. For some inexplicable reason her every sense was heightened to the point where each little sound was increased a hundredfold.

Her senses of sight, touch, and smell had increased as well. The sounds of the hall beyond were near deafening, a loud cacophony of voices, laughter, the simple sound of a mug suddenly set upon the table, the scrape of a blade across a metal trencher. All of it an uproar that exploded painfully inside her head. And within that chaos of noise she could still hear each individual voice, each conversation, each whisper. Her head began to pound violently as she struggled to control it.

The passage outside the hall was lit by dozens of torches, yet they all seemed to fade to darkness. The torch nearest at the wall suddenly spasmed and quivered as if smothered by some unseen current of air that almost extinguished it. And within that quivering flame she saw a growing darkness that pulsed with each pulse of the flame like an evil heart that grew steadily stronger until it seemed she could hear it beating.

"Megan . . ."

From somewhere distant she heard Connor's voice. When she looked at him it seemed as if he, too, faded in that growing darkness, oblivious as it closed around him, reaching out to her but from far away as if some great distance now separated them, pulling them apart.

Pain stabbed at her eyes as she stared at the torch, the pulse of the flame kept beating stronger until it became the sound of her own heart pounding in her head. She pressed her fingers against the side of her head.

Dizziness swept over her. She squeezed her eyes shut, trying to block out the pain, refusing to give in to it, pushing it back until she could breathe again and the pain receded.

"Meg!"

Urgent, nearer now, she heard Connor's voice. Then felt the warmth of his hand against her cheek.

"The torch," she whispered.

"Aye, 'tis a torch," he replied with a bemused expression.

"It nearly went out."

And with that same bemusement, "A frequent occurrence in drafty halls."

Meg realized that whatever she had seen and experienced, she alone had undergone.

The roar of chaos gradually receded until the sounds from the hall were normal once more. The darkness receded as well, escaping along the walls to hide in the shadows. All of the torches burned steadily at the wall. No currents of air threatened to smother them.

Both men were looking at her, Connor with a worried frown while Simon watched her with avid curiosity.

"No doubt you are tired. 'Tis a long journey from Monmouth," he commented, something in his tone drawing her attention. An ease of familiarity that had not been there before. Connor seemed not to notice.

"You'll feel stronger once we've eaten," he suggested.

" 'Tis nothing. It will pass," she replied. At least nothing that she could explain.

"I must find Dannelore. Perhaps there is a curative she has not yet thought of which might be made for Master Merlin."

"You're certain?"

"Aye, most certain," she replied. It was the only thing she was certain of at the moment.

He made no objection. Already she sensed his thoughts turning to the more urgent matters that awaited him. Yet the warmth of his fingers lingered at her wrist, and there was no disguising that parting look in his eyes—that flash of sensual heat that caressed her before he turned to join Arthur in the main hall.

Simon had seen it as well. She saw it in the expression on his face as his eyes narrowed with speculation. And felt it when he continued to watch her as she climbed the stairs to the second-floor chamber in search of Dannelore.

The changeling was not in the chamber they shared, nor had Meg seen her in the main hall. Yet she sensed her presence. Dannelore might be anywhere, for her duties in the kitchens as well as taking care of the wounded kept her busy. She would speak with her later, Meg decided, as she left the chamber.

As she passed the large chamber which Morgana now occupied, something stopped her—an essence of something, like a whisper across her senses almost as if someone had spoken or reached out a hand and lightly touched her sleeve.

"Who's there?" she called out, and on a sudden thought, "Grendel? Tristan? You may as well come out."

But neither her friend nor the boy emerged from the shadows

at the side of the passage, grinning back at her with their usual mischief. She slowly approached the chamber entrance.

It had been repaired, the hinges replaced and stout doors mounted with a large metal latch. She had never been one to eavesdrop. She knew Morgana was in the hall below, no one was in the chamber. Still, she was drawn to it.

She laid a hand lightly on the latch. It was cold as ice! No, colder. So cold that her skin burned and the bones in her fingers and hand ached. She jerked her hand away, frowning as she rubbed warmth back into her icy fingers.

"A frequent occurrence in drafty halls," she muttered, repeating what Connor had said about the torches. It seemed fitting that the latch at the door to Morgana's chamber was ice-cold. It suited her temperament.

She returned to the main floor below, but instead of seeking out the changeling in the hall or kitchens, she turned down the short passage toward the chapel and the monk's chamber that adjoined it.

The chamber was softly lit as she entered, with a fire burning at the brazier and an oil lamp on the table beside the high-backed chair. Also on the table was a trencher of food and a goblet of wine. The food was untouched.

Merlin sat in the chair beside the table, wrapped in warm fur skins. A heavy fleece covered his legs. He had dozed off, his chin resting on his chest, a parchment map with detailed notes on his lap. One hand anchored the map. He had obviously been studying it when he'd dozed off. His left arm rested on the chair arm, a writing quill dangling loosely from his fingers.

His chest rose and fell evenly. In the interplay of light and shadows he did not seem changed from the last time she had seen him. Perhaps John had exaggerated Dannelore's concern, she thought. But as she went closer she realized the trick the light and shadows had played on her.

Her brother had always been tall and lean, with an intense inner strength that seemed to burn through him. Though not as ruggedly built as Arthur or his battle-hardened warriors, his was a strength of speed and agility.

Now that leanness seemed almost spare, and there was no

outward sign of the fierce inner strength he had always possessed. And for the first time she noticed flecks of white in the dark, close-cropped beard that could not conceal the gauntness of his face or the sunken hollows at his cheeks.

Though her brother was older than she was, he was still a young man. Yet the sharp angles of his features which had once given him a fierce, lean handsomeness now stood out in sharp relief, as if she stared at a skeleton instead of the man. Fear rose sharp within her at the changes in him in only a fortnight.

She lightly touched his arm. He did not waken. She pushed back the sleeve of his tunic and gently closed her hand over his wrist. Then she slowly opened her senses and, through the connection of her hand at his arm, used her powers to seek out the malady that continued to plague him.

It was dangerous. She risked the possibility that he might remember the connection. But it was a chance she had to take, for obviously he continued to suffer from the wounds he'd received at Amesbury long after everyone else had recovered.

On a single thought she sent her power moving through his blood, pumping through his mortal heart into every part of him, a gentle current of warmth and light, a fusion of the essence they shared, carefully eluding his thoughts lest he remember.

She sensed the wounds that had not healed and the weakness that continued to grow with each passing moment, even as he slept and in spite of Dannelore's best efforts and his own healing powers.

She frowned. He was an immortal, impervious to the ailments and injuries mortals suffered. And yet he grew weaker with each passing moment. She felt it, though she could not find the cause.

He stirred then, perhaps sensing her presence moving through him. She hastily withdrew. But before she could withdraw her hand from his arm he suddenly seized her by the wrist.

His fingers clamped around her arm in a powerful grasp, stunning her. She wouldn't have thought him capable of it a moment before. Now pain shot up her arm and she feared her bones would be crushed.

One moment his eyes gleamed with a fierce, wild light, and an expression that burned between hatred and lust. Then, eventually, the calmness of reason and recognition returned.

His fingers loosened about her wrist, though without looking she knew they would leave marks. He slumped back into the chair, suddenly sinking into himself, his eyes squeezed tightly closed against the remnants of whatever it was he thought he had seen. Then he slowly opened them.

"Mistress Megan," he said with no doubt of it now. "Forgive me. For a moment I thought . . ."

She sensed none of the anger or rage of moments before, and wondered what had caused it.

"What did you think?" she said, gently laying a hand over his once more.

His head went back and his eyes closed once more. When he looked at her again, she sensed that he guarded his thoughts as carefully as she guarded hers.

"I thought you might never return," he replied with a faint smile. Not the answer she might have hoped for, but a careful evasion with pleasantries.

"Caerleon has missed your laughter and radiant beauty." He reached out, gently seizing the end of her plaited braid. "I have sorely missed our conversations. You are well?"

"Aye, milord."

He frowned. "Except for those bruises." He reached for her hand. "I regret that I was the cause of them. Let me take them away."

She quickly pulled her hand from his, but not without noticing the marks at his own arm just above the cuff of his tunic. They were small and evenly spaced. Then the cuff fell back into place, concealing them.

"A few bruises will cause no harm, milord," she assured him, staying just out of reach. Now that he was awake he might sense something in their contact, and she wished nothing to betray her.

"But might cause the Duke of Monmouth undue concern," he suggested, and she realized that he was well informed on the comings and goings at Caerleon.

She smiled. "Perhaps not. He is well acquainted with my stubbornness, and will probably assume it was of my own doing."

He chuckled. "I have missed your wit as well. Everyone at Caerleon seems sorely lacking in wit, especially troublesome healers!"

Dannelore made a sound entirely lacking in wit as she entered the chamber with a small pot of herbal medicant.

"Not nearly as troublesome as those I must take care of!"

"If your skills were all you claim, woman, I would not still be plagued with this weakness."

"If your skills were all you claimed, there would be no need for mine."

Before things escalated into open warfare, Meg took the herbal remedy and set it on the table.

"'Tis good to have you back at Caerleon, young miss," Dannelore said, their gazes meeting over the fragrant brew, and then she added, "Perhaps you will have more success than I have had." She glared over Merlin's head and made a face.

"A shrew perhaps." He considered, his sunken eyes glinting with humor. "It has possibilities, and there is definitely a resemblance."

His meaning was not lost on Dannelore as he contemplated other things he might change her into.

"I do not think John would be happy if you transformed her," Meg confided.

"He might thank me for it."

In spite of her concern over his condition, she couldn't help laughing at the idea.

"Then I will have to be careful where I step," she replied, smothering a smile.

"True enough," Dannelore snapped. "There's a lot to step in around here."

Their lighthearted banter covered her concern for her brother. She even persuaded him to take some of the herbal medicant.

Dannelore lit more candles about the chamber. Though Meg feared that he grew tired, he waved her concerns away with a thin hand.

"If you leave I will be at the mercy of this harpy. Have mercy. Stay for a while."

Dannelore brought another trencher of food, and Meg took her evening meal with him, asking about the recent news of Maelgwyn and Aethelbert.

Arthur now faced the combined strengths of two powerful, kings who each sought the throne. His only hope lay in uniting the rest of Britain against them—those who had waited for his return and believed Arthur to be the true king.

"Will he succeed?" Meg asked.

"He must, or Britain is lost. She will crumble to dust beneath the boot heels of those who would tear her apart. We will all be lost."

His last words seemed especially prophetic, and Meg wondered what greater meaning lay behind them. But it would have to wait for another conversation. There was now no opportunity to ask as the door suddenly opened and Morgana entered the chamber.

"Good eventide, milord." She greeted Merlin with an expression of faint surprise. "I was not aware you entertained visitors. My brother is deeply concerned about you. You mustn't tire yourself."

"Assure Arthur that I am not at death's door. In fact, I feel stronger than I have in days."

"Ah," Morgana said. "Then it seems perhaps the rumors about my brother's counselor are not true at all. He can be charmed by a beautiful girl."

"Morgana . . . !" There was an edge of familiarity in Merlin's warning. "There are times you go too far."

"Just as long as she does not go too far," Morgana replied in silken tones, and then added as though giving advice, "Connor is not fond of sharing his possessions before he has finished with them."

It was inevitable that they would eventually encounter each other sooner or later. Meg had hoped for later. She retrieved the fleece-lined mantle Connor had given her, laying it over her arm.

"I shall rely upon your experience and wisdom in such

matters,'' she replied, then turned and laid her other hand on her brother's arm.

''Good eventide, milord. I hope our conversation has not tired you.''

''I would not have missed it,'' he assured her. ''You must come back soon.''

Her gaze met Morgana's icy glare, and for a moment she was reminded of her experience outside Morgana's chamber.

''I would like that very much.''

Chapter Seventeen

Over the next few weeks Meg tried to keep that promise to Merlin, but much of his time was spent in counsel with Arthur and Connor.

At other times when he was in his chamber, studying the latest messages that had come in from about the countryside or the maps which had been made with the help of Connor and his men, he was not alone.

"Morgana spends a great deal of time with him," she commented to Dannelore one day after approaching the monk's chamber only to hear the woman's voice.

"As she has since she first returned to Caerleon." And then she added, "Or with Sir Simon."

Meg was stunned. "Simon?"

"Aye," Dannelore replied. "Took him to her bed the very day Lord Arthur and his men returned from the encounter with Maelgwyn."

The same day Meg had left with Connor for Monmouth.

"Does Arthur know?" It was her general understanding of things that a highborn woman was not allowed to wed with a commoner such as Simon. But Dannelore explained it had nothing to do with Morgana's choice of a husband.

"It was another she desired," Dannelore tentatively explained, and though it was unspoken Meg knew who it was Morgana had wanted for her husband.

Connor.

"She tried to get him into her bed. She hoped for an alliance, for Monmouth was once far richer than Caerleon. And there were others. 'Tis not the first time, nor the last," the changeling said with sadness.

"But Arthur will say naught against it. For all that they are sister and brother, they are strangers to one another. I sense he feels no small amount of guilt that he was not here to protect her and Lady Ygraine from Bishop Constantine. I suspect he hopes to settle her on one of the nobility to make an alliance."

"What sort of child was she?" Meg asked thoughtfully, for she had often wondered about that time when Arthur and Connor were children. Before her brother came to Caerleon.

"Indulged she was, by Lady Ygraine and the old duke. There were several men of noble birth she might have wed, but she would have none of it. Headstrong she always was and with ambitions of her own."

"Ambitions?"

Dannelore set aside the vial of herbal medicine she'd been mixing. "While Arthur was gone she enjoyed much power at Caerleon." She sighed and went back to her mixing.

"Now her home is in ruins and she is dependent upon Arthur. I think it does not sit well with her. She had once seen herself as mistress of all Caerleon."

A brother who was a stranger to her. A stranger who now claimed Caerleon for his own and who might one day be king of Britain.

Though Meg still found certain aspects of mortal emotions difficult to understand she understood the pain of loss. Connor had lost his entire family. It had made him the man he was. She smiled faintly as she remembered that she had once thought him cold, remote, ruthless.

But ice had a way of melting, that remoteness had been as near as a touch, and as for ruthlessness . . . Her smile deepened and something deep inside her quickened. Aye, he could still be ruthless. And she shivered with remembered pleasure at the ruthlessness with which he'd made love to her at Monmouth.

She shifted her thoughts back to thoughts of Morgana. How, she wondered, might the loss of everything she'd hoped for and assumed to be hers have affected Arthur's sister?

These were busy days at Caerleon, and there was little time for contemplating the reasons for Morgana's spitefulness, just as there was little time for other encounters with Arthur's sister. Except for the evening meal when they were at main hall, and then under increasingly crowded conditions, she saw little of Morgana.

But what fate had denied Morgana upon Arthur's return, she seized for herself as his sister, establishing herself as mistress of Caerleon. And Arthur, deeply immersed in the cumbersome and painstaking task of building an army that could defend against the combined armies of Maelgwyn and Aethelbert, seemed content to leave the matters of his household in her hands.

Meg escaped further confrontations by keeping herself busy in the herbal, a small niche very next to the kitchens, where she spent the better part of most days seeing to the needs of the people of Caerleon who came to her with a variety of ailments and complaints, not to mention the minor wounds Arthur's men acquired as they trained for the forthcoming campaign.

Only once had Morgana cornered her, demanding that she bring her an herbal tisane for a mild head discomfort. There had been no avoiding it, for Dannelore had been called to one of the huts to assist in the birthing of a child.

Meg had entered the chamber to find Morgana reclined upon a pallet covered with luxurious furs. In the steeped shadows that surrounded the pallet, she seemed to be sleeping. The chamber was redolent with the smell of sex and with some other darker essence that Meg could not name, but it had slid across her skin like an ominous presence.

Then she felt those eyes watching her and saw them in the shadows of the bed.

"You keep yourself well occupied these days, mistress,"

Morgana observed, her voice like the edge of a stone. "Or is it *someone* who keeps you well occupied?" she speculated.

She sat up on the pallet, the midnight back hair falling about her shoulders in undulating coils, and for a moment Meg was struck by the similarity of that midnight satin to a dark serpent.

She quickly prepared the tisane and gave the young servant girl instructions for brewing it, eager to escape that cloying scent and the darker one that had no name but seemed to have a life of its own.

Morgana's voice suddenly hissed a sound of surprise and some other venomous undercurrent, the sibilant warning of the serpent before it strikes.

Her hand snaked out, clamping over Meg's wrist like the strike of a serpent, so quick that Meg had no warning of it.

"You wear his ring?" Her nails had dug in, like the fangs of a serpent.

"What could he possibly see in a creature such as you who has no name, no family, no memory, nothing to offer him?"

Meg quietly but with unmistakable warning told her, "Take your hand off me."

Morgana smiled, a cunning expression on her face, and tightened her grasp, her nails breaking the skin, sinking in.

A coldness moved under Meg's skin, into her blood, spreading up the length of her arm. Morgana had no intention of releasing her. Perhaps she intended to break her wrist. Or was it something else?

She did not wish to use her powers. But she had no choice, for Morgana was much stronger than she was. On a single concentrated thought, she focused the power within her and broke Morgana's hold on a burst of energy that made Morgana cry out in pain.

Morgana stared at her with a mixture of rage and incredulity.

"Do not ever touch me again," Meg softly warned, bending close so that only Morgana could hear.

Once outside Morgana's chamber she took a few minutes to regain her composure. She deeply regretted that she'd been forced to use her powers, but Morgana had given her no choice.

The woman's unusual strength had surprised her. Then she looked at her wrist which still bore the marks of it.

Deep red crescents had cut into her flesh. Even though the marks had grown pale and all but disappeared, she would not soon forget the cruelty of those nails digging in, nor the coldness that had spread through her blood.

The experience with Morgana had stirred a vague memory that lay half-formed. Then, like the marks, it disappeared. In the days that followed she was wary and watchful against another encounter. But Morgana wisely kept her distance.

Just as the demands of the forthcoming campaign occupied all of Arthur's time, so, too, they occupied the time of those he relied upon to lead his army—her brother, the men who had returned with him to Britain, and Connor.

The time they had spent together at Monmouth seemed like a dream that might never have happened.

She rarely saw him, and then there was only time for a hasty greeting.

"You are well, mistress?"

"Aye, well enough, milord."

Or a few, brief stolen moments before he was called back to duty.

Well enough, yet Meg was both relieved and saddened when it became certain she had not conceived his child.

The monthly flux, which Dannelore had explained to her and kept a watchful eye for, came the week they returned to Caerleon.

She discovered there were a few minor details the changeling deliberately failed to mention about the curse mortal women were forced to endure. Not the least of which were the tears which came too easily and at the least provocation.

" 'Tis for the best," Dannelore said consolingly, but with obvious relief she made no attempt to disguise.

"If it is for the best, why do I feel so dreadful?" Meg demanded, trying to understand.

Dannelore tried her best to explain. " 'Tis more than what you feel, child. He is mortal. You are not. Such things cannot be."

"You are not mortal," Meg pointed out with uncharacteristic peevishness that confused her and made her even more irritable. She never would understand mortal emotions. And she wasn't at all certain she liked them. At least certain ones.

"I am not one of the chosen. That is the difference. His destiny is at Arthur's side. Yours lies in another world. The world of the Ancient Ones." Her voice softened. "It began as a game. You must now see the folly in it . . . the impossibility of it."

Before she could continue, Meg held up a hand. Her emotions were dangerously close to the surface, and she was perilously close to tears.

"I do not wish to discuss it."

She spent the rest of the day lost in her own thoughts, unable to deny the truth of Dannelore's words, unable to deny the depth of the emotions that churned within her.

Tristan helped ease her sadness. Adorable and mischievous, with far more spirit and daring than caution, he'd taken to training with Connor's men. The smithy had forged a small sword from a much larger one with a shattered blade. It was more suitable to his short stature, and Connor had given him a small shield. Tristan had shown both to her with great pride.

"I am going to slay Maelgwyn and Aethelbert," he announced to her in the yard when she had gone to watch him practice.

"Both?" she asked with mock surprise, taking great delight in the child. "And leave no one for Arthur?"

"None," he announced with the bravado and self-assurance of a true warrior. Or a young boy who knows no better, she mused, thinking the two had much in common.

Only she was aware of the sadness that plagued Tristan's dreams at night—a sadness of loss and the horror of the death of his family—that crept back in unguarded moments to haunt his sleep.

He and Grendel had taken to sleeping in the small antechamber that adjoined the chamber she and Dannelore shared. Grendel had become her self-appointed guardian when he was not entertaining Arthur's men with feats of magic and tales of adventure. He had also become Tristan's faithful companion.

Perhaps, she mused, they were drawn together by their common size, although in a few years Tristan would tower over most men.

As she watched him play at mock battle, she heard a familiar voice amidst the grunts and groans of warriors and the crash of metal on metal as Arthur's men tested their strength against one another.

"Now I see what has distracted my bravest warrior."

Deeply timbered, the words with that blend of coolness and bemusement, were like rough velvet across her senses. She slowly turned around as Connor walked toward them.

From the moment she first saw him in the forest it seemed some invisible bond connected them, a gossamer thread that found its beginning in that cool gray gaze and tugged at some fated destiny deep inside her.

It was there now, reaching out with invisible hands, strong hands, heated hands that reached deep inside her and took hold of that destiny along with her heart.

Troubled by doubt and the turmoil of uncertain emotions, she wanted to look away but could not. Wanted to protect her foolish, mortal heart. But could not.

The sunlight caught at the tips of his hair and gleamed in those cool gray eyes. She remembered those eyes with other, golden lights, the fire of passion turning them to molten silver when he'd joined his body with hers, turning her to molten silver.

He was just a man, she told herself. A mortal. Weak, vulnerable, not immune to pain and death.

But she was weak, vulnerable, and at that moment not immune to the pain of seeing him again and wanting him again. And that was a little like death.

She reined in her chaotic emotions. *Impossible,* she reminded herself. Yet the word slipped away from her with every step he took toward her.

His leggings and boots were covered with mud from the practice yard. In spite of the sharpness of the day, he'd peeled off his tunic and moisture beaded across his chest and shoulders beneath the welcoming warmth of a rare winter sun.

There were splatters of mud across his belly and up the lengths of his arms, a splatter of dried blood at his shoulder where a blade had slipped his guard and nicked the flesh. He was carelessly unaware of it, wearing the wound like a badge of honor.

She pressed back the need to touch his sweat-slick flesh, to clean the blood from the wound, and then press her mouth tenderly against it in a healing kiss.

Dannelore's warning whispered to her. *Impossible.*

"You must hold the sword just so," he explained to Tristan with the calm demeanor of a wise teacher, but it was her gaze his found and held with unrelenting, ruthless heat over the child's head.

Impossible. She clung to that word, knowing in her logical mind that it was true.

"Straighten your wrist," Connor continued. "Think of it as an extension of your arm. It reaches where you cannot."

His voice reached where he did not. Into her soul.

Impossible.

Then he stood behind Tristan, his large hands gently closed over smaller ones, moving with him step for step, familiarizing Tristan with the weight and balance of the sword, letting the boy feel the movement of his body, the power of each thrust that controlled the movement of the sword.

"You must command the sword," Connor explained. "Or you may very well be its next victim." He released the boy's wrist which bobbled, the sword out of control.

"It is easy enough now for your adversary to take it from you and use it against you. Do you see?"

Tristan nodded.

"Now you must practice."

Tristan made a face and balked. "I know how it is done." And he made a perfect lunge and thrust to show that he did indeed understand. Even with the unfamiliar weight of the sword and his untrained muscles, he showed remarkable skill.

"I do not need to practice."

Connor realized they clearly needed a meeting of the minds.

"Look across the practice yard," he instructed as he squatted down before the boy, putting them on an even height.

"Do you see? Over there. The Viking, Radvald?"

Tristan's eyes widened and he nodded. Of all Connor's men, Radvald was the one who commanded the most respect and fear, even from a reckless young boy.

"He is the oldest warrior," Connor explained. "Old enough to be my father."

There was something in his voice that drew Meg's gaze back from the boy, a subtle lowering of it at the word *father,* and Meg sensed a tightening of old emotion within him, the emotion of a young boy for the father he had loved.

"He first held a weapon in his hand at a lesser age than yourself," Connor continued. "And all these years later, he practices harder and longer than any other man. Why is that so?"

Tristan thought about it for several moments, and then replied with absolute certainty, "Because he is old and addlepated."

Meg made a small strangled sound as she swallowed back laughter and received a warning glare from Tristan's teacher, who seemed to have equal difficulty maintaining his own composure.

"Do you think you could best him?" he asked Tristan.

"Aye! He is not nearly so fast as the others."

"It is not speed that wins a battle," Connor counseled. "Radvald knows that he is not as young as the others. His strength is not what it once was, but what he lacks in youth and speed, he makes up for in cunning and endurance. And he stands the field after younger men have fallen around him. It is because of his cunning and endurance that he fights at my side in every battle."

Tristan thought about that for a moment. "Then I would like to have cunning and endurance."

Connor let out a sigh of relief that the lesson had taken the direction he intended. "If so, you must practice every day until you are as cunning and strong as Radvald."

"I can do that," Tristan declared, squaring his shoulders

and setting off to do what few others dared—challenge the old Viking.

"You have a way with him," Meg said, watching Tristan redouble his efforts with the sword as he swung at Radvald. "The way of a father, I think. Or what a father should be."

His gaze locked with hers, no longer cool, but shades of gray, heated, searching.

"And is all well with you, mistress?"

In the careful question she sensed the deeper question that lay beneath it.

"Well enough, milord," she replied.

"I have seen you so rarely these past weeks I was concerned you might have taken ill."

"Nay, milord," she assured him. "There is no malady." Only the malady of her heart. She sensed an unmistakable disappointment that she had not conceived a child in their time at Monmouth. And oddly, an answering ache of emptiness within herself that no child grew there now, conceived in passion.

She pushed back the feeling.

Impossible.

"I have seen *you* so rarely these past weeks," she said, forcing a smile past the unexpected sadness. "I was concerned you might have found other company preferable, or another to warm your bed."

He flashed her a smile—a smile of remembered moments at Monmouth when he had wrestled her into the snow and tickled her until she cried. Then it shimmered with the heat of the moments that had followed. Frantic. Needy. Wanting.

A rare smile for there was little cause for it these past weeks as they all prepared for the forthcoming war against Maelgwyn and Aethelbert. Only that morning yet another messenger had arrived carrying a dispatch.

Connor made a sound somewhere between that shared memory and that shared need. "The *company* I share fills this yard," he gestured across the muddied practice yard with snow piled up about the high stone walls and the men who honed their skills with their weapons.

"My bed is in the stables, and my companion is my horse." A sound of disgust. "But I swear the beasties are preferable to these louts. They are most foul to sleep with." His gaze darkened.

"I much prefer a softer, sweeter heat."

Because it was safer than the unsettled emotions that churned inside her, she laughed as she imagined him and his men bedded down with the livestock.

"What of Radvald?" she asked, for the man was known for his aversion to horses. A true Viking, he much preferred the firm deck of a ship underfoot, or the solid feel of the earth, to the back of a horse.

"Especially Radvald," Connor quipped. "He has developed an affection for sheep." He rolled his eyes. "I do not even want to think about *that.*"

She smothered laughter behind her hand as Radvald approached. By the expression on his face it was obvious he'd heard at least part of their conversation.

"Sleepin' among the woolies, I'm warmer on a cold winter night than the rest of you. And they do not smell near as foul." As he approached, they realized he dragged something behind him. Tristan.

"I believe this belongs to you." He pulled the boy forward and thrust him toward Connor.

"He has a bit to learn about the sword—and the opponents he challenges." Radvald's eyes twinkled in spite of his fierce expression.

"The lad shows a bit of promise."

A bit indeed, Meg thought, as she saw the nick at Tristan's chin.

With a grumble Radvald turned on his heel. "Come back and see me, boy, when you're taller and you know how to use that pigsticker."

Meg gently took Tristan in tow. "Come with me. We must see to that wound."

His embarrassment and humiliation momentarily forgotten, Tristan brightened.

"Will I need stitches?"

Meg smothered a smile. Why is it, she wondered, that boys—all boys no matter their age—seemed to flaunt stitches and scars like badges of honor?

"Aye, so it seems."

Tristan whooped with delight.

It was a wonder to her how he could be excited about a wound that was bleeding profusely and must no doubt be painful. But neither she nor Connor pointed out the fact that this first battle had been in the practice yard at Caerleon, not against a true adversary but against his own man.

As she turned toward the main hall with Tristan, Connor's warm fingers brushed her wrist.

"Meg . . ."

In the sound of her name, low, like rough velvet, she heard something else, along with the need to do more than touch. The laughter was gone from his eyes. There was another expression in them, something resolute and ominous.

"We leave in three days' time."

The messenger who had arrived that morning. She had sensed it and felt it.

"So soon?" She heard the fear in her own voice, a fear that came from uncertain visions she could not clearly see.

"I am bleeding!" Tristan called out, demanding her attention.

Between her and Connor the air quivered with unspoken words, unspoken needs.

"Will I see you at the evening meal, milord?"

He nodded. "Arthur will meet tonight with the nobles afterward to secure their loyalty and make his final plans. I had hoped . . ." It went unspoken as Tristan called out again impatiently.

But she heard it, and felt it, that need to hold on to what they had shared at Monmouth. He had wanted to return. And she knew she would have gone with him if there had been time.

"Meg!"

She heard a quiver in Tristan's voice that had not been there before as his courage slipped a notch. She had no choice but to follow. But she felt Connor's gaze all the way back to the main hall, and fear knifed through her in tiny slices of pain.

Three days.

Her thoughts scattered. She did not see the man waiting for her.

"Good day, mistress."

As she stepped into the dimly lit hall, she felt something brush her sleeve. Then a gliding, possessive heat as a hand closed over her arm.

Stunned by the unexpected encounter and a faint, sibilant warning that slid along her senses, Meg jerked back with alarm.

"Forgive me, I did not intend to frighten you," Simon the Wise apologized as he stepped from the shadows. He glanced down at young Tristan and added, "Or the boy."

She was reluctant to admit that he had. Not only that, but she was completely unaware he stood there before stepping through the door.

"You did not frighten me," Tristan informed him, frowning up at the tall warrior.

"Ah, another brave consort who has fallen at your feet," Simon speculated with a glance at the boy.

"He was injured in the practice yard," Meg explained. "The wound must be tended."

He caught her unaware again, seizing her hand and covering it with his.

"If only a wounded heart healed as quickly."

She frowned at the absurd comment. "Surely you have found the cure, Sir Simon. 'Tis said Lady Morgana possesses rare healing skills."

A keen glint leapt into his eyes. He leaned closer. "The cure is rare and hard to find, impossible to live without."

"Be careful of rare cures," she cautioned, looking down at her trapped hand, then extricating it. But not before she saw the three small wounds at his wrist, just below the sleeve of his tunic. His gaze followed hers, and he withdrew his hand.

"Such rare cures can often be more dangerous than the wound," she said thoughtfully, wondering about those precise, evenly made wounds, not unlike the ones she'd received in her encounter with Morgana.

Standing between them, Tristan looked from one to the other, not at all certain of the meaning of the conversation but doubtful that he much cared for it.

"I am bleeding!" he announced, removing his hand from his chin to show that he was indeed bleeding all over the place.

"Excuse us, milord," Meg said, "but I do not want him to lose any more blood."

Simon reluctantly stepped aside. "Will you then see to my wounds, mistress?"

"I see no wounds that need my skill."

As she angled young Tristan across the hall, where even now Arthur sat in counsel with Merlin, she knew Simon dare not follow, and she saw a flash of color at the bottom of the stairs to the second-floor chambers.

It was brilliant scarlet, the color of bright blood. Then it was gone.

"Men!" Dannelore exclaimed when she finally put the finishing touch to Tristan's chin, which quivered slightly.

There had been no tears as she applied the neat row of stitches required to close the wound. Although there was a moment when Tristan's eyes grew big and round when he first glimpsed the needle she intended to use.

"Do not look at it," Meg had told him. "Hold on to my hand and squeeze as hard as you like."

"I am not afraid," he declared with false bravado. "I have my lucky coin."

"Lucky coin?" she asked, smothering a smile for she knew there was no such thing as luck. Tricks, magic, conjurements, and spells to be sure. But not luck. And coins were rare. Things were usually purchased through trade or barter. Rarely was there the exchange of any currency, for no uniform currency existed in Britain.

He dug in the pocket of his tunic and retrieved a medallion that measured the palm of his hand and was suspended from a thick chain. It was made of gold, hammered flat, and embossed with twin ram horns surrounding a fierce mask.

"Where did you get this?"

"Found it."

"Where?"

He looked past her to the door as if fearing that someone lurked there. Then he leaned close and whispered, "Lady Morgana's chamber."

She was stunned. "You should not have been in there."

"She left the door open."

A thief in the making. She shook her head and wondered if Grendel had had anything to do with this.

"You may have it if you like," he said with a shrug and a generosity uncommon to thieves. "If it was truly lucky I wouldn't have been injured."

She couldn't fault his logic there, knowing such things as lucky coins did not exist. And she thought it safer if he did not have the medallion in his possession.

"I will try to return it without her knowing of it," she told him, forgetting about the medallion as she slipped it into her pocket.

"Now, I promise it will not hurt if you hold my hand."

And he did, her hand almost turning blue. Through that fierce, small grasp she used her powers to ease his pain and discomfort.

He looked up at her in surprise when it was all over.

"It didn't hurt at all." He frowned at her. "Why are you crying, mistress?"

"Because I'm glad you're better now."

He shook his head. "You make no sense." And he immediately picked up his sword and returned to the practice yard, the hound Dax wagging after him.

"He would have fainted dead away if you had not taken away the pain," Dannelore said with a shake of her head, then repeated, "Men! Bah! They have no brains and they are completely helpless. I cannot understand why we let them live."

Meg arched a brow. "Including John, of course?"

She was aware that just the day before John had informed

Dannelore that he intended to leave with the rest of the men to fight with Arthur against Maelgwyn and Aethelbert in the forthcoming battle. The changeling had been in a peevish mood ever since.

"All men!" Dannelore included him in her tirade, but Meg knew that fear was the true emotion that lay beneath the angry words. It was a fear they shared.

The main hall at Caerleon was even more crowded that night. Lord Tarsan and the Duke of Sorgales had arrived late that afternoon with their men. They were now encamped within the walls of Caerleon, along with other nobles, warriors, and knights who now swore their fealty to Arthur. Among them were the knights Sagremore, Bors, Sandor, Cadog, and Gaheris.

But the atmosphere was hardly festive. The nobles, none powerful enough to stand alone against Maelgwyn and Aethelbert, faced the loss of their lands, titles, and their entire fortunes unless they joined Arthur.

They had brought with them war chests, wagons of supplies, armaments, horses, swordsmen, archers, and warriors who all had their own stories to tell of encounters with the cunning Maelgwyn or Aethelbert who was called Aethelbert the Red for the blood of the countless men he'd killed.

Over a lengthy supper, platters of food were brought, followed by desserts of sweet cakes swimming in peach sauce, and the Duke of Sorgales had brought casks of wine from the Loire Valley on the continent, taken in trade at his coastal ports. The narrow spaces between the long tables were crowded with a steady stream of serving women who moved back and forth between the kitchens and the main hall.

On this particular night Merlin occupied his usual place at Arthur's side. Like a queen at court, Morgana sat at her brother's other side, dressed in a flowing scarlet gown—the color of bright blood.

As Morgana took her place, she demanded that Connor be seated beside her at the long table, forcing Simon to take a place farther down, which placed him directly across from Meg.

His displeasure at the place he'd been forced to take—a reminder of his subservient status to Morgana—turned to open appraisal as Meg was forced to take the place across from him.

"Good eventide, mistress," he said with narrow-eyed pleasure. "We meet again."

His gaze then angled down the length of the table to where Morgana sat with Connor.

"It seems we have been cast aside, at least for tonight. And in a matter of days, we ride to war. So little time."

Her glance followed his down the length of table. Her look met Morgana's, and in that dark gaze she saw unmistakable triumph.

She watched as Morgana leaned against Connor and whispered. He made some response. Then Morgana placed her hand on his arm, an intimate, claiming gesture, her mouth curving in a sensual smile as she lifted a goblet of wine.

"Perhaps not," Meg commented.

It was beneath her she knew, a petty trick, a simple conjurement. Something far more suitable to Grendel's skills. And completely irresistible.

The goblet suddenly wobbled unsteadily, slipped from Morgana's fingers, and the entire contents spilled down the front of her gown, deep crimson staining bright scarlet.

When Morgana reached for a cloth to soak up the wine, her hand bobbled the nearby decanter and very nearly tipped it over as well. And when she abruptly stood, calling for one of the serving girls, her heel caught in the hem of her gown and she tripped.

If Connor had not caught her she would have pitched over backwards and landed on her backside right before her brother and the assembled nobles. She made as graceful an exit as possible, two young servant girls trembling in her wake.

" 'Tis a pity," Simon commented with sarcasm.

"Aye, a pity," Meg commiserated. A pity she had not thought of it earlier.

" 'Tis almost as if ..."

Her gaze met his. "As if, milord?"

"If one believed in such things ..."

Meg refilled his goblet. He sipped the wine, certain it was the wine that burned through his thoughts. Whatever it was he had been about to say was suddenly forgotten.

Meg refilled his goblet several more times and he continued to drink, draining the goblet each time.

"Come, my friend." A warrior prodded Simon sometime later when it was apparent he'd had more than enough to drink. "Let us leave." He winked and indicated the cask of wine tucked under his arm. "We will find a darkened corner and a willing wench."

He eventually persuaded Simon to quit the table. But before he left Simon leaned across, his face very near Meg's. He seized her chin and planted a crude kiss on her mouth.

"I prefer unwilling," he snarled with drunken pleasure.

His companion finally dragged him away, and Meg drained her goblet of wine to rid herself of the foul taste of him.

The evening meal had ended, Arthur and the nobles, along with Connor, had retreated to the round counsel table.

Morgana eventually returned. The servant girls returned with her, their heads hung low as they slipped off to the kitchens, but not before Meg glimpsed a dark bruise that closed one girl's eye and wished she had done more than spill wine on that scarlet gown.

Morgana was forced to join the wives of the lesser nobles rather than intrude at the round counsel table, for the conversations were now of the forthcoming campaign and had turned most serious.

It did not sit well with her, her slender nails raking across the surface of the table in frustrated stabs as she was forced to endure the gossipy conversation of the women. But Morgana was not so bold or unwise as to interfere. Instead she sat at a distance, her hungry gaze fastened on Connor.

At the round table the Duke of Sorgales proposed a toast and with great solemnity pledged his fealty to Arthur. It was an important and crucial step, for it acknowledged Arthur's power as supreme commander over the armies of the other regions. The other nobles stood, and one by one, they, too, pledged their loyalty.

The evening grew long. The wives of the nobles took their leave and retired with their servants. The warriors and those recently knighted by Arthur drifted off to seek their pallets, the warmth of a lover as time grew short, or an encounter with one of the willing serving girls.

Meg felt a stab of despair. She had hoped she and Connor might find some time together. He had glanced at her often, and she had seen those same thoughts in his eyes. But he was deep in conversation with Arthur and the nobles.

Simon saw her as she stood, a shimmering golden flame in the dimly lit hall as oil lamps were doused one by one and others made their way to their pallets. And the hunger to possess burned through him.

Meg stepped carefully over sleeping warriors who had made their pallets at the edge of the hall. Loud snoring was heard along with furtive whispers and an occasional feminine giggle.

As she stepped discreetly around others who slept, two shadows came together under a fleece blanket, pleasure taken quickly in the darkness beyond the reach of light from the fire at the hearth. And she thought of that brief time at Monmouth when she had spoken to Connor of things she had seen in the shadows.

As she reached the edge of the hall and stepped into the passage across from the chapel a hand closed around her wrist. She was pulled across to the chapel and then into a secluded alcove.

A hard, muscled body pinned her against the wall, a powerful hand anchored her arm behind her back while another smothered the startled sound she made.

"Did you think you could escape so easily?"

Chapter Eighteen

"Did you think I would *let* you escape?"

That first feeling of alarm became one of sensual heat where his hands touched.

Hard hands, desperate hands. Hands that shook with need and something else as Connor released her and his fingers skimmed across her cheek. Something tender, longing, and a little bit anxious.

He told himself a touch was all he wanted as his blood burned through his veins at the feel of her, her body soft and yielding beneath his hands, beneath his body.

But it was not enough.

He told himself a taste was all he needed as he skimmed his mouth across hers, then forced his way past the startled sound she made and tasted soft, broken sighs.

Not nearly enough.

Impossible. The word quivered in the air between them.

She breathed him, tasted him. Her heart tumbled and her thoughts scattered like ripples across the surface of still water, impossible to hold.

Then it was all about some darker, more primal need.

His body pinned hers, his hands plunging back through her hair, fisting in shimmering gold satin.

He trapped her mouth—sweet, tender, needy—and plunged into velvet heat.

His hips pinned her hips, hands fisting over layers of soft fabric until he found her—wet, quivering, wanting—and, freeing himself, plunged into her.

It was all about want and need and hunger. Wanting to feel alive, needing it, hungry for it. From the moment she took that first fateful step through the portal until now, pushing back all logic, all reason, all doubt, reaching for him.

He was ruthless, brutal. She was just as ruthless, just as brutal, holding back nothing, meeting each thrust with a primal need to seize life and hold it within her.

A mortal life. A child. His child.

And that need, whispered in fevered words, shimmered at her fingertips as she tore open his tunic, burned at her lips as she pressed her mouth against the scar at his shoulder, then shattered when he poured himself into her.

He held her tight against him. Long past that moment when she cried out against his shoulder, past the moment when her slender body shuddered against his, past the silent tears that spilled down her cheeks, until her breathing whispered gently against his heart.

The sounds beyond those walls ceased to exist; someone passing on the way to the chapel, another stumbling toward the stairs, hasty whispers, and dark promises as time slipped away like the beating of a fragile heart.

Then he pulled her from that alcove and, holding her tight against him, left the hall, crossed the snow-crusted yard beneath a moonless sky, and slipped into a secluded corner of the stables.

There were no words spoken, nor any needed.

He made a pallet of soft furs spread over thick straw. She unlaced the bodice of her gown. He spread his mantle across the gate to give them shelter. She edged the gown from her shoulders. And when he turned to tell her that he had wanted more for her, that he had wanted to take her back to Monmouth, she let the gown drop to her feet.

"Have mercy," he whispered, his throat tight as he remembered how she had once breathlessly begged him with just those words.

"Never," she whispered, the same answer he had given her then, as she went to him now.

Merlin sat in the chair before the brazier in the monk's chamber. He could never seem to get warm. The wound at his side ached. He ached.

Long hours had been spent with Arthur and the nobles. Fatigue pulled at him, made his thoughts slow, dulled his senses. Like a drug that seeped through his veins, squeezed at his heart, and gnawed at his soul.

He felt that stirring of air, heard the creak of the door closing, sensed another presence.

She was there, in the shadows. A shadow within shadows.

He heard the whisper of soft satin, saw the bright flash of color as it puddled at the floor of the chamber.

She slowly walked toward him. Her hair was as dark as night against the bloodless alabaster of her naked body as she came to him.

He rose from the chair, fighting her with the last of his strength. Her soul was as dark as the depths of hell as she claimed him.

"You must come, quickly!" Grendel insisted, pulling at Meg's hand.

"What is it?" She looked up with a distracted smile, from combing the last of the straw from her hair. The night before with Connor a sweet-sad memory that she tried to hold on to.

She'd stayed with him until just before dawn and then left while he still slept so that there would be no parting words, no talk of what he faced when he left with Arthur, no wistful words of what he wanted or promises that might never be kept.

And she had returned to the main hall unseen, slipping past the guards at the door like morning mist. Up the stairs with no one the wiser, and had returned to her own bed just as she had heard Dannelore and John stirring awake behind the partition that provided meager privacy so that there would be no questions, no recriminations, no reminders of what was impossible.

But Grendel persisted, forcing her to tuck the memory back into her thoughts.

"You must come!"

There was an urgency in the little creature that convinced her this was no trick he played, no foolish prank.

"Has something happened?"

" 'Tis Master Merlin," he said with that same urgency that had her throwing the comb aside and running after him down the curve of stairs.

She sensed it even before they approached the chamber, a coldness like the coldness of death that momentarily stopped her at the threshold, a sense of something that whispered faint and illusive across her senses, and then was gone.

She pushed open the chamber door.

Merlin sat in the chair before the brazier. The coals had long burned to ash, and the room was deathly cold. He was deathly cold.

His head was slumped forward onto his chest. His breathing was shallow and ragged, and there was a pallor of death on his skin.

"Find Dannelore," she told Grendel, the coldness of dread closing around her heart. He was already out the door.

Meg gently touched Merlin's hand.

"Dear brother," she whispered. But no amount of words could rouse him. Not even the thoughts she reached out with.

Dannelore gasped when she saw him, her hand covering her mouth, the expression at her eyes stricken.

"Do something," Meg implored her. "There must be something you can do."

But there was nothing within the changeling's ability. No herbal concoction, no medicant known that could reach through the deathly sleep. He was neither dead nor alive, but at a place in between where it seemed nothing could reach him.

Meg refused to leave him, refused to believe that he would die, refused to lose this brother she had hardly known but had loved, been in awe of, and respected. Refused to believe nothing could be done.

Arthur was devastated when he was told and insisted on seeing Merlin. He came not as a future king but as a man who felt deeply the loss of a friend.

"He was tired last night, but he seemed well enough. He was not yet recovered from the wound he received at Amesbury. I should not have expected so much. And now near death."

"He made his own choices," Connor said later, not unkindly, but not voicing false words of friendship, for he had not felt that for Merlin.

It was small consolation, he knew. And with the time so near for them to leave for Glastonbury or fight Maelgwyn and Aethelbert on their doorstep.

"I relied on his counsel, his guidance," Arthur gravely said. "The plans for this campaign, we made together. How can I replace his sharp logic and brilliant strategy." He sighed heavily under the weight of the task that now lay before him. A task he must face alone.

"I would not blame you if you chose to take your men and leave," he said with blunt honesty, speaking man to man in the privacy of his own chamber. And knowing that if Connor of Monmouth chose to leave, so, too, might the other nobles, and with them would go any hope for victory over Maelgwyn and Aethelbert.

The last thing Connor had expected was such honesty. Once they had been that close, many years ago. Many years, much blood, much loss. He realized how much he had missed that closeness in the years apart.

He considered it. He thought of Meg and wanted nothing more than to return to Monmouth, lay down his sword, and find his life again, with her.

Once it would have been so simple, so easy. He would have left, owing nothing to Arthur or any man. The price paid with pain, blood, and all the years he'd fought alone. Now it was neither simple nor easy.

"When we were lads of ten and too foolish for our own good," Connor remembered, going back all those years in his mind, "I believed in you.

"When we were ten and four and no longer lads, with foolish dreams of what could be," he continued, "I believed in you."

"We are boys no longer," Arthur gravely replied. "These are no boyhood games, but we are perhaps still too foolish for our own good. Especially now."

"You are right, 'tis no game," Connor agreed. "And we are no longer boys. But I believe in the man I fought beside at Amesbury and against Maelgwyn." What had been lost had been found again. "And I will fight beside him now."

Morgana's reaction when she learned the counselor had worsened and lay near death surprised even Meg. Though she had made no secret of her resentment of Merlin, of being replaced by him at Arthur's side, of Merlin's being deferred to in all things important while she was relegated to a position of chatelaine, mistress of the household, and left to sit among the women while her brother and his counselor made plans of great import, now she seemed truly saddened and she consoled Arthur.

"You perhaps give too much credit to the counselor, dear brother. And to yourself too little. The plans have been made. It was not Merlin who was to execute them, but yourself with your men. Surely that has not changed."

"It has not," Arthur assured one and all as he sat about the round counsel table and spoke with his war generals, Morgana at his side where Merlin had once sat.

Then he recommitted himself to his men and to the quest they were about to embark upon with a sacred oath that they all shared.

A somber mood hung over all of Caerleon. The nobles quickly learned that Merlin was gravely ill and would not accompany them to Glastonbury. But they held fast in their loyalty to Arthur, repledging themselves to the war against Maelgwyn and Aethelbert.

And hour by hour the time drew closer when Connor would leave with Arthur for Glastonbury without Merlin beside them.

"There must be something that can be done!" Meg insisted. Only Dannelore knew of her fear and anguish. Only she saw it, felt it, heard it. For everyone else, she held it in, concealed it, not daring to let them see lest they learn the truth. Especially Connor.

"I have tried everything I know," Dannelore said, her expression grave. "And still he slips further away."

"I will take him back through the portal," Meg insisted, refusing to think of the consequences, refusing to think that it meant she must leave Connor, perhaps forever.

"You cannot!" Dannelore replied. " 'Tis a dangerous journey for those who are strong. It would kill him for certain. And if he were to die as a mortal, he would be lost to us forever."

She knew Dannelore spoke the truth. The journey was dangerous even for those who were strong enough. Helplessness engulfed her. With each passing hour, her brother slipped further away. She refused to believe there was nothing that could be done.

"He won't die. He can't."

She saw Connor briefly after the evening meal when he met one last time with Arthur. His was calm, resolute, the way she had seen him countless times, his thoughts already turned toward the forthcoming battle.

The tenderness of his touch, the gentle brush of his fingers against her cheek made it all the more difficult to think of what lay ahead, the battle they departed for the next day with no certainty of the outcome. Without Merlin.

It would have been easier if he had remained cool and remote, the resolute warrior, his thoughts with his men, rather than of her. But he said her name, low in his throat, a remembered sound from that last night together when he'd held her until dawn.

"I must speak with you." He pulled her into the small chapel. The urgency followed them even there in that quiet, serene place where he often went to pray to his god.

She sensed that Connor prayed to him now as he glanced past her to the small altar, the air redolent with the smell of candles, old wood, and damp stones.

He turned to her and took her hand. "There are things that must be said before I leave."

She dared not connect her thoughts to his for he would know it, but she sensed the gravity of his thoughts and a tremor of uneasiness moved across her skin like the warning touch of an invisible hand.

"You have no memory of your family," he began. "No name that might protect you."

"I do not need—"

He stopped her. "If I should not return—"

This time she stopped him. "No! I will not talk of it! You will come back!"

She tried to pull her hands from his, to run away from what he was saying. But even she knew the reality of the danger they faced, more so now without Merlin.

His hands tightened over hers, refusing to let her go. "Meg." The sound of her name, tender, pulling at her, refusing to let her go.

"If I should not return . . . I must know that you are safe."

"I am safe here," she reasoned. "There is no cause to worry."

But again he would not be refused in what he had to say.

"It is possible that even now you carry my child."

Her gaze snapped to his. In her heart she had wished for it, but there was no way of knowing. It was too soon.

"It did not happen before . . ."

He smiled indulgently. "You are a healer, surely you must know that once is all it takes. And we made love more than once last night." He kissed her then, a gentle whisper of his lips across hers, and with such aching tenderness that it made her want to cry.

"I pray it is so. I could hope for nothing more than to have my child growing inside you." He stroked a tendril of hair back from her cheek.

"But I must know that you are safe no matter the outcome. My name will protect you. I have made arrangements."

Arrangements? She didn't want to talk about this. She didn't understand what he was saying.

"There is no time for the usual formalities," he continued, "but Arthur has given his permission for us to be wed tonight."

She was stunned. Her thoughts swam. She could not. Dare not.

Suddenly everything she had refused to think of, refused to consider because of her feelings for Connor, suddenly trapped her.

She shook her head. " 'Tis not possible."

"Aye, it is. There is a monk who travels with the Duke of Sorgales. He has said he will dispense with the usual requirements. We can be wed right away."

She shook her head, trying to drag her scattered thoughts into some order.

"You know nothing about me," she protested.

"I know all I need to know." His hand covered hers, his thumb smoothing over the ring he had given her. His ring. His name. Perhaps his child.

"But my family . . . What if I . . . ?"

"What if you are already wed to another?" He smiled again. "No man wed to you could keep from touching you and claiming his husband's rights, little one." And he added with certainty, "You were no man's wife when I took you to my bed."

Then he said tenderly, "Be my wife. Take my name. And if God wills it, give my name to our child."

He was a man who believed absolutely in his god, in the order of things in the world, in what he could see, touch, and fight for. She knew in her heart that he could never understand or accept who she was . . . what she was.

"I cannot," Meg whispered, desperate to make him understand, but knowing there was nothing she could say that would make him understand. For the truth would destroy what they'd shared.

"I must know who I am before I do this."

"I know who you are."

"But I must know. I could not bear to bring you dishonor."

"You could never bring me dishonor."

"You cannot know that. When this is over there will be time enough—"

"There may be no time. But perhaps there is another reason," he suggested.

She heard the pain in his voice and knew that she had hurt him deeply. She could not lie, nor could she tell him the truth.

"Connor, please!" Tears spilled down her cheeks. "I love you. Is that not enough?"

She had never said the words, never thought them. But she had felt them and suddenly they were there, pleading for him to understand.

He reached for her then. Of all the things he'd endured—the death of his family, the loss of good men, the loss of Arthur's friendship, and torture at the hands of Maelgwyn—he could not bear her tears. He brushed his lips across her forehead.

He did not understand, but he would have to accept.

"Aye, 'tis enough. For now. But if you need anything, send word to Thaddeus. He will see that everything is taken care of." That you are taken care of, he thought, but did not say.

He left then. She felt him withdrawing, leaving already for the battle, becoming the warrior with so many last details to be taken care of before he and his men rode with Arthur in the morning.

She remained in the chapel for a while longer. Not for the first time she wondered about the god he believed in, that gave him strength, faith, and courage.

And before leaving, she said a small prayer of her own.

It was almost dawn when Meg slipped past Morgana's chamber and down the stairs to the main hall.

All was quiet now. But within a very few hours Arthur and

his men would leave for Glastonbury where Maelgwyn and Aethelbert gathered their armies.

She crossed the landing to the chapel, then went to the monk's chamber where a candle glowed softly and a fire burned at the brazier.

A young servant girl hovered over her brother. Startled, she jerked back as Meg entered the chamber.

"Oh, 'tis only you, mistress," the girl said, visibly shaken. "You gave me a turn. I had no idea anyone was about."

Meg glanced at her brother to see how he had passed the night. Arthur had insisted that he be carefully watched, and there had been no opportunity to check on him earlier in the evening without Morgana knowing of it. She was vaguely comforted by the faint rise and fall of his chest.

"Has there been any change?"

"Nay, mistress," the girl replied, carefully smoothing the fleece blanket into place. "I gave him the tisane, just as Dannelore said. But he never wakened."

Meg nodded, her thoughts clear and determined. She smiled gently at the girl.

"You may go now. I will stay for a while."

The girl frowned. "I cannot. Milady said I was to stay 'til she sent someone to take my place."

"I am a healer," Meg explained, carefully hiding her irritation at the girl's persistence. "There is no need for both of us to stay." Her voice softened. "Surely you are tired. Get some rest." And with a firmness that tolerated no argument, "I will stay with him."

"As you say, mistress," the girl replied. "But you must remember to give him the tisane at first light."

"I'll remember," Meg assured her.

With a last look back, the girl finally left. Meg set the latch at the door, then turned toward the pallet where her brother lay.

She had no experience with such things, only the certainty of her powers, and the certainty that he would die if she did not use them. She gently laid a hand over his, the heat that burned through him stunning her. If he had been mortal, he would already be dead.

"You will not die, dear brother," she said softly. "I will not let you."

There was no answer, she did not expect one. Nor was there any stirring of thought that reached out to touch hers. Neither had she expected that, for she already knew that he slept in a place where no voice or thought could reach him.

She lifted the bar at the window and opened the shutters. It was almost dawn, stars winking out in the gray velvet twilight, the sky just beginning to lighten at the horizon. An icy wind guttered out the candle.

She waited for that light, the light of the sun, a thousand suns of a thousand worlds, the power of the Light, from which she drew her strength, and from which he would find his strength through her.

The light came, burning at the horizon, burning back the night, destroying the darkness. It played across the sharp angles and deep hollows of his face, his once handsome features now wasted by fever that burned the life from him. She had felt it at his hand.

Then she found the marks. Four small puncture wounds, equally spaced, and fresh blood that still seeped.

She was stunned. They were identical to the marks left when Morgana had seized her by the arm, her nails sinking in and drawing blood . . . identical to the marks she'd seen when Sir Simon had stopped her that very morning.

As she touched those tiny wounds she experienced a stinging pain at her own arm, like a memory of the blood—a whisper of something evil, a darkness that pumped through her brother's veins with each beat of his heart and reached for his soul.

The marks were identical to the ones she'd received weeks ago. But while the marks on her arm had healed, these had not.

Since coming to Caerleon she'd had a great deal of experience with such things. This was not the color of blood usually found at a wound. The blood on his arm was blackened, tainted with the darkness of the poison death that burned through him.

Poison.

The truth was there, in the wound he'd received at Amesbury that had never completely healed but still festered no matter the healing potions used or even the strength of his own healing powers. It continued to poison his blood, making him weak, wasting his body, weakening his mind, and his powers.

And now these fresh wounds. Black death that nothing in Dannelore's skills could stop or heal.

More poison that continued to weaken, destroy, and kill?

She wiped the blood from her hand. An icy coldness swept over her, a premonition of something unseen, insidious, a pervasive darkness that waited just beyond the dawn, reaching out for him . . . reaching for all of them.

She glanced at the open window. It was almost time.

She knelt beside the pallet and stripped open his tunic, baring his chest where that dying heart struggled. Then she placed her hand over his heart, her fingers forming the points of a five-pointed star. The dying beat of his heart echoed the beating of her own heart as she turned her thoughts inward.

Ancient words whispered through her. Words older than the dawn, older than the sky and the earth. Older than time itself. Words of a language known only in the souls of a few, the chosen, those born with the power as the warmth of the new sun spilled through the window opening, pierced through her, and burned deep inside.

She drew on it, seized it, felt the power of the Light burning within her heart, through her blood, through the points of the star her fingers made, burning through him.

It burned the poison in his blood, burned through his heart and into his soul with a cleansing fire, burned away Darkness and death.

His body contorted with pain. Slack muscles that had been too weak to lift a hand for days suddenly spasmed and knotted. His fists clenched as the pain of that fire burned through him, heavy veins visible beneath pallid almost translucent skin. Then his back arched and his head went back, his teeth clenched as the fire burned, searing through his veins and pumping through his heart.

Eyes that had held only the shadows of death for days, now gleamed at her with the power of the life force she gave him, the power of the Light that was the essence of their very existence, the essence of her soul.

And in that fierce blue gaze so like her own, in the hands that suddenly reached for her, closed over her shoulders, and held on as if holding onto a lifeline, she felt the stirring of his own soul as it connected with hers, in a glimmer of recognition and the single word that reached out incredulously from his thoughts to hers.

"Sister?"

"I am here."

There was no time for anything more. A warning quivered in the air of the chamber. It whispered from the walls, across her senses, and through her blood with a new urgency.

Danger was very near, strong and powerful, a shadow moving within shadows. Now it was at the door.

She needed more time! But there was no more.

The door burst open and Arthur's men charged into the chamber. Connor was with them.

"Seize her!"

Arthur's men surrounded her and pulled her back from the pallet. The connection was immediately severed, painful, wrenching, as if cut with a blade. Merlin fell back on the pallet, his body no longer twisted and contorted by pain, his features once more slack and sunken.

Her gaze met Connor's as Arthur entered the chamber. There was no time to explain.

Arthur's gaze swept the chamber and immediately fastened on her, then shifted to the pallet where Merlin lay still as death, his tunic open, the sleeve of it stained with fresh blood from those small wounds.

"What is this about?" Arthur demanded. His gaze fastened on Meg, her gown streaked with blood where she had wiped her hands as she tended his wounds.

"Explain yourself, mistress!"

A movement caught Meg's eye, the presence of another who hung back just beyond the door opening—the servant girl who had been watching over Merlin.

The girl's eyes gleamed with cunning and triumph. Shadows surrounded her, quivered, and then disappeared. And, as she stood at the opening, her features changed, altered, and suddenly transformed.

Morgana!

Oblivious to the transformation, Arthur's men quickly stepped aside as Morgana pushed her way through them, joining Arthur, her expression one of shock and outrage.

"Murderess!" she accused dramatically. "See the blood on her hands even now! She tried to kill Merlin!"

"No!" Connor stepped between them. He shoved aside the swords pointed at Meg.

"This is a mistake. There is an explanation."

Then he turned to her, his eyes searching for answers, wanting to believe in her. She had only to tell the truth and she knew he would defend her, even against Arthur.

"Tell them it is all a lie," he demanded. "Tell them!"

"I did not try to kill him," she answered truthfully. "I am a healer—"

But Morgana cut her off, refusing to hear it.

"I will tell you what my servant saw." Her voice whipped through the air, stinging with accusation. "She came to me terrified. She feared for Merlin's life. See for yourself, the blood on her gown and her hands. God knows how long she has been draining the life from him, weakening him to the point of death. Brother"—she turned to Arthur, hands extended, imploring him—"surely you must see.

"She comes to us with no name, no family. A stranger with no past. We are told she does not remember, but she is a healer. That much she does remember. How easy to gain our trust, to move among us without suspicion while she plays her deadly game. See what she has taken from you with her lies and deceptions."

How easily Morgana twisted the truth, how easily she

deceived them all. Meg could say nothing, dared say nothing that would reveal herself. And knew her silence condemned her.

"Tell them," Connor repeated, pleading now, and in his voice she heard both desperation and hope; his wanting to believe in her and his growing desperation at her silence.

"Take her away!" Arthur ordered, his voice filled with both sadness and anger. "Have her chained."

Meg was taken to a chamber below the main hall. In times of siege, the inhabitants would have huddled there as a last place of refuge. It was like a tomb.

Moisture seeped through the walls and dripped from the ceiling. There was no light and her companions soon became bold, crawling across the walls and scurrying across the floor. They brushed against her ankles, darting in to nip at her. She was bound at the ankles and wrists with heavy chains secured at the wall, making it all but impossible to move when they attacked.

It only added to her misery, for she was constantly watched and could not use her powers even in the simplest manner to protect herself, lest they discover it.

Dannelore tried to see her, but she silently warned her not to intervene.

"Do not!" she silently admonished through the connection of thought.

" 'Tis dangerous. I am well enough." And she warned, *"Be careful of Morgana."*

Morgana.

The discovery had stunned her. What was she? A changeling, capable of altering her appearance or transforming? A trick, an illusion, such as those Grendel performed for the entertainment of others?

Or was it more?

What had happened was more than mere entertainment. The marks at her brother's arm, like the ones she'd received in a fit of anger, had intended far more.

She shuddered, remembering the coldness of darkness within him. That same coldness had burned at the scars at her arm.

Poison!

Meg knew with certainty now that it was Morgana who had slowly poisoned Merlin.

Her powers were such that both Merlin and Meg had been deceived. How many times had Morgana visited his chamber? How many more times in the guise of a servant? And the poison had taken its toll, moving like darkness through his blood, stealing the very essence of life, stealing his soul.

She had been strong enough to fight off the poison of her wound, but Merlin had not. Was it because he already suffered a poisoning wound, received at Amesbury, that had never healed?

She thought of the chamber found at Amesbury, and was certain that it was the bishop who practiced the dark arts, conjuring the spirits of Darkness from the hidden realm.

Myth? Or reality?

Memories of old prophecies stirred. Of stories told by the Ancient Ones. Of cataclysm, death, and destruction. Of the powers of Darkness that had once sought to destroy the powers of the Light.

Eons ago. A score of millennia. Farther back than the memory of the Learned Ones. So far back that it was remembered only in the souls of the chosen ones. A warning of what had once been when the lords of Darkness sought to destroy the hope for the future, a portent of what might happen if the Darkness became powerful once again.

Had the powers of Darkness been summoned by Morgana? But to what purpose? The destruction of Merlin?

She sensed Connor's presence before she heard the grating of a distant door across cold stones. Then closer, and the sound of another door opening. As light from a torch quivered across the walls and across his sharp features. The heavy iron gate that imprisoned her prevented him from coming any closer.

She needed no gift of second sight to know his thoughts. They were there in the lines on his face and the stark expression in his eyes.

She went to him, as far as the chains would allow, just near enough so that she could almost feel his warmth in the coldness of the stone chamber. She longed to touch him, needed to touch him, needed him to reach for her. But he did not.

"I must know the truth," he said, his voice low and desperate. "Tell me Morgana's accusations are all lies. Help me believe you had no part in this."

She wanted to weep. She felt him pulling away from her even now, and there was nothing she could do to stop it. Nothing more she could say.

"I have told the truth. I did no harm. I found those wounds at his arm. 'Tis a poison that has weakened him with wasting fevers. I had nothing to do with it."

"What of the blood on your gown and hands?"

"I am a healer," she reasoned logically. "I have had the blood of countless wounds on my hands since the battle at Amesbury. I did not make those wounds. You must believe me."

He struggled to believe, wanted to. She sensed it.

"What of this?" He held a vial, like any other found in the herbal. But she already sensed what it contained.

"It was found in your chamber. Dannelore could give no explanation for it."

Poison. No doubt the poison Morgana had used. When had she put it there? After leaving Merlin's chamber, and just before she summoned Arthur's guards?

"I do not know how it came to be there."

"What of this?" he demanded, his voice cold, the coldness stinging her as if she'd been struck. He held up the medallion, the light from the torches gleaming across the hammered surface with the image of the ram's horns, no doubt discovered when they'd found the poison.

"I found it."

"Found it? Lying about?" His tone was hard.

She felt belief slipping further away from him. But she dared not reveal that it was Tristan who'd found it, for she could only imagine the punishment Morgana would inflict. Perhaps even death.

"Is this what Maelgwyn paid you? Something rare that he prized, that bears his own seal?"

"How can you think that?" she asked incredulously, trying to make him see. "I had nothing when you found me in the forest. It was your arrow that wounded me."

"You remembered nothing," he continued. "Your family; your name; nothing. Was it planned that I should find you? Or was it a mistake? Did Maelgwyn send you? How do you know him? Is that the reason you refused to wed with me? Are you perhaps wed to another?"

"No!"

The words stung her. How could he think it? It was he who had pushed aside her doubts when they had first lain together and he had known then beyond any doubt she had never lain with another.

Her thoughts reeled and spun into chaos, her emotions shattered.

Maelgwyn?

Had Maelgwyn given the medallion to Morgana?

It was Maelgwyn who had taken Morgana and Lady Ygraine to Amesbury. Dannelore had spoken of Morgana's ambition to be lady of Caerleon and all that title included. Then she'd seen her ambitions thwarted when Arthur returned and she was relegated to a lesser position as mistress of his household, to be settled on some lesser noble in a marriage advantageous to Arthur's power.

Had her ambitions gone further? Perhaps to the throne of Britain itself? And what of Lady Ygraine's sudden, inexplicable death? Had Morgana had a hand in that as well?

Was the accused now to accuse her accuser?

Meg could not tell him the medallion belonged to Morgana. He would never believe it of someone with no past, no family name, no way to prove her innocence. Except with the truth of who and what she was.

Impossible.

The word made her heart ache.

"I have told you all I can. Please believe me," she begged.

But she felt him pulling further away, even before he turned from her.

Then she heard the coldness in his voice, saw it in his eyes, bitter and sharp as a knife thrust through her heart.

"How can I?"

Chapter Nineteen

Meg sensed that Arthur and his men had left Caerleon, even before one of her companions sat up with particular curiosity and regarded her with an intelligence somewhat advanced even for a rat.

"Very clever," she said. "But if you have even the slightest notion of trying to bite me I will turn you into a troll."

The rat immediately transformed, Grendel assuming his true form rather than that of the short, bandy-legged mortal who performed pathetic magic tricks even young Tristan saw through.

"I did not think the guards would be suspicious of a rat," he commented as he came toward her. *"And you have called me one often enough."*

She managed a small smile at the memory of all the times she'd called him one. His own expression was grave.

"Arthur has gone to meet Maelgwyn and Aethelbert."

She nodded. *"What of Connor?"* But she knew even as she asked.

He had pledged his loyalty to Arthur, the wounds of youth healed. And Connor, a man of pride and honor, would not abandon that pledge. Especially now, when Arthur had not even his counselor to rely upon at the gravest moment of his life.

"Gone as well," Grendel replied. *"Along with all of Arthur's knights, and the armies of Lord Tarsan and Sorgales. He left only the household guard and those men."* He gestured to her guards.

"John has gone, given a knighthood this morn," he continued. *"Dannelore is beside herself with worry. All Lord Connor's men have gone as well, including Sir Geoffrey, Sir Simon, and that dreadful, nasty Viking."* He shuddered. *"Vile man, even for a mortal."*

Simon.

Where did his loyalties lie? Meg wondered. In Morgana's bed? And what of the marks she'd seen?

Morgana had used her poison on Merlin and had attempted to poison her as well. A poison of evil that destroyed the soul. Had she also poisoned Simon? And to what purpose?

Was it enough to give Maelgwyn a greater advantage by removing Arthur's trusted counselor from his side? Or was there more to Morgana's evil plan?

It was Arthur's destiny to unite Britain. But what if Arthur did not live to fulfill that destiny? What if he was mortally wounded at Glastonbury? Then Britain would fall into chaos once more, prey to Maelgwyn's ambitious plans.

Simon rode with Connor. And Connor was to fight at Arthur's side. She shivered with a foreboding of danger and death.

"What of Merlin?" she asked.

"Dannelore is with him. He has not awakened."

She stood and easily slipped free of the iron manacles and chains with a single thought. Her senses reached throughout stone, mortar, and wood, but she sensed nothing of Morgana and her worry deepened.

She could not know the extent of the woman's powers. If she was capable of transformation she might be capable of almost anything. But how? What was the source of her power?

"What of Morgana?"

"She retired to her chamber with orders that no one was to disturb her," Grendel replied.

He leaned closer still. *"There is an evil about the woman."*

"Aye, Grendel. A dark evil, I fear the like of which we have not seen for longer than memory."

He was almost afraid to ask. *"What is to be done?"*

"I intend to pay Morgana a visit."

Grendel shook his head and turned away, arms crossed defiantly across his chest.

"I have no wish to encounter that one."

Meg shrugged. *"Then you may stay here,"* she replied as she turned her thoughts inward and drew on her power.

The guards stood at their positions outside the chamber. But when they glanced inside, they saw an illusion—one she created in their minds. To them it seemed she still remained huddled at the wall, bound in chains.

Then she focused her power once more and stepped through the stones at the wall, easily escaping her dungeon prison.

"Do not leave me here," Grendel exclaimed, whirling around to find her gone.

Outside the chamber, Meg channeled her power, moving through stone and earth, emerging in the darkness of the deserted main hall.

Grendel's escape was less efficient. With only the ability of transformations, he emerged from the passage where the opening to those subterranean chambers lay some time later and scurried along the passage wall, his rat nose twitching to pick up any unusual or dangerous scent.

"You left me!" he accused, transforming once more. "You don't know what those rats tried to do to me."

"I know what Morgana will do to you if she hears you with all the noise you're making."

His mouth snapped shut.

A servant passed by, unaware of their presence. Now that Arthur had gone, sound echoed along the empty walls and in the cavernous main hall. From the kitchen came the faint sounds of other servants. A single guard stood at the main entrance. Outside, there were more guards, but here they moved through the passage unnoticed.

She stepped to the stairs, her senses sharpened to everything about her. She sensed Dannelore's presence in the monk's chamber, for the moment safe with her brother. Young Tristan was with them as well.

"Stay with them," she told Grendel as she started up the stairs. For once, he did not argue.

At the second-floor landing she shielded herself with her power. A guard posted there remained impassive and unaware of her presence. He was mortal. It seemed Morgana's evil had not extended here.

She frowned at the unexpected discovery. What game did Morgana play?

Meg used her senses to probe beyond the stone walls and into Morgana's chamber, but she sensed nothing that either warned or alarmed her. No essence of the cold evil that she'd felt when Morgana's poison had moved through her, nor that evil Darkness that she'd felt within her brother.

As easily as she'd escaped that prison chamber, she moved through the wall of Morgana's chamber. Transforming once more into her mortal form, she discovered what she had feared.

Morgana was gone.

She sensed that lingering presence, a coldness of evil that clung to the walls, slipped across the floor, and disappeared into the corners. But she sensed it strongest at the window where Morgana had fled, her essence left behind like a footprint in newly fallen snow. It betrayed her, for Meg realized the way she had gone.

Toward Glastonbury.

With growing urgency, she returned to the monk's chamber, and confronted Dannelore, Grendel, and young Tristan who stood guard with sword drawn. He lowered the sword.

"Morgana?" Grendel asked.

"She is gone," she replied.

"Gone?" Dannelore's voice was equally grave.

"Aye, to Glastonbury to finish what she has begun."

Meg moved to her brother's side. As she took his hand in hers, her thoughts sought his in the old way, reaching out.

"Dear brother, I need you."

The fever no longer burned at his skin. The poison no longer burned through his blood. He slowly opened his eyes, as blue as her own, unfocused at first, trying to see with inner sight.

"You," was all he said, even that small word seeming to take more strength than he had.

"Yes, brother," she whispered, giving him her strength in the connection of their hands and their thoughts, refusing to let him slip back into that darkness of sleep.

He closed his eyes. She sensed him gathering himself, drawing on her power, welcoming it like the warmth of the sun after a cold winter's sleep.

When he looked at her again it was with recognition instead of the madness of the evil that had burned through him.

"Morgana . . . !"

"She is gone," she assured him.

"It was Morgana . . . the poison . . ." And then, "You were there. I felt you . . . You gave me your power and strength."

She smiled gently. "I thought perhaps it might temper your anger, when you realized who I was, for I knew it was a secret I could not keep once our power was joined." She shrugged. "It seemed the thing to do at the time. Now you must save your strength. Give me your thoughts. Tell me everything."

And in the connection of their thoughts, like a warmth of light that moved between them, she learned what she had feared— Morgana had plotted to seize the throne for herself even before Arthur returned to Britain.

A marriage had been arranged by her father, an alliance that would have strengthened Arthur's holdings at Caerleon when he returned to claim them, but left her with nothing. Lady Ygraine was to retain the holdings and title of Caerleon until his return.

But Morgana had other, darker ambitions. She made an alliance with Maelgwyn. Together the holdings of the north allied with those of Caerleon and the lands to the south, guaranteed the defeat of Aethelbert.

A raid on Caerleon was planned during which the old duke was killed. Morgana and Lady Ygraine were taken prisoner by Maelgwyn's ally, Bishop Constantine. Then only Lady Ygraine remained an obstacle to Morgana's ambition. Her death came quickly. She never knew that her son was already in Britain, and within only days of returning to Caerleon.

Morgana was enraged when Arthur freed her at Amesbury. His return jeopardized everything she'd hoped and schemed for.

"She summoned the powers of Darkness," Merlin continued. *"For longer than memory the Darkness has dwelled beyond the great domain, its power destroyed in the great cataclysm when only a few of the Ancient Ones survived. It no longer sleeps. Now it is alive in the mortal world."* His thoughts took on a greater urgency.

"Nothing is safe . . . No one is safe while Morgana lives. She is Darkness incarnate."

Meg sensed the extraordinary effort it took just to give her his thoughts. He was physically and mentally exhausted.

"Simon is part of this," he continued, speaking in the mortal way, as the strength of his power failed him.

"He is the greatest threat to Arthur at this moment. He will strike at him in the midst of battle." His eyes closed for a moment, his breathing rapid and shallow.

"If Arthur falls at Glastonbury, then all is lost!"

She sensed still more. Far more. A deep ache of the soul, a wounding so deep that it tore him apart with its enormity. His hand covered hers, trembled, and then tightened with a strength that came from the agony he'd endured.

"I saw it when she came to me the last time. It was my death she intended, for by then she had filled me with her poison and left me with little to fight her with."

"Don't," Meg gently told him. "Please do not tell me any more."

She sensed this was more than she wanted to know, something that tore him apart, the price he'd paid for fighting Morgana. Her evil had gone far beyond the poison she'd poured into him to slowly drain the mortal life and the immortal powers from him.

Meg saw it all in his tormented thoughts. How Morgana had come to him. Beautiful, naked, tempting beyond anything he could resist, evil incarnate. He fought her but he was weak, his powers unable to protect him by then. In the end, she seduced him and then seduced his soul.

Tears streamed down Meg's cheeks.

"There was a moment," his voice filled with self-loathing, broke, and broke her heart, "when I would have surrendered everything to her. All that I am, everything I ever will be, but there was one thing she could not take from me, nor could she give it . . . because an evil such as hers has no understanding of it. 'Tis something mortal of all things."

She lifted her tear-streaked gaze to his. She heard the irony amidst the sadness. He touched her cheek.

"It was hope."

A single fragile word that seemed to hang suspended like the tear that hung suspended at the end of his finger.

"My hope that I might one day feel what you have felt with Connor."

A great sadness moved through him. "Love. 'Tis part of this thing unique to mortals—their humanity—which we, with all our wondrous powers, can never possess."

She gave him a watery smile. "Love is a very fragile thing, dear brother."

"Aye, but I have learned in this world that sometimes the most fragile thing is also the strongest. The powers of Darkness have no understanding of this. 'Tis impossible for them to understand a thing such as love, or hope. In the end it is what she could not destroy. Now I must destroy her."

He struggled to rise from the pallet, and she realized that even now, weak as he was, he intended to go after Morgana. But the poison and the fever had taken their toil. His weakened powers could not summon the mortal strength. Meg gently pushed him back down.

"You cannot. Surely you must see that," she reasoned, and as his strength ebbed and flowed, he sensed what lay in her thoughts.

"You cannot! You must not follow her! You have no idea what she is capable of." But his waning strength was no match for hers. She gently pressed him back down onto the pallet.

"You have not the strength to fight her again. You know I

speak truth,'' she reasoned with the logic that bound them together. "We waste time arguing, brother. I need your thoughts, everything you know about Morgana. Everything you saw when your thoughts were joined with hers.''

He gave her a long look, his eyes—the same color as hers— large and sunken in his wasted features. But they were clear and lucid with no sign of the Darkness that had been there before. His hand tightened over hers, and she felt the flow of his essence.

"All that I am, all my knowledge, and the knowledge of those who have gone before, goes with you.'' He paused. His hand remained closed over hers.

"It will be dangerous. You risk much. Your greatest strength against Morgana,'' he continued, "lies in the fact that she does not know who or what your are. Just as you kept it from me, you kept it from her as well. 'Tis a weapon you must use wisely.''

Meg nodded with understanding.

He had paused, as if troubled by something with which he struggled.

"When you joined your power with mine and saved my life, I sensed something . . .''

He had grown stronger, and she felt the gentle touch of his thoughts once again.

"You do not know . . . you carry his child.''

The thought stunned her and then brought new tears. She had hoped that it might happen, but then it had not, and afterward their time together had been so brief.

She remembered Connor's words with a tender smile. After all, she was a healer—*it only took one time.*

She was filled with such a sharp poignancy as she remembered their parting only hours ago, his coldness, the look in his eyes, the certainty that she had betrayed him. And she dared not tell him the truth.

Love. It was indeed the most fragile thing. Was it also strong enough, as her brother said, to endure such a wounding, to endure the truth when he learned it as he surely would.

How, she wondered, was it possible to feel so much joy and so much pain and sadness at the same time?

Merlin's hand moved comfortingly over hers. She turned her own hand, holding on.

"The child is part of both you and Connor." His thoughts were gentle, moving through hers. Yet, grave when he continued, *"Because your child is also mortal, you will be vulnerable to Morgana's power. You must guard against her learning of this for she will use it against you. Protect yourself at all times! For your sake, and the child's."*

There was so much at stake. Arthur's life. Connor's life. Their child—a fragile life made of mortal flesh and blood and unknown powers.

She squeezed his hand. *"In all ways, you will be with me brother. How then can I fail?"*

Dannelore and Grendel were to remain at Caerleon. Their powers would be of little help to her. Better that they stayed and protected Merlin. She took Grendel aside and spoke so that only he heard her words.

"If I do not return you must take them back through the portal."

"But, mistress . . ."

She adamantly shook her head. "If I should fail, no place on this earth will be safe. You must promise that you will do as I ask."

It was not a matter of choice. He was bound by laws older than this world which bound his very existence to hers, his duty and loyalty to her. Once it was asked, he could not refuse. He nodded, his mouth set in a grim line.

"I'll do as you say, but I don't have to like it."

"I'm going with you," Tristan flatly declared when she turned to him. The sword Connor had had made for him was belted at his waist.

For all that he was only ten years of age, he seemed somehow taller than before. Less the boy and more the man he would one day be, rich dark hair spilling over his forehead, the expression in his dark eyes somber, resolute, brave. And he had absolutely no notion of the grave danger that awaited them all.

Yet Tristan had seen much and lost much. And she sensed that even had he known what awaited, there would be no fear, no hesitation. Like someone else she knew and loved. If they survived she could want nothing more than to have such a brave warrior one day protect her child.

She did not treat him like the young boy who had been injured in the practice yard, but like the warrior he longed to be, who must now hold steadfast in his duty.

"You must stay with Grendel and Dannelore," she said, knowing it was not what he wanted to hear. When he protested, she explained, "There is no one else I may rely upon in this."

"They do not need my protection; they have Master Merlin. He will protect them."

"He is gravely ill," she replied, and then explained, "All may not go well at Glastonbury. If it does not, Grendel is to take Merlin and Dannelore to a place where they will be safe.

"I can rely on him to do as I have asked but I am less certain of Dannelore . . ." She paused, thinking how best to do so. There was no need to explain. For all his youth, Tristan understood.

"She cares deeply for John, and may refuse to go?"

Meg looked at him, love swelling in her heart for this man-child. It seemed to come so easily now—this mortal emotion that she had found with Connor—and she realized there were many ways to feel love. Like the love she felt for Tristan.

Yet at the same time she knew a pang of loss for the innocence of the boy who had once challenged Radvald in the practice yard, and wondered if he had perhaps lost that innocence long before with the deaths of his family, for it had taken the courage of a man to survive what he had. And it would take a man to do what she asked.

"Aye, that she does. They had hoped to wed, but John has gone to Glastonbury with Arthur. 'Tis the reason I ask this now."

"You fear she will refuse to leave if all does not go well," he replied.

She nodded. "She has been a true friend. I could not bear

her loss.'' Nor yours, she thought to herself. This was a way of guaranteeing the safety of both.

"You must see that she goes with Grendel and Merlin."

He finally agreed, though he was not pleased that he must remain behind.

"I will see that they are all safe."

She wanted to put her arms around him and hold him tight. She sensed the need for it, in the boy in him. Or perhaps it was her own need, for she again felt the tug of those mortal emotions—the pang of loss that she might never see him again.

In the end she did not hug him, but made her heartfelt gratitude known as she would to Geoffrey, Agravain, Sagremore, or any of the other brave knights who now rode toward destiny with Arthur.

"Thank you, *Sir* Tristan."

Dawn, their second day from Caerleon. High atop the hill at the confluence of two rivers, Connor scanned the broad flat plain that lay before them.

The twin glittering ribbons of water caught the reflection of the rising sun, the birth of its fiery glow turning their surfaces red as if the rivers ran with blood.

For once the weather favored them. They had left the snow and mud behind at Caerleon. The old Roman road had been dry and now gave way to a flat plain of dry winter sedge that, come spring, would give way to lush green meadows and verdant hills.

A spring they might not see if Maelgwyn and Aethelbert prevailed.

It was not doubt that intruded, but the cold voice of reality. Twice before Maelgwyn had had Connor within his grasp. Twice he had escaped. Now they met again, two vast armies poised at the edge of destiny—the battle to rule all of Britain.

Arthur's destiny, born in myth and legend, ordained by Merlin, to be fulfilled or lost with the coming battle.

What did Connor now believe?

He had always believed in God, and his sword. He had lived

by them, and would have willingly died by them. But he had learned that there was more to the world than what he had once believed. There was honor, faith, and trust.

Once trust had been lost, when he'd lost Arthur's friendship. But he had found it again, ironically in the midst of battle. And more. Something else he'd lost the ability to believe in.

Love.

It ached inside him now, a thing of immeasurable value, but also a thing of pain and loss. He had survived that loss before in the loss of his family, and he told himself that because he had, he could now bear this pain, this loss. But perhaps, also because he had borne it, this pain, this loss was now all the more unbearable.

Meg.

The memory of her took hold and twisted deep inside at a place where he had thought he would never feel anything again. She had given that back to him. Even now, his first thoughts of her were of what she'd brought him—fierce passion and sweet laughter, easing the pain in his soul, taking hold of him in ways that were tender and fierce just as she had loved him, both tenderly and fiercely.

He had to remind himself of her betrayal, to hold on to the coldness of the rage he'd felt when he discovered it, like a shield that held those other memories at bay. In the past, his rage had been that shield. As it must be now, or he would lose his soul as surely as he'd lost his heart.

Arthur joined him, astride his warhorse. At Connor's other side were Simon and Geoffrey also astride. He had been contemplative, withdrawn with his own thoughts, as they had ridden nearer to Glastonbury.

In spite of the well-made battle plan and the support of the other nobles, Connor knew Arthur was deeply troubled by Merlin's absence. As if it might be a portent of what was to come.

Connor had never believed in such things. But he believed in his instincts. They had served him well his entire life. And his instincts now made him uneasy and wary, as a warning moved across his senses, a restlessness that kept his hand constantly at his battle sword and his gaze constantly scanning the horizon. As if there was something more he strained to see, but could not.

The others seemed to sense it as well, Simon's gaze constantly drawn back to that same place. Perhaps it was that instinct that came from the shared experience of battle, that frisson of energy that burned through the blood, the anticipation of what was to come, mixed admittedly with fear.

Every man he'd ever fought beside had felt it, understood it, confronted it, then summoned from deep within himself that essence of courage that it took to face what they now faced.

The sun gained the morning sky, and Arthur's gaze narrowed as he scanned the inky patches of activity below.

They had encamped the night before a distance away, rising two hours before dawn to take up the positions Arthur and Merlin had laid out after receiving the final dispatches two days ago at Caerleon.

Riders sent ahead earlier had returned and confirmed that Maelgwyn and Aethelbert's combined armies still held their positions, spread out on the rim of the plain like a serpent.

"Perhaps the enemy numbers were exaggerated," Geoffrey now suggested. "They do not seem so many. At least we are only outnumbered two to one." He grinned, his humor dispelling the taut silence.

"Two to one?" Radvald roared with laughter, and then spat. "Bah! Child's play. We'll be back at Caerleon by eventide."

Connor acknowledged it with a grim nod. Laughter, he knew all to well was a weapon against the fear. His own gaze was drawn back to the armies gathered before them.

"We attack as planned," Arthur ordered. "Spread the word to await my signal."

In his time in the middle kingdoms with Merlin, Arthur had learned the advantages of a mounted attack and had acquired as many horses as possible for his men while neither Maelgwyn or Aethelbert had horses.

The battle plan was to be an offensive attack in three waves. Archers were to first take out as many of Maelgwyn's frontline warriors as possible. They were to be followed by foot soldiers armed with spear, ax, and sword.

After the second wave of the attack, mounted warriors were to sweep in behind, charging the enemy, cutting their line into small groups, breaking their strength—breaking the back of the serpent so that it could not defend itself. And then destroying it. Connor and his men were to fight beside Arthur.

Signal fires were lit along the enemy line. Muscles tensed and hands tightened over weapons. All thoughts became one thought as all eyes fixed on that line of enemy warriors.

The battle cry went out as the enemy swept forward. And the answering cry was heard as Arthur's archers let loose a volley of arrows that darkened the sky. Then his warriors charged.

The two massive armies collided like waves crashing on the shore, the sounds of battle exploding in a chaos of steel, blood, and death. Then Arthur gave the final signal, and his mounted warriors and knights, including Connor's men, swept from their position with battle swords gleaming in the morning sun.

They charged into the heart of the fray, swinging their swords into the mass of embattled warriors. To Connor's right and left mounted men fought, hacking and slicing their way through the enemy, cutting the serpent into dozens of smaller embattled groups. Reaching the back of the line, they swung their horses around and charged back into the thick of the fight.

No matter how many battles Connor had fought there was that first moment, that first blow that struck deep into a man's soul; the shudder of the blade as it met the resistance of leather, then the fatal yielding and the sinking of the blade into another man.

It was seen and felt in flashes of images that exploded around him, every man driving past that first blow to the next and the next. All thought, all feeling ceased to exist as numbness set in.

Then they were fighting on the ground. Simon and Geoffrey fought to Arthur's left. Connor fought at his right. They moved in a wedge, their backs protected by each other as a wave of enemy warriors swelled against them.

The battle seemed to have a pulse, beating then resting, then beating again as metal struck against metal and fierce war cries were heard amidst the cries of the dying.

The bodies of their own men and of the enemy lay around them. Simon and Geoffrey were both embattled at Arthur's other side. Connor took a glancing blow that staggered him to one knee and momentarily numbed his right arm from shoulder to fist. As his attacker closed in for the kill, Arthur's blade blunted the blow and he ran the man through.

There was a brief moment of acknowledgment. Then Connor shifted his sword to his left hand and was already pushing back to his feet to meet the next enemy warrior. The heart of the battle beat fiercely about them once again.

Orders were shouted, positions were adjusted, over the screams of the wounded, the pulse seemed to change, faltering, skipping a beat as they seemed to gain the upper hand.

Then, low and urgent, Connor heard a warning amidst the chaos of battle. As if someone stood at his side and whispered it.

"Beware! Arthur is in great danger!"

It was like that voice of instinct, only different. Stronger, urgent, moving through his blood. He spun around and saw Arthur.

Geoffrey and Simon fought beside him, driving back yet another attack by two of Maelgwyn's warriors. Yet the warning still burned through his blood, stronger than instinct. And he heard it again. Insistent, refusing to let him go.

"Arthur is betrayed!"

Then he saw the danger in flashes of images: the protective wedge about Arthur was suddenly broken by a new attack; his attention focused on that attack; Geoffrey overcame one warrior, then turned to help Arthur; the sword at his back that cut Geoffrey down—Simon's sword; the look of dismay on Geoffrey's face as he saw the face of his attacker; and Simon raising his sword for the deathblow—against Arthur.

Disbelief turned to rage. Connor cut his way past an enemy warrior and ran two others through as he fought to reach

Arthur's side. Then rage turned to helplessness as he watched that blade fall.

He shouted a warning, but Arthur never heard it. It was drowned out by the sound of metal ringing out against metal as another blade deflected Simon's blow—a blade that glinted like blue fire beneath the midday sun.

Simon was staggered back by the blow, momentarily stunned. He snarled as he fought his way back to his feet and coiled to strike again. But Connor stopped him this time, lunging between him and Arthur, deflecting another blow.

Now Simon came at him, slashing at him with his sword.

"For the love of God, man! Are you mad?" Connor shouted at him.

But Simon didn't seem to hear. He lunged again, and this time Connor met the blow, and the next and the next, driving Simon back. But still he kept coming, long past the point of reason, past the point of endurance, to the point of madness.

In his eyes were madness, darkness, and unbelievable rage as he struck again and again. He *was* mad.

For all the campaigns they'd shared, for all the times they'd saved each other's lives, Connor beseeched him, "Do not force me to kill you!"

Yet, Connor couldn't erase that last image from his thoughts—Simon's sword raised to kill Arthur, the blow stopped barely inches from severing Arthur's head from his shoulders.

Simon would not yield nor lay down his weapon. Instead, he continued to meet each blow with almost inhuman strength. The battle around them all but ceased to exist. It was kill or be killed.

In the end when death came it was as if a part of Connor died as well. And for a moment there was only silence as if everything around him ceased to exist. As if time stood still and the pulse of the battle paused, and he saw the warrior who had wielded that sword of blue fire and saved Arthur's life.

I know you, Connor thought, remembering the warrior he'd encountered at Amesbury.

And as if he had heard his thoughts, the warrior nodded in acknowledgment.

Was it a dream? An illusion in the heat of battle, like waves of heat that swell across a dry plain on a summer's day? Or was it real?

Mist swirled around the warrior as the sun beat down on the cold winter earth of the battlefield. He was slender with a lean strength. He wore a leather tunic, leggings, and boots, and his features were obscured by those unusual painted markings he'd worn before.

Once before he had intervened and saved Connor's life. That had not been on a sweltering plain but in the abbey at Amesbury. Now he'd appeared once again, like before as if out of nowhere, and he had saved Arthur's life.

What did he want? Whom did this warrior serve?

And again, as if he knew Connor's thoughts, the warrior answered them. *"Morgana has betrayed Arthur to Maelgwyn. Simon was part of it. Even now Aethelbert's warriors surround you."*

Connor's gaze followed the warrior's line of sight to the east and saw the enemy warriors gathered there. A quick glance to the west confirmed the same.

Morgana.

She was ambitious. Once she had hoped to be mistress of Monmouth. He had known of her affair with Simon. At the time it made no sense. But now Simon was dead, and his death was proof of his betrayal. Those massed enemy warriors were further proof that Arthur's battle plan had also been betrayed.

His thoughts spun back to Amesbury, to Lady Ygraine's tragic death at the hands of her abductor, yet Morgana had somehow survived unscathed.

It was insane to believe it. Insane not to. It was all there if one chose to see it.

Lies, deceptions, betrayal. Had Morgana also lied about what she had seen in Merlin's chamber?

Something twisted deep inside Connor, an anguish of pain at what now seemed so obvious, and what he had refused to see.

His gaze scanned those flank positions once more. If Arthur acted swiftly there was still time to send mounted warriors to stop this new attack.

As if the warrior had heard his thoughts, he lifted his sword. The blade glinted like blue fire in the sunlight, and he bowed his head in silent salute.

The battle suddenly came alive around Connor once more. Again he heard the sounds of weapons and the shouts of his men. He spun toward Arthur. He was safe, moving swiftly toward Geoffrey who had fallen.

"You saved my life," Arthur said to Connor as they knelt beside the fallen warrior. "That is twice."

Connor barely acknowledged it as he grimly said, "We've been betrayed. Maelgwyn knows of our battle plan. Even now he prepares to attack our flanks."

Arthur was stunned. He had struggled to comprehend Simon's attack, refusing to believe it of one of Connor's men. There was a flicker of doubt. Connor saw it and knew it for what it was, the years of estrangement between them long, the time reconciled brief. Then he knew the moment Arthur brushed it aside.

Arthur nodded sharply as he pushed to his feet and called for his horse. He acted swiftly. Orders were quickly given for all those still astride their horses to form two groups to meet this new attack. He rode with them, leaving command of this position with Connor.

But even now the battle waned as Maelgwyn no doubt caught sight of the counterattack that was being mounted, and rushed to fortify those positions.

Connor gave instructions to Sagremore and Agravain to support Arthur's attack with foot soldiers to close behind Maelgwyn's warriors as they changed position. Then his gaze sought the warrior who'd given him the warning.

He stood at the edge of the battlefield now, clouds of mist and smoke from those dying signal fires swirling about him.

"Who are you?" Connor whispered, impossible for the warrior to hear across the distance and pockets of embattled warriors that separated them.

Yet, the warrior hesitated as if he had heard, and his stance, the way he lifted his head and looked back at Connor pulled at something deep inside him.

An instinct, a feeling, a certainty of some emotion—sadness, regret, the ache of loss that Connor knew so well.

The warrior's gaze met his. They were brilliantly blue exactly the same as eyes that had once looked back at him with love and passion.

Then the warrior turned, and just before he disappeared into that cloud of mist and smoke, Connor caught a glimpse of something that gleamed at the front of warrior's tunic—a flash of sunlight shimmering on the crystal runes that hung about his neck.

When the smoke and mist cleared, the warrior was gone.

He found the imprint of soft boots at the edge of the battlefield where he had last seen the warrior. The man had not rejoined the fighting. Instead, those tracks led away from the battlefield.

The pulse of the battle had now become a roaring of blood through veins as Arthur commanded his men in a hastily altered plan. Victory had been snatched from defeat. It was now within his grasp as he fulfilled the destiny Merlin had predicted all those years ago.

A pennant bearing Arthur's colors was raised in the midst of the battle. It caught the breeze and snapped as the serpent writhed below. As when a spear has struck the death blow, the serpent's struggles became nothing more than dying spasms.

Connor was no longer needed here. His presence would change nothing now. And there was another threat that still existed. That was where the warrior had gone.

He shouldered the heavy battle sword into the scabbard at his back, his gaze turning north. Then he set off, following those tracks as the first victory cries were heard beneath that clear December sky.

Chapter Twenty

Meg needed no gift of second sight to know where Morgana had gone.

She had gone to Maelgwyn, her co-conspirator in betrayal. No doubt to watch the battle from some safe place apart, to gloat over Arthur's defeat, and then claim the spoils of war.

With Merlin's dire warnings strong in her thoughts, she found the remnants of Maelgwyn's war camp atop the tor, a high craggy hill that looked out across the gently rolling terrain, embers still glowing at the remains of the morning fire. But Maelgwyn was not there. He had gone to join his men in that final campaign that had once assured victory and now had all but ended in defeat.

She sensed that he had seen the course of the battle change as Arthur sent his mounted warriors to his flanks; sensed when he ordered the last of his men, who had watched with him, down the slope to join the battle; and then sensed also when Maelgwyn had followed, knowing even then with a warrior's instincts that he rode toward his own death.

Morgana would have seen it as well—all of her ambitions and plans slipping through her grasp.

Meg sensed her presence, the foulness and coldness of evil

that lingered even beneath the warmth of the midday sun, the last traces of it like something glimpsed more clearly at the edges of sight—like stars in a night sky. And with it Morgana's desperate rage, sharp as the blade of a sword, that now made her so much more dangerous.

But just as Meg sensed she would find her in that encampment, she also sensed where she had fled from Arthur's now certain victory and her own certain defeat. Out across the gaping emptiness of the Salisbury Plain, disappearing, cloaking herself in her darkness, escaping the death and destruction she had wrought.

But to what purpose? To wait? To gather those powers together, nurturing them, feeding them, growing stronger until no one was safe? Not Arthur, nor anyone in his kingdom. If Morgana lived, there was no future.

Her hand smoothed over the place where life now grew. A child of flesh and blood, and immortal powers. If Morgana lived there was no future for the child.

She closed her thoughts to all thoughts of the child that might betray her, closed a small part of herself protectively around that fragile life like a delicate yet strong cocoon. then she reached out with her senses, searching for Morgana.

Connor followed those tracks to the edge of the tor, discovered where the warrior had paused beside the ashes of a smoldering fire. Then found where one set of tracks became two sets . . .

Morgana had passed this way, through the brown winter landscape where a copse of trees nestled against a hill.

Meg sensed it, even if she had not seen those soft impressions, felt it with that same aching coldness she'd experienced at the tor. Even now Morgana's presence clung to the air, fouling it, a smothering presence of evil that grew more pervasive, became nearer with each step, beyond the copse of trees, out across the sedge.

* * *

Connor found where the two sets of tracks paused beside a stream. One set made some time ago. And the other more recent, the clean edge of a boot heel sinking into the mud at the embankment. Then he found where one led and the other followed at the other side . . .

Morgana whirled around, certain she heard someone as she passed through the heavily wooded copse. But it was only the wind in the trees. With winter hard upon the land, the trees were like beggars huddled at the base of the hill, their denuded limbs rustling like the dry cackling of old women.

She started across the expanse of dry sedge and sensed it again, a presence that pressed in on her. She spun around but saw nothing.

Damn Maelgwyn! For his failure. Damn Arthur a thousand times! But it was not finished. It was not over!

Then she felt that presence again, a rising urgency, and along with it the warning of some danger closer now. The sedge was flat, barren, completely exposed. Behind her was the copse and those hills at the edge of the narrow Salisbury Plain. She would not go back.

The warning slipped across her skin and moved through her blood. She turned and ran. As she ran the earth trembled beneath her feet and a deafening sound rent the air. The ground before her suddenly broke open and a huge stone heaved out of the earth, rising to tower over her, blocking her escape.

Morgana slowly backed away, then ran in another direction. Again the earth rumbled beneath her feet, a second stone rising out of the ground before her. She turned and darted in yet another direction and another monolith shot out of the ground.

Each way she turned a great stone appeared, huge, glistening, shining monoliths that reflected the sun, until she stood wild-eyed in the center of the ring of standing stones, her heart pounding fiercely, her thoughts racing, the dark forces of evil within her churning violently.

"There is no place to run, Morgana. You cannot escape."

She whirled around and came face to face with the warrior. This was the danger Morgana had sensed.

He was tall and slender, dressed in leather tunic and leggings. His features were obscured by unusual painted markings, and he carried a sword. He entered the ring of stones and slowly walked toward her.

She attempted to escape between two of the upright stones but found her way blocked, then was thrown back by some unseen force that bound the stones together. She tried again, and again was thrown back. Her fury grew, and with it the power of the Darkness within her.

She was trapped. Caught within the circle of those standing stones by some invisible power. She whirled back around, her gaze narrowed on the warrior.

"You cannot stop me. No one can stop me." Her eyes gleamed black death. It was like looking into the darkest soul.

Meg sensed the spellcast, the sharp gust of bitter wind that cut like a knife, the gathering darkness that rolled over the ring of stones like a rising storm, then the explosion of lightning that shook the earth and made the stones tremble.

The first flash of lightning blinded Meg, pain stabbing into her eyes, leaving nothing but darkness and Morgana's harsh cruel laughter ringing painfully in her ears.

The second flash of lightning stabbed her sleeve, slicing through soft leather and the skin beneath, the warmth of blood trickling down her arm.

She anticipated the next flash of lightning, and using her powers to guide her, deflected it off the blade of the sword. She sensed the next one, and the next as well, the ring of stones exploding in a primordial battle between the powers of the Light and the powers of Darkness.

Then the next bolt of lightning was deflected off the tip of her blade at just the right angle and caught Morgana at the shoulder. The blow staggered her. She screamed furiously, turning on Meg like a wounded animal.

Gone were the beautiful features, transformed instead into harsh lines and angles as the Darkness staked its claim in a hideous visage. Evil pumped through her blood. With each beat of her heart she was less mortal and more dangerous.

Now she called on those powers of Darkness, using them to transform into a Death Stalker, one of the ancient winged creatures that existed only in myth. Until now.

Meg smelled its foulness, felt the bitter cold death of those wings churning the air within the circle of stones, sensed its image with the gift of inner sight that protected her. Then sensed when it came at her, its hideous cries like the screams of the dying on that distant battlefield, the sounds of those deadly talons slashing the air very near her face as it swept toward her.

She swung the sword. But the creature dropped low and caught her at the knees, powerful wings sweeping her feet out from under her in a painful blow that sent her sprawling and the sword flying from her hands.

Meg rolled across the earthen floor of the stone ring. She was disoriented, her senses stunned by the noise and the fierce wind that came from all directions, as if she were surrounded by Death Stalkers. She pushed painfully to her feet and immediately discovered the loss of the sword.

She sensed the gathering force of Darkness as the Death Stalker again hunted her, felt the churning of air, heard the beat of those wings as the creature came at her, suffered a stunning blow that swept her across the hard ground.

Pain swept through her, tore at her thoughts, squeezed at her heart like an angry fist. The transformation that protected her wavered as the creature gathered its strength for the death blow. It circled high within that ring of stones, then plummeted toward her, those deadly talons outstretched to tear her apart.

Meg turned her thoughts inward, the transformation of the warrior receding altogether as she focused the power she'd been born with in a sudden burst of intense light that exploded just as the Death Stalker reached her. The creature was hurtled back across the circle of stones, thrown against one of those upright monoliths with a sickening sound as easily as she had once hurled pottery against a hearth.

Stunned and wounded by the blow, the power of Morgana's

spellcast faded, until the creature disappeared and she lay dazed, confused, and bleeding at the base of the stone.

Meg struggled up on bent elbow. Nausea and pain swept through her. She felt battered and bruised, her senses equally bruised.

The power of the Light within her was weakened by Morgana's attacks and the effort it had taken to stop the Death Stalker. Blinded by that first flash of lightning, Meg had not recovered her sight. She felt weak and helpless as a newborn child.

She heard rather than sensed that Morgana struggled to drag herself to her feet. Then heard her exclamation of surprise when she discovered what Meg already knew—that she was no longer protected by the transformation of the warrior.

"What have we here?"

And then surprise turned to speculation as that coldness of evil crept into Morgana's voice.

"A witch? Spellcaster? Conjuror? Mage? Which is it?"

She drew closer, circling around Meg like a wolf circling its prey. Then made a startled sound as she slipped into Meg's thoughts slicing away the protection Meg weakly clung to with the precision of talons cutting through flesh.

"Merlin!" Morgana's eyes widened with incredulity at the secret that was no longer safe.

And then, with disbelief, "Sister?"

Her dark eyes narrowed and gleamed, twin pools of evil, as incredulity and disbelief gave way to discovery.

Her evil laughter rang out across the circle of standing stones, making those monolithic giants that no score of mortal men could have moved tremble.

"You are Merlin's sister! I should have known! I should have seen it." Then discovery turned to gloating triumph.

"Did you really believe you could stop me? That you were powerful enough?" She laughed. "You little fool. Merlin was no match for me, and you are no match for me. I will destroy you as easily as I destroyed him."

"You're wrong." It gave Meg great pleasure to tell her.

"My brother lives. Even now, he recovers from your evil

poison at Caerleon. You have lost, Morgana. You have lost everything.''

And then with a deepening sense of satisfaction, she added, "Arthur is victorious. He will take the throne and fulfill his destiny as king of Britain. You cannot stop it now.''

It was true. Morgana sensed it. Had sensed it when she'd fled Maelgwyn's encampment.

"Perhaps not,'' she replied. "But there is still something I can do . . . I can destroy you!''

"No!'' Meg cried out as she felt the cold hand of Darkness moving through her thoughts, peeling back the layers of the cocoon, finding what she protected there. Then she sensed the gleam of knowledge in Morgana's evil gaze, the cold hand of death closing around the child. But Morgana only laughed, a cruel harsh sound that tore at her soul.

"Now I will destroy you and your child. Then I will finish what must be done.''

Morgana reached out, her evil thoughts wrapping around the warrior's sword, lifting it where it had fallen across the stone circle, then commanding it to her.

Connor saw everything as he reached the circle of standing stones. He watched with stunned disbelief as the sword flew into Morgana's hands, then watched with horror as she raised it.

"No!'' He charged into the circle of stones, his battle sword swung high overhead in a death blow.

Morgana turned, the coldness of evil gleaming in her dark eyes as she looked at him. Then she turned. Knowing he watched, knowing he saw everything and could not reach her in time, she raised the sword and plunged it deep.

Connor's sword caught Morgana above the shoulders, severing her head from her shoulders. It rolled across the circle of stones, coming to rest at the foot of one of the stones, eyes staring and mouth agape, frozen at the moment of her death.

Her body collapsed, falling across the bloodied sword. It disappeared in a flash of blue flame that leapt around Morgana's body, consuming it. Across the ring of stones, her severed head also burst into flames of white-hot light that consumed it, peeling back the layers of skin, melting away those evil features.

Connor went to Meg.

She was pale as death, her skin cold to the touch. Her hair was tangled beneath her, both arms wrapped protectively about her as she'd curled into herself when Morgana struck, protecting the child. His child.

He pulled her into his arms, then pulled her away from that evil stench of death that rolled into the clouds that hovered over the ring of stones.

He was covered with blood—her blood. He tore open the front of her tunic. The soft linen of her gown beneath was soaked with blood from the wound at her shoulder.

"No!" he whispered hoarsely, fighting back rising panic and desperation.

He tore strips of linen from the skirt of her gown, wadded them and pressed them against the wound.

She whispered his name. "Connor."

"You'll be all right," he told her fiercely. "I'll take you back to Caerleon. Merlin is there." The name slipped out before he realized how easily he'd said it, clung to it.

"Hold me."

"I am holding you." Didn't she realize that he was holding her? Didn't she feel it . . . see him?

The eyes that looked back at him stared past him. The hand that lifted to him couldn't seem to find him. The sudden coldness in her reached out to him, sinking deep inside.

"Please, hold me."

"Aye, little one," he whispered.

"There was something I wanted to tell you . . ."

"I am here, Meg. I am listening."

Her hand brushed his cheek. "What is it? What did you want to tell me?" He looked down into those blue eyes, now clouded with blindness.

Her fingers touched his lips. "I wanted to experience life. I found it in you."

Tears filled his eyes. He wrapped his hand around hers. "As

you gave mine back to me. Stay, and share it with me now. Stay!''

"I want to. Hold me, Connor. Please, hold me.''

He fiercely pulled her against him, as if he could pull her inside and protect her there. As if he could hold back death.

Meg felt the warmth. Then she saw it. A faint golden glow of light that gradually expanded, filling the ring of stones, surrounding them both, then reaching for her. The power of the Light reaching for her, wrapping around her, taking away the coldness and pain, enveloping her in golden warmth, stealing her away from death. Taking her home.

The storm clouds were gone. Blue sky blanketed the ring of stones. Warm sun beat down on him. A light wind lifted the hair at his forehead. Connor slowly lifted his head.

Gone. Everything was gone. All that remained was that ring of towering stones and the blood that soaked the front of his tunic.

He wept. Until the sun sank toward the horizon. Until the coming night settled over those stones with a blanket of stars. Until he could weep no more.

What did he believe?

He had always believed in God . . . and the sword in his hand. Those two things defined who and what he was. Then he lost everything, perhaps lost himself as well. He no longer knew who he was, or cared.

She had given that back to him with her laughter, love, and sweet passion. She had given him back his soul.

It was not enough. Not nearly enough.

Merlin sensed when he returned. Alone, riding through the night, ruthless, uncompromising, unbelieving mortal. And sensed when he entered the gates of Caerleon, the news of Arthur's victory at Glastonbury harsh at his lips as he pushed his way into the main hall. Then sensed when Connor's hand reached for the door, sending it crashing back on its hinges.

"Damn you!" Connor burst out. "Damn you to the fires of

hell!'' Years ago, the conjuror had taken from him. Now he had taken again.

"That may well be," Merlin replied, struggling with the same pain of loss he now sensed in Connor of Monmouth.

She was gone. He had felt it when it happened, that moment that shimmered between them, bound together by the power they shared. Then, like the flame of a candle suddenly extinguished, she was gone.

The woman, Dannelore, had sensed it as well and had been inconsolable. Feeble mortal emotions, he thought as a great sadness washed through him, unlike anything he had ever felt, or might possibly ever feel again, and he silently cursed mortal emotions that were part of him now.

"You could have stopped her," Connor spat out at him. "But instead, you sent her to find Morgana, knowing what she was."

"Aye, I knew what Morgana was. I had learned it well from all the times she filled me with her vile poison, robbing me of my powers, making it impossible for me to help Arthur, guaranteeing Maelgwyn's victory with her betrayal.

"But you are wrong. I could not have stopped Meg. Nothing I could have said or done would have prevented her going after Morgana. If she had not, Arthur and his entire army would have perished on that field at Glastonbury. You would have died there as well. She knew that. *That* is the reason she went, because she knew Morgana's evil must be stopped. It was her destiny."

"No!" Connor refused to accept it. "It was your destiny, not hers." He drew his sword and leveled it at Merlin.

"Change it. Bring her back. You have the power. I saw it in her. You possess that same power. Damn you, bring her back!"

Merlin sadly shook his head. "Do you not think I would if I could? But I cannot create a mortal life, nor call it back once it is gone. 'Tis the one thing I cannot do. What she was is not truly gone. What you saw, what you thought of as Meg an illusion, a transformation that she created. It was not mortal flesh and blood."

Connor shook his head. "It was real. Damn you, *real!* Her laughter was real." His voice broke. "Her blood was real." The sword quivered in his hands as helplessness washed over him.

He stared at the conjuror. For the first time he saw him as a man, fallible, ravaged by the darkness of Morgana's evil and the very mortal grief at what he could not prevent.

Connor eventually lowered the sword. His shoulders sagged with helplessness, bone-deep weariness, and soul-deep pain.

In the main hall the word he'd carried back had spread, jubilant cries from the watchtowers echoed across the yard and spilled into the main hall.

He felt none of it. He felt nothing except the familiar ache of loss. He turned to leave, pausing at the door of the monk's chamber.

"She *was* real. What we shared was real. You cannot take that away from me."

"Has she spoken?"

"Not a word."

Meg heard the whispers and sensed the presence of the Guardians. Voices that moved about her, thought her thoughts; part of her, yet in some strange way no longer part of her.

"What are her thoughts?"

"Very strange. Mortal thoughts. Emotions—sadness, joy, pain, and loss. So deep that I could almost feel it myself. And others . . ."

"Others?"

"I sense them. Very powerful. But I have no notion of such things. Still, it is quite sad. She has not laughed since she returned."

"She just needs time."

"How much time?"

Time. In a place where time did not exist.

"Until she forgets. 'Tis best. You will see. She should never have gone."

"If she went back—"

"She would have to live as a mortal. Her powers would no longer exist. She would be no more than a changeling. 'Tis not a bargain anyone with powers such as hers would make."

"And the child?"

"Does not exist in our world. It was part of the transformation. 'Tis not part of her now."

"Yet, she feels it . . . feels that loss. I hear her crying at night."

"Crying?"

"Yes, tears. Real tears. How is it possible?"

"It is not possible."

Impossible. Impossible emotions, impossible love, impossible need . . .

"You must begin again, mistress," the Learned One instructed. "Focus your power."

The earthenware bowl streaked dangerously close to the wall, sharply banked the corner, and nicked the adjacent wall.

"You must concentrate, mistress!" the Learned One admonished, for all the good it did.

"Visualize!"

The bowl circled the room, no more than a blur. This time it careened too close and the Learned One was forced to dive for cover under the table. The bowl whirled past Cosmo and Grendel.

"Perhaps she is better suited to herb gathering," Cosmo commented. "Some simply do not have the talent or the ability."

Impossible.

"This one possesses both the skill and the ability," Grendel replied. "We are not talking about a mere changeling. You forget whom she is descended from."

The argument sounded vaguely familiar.

"I forget nothing. She is no better than the last time," Cosmo complained.

Impossible.

"Aye, she is much better than the last time. And stubborn."

"Stubborn?" He was confused. "That is a mortal trait. You make it sound as if it were deliberate."

The bowl headed straight for them, shattering against the stones at the hearth just overhead.

"Aye." Grendel smiled. "She's really done it this time."

Epilogue

Connor sat with the rest of his men astride their warhorses, buffeted by the sharp wind in these northern climes that made a mockery of the fact that it was spring at Caerleon.

Snow still blanketed the earth at Dumonia, Maelgwyn's northern stronghold. For years he had ridden from these craggy, forbidding mountains and swept into the southern regions, spreading his reign of terror, blood, and death.

Too much blood. Too much death.

Now that reign had ended. Not as Maelgwyn had hoped and conspired to bring about. Not with his new reign over all of Britain as her one true king. But with his ignominious death on that distant battlefield at Glastonbury.

Now another claimed the right to reign. His destiny, prophesied all those years ago when two young boys battled with their small swords for riches and imaginary kingdoms, fulfilled that day when Maelgwyn fell and Aethelbert was finally deposed to rot for the last of his days on a distant island.

Arthur, King of Britain, led the way now, dismounted and walked up the steps of the abandoned fortress that seemed to be part of the mountain itself. A place of legend and myth, nearly as old as the legend that surrounded Arthur himself.

The inhabitants gone now, except for those who cringed in the rocks or cowered before Arthur's men and begged for mercy.

Connor followed because it was expected, dismounting from his own horse. His men followed as well. They had fought for this day, bled for it, and now by right of that blood were part of it.

Arthur did not seek riches or retribution. He had not come there to loot or pillage. He had come to fulfill the legend. To seek what few had seen and fewer still had ever touched—the ancient sword of Dumonia, its blade buried in stone.

It was rumored to be made of gleaming metal that reflected the midday sun, and fixed in the hilt of the sword was said to be a magnificent blue stone, placed there long ago by the one who proclaimed that only the true king of the land could draw it from the stone.

Over time, the sword had fallen into many hands, but none had ever drawn it from the stone. Not even Maelgwyn in spite of all his treachery, ambition, and betrayals.

The sword was in a large chamber deep within the fortress. Its secrets buried with the blade in the stone. It gleamed when the light of the torches fell upon it, the reflection burning like blue fire in the jewel at the hilt as if it burned within.

Merlin slowly walked forward. His recovery had been slow, but he had insisted that this he must do.

The expression on his face changed, the weariness and exhaustion slipping away. He whispered ancient, long-lost words as Arthur approached the large block of stone where the sword was embedded.

Destiny. Hope. Prayer. They all came together as Arthur closed his hand around the hilt of the sword and then slowly drew it from the stone.

It was done. The long battle had been fought. Arthur was king.

Now all Connor wanted was to go home. To Monmouth, to try to find the pieces of his life.

* * *

"Where do you think you're going?" Connor asked, the breeze blessedly warm after the journey from Dumonia.

Two months now, and still Arthur had not demanded that he return to Caerleon. Instead, he had suggested that Connor build up the garrison at Monmouth, insisting he preferred the comfort of an ally so near to Glastonbury where he had decided to build a new fortress to be called Camelot.

"I'm going with you," young Tristan replied. "To hunt in the forest."

Connor shook his head. "That was not the agreement. You have not yet finished your lessons."

Tristan made a face. "I'm tired of practicing. Radvald makes me practice the same thing over and over."

"And he is right."

"The war is over. What need is there?"

Connor smiled gently. "It is never over. There is much that must be done, and Arthur's struggle is not over. Many would still make claims against the throne. That is why we must be vigilant. That is the reason you must practice."

"Did you practice this morning?" Tristan demanded.

"Before you rose from your bed. If you wish a knighthood from Arthur you will have to be as good as Arthur."

"All right then," Tristan said morosely, scuffing the toe of his boot in the soft dirt. "But I still don't see the need of it."

"And I pray you never will," Connor replied, even though the boy could not hear as he returned to his practicing.

Connor whistled for the hound and set off across the greensward.

By nightfall he had reached the edge of the forest. A rabbit provided supper, the hound provided all the companionship he wanted. At first light they set off, leaving behind for a while the years of fighting, bloodshed, and loss for the more pressing need of stocking the pantry at Monmouth.

The hound caught a scent and bounded on ahead. Connor slipped an arrow from the pouch at his back, and nocked it at the bowstring as he silently followed.

He moved deeper into the forest, following the spore of the deer and the hound's persistent call. A meandering trail of neatly nipped leaves from favorite plants and low-hanging branches suggested the deer was unaware of their presence.

Following the trail, he found more fresh spore, indicating there was more than one deer and only a short distance ahead.

He heard the distinctive sound of an animal moving through the underbrush. Warm sun slanted through the trees, providing a glimpse of movement, a fleeting glance of tawny hide.

A deer gradually emerged from the thick cover of trees, moving slowly as it searched the undergrowth for tender leaves and shoots. Eventually, he spotted a second deer as it made its way toward the bank of a nearby stream.

As Connor raised his bow, the hound let out a loud bark and a flock of birds suddenly burst from a nearby thicket. Their frenzied flight startled the deer. Its majestic head shot up, its eyes wild with alarm. Too late, Connor pulled back the bowstring. The deer bolted, crashing through the underbrush.

Then he heard the sound of the second deer very close by. He again pulled back the bowstring as he sighted along the deer's frenzied flight. There would not be another opportunity.

He released the arrow.

He heard the stumbling and crashing of the animal, and followed it through the trees. The sounds of the hound suddenly ceased. Connor tore through the underbrush, certain of the direction of the arrow, certain it had found its target.

He heard the deer thrashing, much closer now. The hound barked wildly. Connor scrambled over a tree trunk, found Dax, and hauled him back.

He went down on one knee and pushed aside thick branches, exposing the pale curve of a bare shoulder. More leaves and branches were pulled aside, revealing the fall of long golden hair.

The forest was silent around him. Even the hound was silent as Connor swept aside more leaves, twigs, and debris, and then swept her into his arms.

Meg heard a voice, felt the sudden, stunning warmth of human touch. It was tender, gentle, and oddly reassuring. Not at all what she had been taught to expect of mortals. She wanted far more.

She opened her eyes, but no image formed. She had been blinded by her encounter with Morgana. That would remain. But that was the only wound she'd suffered.

The wound at her shoulder was no more than the scar from her first encounter with Connor, and his child rested safe within her, both of them snatched from the mortal world by the powers of the Light in that moment before death as Connor knew it.

Yet she saw him, with a changeling's gift of inner sight, one of the few things that remained to her as part of the bargain she'd made to return to him.

And she knew that his face was smudged with all the colors of the forest and the earth. He seemed to blend into the forest that surrounded them so that she wasn't certain she saw him at all. Except for his eyes. Not brown or blue, but the color of the sky before a storm. Or perhaps after it. Soft gray, not cold, but brimming with tears as he crushed her against him.

His arrow had found its mark, in the trunk of the tree beside her, perhaps because of some last-minute change in the breeze or a last-minute change in the world.

He did not ask, he did not question, he simply believed in what he held in his arms. A man who believed in God, his sword, and the love he had found in her laughter.

"Have mercy, milord," she sighed breathlessly through tears and laughter.

"Never," he breathed into the fiery sweetness of her kiss.

In the summer of 1999, Zebra will publish the sixth book in the magical saga of MERLIN'S LEGACY. Here's a taste of what's in store for the daughter of Meg and Connor . . .

MERLIN'S LEGACY: *DREAMS OF CAMELOT*

by Quinn Taylor Evans

"I have no mother or father," Rianne said defiantly. "They're dead."

She squared off against the warrior, feet spread and firmly planted, ready to do battle if necessary in spite of his imposing height, the crest he wore that identified him as one of Arthur's knights, and the ripple of uncertainty that moved through her blood—like liquid fire, unsettling; stealing her breath away—under the scrutiny of that dark, penetrating stare. As if he saw beneath the disguise of grime, ragged clothes, and anger that she held before her like a shield.

"They're very much alive," Tristan assured her. "And make no mistake about it, you are going back."

At least Connor was still alive when he'd left Monmouth with Meg's urgent request that he find their daughter and bring her back before it was too late.

But in spite of the trail he'd followed, in spite of the crystal rune the girl wore about her neck—a protective talisman given by Meg to the infant daughter she was forced to give up—there was nothing in this angry, dirt-smudged girl that even suggested a bond of kinship.

Surely not in the anger that curled the slender fists at her sides, not in the curses that fell too easily from her lips, nor in the bruises she'd inflicted with undisguised pleasure. And there was every possibility the crystal rune had been stolen since she'd also shown a remarkable talent for thievery in so easily lifting the pouch from his tunic.

There was absolutely nothing about her to suggest that this was Meg's daughter. Except for the color of her eyes, a startling contrast amid the grime and anger.

They were that same unusual color; brilliant blue surrounded by soft gold bands, like the heart of a flame, and—he had a disquieting feeling—capable of looking right into a man's soul; perhaps capable of withering a man's soul as easily as she'd withered his manhood.

Nausea still churned in his stomach from the last blow. It was insulting being caught off-guard by a mere slip of a girl. At that moment he could have joyfully strangled her.

Meg and Connor longed to see their daughter, a child raised in seclusion and obscurity in the care of a trusted Guardian, gently reared and protected, who embodied the traits of both her parents whom Tristan loved as his own.

But the Guardian was long dead and their daughter was no longer a child. Nor had she been gently reared or protected. She'd been left to fend for herself, oblivious to the legacy she'd been born to, with a survivor's instincts, the anger to go along with them, and absolutely no idea of the power she possessed.

How could he possibly take this girl back to Monmouth? It would have been easier, and perhaps better for everyone, to leave her in this disreputable place and tell Meg and Connor that he'd failed.

But he knew he'd never be able to lie to Meg. She would know the truth in spite of her blindness, and the pain of that betrayal would be worse than the truth he must take her.

"You can't make me go with you," Rianne replied, clamping her teeth together to stop the quivering of her chin. "And I won't change my mind."

She refused to be intimidated or told what she could and could not do. In spite of the hard, set angle of his jaw that suggested she'd perhaps pushed too far; in spite of the warning that glinted in those dark eyes that had gone from soulful heat to grim determination in less than a heartbeat; and in spite of the instinctive warning that slipped across her senses.

Tristan almost smiled then. He was glad she wasn't going to make this easy.

"I thought that was what you'd say," he replied, and saw the confusion that leapt into those lovely eyes to be followed by growing suspicion.

"Stay away from me," she warned, slowly backing away from him.

"You give me no other choice, milady," he calmly replied as he took an equal number of steps, easily closing the distance with his longer strides.

Cornered and with all escape sealed off, Rianne whipped the short-bladed knife from the sleeve of her tunic and held it before her.

Now Tristan did smile.

The transformation caught her completely off-guard. Tristan was no longer fierce and scowling. The smile transformed his features, and his dark eyes gleamed with stunning heat. She stared at the beguiling sensuality that curved his lips when she should have been watching his hands.

Quicker than she could even think about it, his hand snaked out and clamped over hers. A brutal squeeze of those long fingers made pain shoot up the length of her arm. The knife fell from her stunned fingers and thudded to the earthen floor of the inn.

He scooped up the weapon, then scooped her up and flung her over one shoulder like a sack of grain. A well-shaped sack of grain to be sure, a slender waist clamped beneath his arm, full breasts flattened against his back, and the soft curve of her bottom anchored beneath his hand.

She was going to need water, soap, and quite possibly a good thrashing. Though in what order Tristan was not quite certain as she cursed, making the air blue.

She was not a child, nor was she the daughter Meg and Connor hoped for. But one way or the other, either astride a horse or trussed and flung across the back of one, she was going home.

He prayed to God they both survived the journey.

ROMANCE FROM JO BEVERLY

ROMANCE FROM JANELLE TAYLOR

ANYTHING FOR LOVE   (0-8217-4992-7, $5.99)

DESTINY MINE   (0-8217-5185-9, $5.99)

CHASE THE WIND   (0-8217-4740-1, $5.99)

MIDNIGHT SECRETS   (0-8217-5280-4, $5.99)

MOONBEAMS AND MAGIC   (0-8217-0184-4, $5.99)

SWEET SAVAGE HEART   (0-8217-5276-6, $5.99)